This was no prim and proper kiss for the cameras. This was him staking his claim and leaving no room for doubt. They wanted sordid tales to carry to the gossip magazines, did they? They waited in the distance for Becca to show a moment of weakness, a single human failing so they could immortalize it in print, huh?

Well, here it was. They could have pictures of his arms crushing her body to his. They could take as many shots as they wanted of his lips moving firmly over hers, forcing her to open up beneath him. They could walk away with the falsely solid belief that this woman was his, and all of the shit they got away with before was about to come to a screeching halt.

And if he maybe got carried away in the middle, softening his assault so that the kiss turned deep and slow, well, that was only to be expected. He'd denied himself the pleasure of this woman's mouth for days now. He was going to take a minute.

It was a hell of a minute.

When I Fall

TAMARA MORGAN

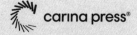
carina press®

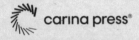 carina press®

ISBN-13: 978-0-373-00320-4

When I Fall

Recycling programs
for this product may
not exist in your area.

www.CarinaPress.com

Printed in U.S.A.

Dear Reader,

I like to believe that every author writes at least one couple who refuses to go away. Months after the book is complete—years, even—they linger on, staunchly sitting under the always-setting sun that was meant to be their final farewell. "Feed me," they call. "Visit me," they demand. "Don't you remember how much fun we had together?"

For me, that couple is Jake Montgomery and Becca Clare, and that book is *When I Fall*.

Perhaps it's because it took a while for me to warm up to this particular pair. As the upstairs characters in my *Downton Abbey*–inspired series, these are two very rich people, born into lives of privilege and ease. They have wealth most of us can only dream of, and as often happens in such cases, don't always use that wealth wisely.

Of course, love changes everything, which is why I'm having such a hard time letting them go. When two imperfect people can grow and become perfect together, it feels as if something clicks into place and all is right with the world.

I read romance for that click. I write romance for that click. I refuse to let go of characters for that click.

But let them go I must. Jake and Becca are now in your hands, and I hope you come to adore them as much as I do. And if they stick around afterward, refusing to leave you alone, you have my sincerest apologies. Fortunately, they don't eat much.

Tamara Morgan

For Alisha Rai, who sparked the idea for this book
(and is a generally awesome human being)

When I Fall

ONE

IF THERE WAS an art to holding someone's hair while they puked, Becca deserved her very own gallery opening. Or a wall at MoMA. Maybe even a chapel ceiling somewhere.

"You'll be okay, sweetie." Becca pulled Livvie's signature dark silken strands out of the way and rubbed a soothing pattern on her back. "It's almost over."

Although Becca was the last person to comment on another person's life choices, she knew from past experience that almost an entire bottle of vodka was rarely a wise decision. She also knew Livvie probably hadn't eaten much in the way of absorptive calories today.

"I have a water bottle in my purse with your name on it," she promised. The deceptively tiny beaded clutch also contained breath mints and an energy bar, both of which were going into her friend's stomach as soon as the opportunity presented itself.

This happened sooner than expected, Livvie rising on unsteady legs and bracing herself on Becca's arm as she righted herself in six-inch platforms. She glanced down at the front of her outfit and groaned. "Oh, no. You let me get sick all over my skirt."

Darn it. Even da Vinci only had two hands. There was no way she could have saved the hair and the skirt at the same time.

"Don't worry," she said, eyeing the stain doubtfully. "We can wash it out in the sink. No one will ever know."

She helped Livvie out of the stall and led her to one of the overstuffed ottomans arranged in the adjoining lounge, which was plush seats and velvet walls as far as the eye could see. Ma Petite was great at offering restrooms that emphasized *rest*, even if most people only used this area to snort a line or two before heading back out into the fray. Cocaine had never been Becca's thing, but she tried not to judge.

Livvie took a grateful swig from the water bottle Becca handed her and tugged unhappily at her skirt, a frown marring her otherwise perfect exterior—cheekbones to die for, those heavy Slavic brows only the most gorgeous women were able to pull off. "There's no point in washing it. It's ruined. It's Italian silk."

"Is it?" Becca took a step back and examined the overall effect. She'd seen Livvie when she came into the nightclub, already well on her way to the summit of her alcohol-infused heights, but she hadn't bothered taking note of her outfit. Becca'd had a particularly arresting man on her arm at the time—one of those dark, beefy types who could have been a gangster but probably worked on Wall Street—so her attention had been somewhat distracted.

She could see now that Livvie was seriously working her look, her tight white skirt shimmering under the low bathroom lights, a sparkling purple tunic top falling artfully off one shoulder.

"Then lose the skirt altogether." She circled her friend, eyes narrowed as she gauged the distance between the bottom of her ass and the hem of the shirt. *Hmm.* Becca might never make it into the Guggenheim with her hair-holding skills, but fashion was another matter altogether. She couldn't sew, mind you, or cobble shoes or even sketch designs—but she was excellent at getting dressed. "If I lend you my belt, I think you can pull that shirt off as a dress. It's scandalous, but doable. You've worn less." She giggled. "*I've* worn less."

"Yes, you have, you dirty slut."

"Take that back. I'm a clean slut, thank you very much." Becca handed her friend the energy bar from her purse. "And if you eat this, I'll let you have a breath mint for dessert."

Livvie wrinkled her nose. "Those things have half my daily calorie intake and they taste like glue. Can't I just have the mint?"

"Nope. You need the carbs and protein."

"Ugh." She dangled the package between two fingers. "Carbs go straight to my stomach, protein right to my ass. The agency will have a fit. You must be drunker than you let on if you think I'm eating this."

Becca paused. *Am I?* She straightened her stance and extended her arms. Since she never did any driving her-self—she never did *anything* herself—she'd never had to perform a sobriety test before. She'd seen them done in the movies though. She brought a finger to the tip of her nose and switched hands. Finger, nose. Finger, nose. This was pretty easy.

"Nah. I'm good," she said. Her current state of non-intoxication probably had less to do with the amount of vodka tonics she'd consumed and more to do with the fact that she'd remembered to have one of the en-ergy bars before she came out tonight. Mean Max, her personal trainer, made her eat one every six hours like clockwork, and she had to promise to carry a spare for emergencies of this nature. He was a cruel son of a bitch on the treadmill, but her ass had never looked better.

"Well, at least help me out of this skirt. I smell awful."

She really did, though Becca doubted anyone on the dance floor would notice above the general aura of substance abuse. One person sweating eighty-proof alcohol was unpleasant. But one hundred people sweating eighty-proof alcohol? That was a party.

"Uh-oh." Becca stopped the zipper halfway down and peeked over Livvie's shoulder. "Sweetie, are you wearing any underwear tonight?"

"Oh, shit." Livvie slapped a hand over her mouth to cover her laugh. "No. You know how I feel about panty lines. I got reamed by that fashion magazine last year for always announcing my cut to the world."

"Call me old-fashioned, but I think the alternative is worse." She was *not* letting Livvie go back out there with her cootchie showing. Even clean sluts had their standards. "Maybe I can sneak you out back and have my driver come get us."

"Your driver always looks at me like I belong on his shoe."

"Yes, but he's very reliable." And Becca had long ago learned not to let his disdain dictate her actions. She'd learned not to let *anyone's* disdain do that. According to the collective judgment of the world, the only place she belonged was in the gutter, broken and beaten down. Or locked up somewhere the walls were soft and the meals bland.

The world was kind of mean.

"It'll be fun. You can come hang out at my place." She tried not to let her desperation show as she casually added, "You can even sleep over if you want. We'll make it a girls' night."

Livvie shook her head, all those dark strands swirling and taking Becca with them. It had been a long shot anyway. No one past the age of thirteen had sleepovers. Then again, no one past the age of eight had to sleep with a nightlight—and her light fixtures were permanently taped in the *on* position.

"It's too early to go home." Livvie extended her hand. "Just give me your underwear."

"What? Ew. No."

"Come on. It's not like you need anything under that dress. It practically goes to your knees."

First of all, *no*, it didn't. The black cage corset dress was longer than many of the outfits she wore, but it still only hit mid-thigh—and that was assuming she wasn't in motion at the time. The falsely modest skirt made up for the fact that the top was basically bra cups and some tightly wrapped bands across her torso.

Second of all, there was no way she was risking her own cootchie making an impromptu appearance tonight. Not that anyone could accuse her of being overly modest, but she was under strict orders from her mother. *The world has seen enough of your lady garden for one lifetime, Rebecca Louise. Wrap it up or I'm shipping it out.*

She would too.

"Livvie, I love you. You know I do, and I'd do anything to help a girl out. But I absolutely draw the line at giving you my panties."

"Please? You always have such cute underwear."

"That isn't even close to the point right now."

Livvie stuck her lower lip out in a pout. "I'm not

ready to call it a night—now that I've purged, I'm getting my second wind."

"Maybe we can still salvage the skirt," she suggested. But the crumpled fabric wrapped around Livvie's lower half looked sad and dirty, and they would both rather walk out of there buck naked than lower themselves to wear crushed, stained silk.

"If you give me your underwear, I'll eat the energy bar," Livvie promised. "I swear."

Becca examined her with renewed interest. "Every bite?"

"Every bite. My stomach is growling just thinking about it. I bet it's delicious."

"Now you're overselling it," Becca said, but she felt her resolve weakening. "How about you eat the energy bar *and* you come out with me and my trainer one day next week? He'll change your life, Livvie, he really will."

"You know how I feel about exercise. I can't afford the bulk."

"What he does is way more than exercise," she said, but she didn't press the issue. Opportunities to get Livvie to consume food products that weren't green olives or pearl onions were rare. It seemed wrong to let this one slip by while she had the chance.

"Pretty please?"

"I can't believe I'm actually doing this." With a quick and fervent prayer to whatever deity oversaw sanitary codes and really bad ideas, she pulled her underwear off and tossed the boy-cut lace shorts to her friend. "Please don't ever mention this again. Or try to give them back."

"You're an angel." Livvie leaned in to give her a peck on the cheek, but Becca took a wide step back. She'd never turn away from a girlfriend in need, but no way was that mouth coming anywhere near her.

She helped Livvie exchange clothes, not displeased with the end result. Livvie was short in the torso, which meant the shirt's hem skimmed the tops of her thighs, offering brief flashes of the black underwear and nothing more. And on her model-thin derriere, they looked like upscale hotpants. With the addition of Becca's wide silver belt, she looked put together and chic—and not at all like she'd just been hauled up from the bathroom floor and force-fed compact protein.

"Bitch." Becca pulled the belt a notch tighter and circled to make sure everything was tucked in. "You'll start a new trend tonight—see if you don't. I want partial credit."

Livvie made good on her end of the promise and took a bite of the energy bar. "Darling, if we make it through this night alive, we can name this outfit after you. Now come on. I think I owe you a drink."

Becca thought about the amount of alcohol she'd already consumed, factored in her body weight and deducted the fact that Livvie had eaten most of her food. Ha—who was she kidding? She couldn't perform complex mathematical calculations under the best of circumstances, but she *could* still touch her nose. That meant she wasn't even close to wasted yet. If she wanted a chance at actual sleep tonight, she was going to have to try a lot harder than this.

Pausing only a moment to toss the discarded skirt into the garbage, she grabbed her clutch and followed Livvie out the door. *Just one or two more hours*, she promised herself. *Then I'll have Liam pull around and take me home.* In bed by sunrise, when the dark wasn't an issue anymore. Up and sober by noon, ready to face another day.

Who knew? She might even try to make it to her mother's house for tea tomorrow.

Stranger things had happened.

"WHY IS THERE such a crowd in the VIP lounge tonight?" Jake Montgomery craned his neck to see past the crush of bodies, but he couldn't make anything out beyond the usual writhing and overconsumption that went on behind the velvet ropes. "Is there royalty in our midst?"

Dana followed the path of his gaze, his face pulled down in a sneer that made him look like a gargoyle. "It's nothing but the usual drunk socialites. Why? Were you hoping for something better?"

"*Is* there anything better than drunk socialites?" Jake asked. Beautiful young women with more money than common sense were his favorite kind. They demanded charm and wit and little else from him—unless you counted the occasional purse hold. Charm and wit were all he had to offer, and he'd long ago mastered the ability to dangle a sparkling bag from his fingertips without losing credibility. It was all in the posture.

Dana clearly disagreed. "This place is getting tedious. I think it might be time for us to find a new venue to patronize."

"Uh-oh." Jake shook his head in mock sympathy. Without fail, Dana got tired of a new club every month around the same date. The moon waxed and waned to his apathy. "Sounds like somebody hasn't been having much luck with the socialites lately. Maybe we should head up there and see if we can't find one willing to lower her standards for the night."

"If you'd been here all summer, you'd realize what a bore the city is becoming."

"And if you'd spent all summer sequestered with your family, you'd realize there are fates much worse than boredom."

Jake's misery eked a smile out of Dana's stony visage. "Still cut off from the hand that feeds you, eh? I wondered why you were staying with me instead of one of your father's hotels."

Jake didn't allow the smile to fall from his face. If the world considered it a grand joke for his family to freeze his accounts and reduce him to penury, then he intended to laugh longest and loudest. *It's all in the posture.*

"I'm proving a point," he said mildly. "Monty suggested I'm incapable of supporting myself for any length of time. I suggested he select his favorite condiments to make his words go down easier."

Dana laughed. "How'd he take that?"

"I believe he might still be sputtering."

"Your brother never did have much of a sense of humor."

Jake didn't respond. While Monty wasn't so much a stick-in-the-mud as he was a log in the whole fucking swamp, Jake preferred the aspersions on his brother's name to be cast by him and him alone. He had *some* family loyalty.

Dana cast one last look around the club, blinking in time to the heavy bass emanating from the dance floor. "I'm officially calling this place a bust. Ready to head out?"

"Sure." Jake got to his feet and shook out his slacks. It didn't matter to him if they sat at Ma Petite and talked about how bored they were, or if they found a new, out-of-the-way hole to grow bored with. The truth was that he'd only been in town a few days and he was already beginning to falter. Without funds—or any immediate means of acquiring some—city life lost the majority of its appeal.

He'd just grabbed his jacket and folded it carefully over his arm when a trill of feminine laughter broke free from the VIP room, whipping his interest. He leaned back and tried to peer in once more. He *knew* that laugh.

"Are you coming?" Dana asked irritably. In addition to reliable apathy, Dana also maintained a strict quantity of impatience at all times. If it was possible to bottle up dissatisfaction and sell it, it would smell exactly like Dana's Clive Christian cologne.

"Wait a minute." Jake stepped away from their table, moving closer to the back of the club. Like most of the dancing/drinking/any-vice-you-want-as-long-as-you-pay-for-it establishments in Manhattan, Ma Petite was set up so that the Very Important Persons in attendance were entertained away from the riffraff, gods and demi-gods on high. They were kept quarantined by a rope and a burly security guard dressed all in black, neither of which Jake feared.

"Anyone interesting in there tonight?" he asked.

The guard sized him up in less than five seconds. Jake never knew if it was his face people recognized, or if the cut of his clothes was enough to ensure entry, but the man loosened his stance and nodded toward the back. "See for yourself."

He intended to. The laughter sounded again, and Jake's gaze was drawn toward a table in the middle, where two women in an obviously intoxicated state danced while a throng of onlookers catcalled from the floor.

"Like I said." Dana's voice brushed his ear. "Drunk socialites. I think the one in the short purple dress is Olivia Winston."

Jake nodded. He'd met the runway model a few times, usually in situations similar to this one, though the location varied. Dana wasn't being cynical when he said these places were starting to suffer from a cycle of sameness. Same people, same sins, same hangover the next day. When Jake was in the thick of it—when he was the catcaller and, he wasn't going to lie, the one dancing on the table—the invariability didn't bother him. There was always something to enjoy about a roller coaster when you were on the ride. It was only now, as the guy standing on the fringes waiting for everyone else to disembark, that he was beginning to feel jaded.

And old. Christ, he felt old.

"I can't tell who the other one is—she keeps turning her face." Dana tilted his head. "Not a bad little body, though. She's a bit young for me, but you like them that way, don't you?"

Jake didn't grace that barb with a response. He enjoyed the company of women of all ages, and he wouldn't apologize for it. Everyone needed a hobby.

The girl turned and performed a shimmy, the sway of lithe hips draped in black making the most out of that nice little body. He dropped his shoulders as recognition settled in. "Oh, hell."

"What? You know her?"

He firmed his jaw and watched her make another turn on the table, inches away from catching her heel on the edge and plummeting off. "I know her."

Dana pointed his dark gaze at Jake. "You sleep with her?"

"Once."

For the first time that night, Dana appeared to be interested. "Oh, yeah? Who is she?"

Jake heaved a sigh and moved toward the table. "She's my aunt."

TWO

JAKE PAUSED AMONG the lookers-on and watched as Olivia and Becca bounced and shimmied their way into a full tabletop party.

In true nightclub fashion, it was mere minutes before their quest for attention was expanded by several more women in tight, expensive dresses and, as was inevitable, a few men eager to enjoy the dresses from a closer vantage point. An entire dance floor rested empty and unused a few feet away, but that was hardly the point. With this crowd, being the center of attention was all that mattered.

In theory, Jake didn't object to being the center of attention. Discretion had never been one of his favorite virtues, and there were enough photographs of his iniquity floating around to wallpaper the White House. But Rebecca Clare—littlest sister to his father's painfully young second wife, media train wreck, recent rehab patron—took indiscretion to whole new levels. Evidence of her iniquity could have wallpapered the Louvre.

"Gimme a boost?" A short blonde in a dazzling array of glitter from head to toe appeared at Jake's side. He gave her his hand and helped her to a chair before she was hoisted the rest of the way up. The addition of her body displaced the rest of the tabletop mass in true scientific fashion, and Becca teetered somewhere near the edge, her dress swaying, the rest of her not too far behind.

His first thought—one of alarm—had him stepping forward, prepared to catch her as she fell. But she managed to maintain her upright position through a particularly impressive gyration, leaving him with empty hands and a considerable dose of respect.

Becca had never been what Jake would consider a *striking* woman, whether dancing on a table or more appropriately seated at the edge of it. She wasn't particularly tall or well-built. Her hair was a nondescript shade of brown that hit her shoulders during those rare moments she wasn't in motion. She had the sleek skin and smooth limbs that all women in their twenties and in this circle had, her eyes a muddy green that most people would have lazily called gray. In fact, there was nothing about Becca that stood out in a place like this, and she could have been any number of rich, pretty white girls out for a night on the town. One of Dana's drunk socialites, another face in the crowd.

But it was impossible not to notice her tonight. Not because of her good looks or because her dance movements were calculated to appeal to anyone with functioning sex organs—though both of these things were true. This had much more to do with the fact that she would cheerfully dance on the table, her skirt swishing around the tops of her thighs, for the next eight hours. And not once would she give a flying fuck that she was totally commando underneath.

With a sigh and another eyeful of the curve of her naked ass, Jake realized it had become his official responsibility to get her down and home in one piece. He might be flaunting convention and his family's wishes by refusing to bend to their will, but that didn't mean he wanted to see his step-aunt come to any harm. He liked her. She was a good kid, if not always of sound judgment.

"Jake! What are you doing here?" Becca caught sight of a familiar face at her ankle and stopped dancing. The sudden halt to her movements was a mistake, because even though her body stopped spinning, the room took over for her—and the room was moving a lot faster than she had been.

"I'm here to help you off that table."

She puzzled over the stern note in his voice for a second before taking the hand he held up to her. If the room was going to start taking off into space—which seemed likely all of a sudden—perhaps it was better to be on solid ground again.

"I didn't know you were back from Connecticut," she said happily. She wasn't entirely sure *why* she was happy, but she suspected it had something to do with the way his arm wound naturally around her waist, helping her to stay standing and move through the blur of a room. A familiar arm was always nice when you were feeling tipsy. So was the man attached to it. He could do helpful things like call your driver and find your shoes and tell you if there was lipstick on your teeth.

If one planned it right, a man on the arm also meant not sleeping alone.

"How long have you been in town?" she asked.

"Not long and obviously long enough." Jake stopped her and peered carefully into each eye. "What are we dealing with?"

"Um, a good time? I'm here with my friend Olivia. Do you know Livvie? I'll introduce you. She's great."

"I've met her." He shook her shoulders, causing her head to flop and the familiar creep of a headache to begin at the base of her skull. "I mean it, Becca. I can't get you home safely if I don't know what you're on."

She wrinkled her nose. Did he mean drugs?

"Yes. I mean drugs."

Since when did Jake Montgomery sound so stern? "Oh, don't worry. I'm totally fine. Watch."

She took a step back and showed him her move with her nose and her fingers. Except she might have missed on that last one. And, *ow*, was that her eyeball? "Okay. Maybe I'm a little drunk."

"A little?"

"I'm sober enough to admire your tie." She reached up and tugged on the dark blue knot, pulling the fabric tight around his neck. "There. Now you're turning the right shade of red to yell at me. You look just like your father."

He sighed and loosened his tie, continuing his close examination of her face. She knew what he was looking for—dilated pupils, chattering teeth, sweat beyond the usual signs of exertion—and stood still to give him a better look. He wouldn't find much. Contrary to very popular, very widespread opinion, she preferred to stick to legal vices.

He nodded once, apparently satisfied with what he saw. "Come on. Let's call a cab and get you home to sleep it off. It's long past time for this Cinderella to be tucked in bed."

"Why, Jake Montgomery. Are you trying to lure me into the sack?" She batted her eyes at him, but the mascara on her right eye was clumped, so it was more like clunky winking. "That's a terrible line. Last time you told me I was a goddess of the night."

He frowned. "Did I really say that? How awful."

She giggled. "I dunno. I thought it was sweet. It worked, didn't it?"

"Is there anything that *doesn't* work on you?" He didn't give her a chance to reply. Gripping her elbow, he ushered her toward the back door of the club. Good call. That was the clandestine door, the door you snuck out when you were too shitfaced to face the press at the front—or when you didn't necessarily want your mother to find out you were being escorted home by your nephew.

Well, sort-of nephew. By marriage. One who was seven years older and had pretty hair.

She dug her heels into the floor. "Hey, you. Pretty Hair. I forgot."

"What did you just call me?"

"It's so pretty." She reached out and gave his tall coif a pat. A rich, thick, burnished auburn, Jake's hair was a thing every woman under the age of forty coveted for her own. The locks flattened under her ministrations and bounced right back again. "But that's not what I forgot."

He waited next to the bouncer while Becca tried to remember what it was she'd wanted to say. It was in there somewhere, buried underneath energy bars and vodka tonics and Livvie's bathroom disaster. She snapped her fingers. "Oh, I know. I have Liam tonight. There's no need to call a cab. He'll make sure I get home safely."

Jake blinked. "Who's Liam?"

"Liam is the boss of me."

"I find that hard to believe. It doesn't seem to me that *anyone* is capable of restraining you."

Coming from Jake—a man famous for doing what he wanted, when he wanted, and without a care for the consequences—that was a compliment. Patently untrue, but a compliment all the same. "I left my purse over on the banquette. Be a doll and get it, would you? Liam's number is programmed in."

Ever the gallant, Jake nodded once and went to retrieve her bag. She closed her eyes and let the room spin around her, taking comfort in the knowledge that for at least tonight, she'd be safe in the care of someone she trusted.

"Well, well, well. What do we have here?" A man who wasn't Jake approached her from the side. Under normal circumstances, she'd have ignored him and let her disinterest carry him away, but there was something about his overt familiarity that twinged in her stomach.

Becca made it a habit not to overlook those kinds of twinges. You could call it instinct, intuition or indigestion—she didn't care. It was never a good idea to ignore the universe when it was trying to tell you something.

She opened her eyes to find a bulldog-like face surveying her with interest. "I'm sorry. Do I know you?"

"Rebecca Clare, right?" He leaned close in a deliberate way that pricked at her skin. "I didn't recognize you before. I believe we met at the Callahans' Christmas party last year."

"Did we?"

"Yes. I remember now. You dared me to eat the mistletoe."

This was an inauspicious start to the conversation. Challenging men to taste the poisonous plant was her standard response when they got overly friendly with the holiday traditions.

"It looks like you didn't take me up on it," she said blandly.

He laughed, his expression taking on a distinct leer.

"No, but it was a close call. Your friend saved me right before I was about to take a bite."

Recognition hit her like a brick to the heart. Although her memory was never at its best when she'd been drinking—thus its appeal—flashes hit her from all sides, sending her into physical recoil.

She and Sara in matching reindeer sweaters, which they'd found in the kids' section at Bergdorf's and forced their adult-sized torsos into for the party. Sara saving her from some bulldog-faced creeper under the mistletoe, saying she'd met him once at a party and wouldn't mind following up. Sara disappearing into yet another relationship a few weeks later, the same way she always did whenever a new man entered her life.

No way. *This isn't happening.* Not here. Not like this. Getting hit on by Dana Carstairs in a nightclub couldn't possibly be what the universe wanted for her right now.

"It's you." The word was venom on her tongue and in her veins.

"Yes, it is," he agreed, seemingly oblivious to the explosions taking place behind Becca's eyes. "And even though it's a little early for mistletoe, I still wouldn't say no to that kiss."

She snapped, instinct and anger and an overpowering sensation of loss taking over. The bastard wasn't expecting anything but a gentle rebuff, and he fell to the ground, his body hitting the black carpet with a thud. Pausing only long enough to take a breath and double check to make sure it was actually Dana Carstairs she had pinned beneath her thighs, she lifted her arms and started landing her fists wherever she could get them.

Face, shoulders, head. "Fucker, fuckface, dirtbag."

Arms, hands, stomach. "Limp-dick hosebeast bastard."

As she hit her intended marks, she felt a mounting sense of both frustration and satisfaction fill her. In the non-fuzzy part of her brain, she knew there were better ways to handle her feelings. Ladylike ways. Rational ways.

But rational behavior didn't begin to touch the rage that swelled in her throat, choking her. Rational behavior wasn't going to make her feel whole again.

"Somebody get her off me!" Dana cried. "I was kidding. It was a joke. A pickup line."

A pickup line? He thought this was about a poor attempt at getting in her pants?

Without pausing for a breath, she shoved her face close enough to rip his ear off with her teeth. Strong arms manacled her from behind and tried lifting her off his body, but Mean Max had been having her work double time on her quads lately, so she was able to keep her grip tight long enough to land something much stronger than a physical blow.

"It was you. You killed her. You pushed her over the edge."

At the sound of her words, cold and hard, the only lucid thing coming out of her right now, Dana's movements came to a sudden halt. So did hers, the pair of them breathing heavily as their eyes met and she was able to see his fear glinting up at her.

She recognized that fear. She understood that fear. He was panicked, trapped, exposed.

Which was why she shouldn't have been surprised when he raised his arm and struck his fist out, catching her on the side of the head and splitting her burgeoning headache in two. Water filled her eyes, and the entire room took on an eerie, ringing silence as though she'd been plunged underwater.

Strong arms wrapped around her again, this time accompanied by Jake's low, murmuring voice, which did more to calm her than fifty punches to the side of the head ever could. "Come on, Tiger. Relax. He's already covered in blood and weeping for his mother."

"Oh, I'll make him bleed," she said, her voice coming as if from a distance. "I'll make him wish he'd never climbed out of his mother in the first place."

"And I'd be happy to help, but this is neither the time nor the place for it."

She felt herself being lifted up and away, her limbs hitting nothing but air. Flashes of light went off in the periphery, and her full capacity to hear returned as voices rose around her. Both of those things were inevitable signals that she'd drawn a crowd. Somewhere deep inside, a place where the rage hadn't touched and the pain sometimes slept, Becca realized Jake was right.

You're making a scene again. You're giving them exactly what they want.

"Get that crazy bitch out of here." Dana struggled to his feet with the help of a pair of men in dark shirts, the back of his hand held to his lip where she'd managed to land a solid enough blow to cut him open. "And have her tested for rabies while you're at it. She's obviously on something."

"I'm not on anything, you fuckwit." Since Jake was still holding her aloft while she struggled to kick herself free, she had to settle for a solid glare. "And you know it. Otherwise you wouldn't be so scared—"

"What say we walk this one off, Tiger?" There was Jake's voice again, crooning in her ear. He used the clipped, carefully practiced tones not uncommon among this crowd, but there was a gently soothing undertone to it that didn't feel fabricated. "You've got about fifty witnesses and ten cameras to prove you won this round. Take it from an expert gambler and let it ride."

She dropped her feet to the ground, surprised when they wobbled at the knees. Jake's arm wrapped around her waist, strengthening her stance and causing some of the red to ebb out of her line of vision.

See? Men's arms were always good for something.

"Don't look at him. Don't look at the crowd. And don't you dare look at your feet."

But she had to look at *something*.

"Right here, Becca. Look at me."

She did. His eyes, a virulent blue, glittered at her under the nightclub lights. She thought she recognized a flash of something—maybe appreciation, more likely disdain—before she realized it was actually the dozen or so paparazzi cameras going off in the distance.

So much for the discreet backdoor exit. Not even the surly man standing guard could keep the vultures at bay in the face of such a tasty story as Rebecca Clare pouncing on Dana Carstairs in the back of a nightclub. Nine nights out of ten found them in that exact location, waiting for the moment she exposed herself as the useless, hot mess of a human being she really was.

But Jake's arm was firm at her waist, his voice a swipe of authority she didn't have the energy to fight. "You've got this. You're going to hold on to my arm with your head held high. We're walking out that door and going three blocks."

"Why three?"

"Because there's a quieter club where we can call your Liam."

"Liam." She whimpered. "I want Liam."

He lifted her chin with one finger. "And don't you dare cry."

She clamped her mouth shut and swallowed the millions of shards of glass that seemed to suddenly lodge in her throat. "Okay."

"Good girl."

Jake's arm proved useful once again as they pushed their way past the hangers-on and into the crisp night air, which smelled of fall and asphalt and rotting waste, a scent that belonged entirely to New York in September. But as they got farther from the noisy press of the club, Becca realized that *pushed* wasn't the right word for it. Jake didn't have to place a strategic elbow here or offer a polite cough there—people just sort of parted to make way for him. He was like some Biblical leader of old, except instead of serving as one of God's chosen, he seemed much closer to the devil. Flaming hair, lithe form, expensive tailoring that fell in perfectly geometrical shapes around him.

She was so busy paying attention to his close-fitting slacks she almost missed the sleek black car emerging stealthily from a block away. Jake's eyes—sharp and on point, the way a devil ought to be if he possibly could—spotted Liam the same time she did.

"Your chariot?"

She nodded, never more grateful at the prospect of Liam's grim, disapproving face than she was in that moment. She'd always thought her driver could be handsome, what with his silvery hair and deep-set eyes, if only he'd smile every now and then. But in the almost five years he'd worked for her, she'd never seen him look at her with anything but a bizarrely touching mixture of pity and censure.

She knew where that look came from. Even though Liam would never do anything to hurt her, it was clear he found her reckless and thoughtless. He believed her entire life was a testament to bad decisions made in the public eye.

He wasn't wrong.

"They're still watching," Jake said grimly, as if reading her thoughts. "Make it a few more feet without attacking anyone, and I'll let you claw my eyes out in the car all you want."

She laughed, as she was sure he intended. The idea of doing *anything* to Jake Montgomery against his will, of ruffling the imperturbable calm that mantled him, had a way of sending her off into giggles. She'd once seen this man fall into a pond and emerge, godlike and soaking wet, without so much as a wrinkle of concern on his brow. And he'd been wearing white pants at the time.

"Evening, Mr. Montgomery." Liam was ready and waiting, also as calm as if they were all finishing brunch. "Ms. Clare. I hope you don't mind that I didn't wait for your call. I saw the excitement outside the club and assumed you'd be in need of a quick getaway."

Becca searched for the appropriate words of thanks— for being there, for his concern, for being her constant in a life that was anything but—but Jake took over for her.

"Your astuteness is appreciated. Let's get her out of here, shall we?"

Jake gestured for Liam to open the door and helped Becca inside before sliding in behind her. The closeness of the familiar gray interior felt like a coffin being nailed around her. A leather-scented, silver-paneled coffin with windows so tinted no curious passersby could peek in, yes, but a coffin nonetheless.

She leaned back against the headrest and closed her eyes, more to fight tears than fatigue. The side of her head where Dana had hit her ached with a dull, persistent throb. She'd broken at least two nails in the attack, leaving her bloodied and stubby and longing for the deep oblivion of a *real* coffin to rest her head. And worst of all, she was no closer to feeling sleepy than she'd been two hours ago.

Becca would have done almost anything to make those feelings go away—drink too much, dance too hard, fight her battles in a highly public venue. So when Jake's voice rippled over the short distance between them, a smoothly drawled "Well, you sure know how to make an exit, don't you?" she could hardly be blamed for flying over the seat toward him.

She'd already attacked one man tonight. What was one more?

THREE

Jake wasn't accustomed to being the better man.

The world was filled with men who were richer than him. Stronger than him. Better in bed and kinder to others and more likely to end up as a statue two hundred years from now. In fact, his one true accomplishment was his ability to accept his failings with good grace. At least half of the corruption in this world came from men who shared his weaknesses but refused to recognize them.

He was practically a public servant.

"Becca." Her name came out jumbled, lost as it was somewhere between the tangle of tongues and the open press of her sweet, vodka-scented lips against his. He didn't repeat himself right away either. The better man—the *decent* man—would have said something more. He wouldn't have run his hand up her naked thigh, knowing full well that there was no scrap of silk at the top to slow him down. He wouldn't have torn his fingers through her hair, tugging her head back to give him better access to her mouth, her jawline, that sweet spot along the side of a woman's neck where her pulse came to life under his lips. And he definitely wouldn't have lifted her off his lap and laid her out on the seat next to him, reveling in the dazed expression and flushed skin, which practically dared him to turn her down.

Goddammit. He really, really hated being the better man.

After taking a moment to adjust the cuffs of his shirt and smooth his slacks—unquestionably askew in the front—he moved one careful seat over. Becca frowned and got up to follow him, but he put up a hand to stop her.

"Stay where you are."

Her lower lip came out in an attractive pout. For all the rest of her charmingly unremarkable features, Becca's lips were a sight to behold. Soft and slick, always in some state of openmouthed promise, they had a mesmerizing quality that made a man forget just about everything else.

But only *just.* Not even the sight of her sweet mouth parting to let him in could erase the fact that she was highly intoxicated and in a state of emotional distress. He was no stranger to taking advantage of women—or to taking advantage of *this* woman in particular—but even he had to draw the line somewhere.

It was liberating, in a way. Now he knew where his line was. It rested just shy of drunk and mauled, on the right side of a few months out of a rehab stint.

Hurting. It rested on the right side of hurting.

"I mean it," he warned when she made a move to draw closer. "I forbid you from crossing this line."

"But I don't see any line."

"Then imagine one. It's thick and impenetrable—and you don't want to find out what happens if you cross it."

"Ooh, that sounds kinky." She licked her lips. "I like it."

He sighed. He liked the sound of that too, which was all the more reason to stop her before her tongue made any more of those provocative darting movements. "That wasn't a challenge. It was an order. I'm hereby putting an embargo on all sexual relations in this car."

"I promise Liam can't see back here. The window is tinted."

"Your modesty is touching but misplaced. It's not your driver I object to. It's you."

She winced, and he immediately regretted his words. *Oh, hell.* That wasn't what he meant. Of course he didn't object to her. He'd slept with her before, enjoyed it very much, wouldn't mind enjoying it several more times. But not like this.

He placed a hand on her leg to show he meant no harm, realizing as he did that physical contact of any kind was a mistake. Her skin burned hot and forbidden, and memories of the fit of her body fanned the flames even higher. Which was precisely why he forced his hand to stay in place. It was proof of his ability to master his baser urges, a promise to Becca—and to himself—that he could do the right thing. For once.

"Another time, perhaps," he said.

"You kissed me back."

"Yes, I did," he admitted, "and I'd love nothing more than to do it again. But what I'm going to do instead is take you home, put some ice on your face and hear what it is that made you almost extract Dana's eyeballs through his groin."

Becca's pique disappeared in an instant. She sat up, not bothering to adjust the skewed lines of the top of her dress. Jake could just make out the hint of a nipple peeking over the tight black band across her breasts and swallowed heavily, determined to avoid even thinking about it. For the duration of this evening, Becca had no nipples. No sex organs. She was a pod person.

"I wish I *had* done that," she said. "He deserves it. Is he a friend of yours?"

Jake paused. *Friend* was such a strong word, and one he wasn't sure fit his feelings toward the man. He sometimes found pleasure in Dana's company, and he preferred his abrasively callous honesty over plenty of other people he could name, but his wasn't the face Jake sought after a long, trying day.

To be fair, there was *no* face he sought after long, trying days—least of all his own, reflecting back at him in the mirror.

He decided not to answer that question. "What'd he do?"

Becca toyed with her skirt, plucking at strings that weren't there. "I don't want to talk about it."

He could understand her reservations, but he still had to ask. "Becca? Did he hurt you?"

She set her jaw and then winced, lifting a hand to her temple. "He punched me."

That would be a yes, then.

Aware that his question—and her answer—went a lot deeper than a fist to the side of her face, Jake nonetheless turned her cheek so he could better examine the wound. Her face was heart-shaped, her chin a tiny jut that he'd heard her lament on more than one occasion as being weak. For his part, he liked the dainty collection of bone and skin that composed her features. She wasn't an imposing figure, like so many of the women in his life, all of them looming large and finding fault. His stepmother, his sister, his cousin, the unsated masses. Sometimes he thought the feminine half of the world wouldn't be happy until he was broken under the collective weight of their disapproval.

But in all the time he had known her, Rebecca Clare had never been like that—mostly because in the land of family fuckups, she was the undisputed queen and leader. If he wrecked his yacht off the Spanish coast after a dangerous storm, Becca took over the spotlight by stealing a Maserati and taking it for a joyride with her friends. If yet another of his ex-girlfriends leaked a sex tape to the tabloids, Becca was caught in a compromising position with a public official. And she'd more than taken the cake a few months back, when she'd been sent to an upstate rehabilitation clinic.

The way he figured it, he owed this woman quite a bit for services rendered—and the one-time fling they'd shared the night his father married her sister three and a half years ago didn't count as payment. No matter how much fun they'd had sneaking out for a quickie in the vestry.

"I don't think it's going to bruise." He ran his thumb softly over the side of her face. Before he could stop himself, he was leaning in again, those sleek lips inviting him to come closer, nibble gently, fall back into the easy promise of the flesh. Because that's what Becca was—not easy in the cruel, misogynistic sense of the word, but in the understanding that there would be no complications afterward.

The lurch of the brakes jostled them both into awareness, saving him from making the mistake of landing the kiss. He was almost tempted to consider it divine intervention, but he made it a habit not to deal with deities of the northbound kind. This was damned good timing, plain and simple.

As if to reinforce the idea that he was a complete and utter ass, Becca grabbed his hand and clutched it tightly, transformed from a seductive woman writhing on the seat to a little girl afraid of monsters under the bed. "Come up with me."

"I'm not so sure that's a good idea."

"Please?" Her eyes opened wider, wrenching sympathy from unlikely places. "If you don't, Liam will feel it's his duty to check the locks on the windows and make me tea. It's impossible to drink tea while he's hovering there, afraid I might slip twenty sleeping pills in while he's not looking."

When he didn't respond right away, she sighed. "I'm not going to slip twenty sleeping pills in when you're not looking, Jake, so you can stop frowning at me like that. My suicide watch ended months ago."

It wasn't that. Well, it wasn't *only* that. Going up to Becca's apartment was a bad idea. He knew that on every level of comprehension he possessed. She was too tempting. They had too much history. The last thing he needed in his life right now was to heap her drama on top of his own.

But there was a cloud lined in silver hovering up those stairs—a cloud he might need to camp out under for a few weeks. He'd left Dana fuming and bloodied back at the club. Dana, the man he was staying with while he tried to figure out a more permanent solution to his financial problems. Dana, who'd punched a twenty-four-year-old woman in the face without so much as a twinge of conscience. The idea of crawling back to him and begging entry for the night wasn't one he relished by any stretch of the imagination.

Becca had space. And money. And she was a hell of a lot of fun. If he was going to have to earn his living as a parasite, he couldn't think of a better host to affix himself to.

"Sure thing, Tiger. I'll come up." He slid out of the car and extended a helping hand to extract his tipsy step-aunt, battling the somewhat new sensation of desire and guilt mixing in his gut.

She released a relieved sigh and looked up at him with such a pleased, beaming expression that the guilt took a clear lead in the stomach-churning department.

"Thanks, Jake. You're the best."

He wasn't, and hearing such a compliment from her lips was almost enough to send him running back to Dana's. But she was drunk and in pain, so he let that one slide.

BECCA'S APARTMENT WAS housed a few blocks outside Gramercy Park in a gaudy, garish building that towered over its more historic and brick-laced neighbors. She'd never loved the location—it was too staid for her tastes—but tonight, home had a welcome aura about it that made her happy to be somewhere familiar. And *with* someone familiar too. If anyone could frighten away the ghosts hiding in the corners, it was the devil himself.

She grabbed Jake's arm more firmly and squeezed, allowing his careful pace to lead her into the elevator and up to her third-floor residence.

"Christ, Becca. Don't you have a cleaner?"

She could see Jake's fastidious nose moving up as they crossed the threshold into her mess of a home— though *mess* wasn't quite fair. There wasn't any dirt in the place, not unless you counted things like a few hairs in her brush in the middle of the living room floor or the speckled powder of her bronzer that had shattered all over the kitchen counter before she left. Or the piles of clothes that lay strewn about like party favors gone awry.

She was good at getting dressed, but like all things worth doing well, it was a process. And she was an Aries, who everyone knew couldn't be bothered to clean up afterward.

"Of course I have a cleaner," she said, and wound her arms around his neck, hoping to cajole him another one of those knee-knocking kisses. For all his faults, Jake had always been a good kisser. So precise and intent. "But she wasn't here this evening when I was getting ready. She came in the morning."

"You did this much damage in one day?" Jake didn't seem to care that her lips were mere inches from his as his gaze skimmed over her apartment's interior. Her home was Spartan as far as interior design went—mostly big white couch-like showpieces that looked more comfortable than they actually were and shiny, opaque tabletops that showcased every fingerprint. Her mother's designer thought the minimalist setting and oversized furniture would set Becca off to advantage, as if she was a fairy Alice in her own private winter Wonderland. When she'd gotten the apartment for her eighteenth birthday present, she'd been photographed just like that for *Centerpiece* magazine. Sky-blue dress with a ruffled underskirt spread around her, her hair bound in a ribbon and a fluffy white rabbit in her lap. *How precious*.

"You're a more destructive force than I realized." Jake shrugged himself out of her embrace. "Is there a bed under one of these piles?"

Becca frowned. She'd thought that once Jake was up here, he'd be a little more amenable to seduction. She was warm. She was willing. And, oh, God, how she wanted to feel something right now. *Anything.* Having once enjoyed the pleasures this man offered, she knew the cathartic bliss of fifteen minutes under his care.

Heck—at this point, she'd take ten minutes. Five. A slap and a tickle before bed.

She sighed, resigned to none of the above.

"Good." He placed a firm hand on the small of her back and pushed her toward her bedroom. "Go put on pajamas and get under the covers. I'll bring you some water and an ice pack."

"I don't have any ice packs." She wasn't even sure she had water.

"Do you always argue when you're drunk?"

"I'm not arguing."

He didn't deign to reply, but wandered off in the direction of the kitchen—the most likely holding place for water in its various forms. Left with the unpleasant task of holding her injured head up even though it felt as if it weighed three tons, she shuffled toward her bedroom, where the oversized white bed was decorated with about twenty throw pillows and at least as many discarded outfits.

She unzipped her dress and disentangled herself from the straps, allowing the garment to fall to the floor with a soft thump. Rooting around the piles for something appropriately pajama-like to wear was too monumental a hurdle to tackle, so she lifted the blankets at the foot of the bed and crawled inside, tunneling her way to the top.

The sound of Jake entering her room and looking for her among the piles was muffled but discernible, and she knew the exact moment he realized she was yet another bundle under the bundles.

"Drink," he commanded, and a cup materialized at her head.

She sat up grudgingly, the blanket falling away.

"Christ." Jake pulled back, his movements sharp. "I thought I told you to put on pajamas."

His sudden movements caused a wave of water to splash over her neck and down her bare chest. She fought an urge to giggle at the horrified confusion that crossed Jake's face. He had to have seen his fair share of naked breasts in his day, and discomfiting him with hers held a certain kind of charm—especially since she'd never considered them all that fantastic. They were on the small size, with too-big nipples that made wardrobe malfunctions a real threat when she wore something plunging, but they did the trick most of the time.

She drank. "They aren't going to bite you."

"Here." He exchanged the water for a towel, which was wrapped around something lumpy and cold to the touch. "Slip that under your pillowcase while you sleep. It'll melt, but it's better than nothing. I'll be in the guest room next door if you need me."

"You're not going to join me in this big cozy bed?"

"No, Becca. I'm not." He dropped a gentle and uncharacteristic finger to her cheek. Jake had never been a touchy-feely man—at least, not unless the touching and feeling were directly related to sex or the pursuit thereof—so she appreciated the gesture. "You've had a rough night. Sleep it off."

The mention of the evening's preceding events moved through Becca's head in a blur of images—all of them accompanied by a hollow, aching sensation that settled on her chest. She clutched his hand.

"Stay with me." When she saw his frown, she spoke

faster, almost frantic. "I'll put on pajamas. I'll put on six layers of pajamas and a parka. Just stay in the bed with me. Don't leave me here by myself."

Jake stared at her—at the decent and the indecent parts of her, at the disastrous explosion of crap that covered her bed, at the sloppily drunk mess she was sure her hair and makeup presented. She was hardly operating at her best here, but she brought her hands together in a clasp, her plea evident. *Say yes. Please say yes.*

Time had a way of losing meaning when a person had consumed as much alcohol as she had, and it seemed an eternity before he finally gave in. Heaving a sigh, he began tugging at the tie that pulled all the impeccable lines of his tailoring together.

"Sure thing, Tiger. If it's that important."

Her gratitude wasn't so much a squeal as a long, thankful exhalation of air. She put on the T-shirt that he tossed over her head and laid herself gingerly on the icy cold pillow. It seemed ages before Jake finally joined her, his body long and warm and still fully clothed. The impression of his weight at her back brought a restful kind of comfort. She flopped to her other side and snuggled against him, placing her head on his chest, loving the steady, regular sound of his breathing.

Jake was unflappable and calm, even now. Nothing ruffled this man. Nothing upset his carefully ordered existence.

As he held her close and whispered a long-suffering "Good night" to the top of her hairline, she wondered what it must be like to live in a world like that. Where everything made sense. Where pain came in only when you allowed it.

Dreaming of that kind of existence was *almost*

enough. As the deep reaches of sleep beckoned for the first time in what felt like forever, she was nearly able to banish the images that haunted her every time she closed her eyes, images so eerily close to the ones in the nightclub earlier.

In those images, she was still kneeling on top of a body, still frantically clawing and pushing to get a reaction. But instead of trying to take the life out of that rat bastard, Dana, she was trying to put life back into her best friend, Sara. Trying and striving and failing long after the paramedics pulled her away and ordered someone to *tranq the bitch before she makes things worse.*

Silly paramedics. As if things could ever get worse than that.

FOUR

JAKE HAD WOKEN up in many a strange place in his life—and with many a strange setting in the background. The sights and sounds of the surf in a Tahitian villa were by far his favorite. The bleating of goats outside a hotel room in Mexico fell at the other end of the spectrum, but that was part of a long story he didn't care to repeat.

He wasn't so sure he cared to repeat this one either. This was unquestionably the first time he'd ever heard "Eye of the Tiger" blasted at top volume while surrounded by a cloud of fluffy white bedding.

"What the hell—?" He rolled over and felt the friction of his fully clothed body rustling against the sheets as awareness of his surroundings dawned. The softly curled form pressed lengthwise against him brought understanding even more into focus, but he had yet to determine the source of the god-awful music or why the hell it was so loud. "Becca? Becca, wake up. Someone is trying to *Rocky* us out of bed."

The pitch and frequency of her groan indicated just how intoxicated she'd been the night before—and it was much more than a woman of one hundred pounds should ever be. Her head was burrowed under about three pillows, but as the song slipped into a refrain, she poked one tentative side of her face out. "That's Mean Max. I didn't think he'd come today. Ignore him."

Despite the fact that Jake made it a point never to

ignore a man whose name was preceded by *mean*, he took a pillow from Becca and slammed it over his ears, hoping to drown out some of the noise. He thought it worked as the music came to a stop, but a heavy whirring took its place. It sounded as if someone had put nails in a blender.

He rolled over again, this time taking a moment to swing his feet to the floor. He wasn't an early riser by any stretch of the imagination, but once he was up, he was up. Unlike Snoring Beauty over there, who seemed to have nodded back off to a happier, less hungover place.

His place was far from happy. His clothes were rumpled beyond recognition, and as he brushed a hand over his jaw, he felt a scratchy growth that reminded him all his belongings were still at Dana's house.

"Out of bed, Becca," a deep and annoyingly cheerful voice called through the flung-open French doors leading to her living room. "I warned you about overintoxication and how hard it is to counteract the effects. Right now, your body is grieving for the damages you put it through. It has every right to be upset. Oh—hello. You have company."

Jake didn't move as the man referred to as Mean Max materialized in the doorway. There was no questioning whether or not the qualifier in front of his name was apt. He certainly looked mean. *Big* and mean, composed of layers of flesh that might taste good over an open spit. He was one of those men whose neck and head were virtually the same width, who couldn't quite cross his arms all the way over his chest. A buzz cut and form-fitting athletic gear completed a look of bovine aggression, though he extended a glass of something murky and pink to take the edge off.

The man's eyes took Jake in—wrinkled, frowning, possibly the least rested he'd ever been in his life—and shook the glass. "Your guest looks like he could use a little less intoxication himself. Have a sip and make sure Becca drinks the rest. We're out the door in ten."

"No, thanks." Jake didn't drink pink cocktails. Or take orders from men who seemed perilously close to overstepping their bounds.

Max shrugged. "Suit yourself." He pressed the glass into Jake's hand with a request for him to hold it, and marched up to Becca's bed. With one firm tug, he sent the blankets and all the crap they'd been too tired to move off the bed last night flying. He also yanked on Becca's ankle, expertly flipping her from her stomach to her back.

Jake released an almost unrecognizable growl at the familiar way Max took charge of Becca's personal space. He didn't know who this guy thought he was or what kind of arrangement he and Becca had, but he'd gone from perilously close to overstepping his bounds to plunging headfirst into Jake's angry place.

Jake's angry place wasn't a pleasant place to be. He knew. He spent much more time there than any man should.

"Up and at 'em." Max spoke in the same deep, cheerful tones as before, even as Jake neared his side, prepared to break the glass of pink crap in his face. Max didn't even blink at him. "Step back, if you please. Seven o'clock is my time. You can have her when I'm done."

"I beg your pardon?" Jake asked dangerously.

"Rebecca Louise Clare, you have exactly ten minutes to get out of bed, drink this protein shake and meet me out front in your running gear. Every minute late is an extra mile during warm-ups. Do you understand?"

Jake didn't know about the groggy mess under the blankets, but he was certainly starting to. "Oh. You're her personal trainer."

"Of course." Max's gaze swiped over Jake, and it was clear from the way he shrugged at the end that he wasn't impressed with what he saw. "You should call me. I could fill you out in no time."

Jake gave in and laughed. As much as he'd like to have a reason to crack a glass over someone's head, this fellow—barging in here as if he owned the place, daring to tackle the groaning, hot mess of a woman on the bed—wasn't it. "Thanks, but I don't take orders very well. And you look like a fan of the tough-love method."

"That I am," Max acknowledged with a nod. He slapped a hand on Becca's bare thigh, the crack of his palm on flesh filling the air. "You're down to nine minutes. I don't think you want to push me today. You know I warned you about taking it easy on your liver. If you don't learn to treat your body well, I'll be forced to do it for you."

She was closer to awake now, having twisted around enough to resemble a person sitting up. Her hair hung limp and crooked to one side, her eyes so smudged in black she might have been in stage costume. And the look of abject pleading in the doe-like eyes she turned Jake's way was unmistakable.

Jake put his hands up. "I'm not saving you from this one. I didn't hire the guy."

"I'm really good," Max said.

"He's really good," Becca echoed. Her voice was a mumble, but at least she rolled all the way out of bed.

Although Jake had managed to get her in a T-shirt the night before, he hadn't been able to swing much else. Her legs emerged, lean and catlike, from the bottom of the hem, the shadow of her ass visible if he tilted his head just so.

He didn't tilt his head again. Neither, he noticed, did the personal trainer.

He decided he liked the guy.

"Eight minutes." Max made an obvious gesture at the stopwatch around his neck and left the bedroom, tactfully closing the door behind him.

"He sounds serious. Here." Jake handed her the drink and she grimaced, plugged her nose and downed the whole thing in one gulp.

He did a little gulping of his own. Becca had amazing swallowing reflexes, and his body was eager to remind him that he'd spent the night next to her warm, willing and annoyingly clingy legs, which had wrapped around his own within seconds of her falling asleep last night. Imagining her as a pod person had only worked when he'd been able to maintain actual physical distance. For most of the night, he'd had to lie there and count sheep.

"What's in the drink?" he asked, primarily to distract himself.

"As far as I can tell?" After discarding the glass on the nearest horizontal surface, Becca lifted her hair from the back of her neck and twisted it into a ponytail. The upward motion of her arms exposed the neat line of her bare cunt, but she continued unaware. Or uncaring. Probably both. "Voodoo. I've only ever seen him add about five raw eggs and a handful of strawberries, but if it doesn't contain the menstrual blood of the Virgin Mary, I'd be shocked."

"And you willingly put it in your mouth?"

Becca just laughed and continued tearing around her room. She located a pair of tiny Lycra shorts and wiggled into them while Jake remained in place, unable to tear his gaze from the squeeze and pull of her naked ass into the fabric. Whether being peeled on or peeled off, clothes and this woman clearly had a good working relationship.

"Don't question the magic. Will you be here when I get back?"

He knew better than to read a double meaning into her query. With other women—women who might have been aware of their nudity, women he would have had no problems fucking last night—questions like that were swords with edges on all sides. But Becca had always been blissfully free of ulterior motives. She made no promises and even fewer demands. If she wanted to know whether or not he planned on sticking around, it was because she wanted to know whether or not he planned on sticking around. Her meaning was that simple.

It was also a fairly decent indicator that last night's plan to ingratiate himself into her good graces wasn't a total bust. Her apartment was a mess and she had duct tape on all her light switches that prevented them from turning off. What had begun as a vaguely appealing idea last night now took over his conscience, rendering it void. Becca clearly needed a roommate to keep her in check and save her electricity bill. Who was to say he wouldn't make an excellent candidate?

"Yeah," he said. "If it's okay with you, I'll stick around."

She beamed. "Perfect."

Without elaborating further, she slipped off her shirt and rummaged around in her piles until she extracted a yellow sports bra-like top, bright and firm. Once again, he found it difficult to look away as she pulled it over her head and manually adjusted each rounded breast to fit inside. Less than six hours ago, he'd refused himself the pleasure of those breasts. And the last time—the only time—they'd fucked, it had been quick and hard and loud, not nearly enough time for him to admire the body that had wrapped around his.

He was mesmerized by it now. Everything about Becca was so neat and compact. Body hair so groomed there was nothing but skin as far as the eye could see. Small breasts with decadently expansive nipples in a dark brownish-pink. Her efficient movements as she covered it all up only added fuel to the fire. He knew she could pull out all the stops and lead a man by his balls, but there was something about her innocent acceptance of her nudity that hit him on a deeper level.

She wasn't showing off. She wasn't trying a different tactic after last night's efforts at seduction failed. She was just Becca—take her or leave her or stand around stupefied while you searched for a third option.

Before he had time to come up with one, she leaned in and dropped a kiss on his lips, her tongue flicking lightly inside his mouth, tasting of strawberry menstrual blood and making him feel that perhaps he'd underestimated her. Maybe the past five minutes had been nothing but a peepshow designed to push him into a hot, bothered corner from which there was only one release.

Last night's chaste sleepover to the contrary, he was rather fond of that kind of release.

But then she pulled a one-eighty and frowned, looking again like a little girl who'd lost her way. "God, my head hurts." She touched the side of her face where she'd been punched, no bruise or even a swelling to indicate that anything had happened. It was almost as though Dana knew exactly where to hit a woman without leaving a mark.

"Did I really brawl with Dana Carstairs in the middle of a club last night?"

"Yes. I'm afraid you did."

"Did I win?"

Jake felt his lips quiver. "I think it might have ended in a tie."

She didn't let that get her down. With a quick stab of her fingers under each eye to wipe the smudged makeup away, she offered a wobbly smile and said, "I guess there's always next time."

"Is there going to *be* a next time?"

"There will be if there's any justice in this world." She checked the clock—an assortment of oversized Roman numerals hung on the wall with a set of small ticking hands in the middle—and swore. "I gotta run. Max is going to kill me."

"How long will you be gone?"

"An hour. Two, tops. Be a doll and have the shower waiting for me, won't you?" She bounded toward the door, a spring in her step and a bounce in her ass. She paused long enough to blow him a kiss over her shoulder. "It'd be even better if you were in it at the time. Preferably naked."

JAKE DOUBTED DANA would be up at such an ungodly hour of the day, but he headed to the other man's apartment as soon as Becca and her vigilant trainer jogged out the door. All of the belongings he'd brought to New York were stashed in the sleek guest room he'd called home, however temporarily, and he wasn't about to spend an entire day in last night's rumpled leftovers.

He let himself in with the spare key Dana had provided, moving through the hall without much noise. It didn't take long to pack up the few shirts and slacks he'd brought along, even though he took his time carefully folding them atop one another. Almost a week he'd been here, and he hadn't left so much as a toothbrush in the bathroom. Dana's apartment wasn't the sort that invited a man to make himself at home. Jake appreciated cleanliness as much as the next guy, but living here had been a bit like balancing on a trip wire.

"Your aunt is some kind of fucked up, you know that?"

Jake didn't turn as Dana's voice rose from the doorway, gravelly and hoarse and pissed off. He sounded like a man who'd gotten the shit kicked out of him by a girl.

He sounded like a man who'd deserved it.

"I hate to make blanket generalizations, but my whole family is fucked up." Jake calmly zipped his garment bag closed and folded it over his forearm. "It's part of our charm."

He laughed as soon as he saw Dana. His lip was split open on one side, his eye a puffy red from where Becca had jammed her thumb into the orifice. He could only assume, from the stiff way Dana held himself, that she'd gotten a few solid punches to his midsection as well.

Too bad. Jake didn't care how much Becca had been hitting him. You didn't hit back. Not if you had an ounce of decency in you.

"I'm glad you find this so amusing, but she's lucky I don't press charges. She attacked me out of nowhere. That's assault."

"True. But I seem to recall you landed a fairly telling blow of your own last night—and with plenty of witnesses around. I don't think making an official record of you punching a woman is going to help your image any."

"She could have killed me."

"She can't have been the first woman to try."

Dana scowled, and Jake adopted a casual air, hoping to get him to elaborate on the subject. There was more to this story than a bad pickup line in a nightclub and a woman with too much alcohol in her system. Becca was unstable, to put it mildly, but he'd never seen her turn violent before.

"What's with all the hatred between you two, anyway?" he asked. "Did you have a falling out?"

"Don't be ridiculous. I've only met her once before. She had no reason to fly off the handle like that." The way his face flushed, highlighting the bruise under his eye, seemed to indicate he was playing fast and loose with the truth. "If you ask me, it was drugs. You know how those girls get. They don't eat for days and then stuff their nostrils with anything they can get their—"

"I'd stop there if I were you."

Dana made a motion as if he wanted to ward off the evil eye. "Everyone knows Rebecca Clare is a walking disaster."

"She may be a walking disaster, but she's a walking disaster I happen to be related to. You might be able to saunter away from a fight with her with a split lip and a nasty bruise or two, but you should watch how far you push me."

Dana scowled but retreated. *A wise move.*

"Thank you for your hospitality," Jake said coolly,

"but I've made alternate arrangements for the foreseeable future. You can forward my calls to Becca's."

"I'm not your damned secretary," Dana muttered, but he sighed and dug into his pocket for a slip of paper. "Here. Your brother called this morning and asked you to contact him at this number. Doesn't he know that normal people are asleep at five-thirty?"

Jake had to laugh. "He does it on purpose. He wants you to know that he's already been up and working for two hours. You're supposed to feel ashamed of yourself."

"Fucking Montgomerys," he said, and turned on his heel, retreating back into the dark gloom of the hallway. "It's a good thing you have each other, because no one else can stand you."

Jake didn't disagree. That was practically their family motto.

"Hello, Monty." Jake let himself back into Becca's apartment, his cell phone held in the crook of his neck. His wayward hostess hadn't yet returned from her training session, so he amused himself by removing the tape from all the light switches. It seemed like an awfully dramatic way to keep the lights on. "How kind of you to call. Were you checking up to see how my progress is going?"

"I suppose you think this is funny."

"I find many things entertaining, so I'm leaning toward yes."

"It's all a big joke to you."

"Again, the odds are good enough that I'm going to have to agree. Was there a point to all this, or did you just want to make sure my sense of humor is intact?"

"You have no idea what I'm talking about, do you?"

He didn't, but that was hardly anything new where Monty was concerned. While Jake made it a point to get to know other people—study them, watch them, learn from them—Monty existed almost exclusively inside his own head. It wasn't uncommon for his brother to hold entire board meetings on topics no one knew about but him.

"Not a clue," he said cheerfully. Some of the tape residue stuck to the light switch in the kitchen, so he looked around for something he could use to scrape it off. "But it doesn't matter. I'm in an exceptionally good mood today."

As expected, his positivity goaded Monty into even more gloom. "Oh? I suppose you're trying to pretend you're doing fine on your own."

"That's because I *am* doing fine on my own." He finally found a lone butter knife in one of the drawers. "You told me I wouldn't last a week on my own without robbing a bank, trading on the family name or coming home with my tail between my legs. Tomorrow marks day eight, and I see nothing but smooth sailing ahead."

He could practically hear Monty's scowl. "One week is nothing. You couldn't find a way to support yourself indefinitely. That would require you finding an actual job."

"You always think along such narrow lines." Jake transferred the phone to speaker so he could work on the light switch. "Job. Employment. Time clock. There are other ways to get by in this world, you know."

"Not legal ones."

He scraped too hard, and the knife nicked his thumb, causing him to swear. Even though the knife was as dull as a block of wood, he could see blood forming on the tip. Who put duct tape on the light switches in the first place?

"What's all that noise?" Monty demanded. "What are you doing?"

"Earning my keep," Jake said. "You know what, Monty? I'm tired of you thinking everyone has to spend as many hours behind a desk as you do, or they're somehow invalid as human beings. You'd be surprised at how easy it is to be successful without lifting a finger."

He stuck his own finger in his mouth to stop the bleeding.

"Fine," Monty said. "Prove it. Make it to the end of the year. See how long you can last without me or dad to prop you up."

Jake was startled into a laugh. "Are you asking me to place a wager? You *do* know who you're talking to, right?"

"It's three and a half months from now. I'm not worried. Not even you can coast that long."

There was no denying that Jake had been born with a gambler's blood. For as long as he could remember, he'd felt a rush at pitting himself against any kind of competitor. He'd raced worms and then bikes and then yachts. He'd played blackjack and then poker and then craps. He'd bet lunch money and then his allowance and then small fortunes.

He didn't always win, but he always made good on his end of the deal. And no one ever had more fun losing.

"And if I do?" he asked, unable to avoid picking up the gauntlet. "What do I get?"

"Nothing. You'll be successful. You won't need anything from me."

Jake laughed and accepted his brother's taunt in good

form. His favorite bets were always the ones where the only stake was pride. "Then I gladly accept. Prepare to be dazzled, brother dear. I plan to make it to January on my wits alone."

"Good. And please pick up a newspaper while you're at it. Your wits are all over the front page again."

FIVE

"I DON'T HEAR THE shower going," Becca said, her words a half-groan.

She'd only made it through the front door of her apartment before falling to the ground, her body, mind and soul collapsing together in an exhausted heap. Mean Max had been in a mood this morning. She wasn't sure if it was his disappointment at her treating her body as anything less than a temple, or if his girlfriend—an explosive, fiery redhead who lived up to her hair color in ways Becca could only be in awe of—had thrown all his stuff out their apartment window again. Either way, Becca had never done so many crunches in her life. She'd thrown up halfway through the morning session, and even that hadn't stopped him from yelling at her to keep going.

Her abs had better look as good as her ass soon.

She blinked as Jake's face materialized above her own. He looked as though he'd spent a calm, restful morning brushing his hair, though his packed bags in the hallway indicated he'd been busy.

"And you're not naked," she pointed out. "I thought I told you to be naked."

Clearly, no man had ever wanted to be naked with her less. With a cool kind of appraisal guaranteed to make her aware of every last one of her open and sweating pores, he said, "I'll tell you what. You get up off that floor right now and take my clothes off for me, and I'll fuck you any way you want."

She thought about it for a full twenty seconds, and if Jake had been wearing anything but an Oxford shirt done all the way to the top and pants with an annoyingly complicated belt holding them up, she might have taken him up on the offer. But there were so many buttons. The thought of moving her arms enough to undo each one almost had her throwing up again.

"You're a bastard." She rolled onto her side and curled into a ball. There. That was more comfortable. "A real gentleman would lift me off the ground and do all the work himself."

"Yes, well." He walked away. "I never pretended to be a gentleman."

She was pretty sure she could have started snoring right there on the floor. Despite one of the best, most comfortable night's sleeps she'd had in a long time— or perhaps because of it—the warm cocoon of oblivion beckoned.

Unfortunately, her obligations for the day ahead beckoned harder. Releasing a sigh, she managed to get her arms underneath her and pushed to a sitting position. "You could at least help me up," she grumbled. Her line of visibility didn't include a glimpse of Jake, but she could hear him rummaging around in the kitchen. She hoped he wasn't trying to cook anything. The smell of a piece of toast right now would send her over the edge. She didn't want to think about what an egg might do.

"Hello?" she called. "I'm a lady in need over here. Heave me to the shower. I'm supposed to be dressed and fit to appear at my mother's by noon. She wants me to read the tea leaves for her friends. Did you hear I predicted Wesley's engagement to the oldest Dauphine girl last month? Got the date right and everything. It was in the chamomile."

Jake's head emerged from the kitchen doorway. "It was also in the paper. We *all* saw that one coming."

She narrowed her eyes at him. "Spoken like a true Virgo."

"Spoken like a man who follows rational processes of thought," he countered. He paused before speaking again, his gaze heavy in a way that signaled he wasn't looking forward to the conversation to come. People looked at her like that a lot more than she cared to admit—she was practically a leper of modern social discourse. "And before you go to Grandmama Clare's, there's something you should probably see first."

His words drew a laugh out of her, putting her at ease. Her mom *hated* it when Jake called her Grandmama, which was of course why he continued to make it a habit. It was her mom's own fault in the first place. What did she expect, encouraging her oldest daughter to fall for a man in his sixties? The Montgomerys were a great family to marry into if you cared about things like breeding and prestige, but Serena was three years older than her now-stepson Jake. And she only had about eight months on Monty. Even Jenna, her youngest stepdaughter, was still older than Becca.

It was weird. And a little bit gross.

"Fine, but you have to carry me to the table. I'm not kidding. I'm not so sure my limbs work anymore."

Shaking his head, Jake came to help her. His arms were strong as they hoisted her unforgivingly from the ground and planted her on her feet. She realized that was all she was going to get from him as he pushed her in the direction of the kitchen. She had a lovely alcove overlooking the courtyard in there, sun streaming in and hitting the white lacquered dining set with the kind of brilliance she wished she could capture and save for nightfall.

"What did that guy do to you anyway?"

"Sprints. Crunches. Push-ups. Something called a Brazilian Butt Lift."

He raised an eyebrow in disbelief.

"Go ahead. Touch it." She turned to give him access to her backside. "He's a genius when it comes to a woman's glutes. You could use this thing as a trampoline."

"I can see that," Jake muttered, his eyes flashing. But he didn't touch, not even when she gave an enticing waggle. *Sheesh*—this man was difficult to penetrate. Or to get to penetrate. He pulled out a chair and pushed her unceremoniously into it. "But you've got bigger problems than the elasticity of your ass. You're going to want to read that."

He pointed at the newspaper sitting next to a to-go cup of coffee and the decimated remains of a bagel-and-lox breakfast—both signs that Jake had been making himself at home here. She hoped it meant he intended to make this a long stay. A girl could get used to being wrapped up in those strong, unwavering arms at night. Even without sex or a long, slow goodnight kiss, she'd fallen right to sleep and stayed that way. No shadows. No nightmares. No memories.

He gestured at the paper again with a command for her to read. She complied, but only because she wanted to check her horoscope. Ever since they'd gotten that new woman at the *National Beat*, she hadn't missed a single day. Madame Pernaud was a genius, but only

about half the time. It was as though she was afraid of
revealing too much in something as commonplace as a
tabloidy newspaper, so she always tempered her wisdom
with something ridiculously off the cuff.

> *Aries (March 21-April 19): Now is the time to ig-
> nore petty acts of vengeance and focus on the big
> picture. Ally yourself with an earth sign to further
> your cause, but beware of how deep you can dig
> in this temporary partnership. The 23rd is a good
> day for a party. Wear the pink.*

Becca snorted. As if she'd ever wear the pink. She
looked awful in pink. It made her feel like a lollipop.

The rest of that, though…

She sat back and stared, unseeing, at the words in
front of her. There was no denying that attacking Dana
at the club last night had been a petty act. Petty and
stupid and not at all effective in the long run. Madame
Pernaud was right. No amount of public confrontations
would change the fact that Sara was gone.

Becca needed to think bigger. Look further. Ally herself with an earth sign, apparently.

"You can't miss it." Jake grew tired of watching as
Becca flipped through the trashy tabloid, skimming
over the important pages and spending a few minutes
on the horoscopes with her brows drawn tight. "It's on
the front page."

She ignored him, her fingers tapping restlessly on the
table. "Did you know Virgos are an earth sign?"

"I know I don't understand most of that sentence."

"Virgo, Capricorn, Taurus—you're all earth signs."
When he didn't change his expression, she rolled her

eyes. "It's not complicated. It just means you have a tendency to be heavy and tied down, like the earth. Getting you to change is like relocating a mountain, rock by rock."

"Now that you mention it, I *have* been known to shake worlds."

Her look of disdain indicated his joke had fallen somewhat short of its mark. "Now, me?" she said. "I'm fire."

"That I do believe." Quick to burn, dangerous to touch, hot as all hell. "But if you think you're going to convince me of anything but what a waste of time this is, you're bound for disappointment. Astrology is nothing more than the ramblings of an overpaid writer with a New Age penchant."

"What an original viewpoint you have, Jake Montgomery. I've never heard that one before, and I'm super impressed by your disdain. Tell me more."

He had to laugh. His tiger wasn't against biting the hand that pet her. "It's nothing personal. I just don't think some stranger's fortune-cookie predictions are a great way to make life decisions, that's all."

"They aren't fortune-cookie predictions, thank you very much. Entire civilizations have been founded on the zodiac."

"Name one."

"Sumerians. Babylonians. Egyptians. Mayans. Some people think Stonehenge has astrological meaning, which would also make pretty much all of the Western world based on it." She smiled pertly. "Would you like me to keep going?"

He stared. How much further could she go? "I had no idea you took it so seriously."

"Why? Because I'm some waste-of-space trust fund baby who can't be relied on to know right from left? Don't believe everything you hear. As much as the media loves a good Rebecca Clare scandal, I *do* sometimes stay home and read." She frowned and cast a careful look around her apartment, as if searching for some unknown evil lingering in the doorway. "Or I used to, anyway."

He filed that look—full of distaste, maybe even fear—away for future reference. "I hate to be the one to break it to you, but the next Rebecca Clare scandal is closer than you think. Flip the page."

This time, she obeyed, and her hands stopped rustling the moment it came into view. "Oh. Shit."

"Yeah." Jake lowered himself carefully into the chair opposite her, gauging her response. In his experience, women had a way of reacting strongly when faced with a clear shot of their naked crotch released for public consumption. And yes, his experience was fairly large, all things considered. His was a world where public consumption was an everyday affair—the more sordid the affair, the better.

This picture of Rebecca Clare—twenty-four-year-old heiress, fashionista, famous for absolutely nothing at all—was pretty sordid. In it, Jake stood holding her around the waist and hoisting her off Dana's body, leaving her free to flash her completely underwear-free crotch at the lucky pap with his camera pointed head—or rather *tail*—on.

He braced himself for the worst.

"I like how they blacked my twat out with a star," she mused, tilting the picture so that her legs were vertical to her line of vision. "It's so much more exciting that way. Like the force of my vulva cannot be contained."

Jake had to struggle not to bray his laughter. He should have known better. Becca didn't have to be intoxicated to be indifferent about her public foibles. With an alarming amount of insight and naiveté, she merely accepted society—and her place in it—as it was offered. Society loved her drama. They loved her mistakes. They loved to rip her reputation to shreds.

So she accepted it.

"Unfortunately, I'm afraid this puts us in a not-so-enviable position."

She shrugged, that insight and naiveté rolled up in one careless gesture. "I know it puts *me* in a not-so-enviable position. I was under strict orders to keep my lady garden under wraps."

"That's an actual rule in your family?"

"There are three rules I must stick to at all times. No public nudity. No discussing money at a dinner party. And don't leave the house without lipstick." She lifted a hand to her lips. "I guess I broke that last one this morning. To be fair, I was in a hurry."

"Those are terrible rules."

She tossed her head, ponytail flying, before she remembered her head injury and winced. Jake extracted a bottle of Ibuprofen from the top of the refrigerator and handed it to her.

"They could be worse." She formed the words around the coffee she used to wash the pills down. It was only the cold remnants of his morning cup, and he felt a pang for not offering to grab her one. He wasn't used to taking care of a woman in the morning. He was usually long gone before the coffee beans started to grind.

"I doubt that," he said. "None of those rules have anything to do with real life."

"Maybe not," she said simply. "But they have every-thing to do with *my* life. What about you? What rules do you have?"

"Rule. Singular. Just one." Nothing else Jake said or did in this world mattered. No one cared where he went to sleep at night or whether or not he remembered to visit the dentist twice a year or how he felt about getting a stepmom his own age. "No matter what else happens, our family comes first." Money was secondary. Affection a distant third.

"Aww. That's actually kind of sweet. I love your dad."

Jake didn't bother correcting her. It wasn't sweet at all. What looked like strong blood ties and loyalty to the outside was really a tangled web of deceit and power plays. He was bound by money. Tied by obligation. Free to do whatever he wanted...provided his dad and Monty approved ahead of time.

Hence his current predicament. He didn't want to set-tle down to work in the family hotelier business, hated everything about the idea of sitting behind a desk and crunching numbers for the rest of his life. He'd rather be forced to eke out an existence hanging on to the coat-tails of assholes like Dana.

Or hanging on to the train of sweet, misguided women like Becca. He definitely preferred that one. In fact, if he played his hand carefully here, he could ride her train right through the holidays and into the next year. Poor Monty had lost this bet before it even started.

"So what are we talking?" he asked, indicating the newspaper article. "Will your mom rage at you? Cast you out on your trampoline ass? Slap your hand and tell you to behave like a lady next time?"

Becca's apartment phone rang, and she held up a finger to pause him as she fumbled under the multicolored bras piled on the countertop. "We're about to find out. A thousand bucks says that's her."

The face she made as she held the phone away from her ear, tinny sounds of anger spreading across the kitchen, indicated that it was, indeed, Grandmama Clare. And it appeared she wasn't too happy with the turn of events.

"Yes, ma'am. I did see my recent foray into the mega-whore hall of fame."

More tinny sounds.

"No, ma'am. I'm sure there are still men in this world who haven't seen my vagina."

Louder now.

"Well, who decided that vaginal mystery was the most important attribute, anyway? Maybe some men prefer to know what they're getting ahead of time. It's like reading the spoilers."

Jake cracked a shout of surprised laughter and then quickly covered it with a cough.

"Oh, please. Men are constantly flopping their bits around, begging for us to take a peek. It's like their re-productive organs are a gift the whole world can't wait to tear open. You were at that Mediterranean resort with me. Remember the one in the banana hammock?" Becca held a finger to her lips, warning Jake to stay silent. "You do too know what that is—it was the yellow sling thing with the thong in the back. We could totally see the outline of that guy's glans."

By that time, Jake had given in all the way to his laughter, bracing himself on the table as he did his best to remain silent, so Becca reached over and slugged him on the arm. He yelped his protest and realized it as a mistake when Becca shook her head in warning.

A sharp sound emerged from the general direction of the phone. "It's just Jake. He helped me home last night. Of course I didn't force him to clean up my messes. He happened to be at the club and I drank a little too much, that's all. And I don't see what business it is of Trish Callahan's... Yes, ma'am."

Quieter this time, "No, ma'am."

Even quieter, "Yes, ma'am."

By the time she hung up, what remained of her energy had deflated, wiping at least half a decade off her age and filling Jake with a bizarrely protective feeling toward her—and he wasn't a man who comforted or cuddled. He'd read somewhere that hugging a woman elicited a burst of oxytocin in her system, making her biologically clingy from there on out. He hugged only upon pain of death.

"Have you been handed down a punishment?" he asked, feigning unconcern as he folded the pages of the paper and set them to one side. "I'd offer to take the blame for you, but your mom probably wouldn't believe it. She loves me."

"All women love you. We can't seem to help ourselves."

"It's because I remind you of the one that got away."

She shook her head, considering his words with much more care than he'd offered them. "No, that's not it. It's because we know you're bad for us. You're a big, fat piece of chocolate cake on day six of a juice cleanse."

"Fat?" He smoothed a hand over the front of his shirt. "Now you're just being cruel."

That won him a smile and a laugh, a return to the

carefree girl who loved dancing on tables and astrology and vodka tonics. "So big and fat and decadent." She licked her lips with a painstaking slowness, ending the show by capturing the bottom one between her teeth, shrinking the world to nothing more than him and that lip.

"Not to mention rich," she added.

"Go on."

"Incredibly filling."

"I like the sound of that."

"Creamy." This time, her tongue flicked in and out, a glimmer of pink he could practically taste. But she dropped the game with a sigh. "And most likely to cause regrets in the morning."

He had to will his blood to cool, mastery over his body becoming more difficult with each passing second spent in this woman's company. It was unfair how quickly she was able to turn the sex kitten—no, sex *tiger*—on and off, as if none of it meant anything. She was toying with him. She was toying with his poor, straining prick.

And his poor, straining prick *liked* it.

"You don't seem too traumatized by your past experience with me," he said, his voice only partially strangled.

"Yes, but I think we can all agree I suck when it comes to the issue of sound judgment. Overindulgence is the only thing I'm good at. Just ask my mother."

"Was that her verdict?" he asked lightly. "No more clubs? No more dragging wayward nephews home for the night?"

"Nothing so serious." Becca sighed. "It actually wasn't that bad—not as bad as it could have been. She still wants me to come to tea with Trish Callahan this afternoon. Play the lady. Pretend all is right in the universe. If there's one thing we Clares are good at, it's putting on a clean face and moving ahead as if nothing is wrong. Though she did request I put on proper undergarments this time."

"And will you?"

She put a finger to her pursed lips, playing again—playing the ingénue, playing with him. "You know, I don't think I will. I'm feeling a need for some airing out downstairs."

"That's my tiger."

"And I'm going to read horrible fortunes in their tea leaves."

"Since it's all made up anyway, why not?"

He got a glare for that one. "I usually focus on the positive things out of kindness. No one wants to hear that their husband is cheating on them for the fourth time in as many months."

"How astute of you."

"Mock if you must, Jake Montgomery, but if you'd just polish off your latte over there and let me see the dregs, you might be surprised what I find."

He pulled the cup closer to his side of the table. Becca wasn't getting her hands on his coffee dregs or his fortunes. There was nothing she could see—real or otherwise—that he wasn't already acutely aware of.

"I don't know how I'm going to keep my head up, though. I don't even think I can walk to the bedroom without falling down." She quirked a brow. "Are you sure you won't shower with me? You could prop me up with your extra leg."

His extra leg took on additional proportions at the prospect. He'd seen enough of her trampoline ass that the idea of running his hands over it, water and soap easing his way over curves and inside nooks, was one he found highly appealing.

But as was the case last night, he found himself strangely reluctant to take advantage of her when she was so obviously struggling. *Goddamn conscience.* Next thing you knew, he'd be offering her hugs for no reason at all.

"How about I promise to come to your mom's tea instead," he offered, wondering, as the words left his mouth, who had put them there. If there was one thing he hated more than tea, it was mothers. Together? They were practically the axis of evil.

"Do you mean it?" Becca's eyes lit up and, all exhaustion to the contrary, she bounced to his side of the table to fling her arms around his neck. She planted a kiss— soft and sweaty, her tongue making no apologies as it slid across his—before pulling away with just as much force. "That would be so nice. You can woo them and wink and no one will even notice I'm there."

Her excitement prevented him from backing out, which was what his natural instinct rolled over and begged for. Sleepovers. Hugs. Earth signs. Chastity. He barely recognized himself over here.

"Maybe I could go without underwear too," he suggested, resigned to his fate. "That'll really give them something to gawk at."

SIX

JAKE TIRED OF studying the mild, watery Monet after about five seconds.

He didn't know a lot about art, not in the way his sister Jenna did, with true appreciation for craftsmanship, and not in the way Monty did, with true appreciation for resale value. He knew just enough to recognize the artist and the style and the overwhelming sense of déjà vu that overtook him at the sight of it. Monet had been one prolific bastard, and anyone with a couple of million dollars to rub together seemed to have one on display.

The Clares had opted to hang one in the sitting room. And the dining room. And, unless he was very much mistaken, the bathroom down the hall.

"I don't understand how difficult it is to put on drawers before you leave the house, that's all," Moira said. Her voice, never what one would term soft spoken, carried easily across the room to where Jake continued his bored examination of the painting. "Especially if you intend to brawl once you get where you're going. A scrap of lace, Becca, is all I'm asking for. Even cotton will do in a pinch. I don't think it's too much to ask."

Jake felt his lips lift, grateful that neither woman could see his amusement. Moira Clare had no qualms about the fact that her daughter had attacked a seemingly innocent man in the middle of a nightclub. She seemed delighted that Jake was the one who had come to her aid. And an appearance on the front page of the *National Beat* was always something to celebrate.

But she could not, would not, dared not forgive the sin of Becca having left the house underdressed.

No public nudity. Rule number one.

"When is tea being served?" he asked congenially, turning to face them with his hands deep in his pockets. He *had* offered to be a buffer between the Clare women, rising to the challenge and saving Becca from the passive-aggressive wrath of a mother who meant only the best. He might as well earn his keep. "I'm famished."

It was the right thing to say. Moira, a widow of two decades, had only daughters—four of them in all, his stepmother Serena the eldest at thirty-four, Becca the youngest at a decade less than that—so she took a keen maternal interest in the appetites of men. "Of course you are, poor lamb."

Like all the Clare women, Moira was slim and dainty and slightly washed-out, her features well-preserved but all the more unremarkable because of it. Unlike Becca, whose casually green eyes sparkled with humor and life, Moira boasted irises that were an unnaturally sharp shade of green that made him feel he was gazing at a jewelry case.

"You're too thin," she said, and led him to the seating area. "You and Monty both. I've always preferred a man with a little something to hold on to."

"Like a decadent piece of chocolate cake, perhaps?"

"Oh, no." Moira frowned, the expression leaving very little impression on the lines of her face. "Don't say that. Men should never be compared to desserts."

"Now you've stepped your foot in it. Unlike me, my mother requires that her food analogies stick to strict gender stereotypes. Only women can be desserts, because they're sweet and smooth." Becca flashed him a provocative smile. "And sometimes moist."

He coughed, glad he and Becca had decided against attending this function without proper undergarment support. If she didn't intend to behave properly, they needed every extra layer they could get.

"You know how I feel about that word, dear," Moira said. "Say damp. Or saturated."

"Saturated? Right, because that's so much better—no man can resist a little after-dinner saturation." She caught Jake's eye with a twinkle of humor. "And please don't go force feeding him sandwiches. Between you and Mean Max and dessert analogies, he's going to start developing a complex about his manly physique. I think he looks fantastic."

"Who's Mean Max?" Moira asked.

Jake ignored the question and helped the older Clare woman to the couch, trying not to show how much Becca's compliment affected him. He'd been called a lot of things in his lifetime—some of them more complimentary, some of them decidedly less—but the unaffected way the word *fantastic* fell from her lips made him feel like an asshole.

He wasn't sure he'd ever complimented her without some kind of ulterior motive. She was a goddess of the night when he wanted to fuck her, Cinderella when he wanted to get her home, a potential roommate when he needed her coattails. Thinking back on all the things he knew about her—the lurid stories, the scandalous pictures, the way the world talked about her in hushed tones—he wondered if anyone ever just complimented her and meant it.

"Max is my personal trainer," Becca explained. "And he's very mean. He made me throw up two times today."

Her mom looked horrified. "What on earth is he training you *for?*"

"Life." Becca didn't care to elaborate further. Max—exhausting, pushy, in-her-face Max—was one of the best things that had ever happened to her. She wasn't giving him up. "Oh, I think I hear the Callahans. Did you remember to get the oolong loose leaf tea I recommended? I find it's much more accurate than chamomile."

She tried to avoid looking at Jake, since she was sure he had a mocking sneer in place, but he merely offered a quirk of a grin and rose to greet Trish Callahan and her perfect paragon of a daughter. That was nice of him. This whole thing was nice of him—uncharacteristically so. Jake Montgomery wasn't the sort of man who put himself out for others, especially if he wasn't getting sex out of the bargain.

Though he *could* have sex. Lots of it, and with a woman who was growing increasingly turned on with every hour spent in his tightly restrained company. She was having a hard time deciding if the reason she wanted him so much was because he was determined not to have her, or if there was more to it than that.

She *hoped* there was more to it than that. No one wanted to be the child crying at the candy store over a box of chocolates she couldn't have but didn't even like in the first place. It was a waste of tears. Life was hard enough without making an effort to seek out sadness.

Becca knew that firsthand. Sadness would always find its way to you on its own. It was dependable that way.

Her mom's housekeeper showed their guests into the

sitting room. Trish, a long-standing acquaintance of her mother's, looked the same as she always did, her hair a shellacked helmet of wrought-iron strands, her suit an original vintage Chanel. Her daughter Lulu had changed quite a bit since the last time Becca had seen her. They were the same age and had often played together as kids, but Lulu had not only graduated the top of her class at Sarah Lawrence, but she'd also just returned from a six-month mission to dig wells in Somalia. Her tan was fantastic, even if she was wearing a shade of orange that did nothing to set it off.

Becca preferred her own schoolgirl plaid, worn primarily to provoke both Jake and her mother—though with widely divergent outcomes in mind.

"I'm surprised you're willing to show your face in public, Rebecca dear." Trish leaned down to kiss Becca on both cheeks, her lips barely a whisper on either side. "Though I suppose this sort of thing makes no difference to you—you positively invite scandal. Lulu and I were just discussing how it doesn't seem to matter where you are or who you're with. Some part of you is always exposed."

Becca smiled sweetly, though her fingers itched to get hold of this woman's teacup. The last time she'd read for Trish, there'd been a huge clump of leaves opposite the handle—a clear sign of trouble not of her own making. Since everyone knew her husband had been screwing the newest Lancôme model at the time, Becca had assumed it indicated imminent divorce. Of course, she'd refrained from saying so out loud.

It was cruel to bring attention to someone's worst moments in public. Obviously.

She turned to Lulu, expecting another set of false

kisses and backhanded insults, but the younger woman seemed too nervous to offer so much as a hello. Lulu was, in addition to a digger of wells and sun goddess, a statuesque beauty with dark hair that tumbled down her back. She perched on the edge of the chair, looking regal and condescending, her legs crossed tightly at the knee. You couldn't squeeze a camera up there even if you wanted to.

"It's nice to see you again, Jake," Trish said, taking over the conversation as per her usual custom. "I noticed you also made an appearance in this morning's paper."

"I looked quite dashing, didn't I?" he asked. Even though he had a dainty bone china plate balanced on one knee, he looked competently masculine as he ate his watercress on rye. "I usually do. The trick is to turn in profile whenever you see a bulb flash. It's the dead-on photos that do the most harm."

"Is that so?" Trish asked, taking his sarcasm at face value. Lulu also seemed to perk up as she accepted a proffered cup of tea. "I had no idea there was an art to it."

"Oh, there's an art to everything. Eating. Dancing. Sex." He flashed a disarming grin and took a bite of his sandwich that was so contrived, it might have been the nibble of teeth on rounded female flesh. "Especially sex."

"Jake!" Her mother slapped at his leg ineffectively. Becca hadn't been kidding when she said older women loved Jake. They drank in his casual naughtiness as if they were dying of thirst. They'd probably bathe in it if they could, like the blood of virgins to keep them from aging.

Lulu seemed less interested in Jake's naughtiness and

more interested in his technique. "How did you learn that picture trick?"

"I've had plenty of practice. Here—I'll show you." With a disarming grin, Jake scooted closer to Trish, so close their knees practically bumped. He lifted the older woman's chin and tilted her head to the side, examining her as a connoisseur. "See what I did there? A slight lift smoothes the skin. Elongate the neck and voilà! Your mother is a Raphaelite."

Trish lifted a hand to her face as if she expected the skin of a baby's behind to have replaced her own. The man was downright shameless. If he wanted, he could have Trish dancing a striptease down to her girdle right there in the middle of the room.

"Yes, well. Not all of us had time to preen beforehand," Becca said. "I was a little busy at the time."

She swirled her cup and frowned at the amber liquid. There weren't very many leaves in there. It would be hard to see anything, which was a pain, since she wanted to follow up on her horoscope from the morning. If she was going to solicit Jake's help in figuring out this big-picture-Sara stuff, she needed a better understanding of the role he was supposed to play.

"Did *you* know they were there, Becca?" Lulu asked. "The cameras?"

"Of course she didn't know," her mother answered for her, unconcerned with the truth. "She would have kept things wrapped up if that were the case. We're all just grateful Jake was there to keep her from doing anything irreversible."

Jake chuckled good-naturedly. "I hardly think it was irreversible. It was a minor altercation at a private club. It happens more often than you might expect."

"Surely not at a place like Ma Petite?" Lulu looked at them through wide, alarmed eyes, as if she couldn't imagine such a thing happening at a place she might frequent someday, as if Becca herself was responsible for all the depravities of their social set.

Point taken. She had no self-control. She balked at propriety and binged on excess.

Before she made the mistake of saying something *irreversible*, Jake continued, "Oh, you wouldn't believe the trouble we get into. Love affairs gone awry. High-end escort services. Blackmail. Every now and then you'll get a good, old-fashioned bar fight." A small smile danced on his lips, as if none of those things were beyond him. "But the cameras only capture the Rebecca Clares and Jake Montgomerys in the thick of it all. Not the Lulu Callahans. *Never* the Lulu Callahans. That, unfortunately, is the price of being worth reading about."

"If that's how much it costs to be *famous*, then I'm glad Lulu doesn't carry the right currency." Trish sniffed and turned her attention to Moira. "I don't know how you stand for it. One of these days, you're going to wake up to find Becca on the front page of the *Times* instead of that gossip rag."

"Oh, I don't know," Moira hedged. "You know how careless young people are."

Moira turned to Jake, her eyes pleading with him to step in. Unfortunately, he wasn't sure what she wanted him to *do*. Short of hauling these awful women out the front door and leaving them on the sidewalk, his hands were tied up in platitudes. What kind of a tea party was this? He'd assumed it was going to be all air kisses and scones and love life predictions. This was a witch hunt...

and the witch in question was sitting right there, growing increasingly rigid as the conversation progressed.

Couldn't they see the warning signs? Didn't they know Becca was reaching the limits of her tolerance?

He opened his mouth to direct the conversation to more neutral territory, but Trish interrupted.

"You're right, Moira. Of course I know how careless young people are—and you know who else does? Peter Yarrowgate. If you aren't careful, that's exactly who you'll become. No one was surprised to see his daughter wind up dead in a hotel room, enough pills in her system to open a pharmacy." Before anyone had a chance to get a word in, she turned to Becca, her movements prim and triumphant. "Didn't you two used to travel in the same circles?"

The speed with which Becca flew out of her seat to land in front of Trish was nothing short of miraculous. At least, it seemed miraculous until he caught sight of her face, which carried the same wild-eyed look she had when she'd attacked Dana the night before. He'd felt enough of her fury under his fingertips to know that adrenaline transformed Becca into some kind of superwoman.

"Say that one more time."

Trish's mouth opened and closed and opened again, leaving her gaping.

"Say that about Sara one more time."

Trish was able to close her mouth long enough to speak. "I don't see what you have to get so upset about. She took her own life. It was her choice."

The ringing slap of Becca's hand on the older woman's cheek was a sound Jake wouldn't soon forget. Nor would he be likely to erase the image of Becca's face, pale with fury, twisted up in so much pain it was a wonder they didn't all suffer a contact high.

"How dare you."

"How dare *I?*" Trish looked to Moira as if for confirmation that this was really happening—that Becca was standing in front of her, seething, assaulting, about to do it again. "You might be able to get away with this kind of thing in your trashy clubs, but—"

Jake felt it would be timely to intervene.

Before Becca made the mistake of saying what she thought—or, worse, tackling this horrible woman to the floor—he came up behind her and pressed his hand on her waist. She hissed in a sharp breath, but the direct pressure as he dug his fingers below the hem of her short silk top worked as a deterrent, and she stilled under his touch, a tiger calming beside him.

The ramifications of this cause-and-effect weren't lost on him. Between last night and today, it was becoming clear that he was able to influence this woman's direct actions. If she flew off the handle, he could stop her. If she approached scandal, he could reel her back in.

He could, in a sense, control her.

His head rationalized this as a good thing, acknowledged that becoming Becca's keeper was a great way to make himself indispensable to her. But his gut warned him that *bad* might be a more apt term. Jake was not a man to be trusted with this kind of power.

"I think we've overstayed our welcome, Becca," he said, not lifting his hand. "What say you and I head back to your apartment? Maybe we can call Max and have him come help you work out some of that extra aggression."

She stood poised between rage and retreat, as if unsure which held more appeal.

Moira chose for her.

"Rebecca Louise Clare, you'll apologize to Trish right this minute." She set aside her teacup and stood to defend her guest. "I'm so sorry. I don't know what's come over her—"

"I do." Trish stood and brushed the crumbs from her pink suit skirt, gesturing for her daughter to do the same. Lulu rose on unsteady legs, her hand pressed to her mouth. "If you ask me, it appears your daughter's last trip to rehab didn't take."

"I'm not on drugs." Becca stiffened until he thought she might snap, so he spun her to face him.

"Just breathe," he murmured, forcing her eyes to meet his. They flashed dangerously, but he could still see her in there, lost and hurting and betrayed. "She's not worth the effort. She'll pull your hair and give up too easily. We can maul the next one, someone who's an actual challenge in the ring."

A reluctant sob-turned-laugh escaped Becca's throat. "Do you promise?"

"I'm a man of my word. But you have to stop this nasty habit of physically assaulting everyone you dislike."

"You heard what she said about Sara. About the awful way she died."

He'd heard every unfortunate word. He was also starting to put some of the pieces of this puzzle together. Unless he was very much mistaken, Sara Yarrowgate, a notorious party girl whose father ran one of the largest tech security companies in the country, had died from a potent mixture of antidepressants and vodka a few weeks before Becca had been shipped off to rehab.

Oh, fuck. They'd been friends. Her friend had committed suicide. Of course she was a mess.

"Sara doesn't deserve to be spoken of like that," he said, and wrapped an arm more firmly around her. "No one does."

He directed her to the now-vacated couch, hoping to keep her from noticing where Trish and Lulu stood near the door, sharing a heated discussion in undertones and making not-so-vague gestures toward them every few seconds.

"Want to talk about it?" he asked as she settled in. He took the seat opposite her, leaning on his knees so that he could see her face where it drooped down.

"No."

"Want to cry about it?"

"Is yelling an option?"

"I'd like to say yes, but I don't think now's the time. Your mom's headed this way and she looks as if she's about to murder the first person to blink. I'm sorry to say it, but that won't be me. I have exceptionally saturated eyes."

Becca released a strangled laugh.

"Well, Grandmama Clare?" Jake rose to his feet in an attempt to divert some of the incoming firepower. "You certainly throw one hell of a tea party. I'm disappointed I don't get invited more often, I never turn down an opportunity to watch women brawl."

"Don't you try to sweet-talk me, Jake Montgomery. I blame you for this. What did she take?"

"She was fine when we got here," he said mildly. He allowed himself a brief glance at Becca's face, fearful she was about to attack her own mother next, but she just looked tired and small and... *Christ*. Sad. She looked sad. "Might I suggest the company was at fault?"

"Not if you want to remain on my good side. I don't know what your father would say if he knew what you were up to, but I can't imagine this is how he encourages you to behave."

Jake kept the smile firmly in place. That was where Moira was wrong. This was probably the first time in his life he was doing something his dad *would* approve of. John Montgomery the Second was a large proponent of supporting the downtrodden, of standing up for the persecuted. Staying in this room while Becca was being ripped to shreds by her female acquaintance was one of the few decent things Jake had done.

"And you, young lady." Moira wasn't done yet. She turned her attention to Becca. "You know exactly what this means."

"That I don't have to come to any more of your tea parties?"

Jake almost laughed out loud. His tiger didn't stay down for long.

Moira was less amused. "No. It means you've earned yourself a one-way ticket back to Tranquility Ranch. I'll have my driver escort you home to pack your bags. You have one hour."

Becca shot to her feet. "I'm not going back there!"

"Oh, yes, you are. It's one thing to act up for the publicity—I was willing to chalk last night's activities up to nothing more than an indiscretion. But to physically assault Trish Callahan? You're out of control, Becca. It's for your own good."

Jake found himself at a momentary loss. Tranquility Ranch wasn't an empty sort of threat. It was *the* rehabilitation center of choice for the entire East Coast elite—spacious suites, soothing spa treatments, detox facilities…and bars on the windows. People didn't go there unless they were serious about getting clean. But Becca was *fine*. Emotionally distressed, clearly, but imprisoning her wasn't going to help her get over her loss.

"Drugs are not the problem here, Mom. They never have been, and you *know* that. Give me a test right here, right now. I'll pee in all the cups you want."

"Don't be disgusting."

"It's the only way you'll get me back there. You can't force me without a court order."

"She does have a point," Jake said.

"Then she'll self-surrender."

"No, I won't."

"Yes," Moira said firmly, "you will. Or I'll revoke your trust and close up your apartment. We'll see how long you last trying to figure things out on your own for a change."

Jake reacted more strongly to her words than Becca, feeling the recoil of the threat on a personal level. As a man who'd been punished in just such a manner, he knew all too well that financial insolvency wasn't a joke. And he doubted Becca had anything even remotely approaching real-world coping skills.

"I told you how hard it was for me the last time. I don't think I can do it again." Becca's voice took on a keening edge. "Put down the phone. Please."

Moira didn't flinch as she held her cell phone to her ear. "Gerald? Yes. You're needed around front. You'll be escorting Becca to Tranquility Ranch this afternoon."

"Mom."

"You may need to get Sven to help you."

"*Mom*."

"No, I don't think restraints will be necessary, but you might want to have them on hand just in case."

"Moira." Now it was Jake's turn. He grabbed the phone from out of her hand and pressed the end button. "Stop."

"You know I love you, Jake, but I think it's best if you leave now."

As if he would. As if he *could*. "What Trish said was out of line. You can't hold Becca responsible for that woman's lack of tact."

"I can and I will. You have no idea the things my daughter is capable of, and as much as I appreciate you helping her out last night, this has nothing to do with you."

No, it didn't. He didn't know Becca much beyond a few encounters at clubs and bars, the obligatory family dinners where she provided a much-needed burst of liveliness among his drab relatives. He didn't have the authority to tell these women how to organize their messy, loud, overly dramatic lives.

But he did know what it felt like to be purposefully misunderstood by the people who were supposed to care the most. He did know that letting Moira whisk Becca away to that cold, sterile place with no hope of escape had the potential to subdue the tiger for good.

He didn't know *why* he knew that, but there it was. Maybe it was in the tea leaves.

"Let me be the one to keep an eye on her." Jake set the phone next to the tea tray, a note of finality in the gesture. "Don't send her away. I can promise not to let her come to any harm."

"Jake—" Becca began, but he silenced her with a motion of his finger to his lips. He could help her. He could fix this. And if she didn't like it, she could rip up at him later. Hell, he'd probably deserve it.

Moira saw the exchange but shook her head in a stubborn refusal. "Thank you, but no. Controlling Becca is going to take much more than a well-meaning friend, and I can't ask you to make the attempt. It's not your job."

"But she's not my friend, and it *is* my job." He almost smiled as the word crossed his lips. *Job.* What would Monty have to say about that?

"What do you mean?" Moira asked sharply.

"I'm afraid I can't let you take my fiancée to rehab without my consent." He smiled, enjoying the shocked look on both women's faces. "Be the first to congratulate us, Grandmama Clare. Becca is my responsibility now. She agreed just this morning to marry me."

SEVEN

"I KNOW WHAT you're thinking."

Becca stood, hands on hips, watching as Jake settled himself on her mom's couch and spread his arms across the back. He spoke with a level of calm unheard of in a man who'd recently proposed marriage and been accepted. Kind of. Sort of. Not really at all.

"I highly doubt that," she said.

He nodded at the chair across from him, commanding her to take a seat. There was no denying that the idea of sitting back and unwinding into the upholstery was tempting after the day she'd had. Hungover, exhausted and at her emotional wit's end, she'd still had to spend a good half hour helping Jake calm her mother down after that casually dropped engagement bomb. Her mom was currently relaxing in her room with one Xanax under her tongue and a spare underneath her pillow.

The irony of that wasn't lost on Becca. She never touched anything stronger than alcohol, but because Xanax came with a prescription, it was somehow okay.

"I think I have a pretty good idea." He nodded again. "Sit. You're making me nervous."

"Why? Are you afraid I'm going to attack you next?"

"Yes. And this is a brand-new shirt. I'd hate for it to wrinkle."

Oh, she'd wrinkle it, all right. She'd wrinkle it so much he'd have no choice but to take it off. The cool, composed man who'd brought her so much comfort last night was only ticking her off something fierce now. She'd pretty much opened her veins and bled out onto the ikat rug earlier, and he had the audacity to sit there and act like all was well with the world.

The world was not well, dammit. The world was a seething pit of suckitude.

"Then tell me." She squared her stance, determined not to let this moment go so easily. He'd promised her a chance to fight someone. In the absence of a more appropriate sparring partner, he would have to do. "What am I thinking right now?"

He propped one leg carefully on the opposite knee and tilted his head. God, he looked unfairly delicious when he did that—stern and in control, the perfectly chiseled features of his face cut as if of marble. She was used to associating with attractive people—it was one of the perks of being young and wealthy—but few men were able to carry off Jake's classically attractive looks with such aplomb. He was freakishly fastidious about his clothes, his lips were a touch too full for pure masculinity, and there was a delicacy to his lean strength that would have made many men seem weak.

But not Jake. He made every other man on the face of the planet seem like heavy, awkward clumps of flesh.

"You're wishing I'd let you tell Trish Callahan off on your own terms," he said, as casually as if they were discussing where to go for dinner. "You're pissed as hell that I made up that story about us being engaged. And you're wondering what's in it for me."

"Nope."

He laughed. "Nope? That's it? That's all you're going to give me?"

It was until he offered her something in return. She wasn't after much—a hint of humanity, a chink in his emotional armor, some sort of sign that she wasn't the only one in the room with a heartbeat. She was fairly easy to please that way.

Since he didn't seem to be forthcoming with a pulse, she took it upon herself to find one. Playing coy, she dropped her voice to a huskier, more obvious tone. "Why? What else do you want?"

His brows lifted a question at her, so she answered. Dropping to her knees, she helped herself down by bracing a hand on each leg. The tensile strength of his thighs under her fingertips felt raw—which was exactly how she felt right now. Raw.

But also good. *And alive.* Alive was a big one. Despite everything—Sara's death and all the drug rumors and the seedy photographs and Tranquility Ranch—she was still very much alive and kicking.

No one ever wanted to give her credit for that one.

"Um, what are you doing?" Jake asked as she slid her hands farther up each of his thighs.

"What does it look like I'm doing? I'm attacking you."

His brows didn't come down, but he didn't try to stop her either. If anything, he was watching with a curious kind of detachment, almost as if he was conducting a scientific experiment. *How Far Becca Will Go in Her Mother's Sitting Room. The Mating Habits of the Fucked-Up Elite.* But no amount of detachment would be able to alter the fact that he liked it. He liked it a lot.

She reached higher, her knuckles grazing the rapidly hardening erection no amount of expensive tailoring could hide. She reached for his belt buckle, her movements purposefully jerky as she pulled it open. He seemed to enjoy the fumbling roughness, hissed when her fingers scraped along the front of his fly.

"Are you sure this is what we should be doing right now?" he asked.

"Why not? Isn't this what fiancées do?"

"Becca." His eyes grew serious as they bored into hers. "You know we're not really engaged, right? I only said that to stop your mom. She was about to have you committed."

She stuck her lower lip out in a pout and began swirling her thumbs in a hard, circular pattern up his inner thighs. "My fiancé is kind of grumpy. I wonder what I can do to help him relax."

"You can stop doing that, for starters."

She complied—and then promptly lifted herself from the ground and settled herself in his lap instead. Her short skirt rode up both legs as she straddled him, and she had the satisfaction of feeling his erection harden the rest of the way against her.

"I mean it." He gripped her thighs, but not with the intention of running his hands all over them. He was holding her in place, preventing her from moving against him. "I need to hear you say that we're not really engaged. I need to make sure you understand this situation."

He was seriously sucking all of the pleasure out of her triumph. "I'm an emotionally unstable media whore, Jake. Not an idiot."

"Say it anyway."

"So stern." She dipped her head down and kissed his jaw, soft with the fine stubble that only redheads seemed to grow, smelling of a heady mixture of sandalwood and rose. "So commanding. I like it. What else should I say?

Do you want me to tell you how naughty I've been and call you Big Papa?"

His laughter hit her ear in a warm, intoxicating *whoosh*. "Please don't." Then, when she landed another kiss at the edge of his mouth, "Although now you have me curious. What did you have in mind? How naughty have you been?"

"Oh, Big Papa, you have no idea how bad. I'm so dirty. So depraved. I need a strong hand to hold me down and teach me a lesson."

He held his palm level and tilted it side to side. "So-so. I was hoping for more specifics."

She reached between them and slid her hand down the front of his pants, fisting the length of his erection, back and forth, up and down, eliciting nothing more than his calm, careful appreciation as he watched.

"Hmm. Okay. How about this?" She tossed her hair over one shoulder and continued her movements against his cock. "Sometimes, late at night, I like to touch myself and remember the way you took me up against a wall. Hard and fast. A man who knew exactly what he was doing."

He murmured his appreciation as she flicked a finger over the tip of his cock. "I like where this is going."

"And when that's not enough to get me wet, I like to imagine there's another guy in there with us. He's beefy and takes turns plowing us from behind."

This time, his murmur was less like appreciation and more like a man who didn't care for male-on-male action. *Good.* She'd finally succeeded in tipping his stupid serenity on its side.

She stopped her movements as suddenly as she'd started. It seemed as good a time as any to clear the air.

"I know we're not really engaged, so you can stop freaking out. I'm not planning an intimate wedding for our families and five hundred of our closest friends. I'm not imagining our adorable, redheaded, two-point-four children summering in the Hamptons. You were coming to my rescue. I get it."

He grabbed her wrist and held it firm. She looked down at where her skin grew white under the pressure—not in pain, but curious. Why was he taking this all so seriously? Jake never took anything seriously.

"Don't worry about it so much," she said lightly. "I appreciate your timely intervention more than you realize. Tranquility Ranch was awful."

"That's where you were before." It wasn't a question.

She answered anyway. "Yes."

"I've heard it's pretty luxurious."

"The sheets were nice." So was her huge suite, the clawfoot bathtub, the yoga instructor who'd once run one of the top studios in Los Angeles. Daily massages and five-star dining didn't hurt either. It was all on their website.

He didn't respond, just sat there and leveled her with his startlingly blue stare, as if he was sending subliminal messages to get her to open up. But she wasn't sure what else he expected her to say. Did he want to know why she went in the first place? Why it was awful? Why the idea of going back there, where they locked the doors at night and lights-out was strictly enforced, made her want to scream?

"I didn't take Sara's suicide well." That about summed it up.

She could have told him more—about how the catalyst for everything had been the Haldol the paramedics used to sedate her at the scene of Sara's death, and how the tabloids took that as evidence of drug abuse and ran wild with it. She could have told him about the terrible nightmares she couldn't seem to shake, daily reminders that she hadn't tried hard enough to save her friend.

She could have also told him about how both of those things meant people watched her out of the corner of their eyes, as if she was one vodka tonic away from joining Sara in the grave.

But what was the point? People didn't care about the realities of her life. They never did. She was an emotional wreck, an object of derision, a great headline. Her best friend in the entire world had *died*, and all her family did was toss her into rehab for three months, hoping to get her out of the limelight and cure her of her sorrow, as though it were a disease or an addiction.

"That really sucks," Jake said simply. "I'm sorry for your loss."

She felt her eyes water. For all her expensive recovery activities and therapy sessions, few people remembered to say that.

"Thank you." She blinked rapidly, refusing to let any tears fall. Jake was not the sort of man on whom tears had any efficacy—at least, not unless the goal was to send him running as fast and as far as his legs would take him. "It's been a tough year."

He looked like he wanted to say more, but he settled for a firming of the mouth as he glanced around, gaze skimming over the surfaces of a room Becca had never found terribly comforting, even when she was a kid. "Want to get out of here?"

"Yes, *please*." She jumped out of his lap, grabbing his hand and giving it an insistent tug. It didn't work, and he got to his feet at his own leisurely pace. "Believe me when I say this is not where I envisioned spending the day of my engagement."

When she saw the panicked warning in his eye, she laughed. "My *fake* engagement. My fake engagement I have no intention of forcing you to see through to the end. God, Jake. You make it so easy. You should see the look of terror in your face right now."

He ignored her, taking her by the elbow and leading her toward the door. "Where do you envision spending the day of your engagement?"

"On my back."

He almost tripped on the edge of the carpet. "Is there a second choice?"

"There are lots of them. New York is such a great place to be young and in love, don't you think? We could rent a rowboat in Central Park. Climb the Empire State Building together. Book a couples massage…"

He did a much better job of hiding his horror that time.

"Or we could pinch a bottle of tequila and sneak into the backstage area of the Artista Theatre. I like to watch them rehearse sometimes. It's all in Spanish, so I have no idea what they're saying."

Jake raised an amused brow. "And they let you?"

She shrugged. "Sara and I used to break in there as teenagers. The janitor would chase us out with his broom, but then he'd leave the backstage door unlocked so we could return when no one was looking."

"Sounds charming. Should I wear all black and carry a lockpick?"

And he would. In Jake's world, breaking and entering was preferable to romance. Jail time probably was too.

She decided to take it easy on him. "We should be good. When Sara died, I gave them a pretty big chunk of money in her name. They only chase me out half the time now."

EIGHT

"WHY ARE WE being so clandestine about this?" Jake took the stubby piece of wood Becca proffered and wedged it vertically into the open windowpane. The frame creaked as it lowered, threatening to splinter the hastily manufactured support beam, but it held. Barely. "We had Liam drop us off out front. The guy at the ticket counter waved at you."

"This is how Sara and I used to do it."

He looked at the tiny window, just big enough to fit the heads and hips of a pair of teenage girls with a greater sense of adventure than common sense, and sighed. The alley behind the theater smelled as if it contained no fewer than three dead bodies, and he was pretty sure what Becca thought was a stray dog was actually some kind of mutant rat, but this was how she and Sara used to do it.

It would take a far stronger man than he to defy that kind of logic.

He laced his hands to form a platform and gestured for her to climb up. "No wonder you end up in the tabloids five days out of every seven. You're practically giving the scandals away for free at this point. And in a dirty back alley, no less."

"Unlike *your* scandals, which are always so classy and elegant." She braced a hand on his shoulder and slipped her foot into his waiting hands. Something wet and sticky transferred from the bottom of her high heel to his palm. "Ooh, this is a lot easier with a strong man to help. I like it. We used to have to drag the garbage over and climb on top of it."

She pushed her arms through the window and hoisted herself up, body wriggling efficiently through. This clearly wasn't her first time, though Jake doubted she'd ever accounted for the flash of her ass, tightly encased in a pair of white lace panties, as her skirt rode high. It would have been a perfect paparazzi shot—he was certainly enjoying the view from his angle—but she slipped through before he could do much more than shake his head in a mixture of wonder and respect.

Becca never did anything without turning it into an endless loop of sex and scandal. He wished he could determine whether that was a virtue or one of the biggest fatal flaws he'd ever encountered in his life. Since there weren't any cameras going off in the distance—this time—he decided to reserve judgment.

Her face materialized where her ass had been just seconds before. "Hand me the bottle. I don't want you to drop it."

He held out the paper-bag-encased bottle of tequila, which they'd thankfully purchased rather than stole at a liquor store farther uptown, and followed it with his jacket. There was no elegant way to foist himself up the side of a building, so he had to make do with getting a good grip on the window's ledge and swinging his legs up in a fairly impressive gymnastic feat. Like moving through the birth canal, his shoulders were the hardest fit, and he had to try several different positions before he was finally able to slip through.

"You know, if this engagement thing doesn't work

out, we could totally head out on the lam and be cat burglars together." Becca waited until he was on his feet again before handing him the bottle, now open and missing an inch of liquid off the top. "We'll be a modern-day Bonnie and Clyde."

He took a grateful swing of the alcohol—cheap and burning and his very first drink out of a paper bag. "You know they were shot to pieces in the end, right?"

"We could invest in a good pair of bulletproof vests first."

He didn't have a chance to reply to that sound bit of wisdom, as a middle-aged woman with several pins sticking out of a band on her hand rushed up to embrace Becca. Jake had to give them a wide berth to avoid being stabbed.

"Hey, honey," the woman said, not the least bit surprised to find them lingering near the propped window. "I didn't know you were stopping by today. I don't suppose you came to help with the costumes, did you? I was just putting together the fabric order, and I could use your opinion before I send it off. You always have such a good eye for colors."

"We're not here." Becca winked at Jake and wound her arm through his. "We're sneaking in today."

The wardrobe matron nodded as if this was a perfectly normal occurrence. "Oh, then don't let me stop you. I haven't seen a thing. You two go on and have fun." She turned before she got too far. "By the way, there's a sandwich tray in the lounge from your favorite deli. You can grab a few on your way down. And maybe you can swing by later this week about the costumes?"

Becca beamed. "I'd love to."

The woman beamed right back and slid off into a

dark hallway, part of the maze of backstage and storage rooms that seemed to make up this part of the theater.

"Just how much money did you give this place?" Jake asked as Becca led him expertly through, several more people appearing to say hello or wave a greeting or otherwise treat her as a benefactress of godlike proportions. To hear them speak, you'd think Becca had singlehandedly written, directed and performed their last twelve shows.

"I think I might technically own it, but I'm not sure." She stopped them at a rickety ladder that led to an unknown abyss. "It was really close to shutting down. You'd have to talk to my mom's financial advisor to get all the details, but I don't recommend that unless you're desperate. She doesn't approve of the arts. She only believes in real estate and securities."

Jake felt a churning in his stomach that had nothing to do with their descent down a ladder that seemed rickety enough to leave them stranded underneath the stage. Becca had a lot more money than he'd previously thought if she was buying businesses and real estate like he might pick up concert tickets. It had never been a secret that the Clares had money—more, even, than the Montgomerys—but this went beyond anything he'd imagined.

These are the lengths to which I've gone. I'm a gold digger. I've proposed fake marriage to a billionaire and been accepted.

"What are you waiting for?" Becca tugged on his pant leg, urging him to hurry. "Did you want to stop and grab some sandwiches first?"

"No, thank you. Food is not my problem right now." He landed on both feet, looking past the coils of rope and set props to a tiny alcove where Becca had clearly made her mark. Colorful pillows created a seating space, a wispy curtain allowed for privacy—and overhead, the muted voices of actors could be heard.

He lifted the tequila bottle to his lips again. "What I need is more to drink."

"WHAT DID HE just say?" Becca tilted her ear toward the ceiling and paused. "Did he finally propose to her?"

"No. He said he'd rather have his heart torn from his chest and tossed into the ocean than break her family apart." Jake rolled his eyes—or close enough to it to count. He probably didn't have the physical capabilities to roll them all the way. It was far too emotive an expression. "This play is terrible. It sounds like it was written by a twelve-year-old who just broke up with his first online girlfriend."

"That's not fair. You'd hate any production where an integral part of the plot revolves around love. I bet you break out in applause when Romeo and Juliet die."

"Of course I do," he said. "It's the end of the play. It'd be rude not to."

Becca giggled. She should have known better. If given the chance, Jake would always demolish sentiment with reason.

"What they need to do is replace that man speaking in baritone with the one wearing clogs and stomping around like an elephant," he mused, mostly to himself. "He's clearly the stronger actor of the two."

She paused for a moment, listening. "You know, I think you might be right."

"Of course I am. I was born for the stage."

"Hardly. You're just really good at pointing out other people's shortcomings." She didn't give him a chance to

point out any more of hers. "How do you even understand all this anyway? I had no idea you spoke Spanish."

"I understand it better than I speak it—lots of listening to foreign language tapes when I was a kid. It was
always my dad's hope that I'd oversee his international
hotels, so he started me young. Fortunately for us both,
Jenna is more than capable of picking up my slack." He
leaned his head back against the wall and closed his
eyes. He'd been grumpily doubtful about crawling into
her lair and mussing up his clothes, but now that he was
here, he seemed perfectly at ease. Long legs extended
casually in front of him, head cocked to hear the sounds
from above, and he sat just far enough away that they
weren't touching...yeah. That was about as relaxed as he
was capable of getting. "I also speak decent French, terrible Italian, and—if you count highly inappropriate ref-
erences to the act of copulation—a touch of Icelandic."

"Really?" She liked the sound of that last one. "Tell
me something dirty we could do in Iceland."

He looked at her levelly. "*Við gætum velt okkur um
með kindunum.*"

She gave an involuntary shiver at the rough way the
unfamiliar words rolled off his tongue. "I have no idea
what you just said, but I like it. Let's do that. Let's do
that right here."

"Not a chance, Tiger. It's the wrong kind of dirty."

"Fine. Keep being annoying." Here they were, bun-
dled in a nest of pillows and low lights, half-drunk on
cheap tequila, and he *still* wouldn't slip her a little foreign tongue. "You win."

He eyed her speculatively. "I almost always do."

How nice that must be. She held up the bottle in a one-
sided toast. "Sara always said I was the most annoying

person she knew, but I think that's because she never met you. To Sara, who's going to miss out on a lot of great things, but who at least had the good fortune never to share a pretend engagement with Jake Montgomery."

"To Sara," he echoed. He paused for a full minute, his unreadable gaze holding her much-too-obvious one, before speaking again. "Why here, by the way? What's so great about this place that you two broke the law to get in?"

Nothing, really. If anything, this place contained more sad memories than good ones. She still remembered the first time she and Sara had come—through the front door and with tickets in hand. Sara had a major crush on the lead actor at the time, a darkly good-looking college guy who was much too old and far too worldly for her.

Nothing had come of it, of course. A kid drooling at a grown man from the front row was hardly the start of a lifelong romance, but it had marked one of the first times Becca had seen for herself how fixated Sara could get on unattainable things—on unattainable men, in particular.

"It was a love affair, of course," Becca said, fully willing to end the conversation there. She wasn't sure how much of this Jake actually cared to know, and how much of it was him being polite. "One that could have been written by a twelve-year-old who just broke up with his first online girlfriend."

"Was the love affair yours?" he asked.

Apparently, he was willing to go a little deeper. "Unfortunately, no," she said. "Sara had a thing for one of the actors. We saw the play he was in at least twenty times during its run. She thought that if we just kept showing up, if he could just see how devoted she was, he'd eventually come around and declare his undying love for her."

"Affection born of persistence?"

"Something like that." Affection born of persistence and obsession and the unerring belief that she could will it into existence, if only she tried. All Sara had ever wanted was for people to love her—and when they didn't, as men and the media and her too-busy father were wont to do—she coped by turning off, usually for months at a time. Her highs were always a blur of parties and fun, but her lows were downright scary. "When the show ended and the actor moved away without so much as a backward glance, the Sara I knew sort of disappeared for a while. She'd skip school to break in here and stare at the empty stage for hours. I got in the habit of coming along to keep her company."

"That was nice of you."

"Was it?" She—and her nightmares—weren't so sure. "Sometimes I feel like it was the exact opposite. I can't help but think it would have been better to make her adopt the Rebecca Clare Method of Problem-Solving instead."

"And by *method of problem-solving*, you mean losing control and making a public spectacle of yourself?"

"Yes," she said firmly. Anything was better than an isolated, pill-infused depression. Her mother and Trish Callahan and even Jake might think it was better to shove the feelings down and put a brave face on things, but look what a brave face had done for Sara. You could only muffle the sound of a heart breaking for so long before it broke everything else. "I know it's not socially acceptable, and I'm always sorry afterward, but I have to do *something* to get it all out. You should try it sometime. It's almost as effective as working out with Max."

"I'll bear it in mind."

They sat in comfortable silence for a few minutes, their bodies not touching but a palpable sense of affinity swelling in the empty spaces between. It would have been the perfect moment for him to kiss her or swoop her into his arms or at least discuss the fact that they were essentially hiding in a hole to avoid the reality of their day's handiwork, but all he did was grab her wrist. She thought for a startled moment that they were going to actually *hold hands*—in which case she'd need to have Jake checked for signs of possession—but he merely turned her hand over, palm-side up.

"Can I show you a trick?"

"A magic trick?" She was oddly tickled at the idea. Was he going to pull a quarter out of her ear? Wow her with fast hands and tight pants?

"Not that kind of trick, I'm afraid. It's more of a technique. It's what I do when I know I'm reaching my limit and need to calm down."

"Oh, please. If you got any calmer, your heart rate would stop altogether. I hardly think we're in the same league when it comes to emotional outbursts."

"Do you want to know my trick or not?"

Was he kidding? She wanted to know *all* his tricks. She wanted to know how he got his hair to look so good without even trying. She wanted to know why people continued to treat him with respect no matter how many times he screwed up. She wanted to know if his famous ability to stay calm in a crisis came at the cost of his soul.

This seemed as reasonable a place to start as any. "Okay, sensei. Show me."

He lifted two fingers in what was either a Boy Scout salute or a promise to start fingering her right there on the cushions. It turned out to be neither. With a quick movement, he tapped lightly on her wrist. One, two, three, four. Pause. One, two, three, four. Pause. There was nothing erotic or even all that intimate about his touch, but she felt each beat of his fingers as if she were a drum he was playing, a minion he was piping to his tune.

"I usually repeat it about five times. If you don't feel any calmer, you can grip instead, like this." He wrapped his hand around her wrist and squeezed tightly, a testament to his strength. "But people tend to look at you funny if you do it too hard. I find the tapping can be done on the sly, especially if you use your thumb."

She watched as he repeated the motions on her other wrist, and then he released her, tossing her hands into her lap as if he was tired of them already. "It looks silly, but it works. Better than counting or breathing or Xanax, anyway."

"I bet it's because there are like six acupressure points in there." She held up her wrists and flexed them. "Some of those points are bound to be related to emotional balance. I had no idea you were so alternative-health friendly. I'm starting to feel like I'm engaged to a stranger."

She couldn't have chosen a better insult if she'd hand-selected it. He scowled. "It has nothing to do with alternative health. It's just a thing I learned from my nanny growing up."

"Sure it is."

"Mind over matter."

"I don't doubt it." When his scowl didn't ease up, she softened. It wasn't nice to poke the devil when he was trying so hard to be helpful. "And thank you. In exchange for your magic trick, I'll do something for you."

"Hire new actors?"

"This company gets fantastic peer reviews, I'll have you know. No one touches the Artista." She'd buy up the whole block if she had to. This place had become her sanctuary, not just because it reminded her of Sara, but because she'd come to learn just how hard the staff worked to make a success of the off-off-way-off Broadway circuit. The Artista reminded her that life went on, that everyone was struggling to find their footing. "But what I will do is call our engagement off whenever you want. We should probably give my mom a few days to calm down and forget about Tranquility Ranch, but she tends to get over these things quickly. It'll be a week, tops, and then you can get back to your regularly scheduled life."

"About that…" For the first time, Jake looked out of place down here. He shifted his position and studied his hands.

"I won't make you look bad," she promised. "We can put all the blame on me. Maybe I can stage a public meltdown or have a diva moment or something. I'm good at those."

"Or—and I'm just throwing this out here—we could eke this thing out a bit longer. Maybe even for a few months. Until after the holidays."

"Oh?" She licked her lips. "Any particular reason?"

"Not that one." He shot her a warning glance. "I hate to show my true colors so soon in our grand romance, but offering you fake marriage wasn't an entirely altruistic move. You've got something I want in return."

She laughed and leaned in to drop a kiss on his nose. One didn't normally treat a man like him with such casual condescension, but she couldn't help it. He really did think she was an idiot on top of everything else. "I know. You need a place to stay while you're in New York, and you're hoping I'll let you shack up with me."

The only sign of change in him was a white line around his lips. "What makes you think that?"

She lifted his hand from out of his lap and studied the palm. His hands were long and lean and tanned, just like the rest of him, no jewelry to mar the perfection of his digits. She traced the path of his fate line right down the center, lifting her fingertip at the break in the middle, where the heart line intervened. "Because it says so right here in your palm."

"Bullshit."

"It's true! Right here. I can read it clearly." She moved her finger as if following a line of text. "It says, *As he approaches middle age, Jake Montgomery will be homeless and desperate, and only fake true love can save him.*"

"I'd hardly call myself middle aged."

"You're thirty-one. Compared to me, you're practically an old man."

He snatched his hand back. "Compared to you, I'm practically a saint. You're nothing but a con artist. You don't read horoscopes or tea leaves or palms. You make things up and cloak it in the occult so people believe you."

"Oh? Then tell me I'm wrong about the needing a place to stay part."

He didn't, because he couldn't. She almost laughed at his frustration upon finding himself stranded at the crossroads of disbelief—a place the devil rarely tread. How easy it was to write these kinds of predictions off as silly and unfounded, an ideal hobby for a woman as deranged as her. But what Jake didn't understand was that there was more to reading fortunes than chance. She paid attention. She understood pain. She knew how to take what the universe gave her and make it fit in real life.

And she was right much more often than she was wrong. That meant something, whether he believed in it or not.

"How did you really know?"

She sighed. Jake obviously wasn't in a place to accept anything more than the obvious, so she rationalized it the best she could. "You moved your bags into my apartment this morning, Jake. I've never known you to stay anywhere but in one of your family's hotels."

"It's not that," he said, his voice grumbling in a way that indicated she'd hit her mark. "Well, not *just* that."

She waited to see if he'd offer the rest without prompting. She wasn't disappointed.

"There might also be this tiny bet I'm trying to win. And before you start yelling at me, let me clarify that it barely qualifies as a bet—I'd define it more as a matter of pride. Monty thinks it's impossible for a man to survive in this world without gainful employment, and I'm trying to prove him wrong. That's all."

"And to win, you thought it might be a good idea to get engaged?"

"So it seems."

"Are you serious right now? Your bet-winning survival method is to trade gainful employment for a sugar mama?"

"I never said it was a *good* method."

Becca burst out laughing at the absurdity of it all. She'd been about two minutes away from a forced return to rehab, and here Jake was, making nonsensical wagers in an ongoing rivalry with his older brother. And everyone thought *she* was the messed up one.

"It's not that funny," he said with a glower.

"It's pretty funny. You could have just asked."

"I was going to. Things got complicated." He continued his close examination of his hands. "We don't have to do it if you don't like it. I was only trying to help back there, and it seemed like the easiest way for us to both get what we want."

"Oh, we're doing it. We're totally winning." Was he kidding? Not only had he saved her from Tranquility Ranch, but he was offering to be her live-in bedtime companion for the indeterminable future. Madame Pernaud had nailed this one. A temporary partnership with Jake was exactly what she needed right now. She could sleep again, relax again, be herself again.

And maybe, just maybe, I can finally put Sara to rest.

She scooted closer, running her hands over the front of his shirt, reveling in the hard wall of chest under her fingertips. And a wall it was—not because of the delicious dips and lines of his musculature, but because he wasn't moving. Not even to breathe.

She dropped her hands. "What? I wasn't going to *do* anything. Your chest was right there. I only wanted to touch it a little."

"If we go through with this," he said, his voice low and intent, "can you promise me something?"

"Well, I'm not giving you my soul, if that's what you had in mind."

His expression wavered between laughter and impatience. The impatience won. "I mean it. This is serious. I can only do this in good conscience if you promise me you won't get attached."

Her urge to laugh wasn't quite as strong this time. Of course *that* was what worried Jake, why he was refusing all her overtures, why he'd become a sexual fortress. Not that he was uninterested in sex or because he didn't want her. He was afraid her instability might leak over and sully his hands.

Poor guy. Her instability did that a lot.

"Don't worry so much," she assured him. "I can safely say I don't stand in any danger of getting attached. You're the last man on earth I'd ever marry."

"What?" His question came out as a bark. "Why?"

"Well, for one, I don't particularly want to. You're controlling and condescending and will probably treat your wife like an accessory only to be worn with the right outfit."

These qualities were fantastic when viewed through a temporary lens. Controlling and condescending men made incredible—if precise—lovers, and she had no objection to being a bit of arm candy from time to time. But long-term?

No way. She wasn't putting her happiness into the hands of a man like Jake. Even if he did somehow transform his entire way of life and become an ideal husband, love with someone who maneuvered his emotions as if they were chess pieces was far too risky. That kind of love—the painful, fruitless, never-ending search for more—was what had killed Sara in the end. She'd given up on ever finding it.

Which was why Becca didn't intend to start.

"I'm not that bad," Jake muttered.

"You're pretty bad—when was the last time you dated anyone who wasn't a supermodel?"

"I can't help that the only people who find me attractive are tall, elegant, photogenic women. I have to take what I can get."

Becca laughed and shook her head. She was definitely neither elegant nor photogenic, yet they both knew he could have her for the asking. "That was only my first objection anyway."

"I'm almost afraid to ask about the second one," he said. "What is it? Does it make you feel dirty to lust after your nephew? Do you have your sights set on a remorseless assassin from the wrong side of the tracks?"

"Nothing quite so exciting as that. I'm sorry to disappoint you, but it all boils down to fate."

"Fate?" The word practically burned on his tongue.

"Yep. You're a Virgo and I'm an Aries. It's the worst possible matchup under the stars."

Jake waited for the punch line, staring at Becca as if he could will her into confessing something more—that maybe she had a secret husband already tucked away, or there was some kind of strange will in place that forbade her from marrying or she'd lose her billion-dollar trust fund forever.

But it didn't come. She just sat there and smiled, purring against his side like a contented kitten, warm to touch and soft to pet. And that was it. The end. The incompatibility of their astrological signs was her actual reason for not wanting to marry him.

And he had no clue how he was supposed to defend himself against that kind of insult. *No, I wasn't born in the month of August? No, everyone wants to marry me because I'm irresistible?*

He didn't get an opportunity to come up with a third option because Becca started moving again. Never content to stay where she was for long, she'd wriggled herself into a more interesting position and was worming her hand inside the front of his shirt, her fingers walking a dangerous line down his abdomen. He was inclined to let her keep going, to show her how little she affected him, but at the first graze of her fingertips under the lip of his belt, his nerve endings got up to make their demands.

They wanted more. And they wanted it right fucking now. It was dark, he and Becca had been drinking, and they were surrounded by pillows. They were also grown adults who'd performed a similar act in the past. There was no earthly reason why he couldn't act on the urge to pull her on top of him and force her to scream his name.

Unfortunately, the only screaming taking place today was inside his balls. As much as it pained him to admit it, he'd somehow fallen headfirst into the only rabbit hole in the world where sex was forbidden to him.

He couldn't bring himself to take advantage of Becca. Not when he was already taking advantage of her.

He lifted her hand away and, with a very clear tap of his fingers against his opposite wrist, managed to get himself under control again.

"Want me to give that a try?" she asked coyly. "I can think of somewhere else I might tap."

"Goddammit, Becca," he said. She was killing him here. "We're definitely going to need to have a talk about personal boundaries for the duration of our fake engagement."

"But I was just getting started down there. Give a girl a chance to prove herself."

"When I want you to touch my cock, I'll tell you." He pinched her chin, drawing her close. So she thought he was controlling, did she? She had no idea. "And you'll do it without a word of protest. Understand?"

Her pupils widened as she bit down on her lower lip,

assent written in the flush of her skin. She'd do it too. She might have all sorts of ridiculous reasons why the incompatibility of their birthdates meant they could never be life partners, but if Becca was good at one thing, it was playing along. She'd play all the way to the bedroom and back again.

He bit back a groan. What had he gotten himself into?

"Of course I'll do as you say." She batted her eyes up at him. "Your wish is my command, Big Papa."

He released her and sighed, any and all of his power in this conversation fleeing as suddenly as it had come. He should have known better. In order to get a normal, female reaction out of her, Becca would have to be a normal female.

"No way." He held up a warning finger. "Not Big Papa. *Anything* but Big Papa."

"Love Muffin?"

"Not if you value your life."

She winked at him and rose to her feet. Without a care as to how much of her skin she flashed at him, she adjusted her skirt, transforming herself from a seductive, half-dressed mess to a seductive, half-dressed woman ready to face the collective weight of the world's disapproval.

"Oh, don't you worry, Pookie Bear." She flashed him a serene smile as she gathered up their things. "I'll find it. Just give me time."

NINE

"I CANNOT BELIEVE you're seeing Jake Montgomery and you never said a word." Livvie pointed at Becca with her champagne flute, which contained much more sparkling wine than orange juice. "You sly thing. I could have sworn you went home with one of the Parker twins just last week."

Becca brought her own glass to her lips with a smile. Brunch with Livvie was a fairly new tradition—part of her one-woman campaign to get her friend to occasionally emerge during daylight hours—and it had already become one of her favorite rituals. It was such an ordinary thing to do, eating and gossiping and flipping off the camera guys who'd camped out across the street, waiting for them to leave. It almost felt normal.

"I wouldn't exactly say I'm *seeing* him," she hedged. That was technically the truth. She was doing both a lot more and a lot less than that. Too much more, and too much less. It was an odd conundrum. "Think of us more as allies united for a common good."

"That doesn't sound very romantic."

"It's not. Unless, of course, you consider it romantic for a man to spend three hours rearranging your closet while calling you the most useless human being ever to touch a coat hanger. He didn't even make me dinner afterward."

Livvie looked incredulously at her. "Are you serious?

A friend of mine dated him about four years ago, and she used to tell us these stories about the lengths he went to for romance. Whisking her away on a private jet to dine in Paris. Kidnapping her and taking her aboard his yacht in the dead of night—and I mean that in the best possible way. Silk restraints, blindfolds, everything."

Becca tried to ignore the twinge of jealousy these images evoked, of Jake binding her hands and using his obsessive compulsive powers for good. *Of course* he'd pull out all the stops when he was wooing a supermodel. That sort of thing required finesse. What the two of them had was a deal, an arrangement, a temporary partnership, just as Madame Pernaud foretold.

"Our relationship isn't like that," Becca said firmly. "He's mostly looking out for me because we're related."

"Oh, that's right. You're like his grandma or something, aren't you?"

She laughed and brought a bite of mango to her lips. "Close enough." There was no need to explain all the gritty details. One of the first things she'd come to learn about Livvie was that nothing could surprise or shock her. At twenty-five, she was only a year older than Becca, but she and her perfect cheekbones had been modeling for at least a decade. No one grew up faster than a teen model in New York City. Some of the stories she told made Becca's heart hurt.

"If I tell you something, can you promise to keep it secret?" Becca asked.

"Of course. You know you can count on me." Livvie smiled, flashing her teeth. "I've worn your underwear, Becca. There's no going back now."

She laughed again, so loud she startled the quietly conversing couple at the table next to them. With an apologetic grin, she scooted her chair closer to the table. "I thought we weren't going to mention that ever again."

"You're so cute when you're being a prude," Livvie said. "Remind me to tell you some time about when a few of the girls and I got trapped on the Prague Metro overnight. You don't know female kinship until you've survived that. I'm pretty sure I'm pledged to bear children for at least two of them."

In that moment, Becca would have willingly worn any item of clothing her friend passed under the table. This feeling of affinity was a good one—much too rare these days—and she planned on cherishing it for as long as she was able. She didn't do this sort of thing nearly enough. In the months leading up to Sara's death, life had been such a whirlwind of parties and prior engagements that Becca had only seen her friend a handful of times, most of them in a social setting that made any real conversation difficult.

Never again. There weren't many people who understood what it was like to live under the constant glare of stadium lights, but Livvie was one of them. Becca didn't care if she had to blackmail her into coming out to a restaurant every few weeks. They would meet. They would talk. They would bitch about the men in their lives and discuss their fears and even share their goddamned underwear.

They wouldn't get so lost they forgot there were people who cared about them.

"Jake and I are going to pretend to be engaged," she said, watching with satisfaction as Livvie's already colt-like eyes widened. "He's not getting along with his family right now, and my mom is threatening to disown me if I don't clean up my act, so we're banding together in not-so-holy matrimony for a few months."

"Pretending to be engaged? In actual public?"

"That's the plan."

"We're talking about the same man who has never dated any woman for longer than two weeks at a time?"

"I know."

"The same man who was quoted last year as saying marriage is 'the weakest, most easily dissolved contract in modern society?'"

"I know."

"The same man who once broke up a wedding because he winked at the bride too suggestively and the groom took offense?"

"First of all, that one was never proved. And second of all, since when did you become such a Jake Montgomery fangirl?"

Livvie shrugged. "He's cute—and his family's hotels are everywhere. You know how much easier it would be to travel if I had a penthouse waiting in every port?"

"I guess relationships have been founded on less." Becca laughed. "*Our* relationship is founded on less."

As expected, Livvie was neither surprised nor shocked by the revelation. "Well, I think it's genius, to be honest," she said, and kicked back the rest of her drink. "Movie stars are always fake dating to get publicity, and you can enjoy all the perquisites of an engagement in the meantime. I bet Jake has fantastic perquisites."

On that subject, Becca remained silent—and it was only partially due to the fact that Jake's perquisites were off-limits to her. For all that he refused to consider the possibility of warming her bed in more athletic ways at night, there was an odd intimacy about the way his even breathing lulled her to sleep, and she was hesitant to shine a light on it just yet.

Since Livvie gave every indication she'd be happy continuing a discussion of Becca's sex life—or lack thereof—for hours, she maneuvered the conversation to less dangerous waters. "Oh! You'll never guess who was at my mom's tea the other day. She's part of the reason all this happened, actually. Do you remember Lulu? Lulu Callahan?"

"Hmm." Livvie tapped on her teeth, her gaze thoughtful. "Tall, right? Great legs? Her family's in finance?"

"That's her. I was thinking it might be nice to invite her to brunch one of these days, if you don't mind. She just got back from some kind of charity work in Somalia, and she seems a bit out of her element. I thought she was going to pass out during tea—and that was before I started attacking people. I'd like to make it up to her."

"Oh, she wasn't in Africa, darling. Not if we're thinking of the same person."

"Of course she was. She graduated from college and went straight off to dig wells. You should have seen her tan. It was incredible."

"That's right." Livvie frowned. "You weren't here. You wouldn't remember."

Now it was Becca's turn to open her eyes in surprise. "What wouldn't I remember?"

"She never graduated—at least, not from college." Livvie offered a sympathetic wince. "She spent her final semester in some sort of residential spa in California, if I'm not mistaken. It was a few weeks after you were sent away. Don't…freak out or anything, but rumor at the time was that her family had her under a lot of pressure. She suffered some sort of breakdown."

Becca's heart sank as Livvie's full meaning settled. "Oh, no. Not Lulu too."

"I'm sorry." Livvie reached across the table and squeezed her hand. There was no need for her to say anything more—it was those stadium lights. Nothing escaped anyone's notice under here. "I wish I'd known Sara better. She seemed like a great person."

Dammit. Now she was going to cry. And those stupid cameras were out there just waiting for her to make a fool of herself again.

"She *was* a great person." Becca blinked rapidly, forcing her eyes to reabsorb the tears. It was a good thing she'd invested in bulk-sized quantities of waterproof mascara lately. "She felt everything so deeply—the good stuff as well as the bad. Did you know she practically ran that battered women's shelter in Queens?" That was another organization that had received a hefty contribution from her trust fund after the clouds of shock had cleared. "I tell myself every day it wasn't my fault, that her problems went a lot deeper than the occasional boyfriend trouble. I mean, she'd been seeing psychiatrists since before she could talk. But I can't help feeling that all it would have taken was one good thing. *One* man in her life who didn't treat her like crap. *One* news article that didn't call her out as being a desperate attention-whore. *One* friend who remembered to call and check in on her from time to time."

That was as far as she could go. Her throat had solidified.

"You know, I'll never understand why it is that people think just because a girl has money and youth and a little bit of fame, she's somehow exempt from having feelings too." Livvie shook her head, summing up all of

Becca's thoughts in a few words and one tiny gesture. "We have hearts, for fuck's sake. And they break just like everyone else's."

Becca wiped at her cheeks with the back of her hand, determined not to turn the morning into a sobfest. Max was constantly telling her to celebrate every milestone and accomplishment. You didn't get stronger by counting the number of sit-ups you *hadn't* done. And she and Sara had made plenty of good memories together too: road trips and parties they'd crashed and sleepovers where men took a backseat to friendship. Those times mattered. They had to.

"Then it's settled," Becca said. "I'm inviting Lulu to brunch next time, but you have to promise not to scandalize her with lurid stories about models trapped on trains."

"Cross my heart. I'll stick to my best PG-13 tales. I'm sure I have one or two."

"You know, we could turn it into a whole thing." She gave Livvie the side-eye. "Brunch. Shopping. And then we can all go out with my personal trainer afterward."

Livvie pointed her fork in a warning. "No way. Stop trying to foist your burdens on me."

"He's not a burden. I'm telling you—he's a godsend."

"Oh, really? And how does your fake fiancé feel about your godsend?"

Becca laughed, picturing Jake's face when she'd confessed that Max liked to keep her on her toes by never making appointments. He just showed up when he felt she needed it. "I haven't asked him directly, but I'm pretty sure he's declared him his mortal enemy."

Livvie gave a delighted shiver. "Is it wrong that I'm totally turned on by that?"

"If it is, then I have no desire to be right."

TEN

"ARE YOU FUCKING kidding me right now?" Jake jolted awake, all of his senses alert.

Becca released a mumbled groan and burrowed her head under the comforter. She also burrowed her arms and her legs and her body, writhing him into a state of early morning discomfort. It went well with his bedtime discomfort. And his middle-of-the-night discomfort. And unless he found himself some kind of portable cold shower, his whole-damn-rest-of-the-day discomfort.

They were *really* going to have to rethink their sleeping arrangements. He didn't care how many heartfelt pleas she buried him under, or how her lip quivered when he tried to take up residence in the spare room. There were very hard, very painful limits to his sense of nobility.

"You have to save me," Becca murmured into his chest. "Don't let him come in here. *Flashdance* days are the worst."

He rolled away and out from under the covers, willing his blood to cool and his body to maintain a semblance of decency. It was easier than expected, thanks to the sound of "Maniac" continuing its techno beat from the living room.

"What I can't understand is why the hell you gave that man a key to your apartment. He's a sadist." Then, more curious than anything else, "What happens on *Flash-dance* days?"

"Usually?" She peeked her head out from under the blankets. He'd managed to extract a blood oath that she'd wear real pajamas to bed from now on, so at least she was covered up, but she still glowed like sex awakening from a long night of satisfaction. "He has to carry me back. They've started keeping a pushcart down by the concierge desk, or I'd never make it home. Want to come with?"

"Not a chance. As charming of a picture you paint, I fail to see the value of early morning exercise. You could at least ask him to come at noon or something."

"Oh, you don't ask Max for anything. He tells you what, when and where—and if you know what's good for you, you don't ask questions. He's a Virgo too."

He ignored the barb as she unfolded herself out from the bed, stretching as she went. Her limbs were strong and catlike, the delineation of her muscles evident under the stretchy nylon on her lower half. He barely had time to appreciate the sight of her as the music switched over to the ominous blending sound of her morning smoothie being made. That man certainly knew how to make himself at home.

"How long has he been coming here?"

Becca pursed her lips, considering. "Three months? Three and a half? Somewhere around there."

Jake didn't have to do the math. "Ever since you got out of rehab."

He couldn't tell if the smile she offered him contained more joy or grief. "I don't know how I would have done it without him. It's nice having a familiar face to look forward to in the morning, you know?"

"No, I don't know. I like waking up alone. Preferably in a soundproofed guest room."

"Mock all you want, but he's been better than therapy. He told me after our first day together—when I was basically dying on the concrete and threatening to sue him for cruelty—that focusing on physical pain and exhaustion is a good way to work through the emotional kind." She paused, only shaking herself off when the sound of the blender came to a halt. "It's like your tapping trick. When my legs and stomach hurt so much I can barely stand, it's easier for me to process everything else."

Christ. She meant every word.

"Oh." She whirled and snapped her fingers. "And he always makes sure I remember to eat, so that's good too."

Jake was unable to move as Becca continued her morning routine, muttering to herself as she rooted through her dresser. He found it impossible to come up with a reply to a confidence like that, so casual, so honest, so fucking unfair it made him boil up with unfamiliar frustration. It was odd how much that frustration felt like lust, as if he wanted to throw Becca to the bed and cover her body with his own, protecting her from everything but his touch. The more time he spent in her company, the more obvious it became that she needed *someone* to protect her. Mean Max, her driver Liam, the costume lady at the theater—it took the combined efforts of a village to keep this woman from walking straight off a cliff.

How the hell did it come about that *he* was the only one to notice this? The day Jake Montgomery was the most observant and caring person in your life was a desperate day indeed. He'd once been given a hydroponic herb garden for Christmas. It had lasted three days before it turned black and died.

The doors to Becca's room opened in a burst of energy. Max planted himself in the doorway, two glasses of pink protein in his hands this time. He handed one to the half-naked Becca, blithely unconcerned that she was in the middle of pulling on a sports bra, and turned to Jake, his hand extended.

"You're coming with us today," he said. "It's not optional."

"Thanks but no thanks. I perform for no man."

Max nodded at Jake's torso, clad only in an undershirt. "I know. I can tell."

Since there didn't seem to be any way to get the better of this behemoth, Jake laughed and accepted the glass. He even went so far as to give an obliging sip. It was sweet and cloying and cold—his three least favorite adjectives in a breakfast beverage—before handing it back. No way was that making its way down his throat.

"You can push all you want, but I have it on good authority it would never work out between us," Jake said. "You and I are both Virgos. We're doomed to constantly lock our cold, unfeeling horns."

Across the room, Becca managed to finish dressing and interrupted their conversation. "Close, Jake, but that's not how it works. Max was born on the Leo/Virgo cusp. He's actually quite balanced."

"There are cusps? You never mentioned cusps before. Why does this astrology stuff get more complicated every time it comes up?"

"Because it's more complicated than you're willing to admit." Becca dropped to the foot of the bed and pulled on a pair of bright white running shoes. "Won't you come with us? You're already awake, and it's to-tally unfair that I have to whip my ass into shape with blood, sweat and tears while you get to saunter around the apartment drinking coffee and looking gorgeous."

There she was again, dropping compliments like they meant nothing. To make matters worse, Max already considered it a done deal, rubbing his hands together fast enough to start a fire. "I could make you carry her across Central Park on your back. It's amazing for the core. Or we could tackle the stairs at the Empire State Building instead. What do you say?"

Becca hopped up, delight lighting her eyes. "Please? No one comes with me no matter how much I beg."

Her expectation filled the room, trapping him. What else could he say? For better or for worse, he'd prom-ised Moira he would take care of her daughter. He might be able to fool himself for a few days that organizing her closets and removing tape residue from her light switches counted, but they were talking about a woman who exercised through her emotional pain, who relied on a personal trainer to get her out of bed in the morning.

This was a much bigger task than he'd anticipated.

"Fine. I'll come." At the excited sounds greeting his capitulation, he held up a hand in warning. Becca fell silent. "But I need about ten minutes to get ready, and I require coffee first. These things are nonnegotiable."

"No can do, my friend." Max shook the protein drink, now melting to an unappealing brown. "Stick to Miracle Max here. Coffee is too dehydrating. Believe me when I say you're going to want to keep all your bodily flu-ids intact for this."

Jake opened his mouth to protest, but Becca silenced

him by holding up her glass, mocking and toasting him at the same time.

She's doing it again. As Max closed the doors—once again, quite tactfully—behind him, Jake felt his control of this situation slipping away. He couldn't tell if Becca was manipulating him or merely holding out a hand, asking for him to help her up.

"If it makes a difference, he's very expensive," Becca offered. "You can tell Monty all about how you spent your day running around the park with a man who makes more money than your family's entire team of attorneys. His head will explode."

Manipulating him.

"And thank you." She got up on tiptoes and brushed a kiss on his cheek, her lips soft and warm. "You have no idea how much it means to me that you're willing to give this a try."

Shit. Asking for help.

JAKE WAS IN better shape than he let on.

From the looks of him, all neatly coiffed and poured into a long-sleeved compression shirt, he was one of those guys at the gym who went for the mirrors rather than the free weights. But the pair of them were about three miles in to a five-mile run, and he'd barely broken a sweat. In fact, he turned backward and began trotting ass-first, watching her with a smile curling his lips.

"You run like a zombie," he said. "Shuffle, shuffle, moan. Shuffle, shuffle, moan."

She flipped him her middle finger. Some people were able to make jogging look elegant, but she wasn't counted among the fortunate ranks. She could pull off leg lifts with the right amount of sex appeal—and Jake had no idea what she was capable of when Pilates came into play—but jogging had always seemed an indecorous sport. All those body parts flopping up and down, lubricated with gallons of sweat.

Max had parked himself at the end of the upper loop in Central Park, where he was waiting to put them through their paces. He liked to get the cardio out of the way first to loosen the body, although Becca suspected it had more to do with training her to use running as a relaxation technique. He was always telling her to focus on the rhythm and her breathing, to turn her mind off and enjoy the sights and sound of New York waking up around her.

It didn't always work, but she tried. Having a running companion with her today was greatly improving her enjoyment level, but she didn't want to think too much about that. She was already growing scarily dependent on Jake for sleep—she'd had to practically tackle him to the mattress last night to get him to stay in her bed, and he'd visibly recoiled when she'd used the term "cuddle."

He might be willing to play along with this whole charade while she had something he wanted, but their careful balance could change in an instant. No one knew that better than her.

"It's all breezy jogging and gentle stretching right now," she warned, "but just you wait. This is only Max's warm-up. The mean part comes only after you've been lulled into a state of relaxation."

"I can respect that. I like a well-planned ambush as much as the next man."

"And he takes it as a personal insult if you aren't in tears by the end. You may want to start thinking of sad things."

"How can I, when I'm out here with you?"

Becca laughed so hard she got a stitch in her side, her hand clasped to her flank to keep it from spreading. "That was worse than the Cinderella pickup line, Jake. You're seriously slipping."

"Yeah, but it still would've worked on you, wouldn't it?"

"That's hardly the point. I'm no conquest. Heck—if you wanted to duck over in those bushes for a quickie, I wouldn't say no."

He stared at her for a long moment, his Adam's apple working heavily, before turning to run in a normal, forward-moving pattern. There was no denying that he'd pictured it—the pair of them scrambling into the bushes with all their sweaty, flopping parts—but he was too much in control of himself to take it further than a picture. The bastard.

"I don't do outdoor sex," he said lightly. "It's unseemly. And I'm pretty sure I could get Max to cry well before he managed to break me. The big ones fall the hardest—and they always make the most glorious crash."

"Don't you dare make my personal trainer cry. I like him."

"Or you'll do what?"

She thought about it. There weren't many thing she could do to hurt Jake—there weren't many things *anyone* could do to accomplish that. Sure, she could kick him out of her apartment, but he was the type who would dive from an airplane only to land gracefully on his feet. She could end their engagement in a gloriously tabloid-friendly manner, but as public opinion had already proven, Jake's foibles were charming while hers were the sign of a raging slut storm. And she couldn't even use him for sex and leave him in the lurch, because none of her feminine wiles were working on him.

He's broken my wiles.

She had to settle for the only thing she knew he cared about. "I'll let the hem out of every pair of pants you own—but only a quarter inch at a time and always under the cloak of night. And I'll do it every day for a week. You'll think you're shrinking."

He pointed a warning finger at her. "You wouldn't dare. You can mess with my life all you want, but mess with my tailoring and I refuse to answer for my actions."

"Then be nice to Max," she said firmly. "He's all I have."

He opened his mouth to disagree before quickly shutting it again. His smile disappeared with the firm press of his lips, and she couldn't help but feel it was her fault. Something about Max made Jake upset. It wasn't jealousy—she wasn't so deluded as to think Jake cared about her enough for that—and it wasn't anger, because the entire way over here, Jake and Max had been chatting like best friends as they discussed more appropriate wakeup songs. Jake would accept 8 Mile's "Lose Yourself" but nothing from *Dirty Dancing.* He was partial to Macklemore and Kanye West. Kid Rock would do in a pinch.

Basically, Jake had the musical tastes of a painfully white, fourteen-year-old wannabe. It was kind of hilarious.

"He's tough, but I promise he's really nice," Becca said, hoping to smooth things over. But Jake picked up his pace as they rounded a corner of the North Woods, leaving her struggling to keep up.

She imagined having a long-term relationship with this man would always be like that—one step behind, watching from afar, never quite his equal. It was probably why he'd managed to stay single for so long. Women knew, instinctively, that Jake Montgomery wasn't for everyday wear. He was a couture ball gown, a lacy garter belt from La Perla, that pair of Valentino pumps you knew looked fabulous but would leave your feet aching before the night was through. You only brought him out for special occasions.

No matter how unsuitable he might be over the long haul, Becca was determined to count today as one of those special occasions. She trotted along after him, enjoying the sight of his ass, high and round, flexing under his loose-fitting track bottoms, and left it at that.

"How'd you get to be in such good shape anyway?" Becca asked, mesmerized by his body's effortless movements. "You don't run or work out or even walk all that briskly. Every time I see you, you're standing around like some kind of predatory animal, conserving your energy for the kill."

"That's because I *am* standing around, conserving my energy for the kill. I just happen to prefer to do my slaughtering after dark."

"Why, Jake Montgomery," she purred, "is that a sexual innuendo I hear?"

"Not this time."

"Then it's a murder innuendo?"

"If by *murder innuendo* you mean a confession, then no. You can't get rid of me that easily."

She pulled her lips into a pout. "Well, it's some kind of innuendo. Those are the only kinds of conversations you're capable of having. Innuendo or sarcasm or, when you're feeling particularly witty, out-and-out insult."

He hesitated. "I have normal conversations. We're having a normal conversation right now."

"Are we? In my experience, normal conversations engender intimacy, if only for the space of a few minutes at a time. And you're the least intimate man I know. You won't even tell me how you find time to exercise."

Jake purposefully slowed his pace, allowing Becca an opportunity to catch her breath.

He didn't know how she did it, but that woman possessed an uncanny ability to smack him flat with her observations. Not only was she painfully astute, but she spoke kindly and meant no harm—both of which made the underlying implication that much sharper. No wonder people turned to her to have their fortunes read. It was like sitting down with a child who'd been taught never to lie, who saw the world without prejudice.

"You really want to know how I stay in shape?" he asked.

"Yes, please."

"Hard work, just like everyone else." He glanced at her sideways. "I run eight miles, three days a week—usually on Mondays, Wednesdays and Thursdays. Every other Sunday, I push myself to do a half marathon."

"That's the best and most disappointing answer ever."

"Don't worry. There's more. The reason you didn't know about it—why no one knows about it—is because I always go for my runs in the middle of the night. And I usually do them in a part of the city where I won't come across anyone I know, because even though my vanity requires that I keep up a rigorous regimen, my pride forces me to do it where no one else can see."

"Are you serious? That's the killing you do after dark?"

"Not so exciting after all, is it? I wasn't playing with innuendo—sexual or otherwise. I'm just a mortal man who has to work hard to stay in shape, but I prefer that no one actually know it."

He braced himself for Becca's reaction—delight at being let in to his secret, mockery at the narcissism that drove him—but wasn't prepared for what followed.

"Are you sure that's *safe?*"

He had to laugh. In all the years he'd been running by cover of night, he'd never once given a thought to the physical dangers that surrounded him. The idea that he might be spotted by an acquaintance had always been the much more pressing of his concerns.

He didn't have a chance to tell her, though, because she sucked in a sharp breath and skidded to a halt. His adrenaline—already moving swiftly—spiked, and he stopped next to her, shielding her body as he scanned the horizon for danger.

Trees. Running couple. Men drinking coffee. Squirrel. Becca tapping furiously on her wrist next to him. "What? What is it?"

"You lied. This tapping thing doesn't work at all. I'm going to kill them."

"At least you're talking about the act of murder rather than performing it. I think that's progress."

Her expression filled with equal parts amused and irritated as all hell. "Do you intend to take credit every time I *don't* physically assault someone for the rest of my life?"

"I should have set it up so I get royalties. Who aren't we killing?"

"My not-so-adoring public. Look natural." She let go of her wrist and pointed in the direction of the men drinking coffee. Gone were the paper cups and the air of casual camaraderie. Each man now boasted a long lens pointed their direction, the beaks of vultures getting ready to swoop in. "And you might want to smile and get that famous profile shot ready. We're about to be immortalized in print."

"Shit. They must have gotten wind of our engagement somehow." Jake did his best to look calm, as if being caught running in the park with his fiancée at seven in the morning was a typical day for him. "Want to get out of here?"

"Yes, but it's better if we give them what they want." She blew the man on the right—a tall, gruff-looking man with a scar across his forehead—a sneering kiss. "If we don't, they'll just be back tomorrow or the next day or when you're skulking along the streets at night running a half-marathon. I should have mentioned it earlier. Those three are my usuals. Gary, Barry and Greg. Greg's the sweetheart with the scowl."

Although instinct urged him to start jogging again and get her out of there, Jake found himself glued to the spot, studying the trio through narrowed eyes. "Do you mean to tell me they're here every day?"

"Not *here*, specifically. But you can find them hanging around my regular haunts. I should probably warn you that Greg might jog along after us for a ways, but he usually gives up after about ten minutes—he has asthma, so he has to take it easy."

Jake could only stare at her, words flitting about five feet above his head, out of reach and colorful enough to paint an entire naval yard. These scumbags actually had the audacity to stand there and wait for Becca to run by, three grown men chasing down a woman who weighed less than a punching bag? In what world was this okay?

She spared him the necessity of a response by pitching him a look of supplication. "Would you mind if we played this whole engagement thing up a little? I know I'm already in your debt a thousand times, but my opportunities for positive press are so rare. It seems like a waste not to use it."

"You want to give these assholes a reason to keep following you? No way."

"They're going to follow me no matter what. They always have. It's what they do."

He didn't know how to handle that. Yes, he'd had more than his fair share of run-ins with the paparazzi, but it was usually restricted to events and situations where their presence was expected. Nightclubs, private parties that got out of hand, anywhere expensive shoulders rubbed. It was the price he paid for having fun.

But this wasn't fun. This was everyday life. This was Becca pushing her body to the limits of its endurance so she could find a way to move past her grief. Who the fuck did those men think they were, chasing her down, waiting for her to fall?

He found himself halfway across the grass to where the men stood before he realized what he was doing and stopped. His hands had formed fists at his sides, and he looked at them curiously, surprised to find how natural they felt. He had never hit another man in anger. He had never hit another man, period. There was something so primitive and unnecessary about pugilism. He'd always found it much cleaner—and far more satisfying—to bring a man down through slow, careful plotting, bringing his whole world down with him.

Where was the fun in it otherwise?

With a deep breath and four careful taps on either wrist—Becca was right, it was a waste of fucking time—he turned on his heel and walked carefully back to her side. Not bothering with preliminaries, he brought his mouth to hers and gave those bastards exactly what they wanted.

This was no prim and proper kiss for the cameras. This was him staking his claim and leaving no room for doubts. They wanted sordid tales to carry to the gossip magazines, did they? They waited in the distance for Becca to show a moment of weakness, a single human failing so they could immortalize it in print, huh?

Well, here it was. They could have pictures of his arms crushing her body to his. They could take as many shots as they wanted of his lips moving firmly over hers, forcing her to open up beneath him. They could walk away with the falsely solid belief that this woman was *his*, and all of the shit they got away with before was about to come to a screeching halt.

And if he maybe got carried away in the middle, softening his assault so that the kiss turned deep and slow, well, that was only to be expected. He'd denied himself the pleasure of this woman's mouth for days now. He was going to take a minute.

It was a hell of a minute.

"How was that?" he asked, ending the kiss long after it passed the bounds of decency. He felt rather than heard the hitch in his own breath. "Good? Or should we give them some more? Because I can do that again if I have to."

After a slightly perplexed look up at him, Becca released a shaky laugh. "There's no need to go to such lengths. I think that one did the trick—but that wasn't what I had in mind when I asked you to play the engagement up. We could have given them a quote."

He waved her off. Maybe it wasn't what he had in mind either, but it was done now. Done and enjoyed and not fucking likely to happen again. Not if he wanted to rebuild the crumbled remains of his self-control.

"How are they taking it?"

She transferred her gaze over his shoulder to get a better look at their audience. "Oh, how sweet. They're so excited. It's like Christmas morning over there and each one of them just unwrapped a pony."

I'll bet it is. Wrapping an arm firmly around her waist, he turned them both so they faced the rapidly clicking cameras, and actually gave a goddamn wave. He felt like a politician parading his affection for his wife in order to secure the conservative votes, but he was in it now. When he gambled, he gambled hard. All in.

"Well, there it is," Becca said under her breath. "My mom is going to have a heart attack when she realizes we just made this thing officially official."

And that was it. She didn't wait for a response or thank him for his sacrifice or ask him to go ahead and punch the cameramen after all. Nudging him back toward the trail, she picked up her earlier pace and resumed her run.

This time, Jake trailed slowly, reflecting on what he'd done. He was all in, resolved, officially official. His relationship with Becca had become about more than winning a bet with Monty, moved beyond a well-meaning urge to keep his step-aunt from harm. He was part of the village keeping her from the cliff's edge now.

No—scratch that. He glanced back at the cameramen, now zeroed in on the movements of her ass as she departed, and scowled. He was going to *lead* the fucking village, rallying the peasants in an uprising to protect and serve.

ELEVEN

JAKE KNOCKED ON the window of the limo, startling Liam into spilling his coffee. With a rolling gesture, he stood patiently by until Becca's driver got himself under control and dropped the window a fraction of an inch. The scent of leather, coffee and suspicion wafted out the crack.

"Don't worry," Jake said. "This isn't a carjacking."

As Becca's houseguest—and betrothed—he'd made fairly quick work of winning over the rest of the people who worked for her. The doorman in her apartment building already accorded him a smile and a nod when he asked to be let in. Her maid, a shy, overworked woman in her late twenties, had gone so far as to stammer out an incredulous thanks when she arrived to find that Jake had hung Becca's discarded towels and lined up her enormous collection of boots by the door.

But Liam hadn't yet decided what to do with him. It turned out her chauffeur was slightly begrudging with his respect—which wasn't going to work for Jake at all. If he was going to be leading this village, everyone needed to be on his side. It was a dictatorship or bust.

"I'm supposed to take Ms. Clare to her manicure," Liam said warily.

"Ms. Clare decided she'd rather paint one of the walls in her apartment today."

"By herself?"

Jake appreciated the chauffeur's incredulity. He'd had a hard time coming to terms with it himself. They'd enjoyed a Max-free morning only to be beset by Becca's sudden urge to become a painter and seven different shades of paint delivered to the door. He hadn't yet decided which was worse.

"She appears to have convinced her cleaning woman to help. It looks like the scene of a recent murder in there, so I thought it might behoove me to entertain myself elsewhere."

Liam gave a reluctant chuckle and popped the locks up. Recognizing it as an assent, Jake moved to the front passenger side and took a seat, his movements only slightly stiff. While Max hadn't been able to coax a tear out of him yesterday—or vice versa—Jake's abs weren't too pleased with the recent turn of events. Nor was his pride, to be honest.

"You want to ride up here?" A horrified expression crossed Liam's face at the sanctity of his front seat being broken. "Next to me?"

"I'm not riding anywhere at all," Jake explained. "I was hoping you and I might have a conversation instead."

Liam grew even more uncomfortable. He wasn't like the Montgomery family's chauffeur, a man who moonlighted as a stunt driver and knew his way around sports cars, a man Jake considered his friend. Liam looked as if he'd rather get out and push the car than give in to the lure of racing. Or camaraderie.

"If Ms. Clare isn't in need of my services…"

Jake dug into his pocket and extracted his phone, his finger poised above Becca's speed dial. "You can call her if you want. I'm sure she wouldn't mind you taking me where I need to go."

"But you don't want me to go anywhere."

"Is that what's bothering you?" Jake buckled himself in. "Then let's make it a tour, shall we? We can start at Battery Park and head to the Lower East Side from there, maybe even swing by Times Square. That should make this a nice, long drive. We can chat. Get to know one another."

A ghost of a grimace crossed Liam's face, but there was little he could do about the situation, so he pulled the car out with a sigh. No wonder Becca regularly attacked people. If Jake had been saddled with intrusive cameramen and a condescending driver and a personal trainer with a death wish, he'd probably start punching anyone who pissed him off too.

"So, Liam." Jake feigned an interest in the passing scenery—the too-close brick townhouses, the shops with striped awnings, New York at its finest. "I don't believe I thanked you for the quick getaway the other night."

"There's no need. It's my job."

Ah, *job*. There was that word again. For thirty-one years, he'd successfully managed to avoid any and all conversations related to employment. Now he was practically running his own human resources department. "And it's a job you do well," he said. "Do you mind if I ask how long you've been driving her around?"

"Five years or so."

He was suitably impressed. Being at Becca's beck and call for that long couldn't be an easy task. "Our family driver has been with us about half that. You'd like him. He fixed up a Triumph TR250 for me over the summer, though I didn't bring it with me. I don't care for driving in the city."

"There is a certain amount of skill to it," Liam agreed begrudgingly. Then, when Jake didn't make a move to continue the conversation, he asked, "Is there a point to all this? No offense, but there are things I could be doing."

"Things like sitting outside Becca's apartment, watching everyone coming and going?"

Liam's mouth lifted at the corner. It was more of a twitch than a smile, but Jake figured it counted. "It never hurts to have an extra eye on things—and she knows I'm out there, if it makes you feel any better."

"It does."

"Technically, it's half my job description," Liam said, loosening up even more. "There was an incident right before I got hired with some jerk trying to sneak past her doorman."

"Of course there was. Let me guess—he had a camera?"

"They're nothing but scavengers, every last one of them. They call her The Paycheck. Did you know that?"

"No." Jake looked down, curious. There were his hands, formed into fists again. "No, I didn't know."

"And I'm pretty sure they have a system of sharing—a kind of stalking schedule, if you will. They all want the night shift, but they've devised a way to take turns. I'll see them moving in rotation sometimes."

Jake forced himself to breathe in and out, concentrating on the motion of the tires over the pavement. *A stalking schedule. For a single woman living alone.*

Apparently, Liam felt the same way he did. "I wish there was more I could do to stop them, but they're careful not to break any laws. The best I can do is keep a regular watch and get her out of the way quickly. Unfortunately, she's not always, uh, eager to be extracted. She likes the attention."

Jake didn't bother contradicting him. Liking the attention and accepting it as a fact of life were two different things. "It's a wonder they don't try to pay you for information. Seeing as how you know more about the company she keeps than anyone."

"Oh, they try. But I won't take it." There was nothing about his demeanor to suggest otherwise. "I have a daughter her age."

Jake was surprised to find that they'd pulled up in front of her building again. He was even more surprised that Liam considered their interview at an end. He stuck his hand out and held it there, unwavering, until Jake slipped his palm carefully in.

"I can't say I was ecstatic to hear of your engagement to Ms. Clare, but I can see now that you have her best interests at heart."

Despite his reservations at hearing *anyone's* best interests might be placed in his safekeeping, Jake smiled. He'd come out here with the sole intent of reassuring himself that Liam could be trusted, but he couldn't help feeling that he'd been the one being tested.

He also couldn't help feeling that he'd passed.

"I THINK YOU should take me out tonight to celebrate our engagement."

Jake didn't, as Becca expected, balk at her suggestion. To be fair, he didn't exactly jump to his feet in excitement either. He was pretending to relax, idly flipping through a magazine, but she was pretty sure he was nursing his sore muscles. He hadn't moved from that spot in over four hours.

"And by *take me out*, you mean you'll choose the place and pick up the tab while I watch from the sidelines, yes?" he asked.

"Aww, poor baby." She ran her hand along the back of the couch, moving seamlessly from cool leather to the warmth of his neck before he could stop her. "Being a kept man is harder than you thought it would be, isn't it? Is that why you won't sleep with me? Is your manhood suffering from all this lazing about?"

He twisted his head to look up at her, his expression stern. "My manhood is working just fine. And I think I more than earned my keep fixing the living room wall you and your maid butchered yesterday."

She climbed onto the couch and nestled next to him, delighted when he lifted an arm to begrudgingly hold her close.

"And you did such good work. I love it." A red so bright it seared the eyeballs, extending all the way up to her twelve-foot ceiling. She should have painted over the boring, empty white years ago. She'd had wonderful dreams last night of swimming in red silk and gorging on candy apples. "I had no idea you were such a good painter."

"It wasn't difficult. I moved a brush up and down."

"But you were so careful with the tape and everything. I guess it was only to be expected, seeing as how you're a—"

"I swear to God, Becca, if you tell me I'm a good painter because I'm a Virgo, I'm going to Picasso the hell out of that wall the second your guard is down."

She giggled and snuggled closer. He sighed but allowed it, which was becoming his standard response to all her overtures at physical affection. She suspected he was trying to keep her at arm's length to avoid the possibility of her getting too attached, but nothing she said or did would convince him she didn't harbor any illusions about the true nature of their relationship.

What Jake couldn't seem to understand was that she didn't harbor any illusions about *anything*. Okay, so maybe she'd thought she'd be better at balancing on top of a ladder with a gallon of paint in her hands, but that was different. Jake had definitely overreacted when he'd yelled at her to get down and let him do it or risk being tied to the couch.

Because the real stuff? The things that mattered? She knew how it worked.

Friends died. People hurt. Horrible things happened while the world sat at home and looked eagerly on. No one would ever accuse her of being overly intellectual, but she knew better than to break her heart over a man like Jake Montgomery.

"I was going to say it's only to be expected, seeing as how you're a perfectionist," she teased. "But yours fits too."

His chuckle shook her, and he lifted a hand to run it negligently through her hair. She wasn't sure if he was even aware he was doing it, so she didn't move, barely breathed, letting herself bask in the quiet comfort of his touch.

It only lasted about two minutes.

"What did you have in mind for this evening?" he asked, dropping his hand. "I suppose we might as well get our first public appearance over with. That article

in the paper didn't leave much in the way of mystery—
though I *do* like that they've decided to call us Jabecca."

"You just like it because your name comes first. I prefer Beccake." Rather than get into an argument about
a name that sounded either like a *Star Wars* character
or a Japanese sex act, she plunged ahead with her plans
for the evening. "I was thinking we could hit Juno—you
know that place in the Meatpacking District? They have
an amazing DJ on the weekends."

Jake stiffened at Becca's words. He didn't have anything against the Meatpacking District, though he found
it a trifle overdone, but Juno was the one place in New
York Dana frequented no matter how much his ennui
plagued him. No way was he taking her there.

"How about that new place on Sixteenth? I've heard
it's good."

"No thanks."

That was it? *No thanks?* "What about Satan's Bou-
doir? I haven't had a chance to see it yet."

"You only want to go there because the waitresses
wear nothing but pasties and devil tails."

"You say that like it's a bad thing."

"I want to go to Juno." The way she said the words—
like a teenager about to slam the door—made him wary.
He lifted his arm out from where she was crushing it
against the couch and watched her for clues.

Not that he knew what he was looking for. Becca
didn't really have tells the way other women did—playing with her hair in flirtation, snapping her brows in
anger. She just *was.* And right now, she just *was* making him suspicious.

"Why Juno?"

"I told you. Good DJ."

"Why?"

"I don't know. Maybe he attended the School of Rock. Maybe he has music in his soul."

"*Why*, Becca?"

"Ugh. You're so annoying. It's not necessary for you to know everything all the time."

He waited. Becca scowled at him for all of ten seconds before throwing her hands up in surrender. "I'm hoping Dana Carstairs will be there, okay? My horoscope says it's a good time to confront the man with the power to hurt me, so I asked around and found out he sometimes goes there on Fridays."

Jake's head clunked with the lopsided rotations of his incredulity, too many of them all at once. "Slow down a second there, Tiger. You want to go out with the sole intention of attacking Dana again? Because your *horoscope* says so?"

"I'll have you know that Madame Pernaud is rarely wrong."

He held up a finger, more to calm himself than to quiet Becca—which was just as well, since she ignored him.

"And I'm sorry to speak badly of a friend of yours, but Dana is a horrible human being who deserves what's coming to him."

"I'm well aware of that."

Her eyes lit up. "So you'll help? I wasn't planning on forcing a confrontation like this, but I figure if Madame Pernaud thinks it's time I got to the root of the problem—"

"Whoa. One step at a time. I'm still dealing with the horoscope side of this conversation. Do you often base major life decisions on the musings of a stranger?"

"Not always." She pursed her lips, considering. "Maybe seven times out of ten? Stop looking at me like that, Jake. It's not that bad. The horoscopes don't tell me anything I don't already know. Madame Pernaud just forces me to put things into perspective."

She meant it. She actually fucking meant it. This woman, who'd almost killed herself and her cleaning woman trying to paint a wall in her apartment—who, minutes ago, had been curled up against him like a kitten purring in his lap—routinely put her fate in the hands of a few random words on a page. And she was *proud* of it.

"Oh, please," she said, that pride coming through loud and clear. "Like you have any room to judge. Your way of making decisions isn't any better."

"My way?" Jake wasn't aware he had a *way*…at least, not unless you counted his tendency to use goddamn common sense. "I'm afraid you'll have to explain what that is. I don't have the wisdom of a tabloid medium to enlighten me."

She clamored off the couch and stood, her back set against the newly vibrant red wall. He didn't much care for bright colors in general—especially on unmoving fixtures like apartments—but there was something about the combination of her appearance, small but resolute and dressed in a striped miniskirt layered with about twelve tank tops, and the powerful red that seemed to fit.

He recognized the fit at once. Becca wasn't a woman who stood out among the backdrop of everyday life and ordinary people, and she could easily get lost in the bustle of the real world. But place her in a harsh environment designed in every way to outstrip her, and she shone.

She absolutely fucking shone.

"What are you doing?" he asked, his voice gruff.

"I'm proving my point."

"By standing there staring at me?" He crossed his legs and rested his arm along the back of the couch, forcing himself to appear relaxed as he awaited her next move. "Did Madame Whatsit tell you to do that too?"

She didn't answer, opting instead to turn her back to him. There was no denying that her backside was a sight to behold—Max knew what he was doing when it came to muscle development—especially when her ass was encased in the tight, stretchy fabric of her practically nonexistent skirt. Without warning, she wrapped her arms around her midsection and pulled off the first tank top, flinging it over her head and allowing it to float to the floor. It was the way women removed clothes only when they wanted to entertain, to seduce, to make a grown man cry.

"Whatever you're doing, it's not going to work. Don't forget—I've seen you in various states of undress before. It's lovely but not life-changing."

She peeked over her shoulder at him, her smile coy. Christ, she did that well. Toyed with him, dared him to do more. He hoped she didn't plan to get all the way naked. Her body might not be able to change his life, but it was more than enough to ruin his day.

"Should I put on some music, do you think? It might make my triumph go down easier."

"No one will be going down in this room anytime in the near future."

She flashed him a bright smile. "That's what you think."

With another seductive sway of her hips, she lifted the next layer of tank top. She moved slower this time, taking a moment to flash the bare skin of her back, perfectly shaped, an instrument tuned to all of mankind.

"It's getting kind of cold," he said. "You might need a blanket."

"Oh, I'm not worried. It's about to get very hot in here."

She wasn't kidding. Not content with the removal of her top layers, she reached a hand up her inner thigh. She paused as she hit the hem of her skirt, lingering in a tiny space of time just long enough for Jake to draw a breath. It was good that he did, because he didn't breathe again for the entire ninety seconds it took her to draw a tiny pair of black panties down her legs. She stepped out of them one foot at a time, the lace snagging on one of her heels in a way that had to be fabricated.

It was exquisite. It was absolute torture.

"You're wasting your time," Jake said, though he couldn't be too sure about that any longer. Since he wasn't sure what her end goal was, she might very well be on the track to victory. Did she want to turn him hard and leave him straining for more? Goal accomplished, though that wasn't too difficult to achieve these days. Did she plan on forcing his hand, getting him to toss aside his tenuous scruples for a hard fuck against that bright red wall? Hmm. She might have him there too. "I've already told you. This is an engagement in name only."

"Just be quiet and watch. I'm almost done."

Almost done? Disappointment twitched in his cock, taking up residence alongside a rapidly growing amount of interest. He wasn't sure which feeling unsettled him more, so he decided to sit back and enjoy the show for as long as his conscience would allow it.

There was only one layer of tank top left covering Becca's upper half, and she spun to the front to give him a front-loading view of its removal—which wasn't a bad thing in theory, but it turned out she wasn't wearing a bra. Jake had been braced for another layer, a few pieces of fabric and well-crafted bits of metal to shield him from the full onslaught of her nipples.

But there they were, drawing tight before his eyes, lifting and beckoning in their voluminous perfection. Those weren't spectator nipples. They weren't sweet, daintily formed features awaiting a soft caress. They begged him to touch them, tug them, clasp them between his teeth and pull.

Dammit. Those nipples took him by surprise. He could handle himself just fine around her if it weren't for all the fucking surprises.

Becca had just hooked her thumbs on the top of her skirt waistband when Jake gave in. He was across the room in less than four seconds, had her breasts firmly in hand in half that. Her skin was impossibly soft under his touch, the warm weight of her body a perfect fit. He pulled her closer, his hand splayed on the small of her back as he dipped his head to take one of those surprise nipples into his mouth.

It was amazing and as far from a spectator sport as you could get, so much to fill his mouth and his senses all at once. He flicked his tongue lightly over the contracting flesh, loving the way her body reacted in an instant. She was pliable and yielding, offering as much as he wanted. And he wanted a lot. He wanted to continue suckling until he could feel the pull echoing in his groin, drop to his knees and worship at the idol of her body until they were both left panting.

But he didn't. He'd taken what he needed—a taste, nothing more—and wisely backed away.

His lips had left a mark, a tint of pink where he'd nibbled too hard, lost an iota of control. As this wasn't something that happened very often—especially where sex was concerned—he met her eyes to gauge her reaction and…blinked. Was she laughing at him? Was she seriously laughing at him right now?

"*Now* I'm done. Thank you for making my point." She reached for the nearest tank top and pulled it over her head. It was the shortest and loosest one, a sort of half-shirt she'd layered over the rest, and he could still see the lure of her nipples underneath the thin white fabric.

He took another wide step back. "Your point is that I'm capable of succumbing to temptation like any other man? This seems a rather cruel way to go about it. I'd think that was fairly obvious."

"My point is that you aren't the type of person who makes any decision at all until you're pushed to extremes. You don't act, Jake. You react."

He opened his mouth and closed it again, startled by her approach, which smacked of feminine judgment. Becca wasn't supposed to be disapproving—that was what he liked about her. She didn't push him to be different or better, she accepted that he made stupid bets with Monty and then did her best to help him win.

"I think you're forgetting one small thing," he said, trying not to let his resentment show. "If I were to perform a similar striptease right now, I bet everything I own that you'd react the same way. Two minutes in, and your mouth would be all over me."

"Well, yes. Obviously." When he didn't respond right away, she sighed and ran a hand through her hair. The lifting action caused her breasts to swell and her body to arch toward his—neither of which was helping his case right now. "But I've been trying to get you to have sex with me since you moved in. I'll have sex with you right now, in any position, in any location. All you have to do is say the word. We could even step outside and you can bend me over the rail of the fire escape, if that's what you want."

"Not amused."

"No. I can see that. But you have to admit that I'm right. The only reason you put your mouth on me just now—which, by the way, was *fantastic*—was because I forced your hand by waving my tits in your face. You want me. You've wanted me since that night in the club. But you won't act on it. You'll only react when I give you no other choice."

A coil of frustration tightened in his stomach, pulling down, growing dangerous with potential energy. "Or maybe I'm trying to be a gentleman and not take advantage of your situation—and you're making it really difficult. Did you ever consider that option?"

"You think that's it?" She pursed her lips. "Because I'm pretty sure you've never done anything in your life that wasn't a reaction to something else. You took up sailing because you won that yacht in a poker game. You go to nightclubs and parties because that's where your friends are. You were mad at your dad for marrying my sister three years ago, so you whisked me away for loud, messy sex in the next room."

She paused, as if waiting for him to contradict her. He wished he could. He didn't regret sleeping with Becca—to regret any of his sexual partners would be a discredit

to each and every one of them—but he did wish there
had been more to their encounter than that.

"Your dad and brother froze your accounts, so you
ran off to the big city to prove it didn't matter." Her voice
grew quieter. "And my mom threatened to have me committed, so you faked an engagement to save me."

He wouldn't regret that one either.

"And even now, you aren't saying anything. You do
that, you know. Listen. Watch. Wait. It's like the other
day at the Artista, when you sat and absorbed the play
just long enough to pinpoint what it was you didn't like
about it."

"They were bad actors."

"They were *rehearsing*. Of course they didn't have
it all down yet." She shook her head. "It's a hell of a lot
easier to critique than it is to create, to react instead of
act. And that's what you do. You let everyone else make
the first few clumsy mistakes so you can swoop in and
dazzle us with a checkmate."

"I don't do that."

"You do too. I'm not saying it's a bad thing—and I'm
not saying it's good either. What I *am* saying is that it
doesn't give you the right to judge me. You might think
it's silly that I make decisions based on what my horoscope says, but I think it's silly that you won't make any
decisions at all." She straightened her shoulders, clearly
proud of herself, and flashed him a wide smile. "So.
Dancing at Juno tonight. It's a yes?"

He'd been so busy processing Becca's striptease and
obsession with star rotations that he'd forgotten the driving force of this entire conversation. It all came rushing
back now—the questions, the concerns, the potential for

catastrophe. Not content with having the scandals come to her, she was actively seeking them out now.

"If I agree to this," he said slowly, "which, by the way, I'm not at all sure I want to do—will you finally tell me what it is Dana did to spur all this aggression?"

"Oh." She blinked and tilted her head. "Didn't you already know? It was Sara, of course."

"Hell—I didn't even think of that." Nothing triggered Becca quite like someone tarnishing her friend's reputation. Trust Dana to make a dick comment at the wrong time. "If you want my advice, don't listen to a word he says. He's even more of an idiot than Trish Callahan."

Becca looked at him as though *he* were the idiot, and he had the sinking feeling that despite all his watching and waiting, he'd missed something huge.

"I'm not mad because of something he said, Jake." She spoke gently, but there was a steely undertone to her words that made her appear larger than her five feet three inches. "I'm mad because Dana is the reason she killed herself."

TWELVE

JAKE SAT ENJOYING his third glass of scotch—neat, room temperature, top shelf, exactly the way he liked it— feeling far more relaxed than he had in a long time. It was a strange sensation, almost foreign in the way it fit, like the first time he'd slipped into a suit tailored to his measurements.

He shouldn't have been relaxed at all. He was living with a woman he didn't love, but who the world thought he intended to marry. He had no money and even fewer prospects for the future. And a man he was acquainted with had just been leveled with what amounted to a murder accusation.

Well, that last one wasn't so bad, actually. Finding out Dana had been dating Sara Yarrowgate in the months leading up to her death had been the least shocking revelation of the past few weeks.

From across the nightclub—which *wasn't* Juno, after much persuasion on his part—Becca lifted a finger and beckoned him to join her in the series of gyrations that were equal parts striptease and dancing. He had no idea how she did it, how she turned the dark parts of her life off and found the joy in what was left, but he was doing a damn fine job of emulating her. For right now, Becca was happy and thriving—not an unstable young woman thrust too often into the spotlight. For right now, Jake was an independent man of means—not a waste of space drinking expensive liquor on his billionaire fiancée's tab.

Becca beckoned again, the short, green spangled dress she'd worn for the night slithering over her body like snakeskin. Since the moment she'd put the dress on and crooked her arm through his, she'd been in constant motion, reinforcing the snake metaphor so firmly in his brain he'd never be able to look at a forked tongue the same way again.

As tempting as she was out there, Jake gave a slight shake of his head and held up his glass in a one-sided toast. He wouldn't *react* to the provocation of her grinding on some douchebag in a popped collar and designer jeans. He wouldn't give her the satisfaction. Tonight, his plan was to sit and enjoy a bottle of scotch. His choice. His decision. Maybe it didn't look like action from where she was standing, but she wasn't feeling the warm, numbing creep of the thirty-year-old alcohol in her veins.

And he didn't need a stupid horoscope to tell him how good it tasted.

Unfortunately, even he had to admit a twinge of regret for not checking the *National Beat* about ten minutes later. A deep, rumbling voice interrupted his quiet contemplation of Becca's writhing form, filling him with a bone-deep resignation. It would have been nice to see this one coming.

"I see your fiancée is about to start fornicating on the dance floor."

The shadow his brother Monty cast as he approached was an impressive one—and Jake meant that in every possible sense of the word. He impressed by size. He impressed by stature. He impressed by the severe, funereal lines of his poorly cut suit jacket and even more severe, funereal face.

Monty had definitely missed his calling. He shouldn't be overseeing the family's charitable foundation, bringing joy and light to the world. He should be burying people. Burning them to ashes and burying them.

"I see you're still using words like *fornicating* in public." Jake motioned at the chair next to him, hoping his brother would take the hint and sit down. He didn't. "And for chrissakes, stop hulking there and turning your death stare on everyone. These people are here to have a good time, not buy coffins."

Monty paused and turned that same death stare Jake's way for an uncomfortably long twenty seconds before finally taking the proffered seat. Jake cast a look over his brother's shoulder toward the dance floor, hoping to hint Becca far, far away from the conversation that was about to take place, but she was oblivious to anything but the music. As there weren't any tables around for her to climb onto and subsequently fall off of, he left her to it.

"So it's true."

Jake twirled the glass in his hand, watching as the tawny liquid rose up and around, leaving viscous ripples along the edge. "Did you really ascend all the way from the depths of Hades to ascertain my relationship status? You could have saved yourself the trouble and picked up a phone."

Monty didn't smile. Monty never smiled unless he could possibly help it. Although only three years separated Jake and his brother, and more than one person noted the physical similarities between the two of them—the same sweep of auburn hair, same wide shoulders, same tall form—no one had ever gotten the two of them confused. Jake was thinner, for one. For another, the sight of Monty's lips curved in a smile was so rare most people assumed it was a myth, like unicorns riding the kraken on their way to Atlantis.

"We'll need to put an announcement in the *Times*."

"Go ahead," Jake said, though his heart picked up at the thought. There were several things in this world that were reversible. Vests. The destruction of the rainforest. Vasectomies. In his experience, a formal engagement announcement in the *Times* wasn't included on that list. "I'm sure Grandmama Clare would be happy to help get that written. Although I wonder...do you think I should start calling her Mother Clare now? I'm not sure what the formal etiquette is. Maybe I could call her both. My mother-grandmother. Double Mee-Maw. That's not creepy, is it?"

"I'm glad this is so amusing for you."

"It's an engagement, not the End of Times. I'm supposed to be happy." He fell into a mocking smile. "Or are you just upset I won the bet? That's it, isn't it? You always were a sore loser."

"I don't count it a win yet. Last I checked, it wasn't January first."

"Oh, come on. You said I couldn't find a way to be successful without your help or some kind of job holding me up. I don't know if you've noticed, but I've got a pretty cushy address right now. And these shoes are new." He extended a foot and admired the glossy black sheen on his Balenciagas. The shoes weren't even remotely new, but Monty didn't have to know that. "Why don't I buy you a drink?"

He made a motion to the bartender, who came prepared with the bottle of Lagavulin that was bearing him company this evening. "My brother here would like to join me in my celebration. What do you think, Monty? Single? Double?"

"What are we celebrating?" the bartender asked, holding the bottle poised to pour. "If it's something big, I'd go with the double. Or I could grab a bottle of the Perrier-Jouet we just got in."

"Water's fine, thanks. I'm not staying long." As soon as the bartender processed the ridiculous order and sauntered away to more promising customers, Monty turned to Jake with a frown. "Those are some costly brands, Jake. Is this who you are now? Is this how far you'll go to avoid real life? I didn't think even you could sink so low as to take advantage of a sweet kid like Becca."

Jake flicked an imaginary piece of dirt from his cuff. "I'm not taking advantage of her. We're in love."

Monty looked like he wanted to say something scathing, but he refrained. "And are you absolutely sure this is the best place for you to be taking her? I spotted about twenty cameras on my way in. I suppose it would be asking too much for you to pick a quiet, out-of-the-way club for once."

Jake's jaw tightened. He *had* picked a quiet, out-of-the-way club. He'd even had Liam drop them off a few blocks down the street. The paparazzi must have gotten wind of their arrival here anyway.

"Is there a reason you came all this way? Not that your input into my life isn't appreciated, but I know how difficult it is for you to tear yourself away from Dad's teat for any length of time. I wouldn't want to keep you."

As it always did, his sarcasm flew right over Monty's head, lodging itself in the wall never to be seen again. "Yes, I am here for a reason. Dad wants you to come home."

"Home?" The word felt dry and starchy on his tongue.

"Yes. Preferably with your betrothed in tow." Monty looked up, his frost melting a touch as Becca wound her way through the tables. A gentlemanly undertaker, he pushed back from the table and stood as she approached. "Hello, Rebecca. You're looking well, as usual."

Despite the chilly reception Jake had received, Monty looked almost pleased as he dropped a kiss on Becca's cheek.

"Thank you, Monty. It's great to see you again."

He pulled out a chair for her, but she chose to sidle up closer to Jake's side and wrap her arms around his neck instead, a show of affianced solidarity he couldn't help but appreciate. She smelled of exertion and a deep, amber perfume he found intoxicating. And she was warm from the dancing, her skin flushed with color he could make out even under the low, intermittent lights in the club.

"What brings you to New York?" Becca asked brightly. "Business or pleasure?"

"Neither." Monty frowned. "Or maybe both. I'm only here to deliver a message."

"Is the message written in lemon juice and/or signed in blood?"

"Um…no? It's verbal."

"Business then." She nodded and made a motion to rise. "Should I give you two some alone time?"

"Oh, no—it's nothing like that. I wanted to offer my congratulations."

"And you came all this way? That's sweet." Becca spoke lightly, but that didn't mean she wasn't aware of the undercurrent of tension currently enveloping the two brothers. *Everyone* within a ten foot radius was aware of the undercurrent of tension. Putting the Montgomery brothers in the same room was like trying to force two planets into each other's rotation. "But you could have just called, you know."

"That's exactly what *I* told him," Jake grumbled.

Becca kept her arms around Jake's neck and leaned to press her lips against his, woodsy with the scent of scotch. He stiffened at first, as if a public display of affection in front of his brother would somehow give his foe the advantage, but she had to do *something* to ease the tension. They were seriously killing the vibe in here.

"I hope you've come as an ambassador of goodwill," she said to Monty. "Did I hear you say something about home?"

"Yes, that's right. Dad was hoping the two of you would be willing to come to the Manor to spend a few weeks with family. Give news of your engagement a chance to settle in."

Becca dropped her arms from around Jake's neck and frowned. "To settle in?" She didn't like the sound of that. It implied an unnatural fit, an element of wrong-doing—and she refused to feel bad about what she and Jake were doing. Her own mother would rather lock her up than deal with her problems, and Jake was constantly being goaded to extreme lengths by a family that didn't understand him in the slightest. Banding together was the best thing for them both.

"Does that mean he doesn't approve?" she asked.

"What? No. No, no, no. Don't misunderstand." Monty leaned over the table and took her hand, giving it a squeeze. He noticed the lack of a ring on the fourth finger of her left hand and raised a questioning brow at Jake. "I see you spared no expense."

Jake countered his brother's look of incredulity with a carefully arched brow of his own. That was how bad the rivalry between them was—they were down to dueling eyebrows. "Why am I not surprised that the first thing you notice is attached to dollar signs?" he asked. "Do you want to head outside and discuss her dowry before we go any further?"

"I didn't say that. You're always putting words in my mouth."

"You should be grateful. Most people prefer talking to me."

Poor Monty flushed red at Jake's words—mostly because it was true. Monty was a nice guy once you got to know him, but he tread so heavily it was hard to feel comfortable around him. He was a Capricorn, of course.

"I don't think it's extraordinary to wonder why she isn't wearing a ring," Monty grumbled. "Forget I asked."

"It's too late now. And it just so happens there's a perfectly logical explanation for it."

What is he doing? Becca scrambled to come up with a realistic lie as to why she wasn't wearing an engagement ring—Jake grossly misjudged the size, she'd hated the cut and refused to wear it, it didn't go with this outfit—and had just decided on the last one when Jake spoke up.

"I'm planning to give her the family ring."

Monty sat up with a start. "You can't mean the Montgomery sapphire?"

"Do you know of any other family ring?" Jake asked. "Unless there's a treasure trove you and Dad have been keeping from the rest of us, that's the exact one I mean."

"But…" Monty's forehead crinkled as he looked

back and forth between Jake and Becca. "It's not… You can't…"

"But…you wanted it for yourself? It's not…my birthright as much as yours? You can't…imagine why I might be interested in giving my future bride the same ring Mom wore?" Jake's voice grew harder with each question, and Becca didn't doubt for a second that he was reacting instead of acting again. Monty had pushed him into a corner, so of course Jake felt compelled to push right back. She would never understand why Jake's family insisted on mishandling him so.

"Now you're deliberately misconstruing my words."

"Let's face it, Monty," Jake said. "The chances of any woman sacrificing her last name to stare at your sullen face across the breakfast table every morning are slim. I figure one of us should get some use out of it."

"You'll have to talk to Dad."

"I'd be delighted," Jake said through his teeth, clearly anything but.

"I don't need anything fancy—" Becca began, but Jake's hand fell to her leg in a vise-like grip, and she clamped her mouth shut. *Okay, then.* She could take a hint, especially when it was cutting off her femoral artery. He wanted her to have the ring. "But I do love things that sparkle. It *is* sparkly, isn't it, Snickerdoodle?"

Jake's hand relaxed, and blood flow returned to her leg. "Yes, Pussy-Cat. It's very sparkly."

She beamed. Even though accepting a ring was not part of the plan, she *would* like to catch a glimpse of the infamous Montgomery sapphire. At eighteen karats and set with a dozen diamonds of impressive size, the ring was supposed to be amazing. They'd all wondered, when Serena had agreed to marry Jake's dad, if she'd be offered the same piece of jewelry that had graced her predecessor's hand, but Mr. Montgomery was much too wise a man to offer her sister a recycled declaration of his affection. The emerald-cut diamond Serena wore had been made specifically for her—a one-of-a-kind piece not even the most exacting collector could fault.

"So it's settled, then? I'll send Ryan out to pick you up first thing tomorrow morning."

"I don't have to come just because Dad whistles," Jake said. "And I'm not going to hide my fiancée away in Connecticut like I'm ashamed of her. We're doing just fine here in town."

"You can save the theatrics for another time, Jake. Given Rebecca's recent, ah, institutionalization—" Monty looked an apology at her, "—and the way the press seems to be slamming you both, Dad thinks it might be best if we show that this engagement has the full family support. We're going to do the changing of the seasons, traditional hayrides, the whole show. With plenty of photo opportunities and parties, of course."

Becca perked. "Parties?"

Monty's eyes crinkled in what might, in a more demonstrative man, be termed a smile. "I'm sorry if I came across as disapproving before. The truth is, Dad couldn't be more delighted to welcome you to the family, and he wants to make sure we do it properly. Serena too."

Jake waited to see what Becca's reaction was before he responded. More watching and waiting, yes—but this time with the best of intentions. A long, semi-enforced stay at Montgomery Manor was exactly what he'd been escaping from in the first place. All that fresh, countryside air and wholesome food cooked at the hands of Serena's grain-obsessed personal chef. The constant reminder that everyone else was busy working the hive while he alone balked at the taste of honey.

But it would get Becca out of the city—and that idea appealed to him so strongly it was almost a physical force. Out in Ransom Creek, there would be no photographers chasing her on her morning run. There would be no opportunities for the Trish Callahans of the world to pop up with snide remarks and judgy faces. There was little chance that her mom's threats of rehab would reach that far.

And of course, a confrontation with Dana would cease to be an issue. Now that he'd committed himself to the task, Jake was willing to do almost anything to help Becca find closure over Sara's death—but he was pretty sure a few more scratches down that man's face weren't the way to accomplish it. Until Becca was able to find a more appropriate solution, he was willing to look on this family intervention as a positive thing.

It could be good for her. Hell, it might even be good for him.

Becca turned an enquiring look his way, her lower lip captured in her teeth as if she was hesitant to speak up. "I *would* love a chance to spend some time with my niece and nephew. And I haven't seen Serena since before…you know. The Ranch."

That settled it. Jake nodded once. "Okay, Monty. You can tell Dad we're in."

"That's it?" Monty's brows rose in suspicion, and he examined Becca as if she held some kind of mystical power. "You'll actually come?"

Yes, brother dear, Jake wanted to say, *sometimes I do think about people other than myself.* It was rare—he'd admit that much—but not altogether unheard of.

"No arguments? No sarcasm? You'll pack your bags and be ready when the chauffeur comes to get you at eight?"

"Well, not at *eight*," Jake said. "Now you're just being absurd."

"Does ten suit you better?"

"We could probably use a few days to settle things here in town first. How about you let Ryan decide when he can spare the time to make a drive to New York and have him call me?"

As he'd hoped, his response flustered Monty to the point of speechlessness. Monty liked to pretend that of all the family, he was the liberal-minded one, the one who cared most about the everyday man. Because he oversaw the family foundation and charitable interests, he somehow felt exempt from having to make an effort with people.

Not that Jake went out of his way to make an effort with people. But at least he didn't have any delusions about his motivations.

"I'll pass your message along," Monty said tightly.

"I'd appreciate it, thanks." Jake kicked back the rest of his drink and stood, lifting Becca with him. He made sure to grab her hand as he set her back on her feet, giving her a delicate twirl. "Now. If you'll excuse me, I believe I owe my fiancée a dance."

As Jake expected, Monty and his cloud of gloom were out the door before he and Becca hit the dance floor. To his brother, dancing was nothing but a shameless display of excess. Energy was expended on something that wasn't work. Body parts touched in unseemly ways.

And—horror of all horrors—people actually enjoyed themselves.

In fact, that was exactly what Jake intended to do. If he was going to spend the next few weeks of his life eating family dinners and basking in the glories of nature, he was going to indulge in a little excess first.

"I've been trying to get you out here all night, Muffin Cakes," Becca cooed. His hands dropped to the curve of her hips, and he let her movements guide his own. It was an easy thing to do, so natural was the sway of her body. "I wish you'd told me earlier that all it would take is your brother's disapproval. I spent an hour attempting to make you jealous with some guy who says he snuck in with the delivery truck. He smelled like beets."

"Good try, Kitten Claws, but you're forgetting one thing."

"Oh, yeah? What's that?"

"In order to make me jealous, our engagement would have to be real."

It was difficult to speak with the noise level, so he had to bring his lips close to her ear to be heard. From there, it was a short step to wrapping one of his hands around her waist, the other holding the back of her neck so that she had no choice but to move against him, her pelvis rocking against his. Each step closer lowered his inhibitions and made him question why, exactly, he was punishing himself so much by keeping her at a distance.

Because I'm taking care of her. Because I'm leading her village. Because it's the right thing to do.

She wasn't helping him stick to his resolve any. Arching to give him better access to her neck, she never once stopped the rhythmic movements of her body to the music. She tasted of sweat and skin, all the artifice of attraction wiped away and leaving nothing but the essence behind. He bit softly at her pulse, unable to stop himself.

"You're right. I guess I'm technically a free woman, aren't I?" She spun around so that her backside was pressed against his groin, his face still buried in her neck. The soft, sensual movements of her ass against him only made him bite harder.

She purred in response. Actually fucking purred.

"Far too free, if you ask me," he muttered.

"Does that mean I get to sleep with the pool boy once we get to your dad's house?"

Arms lifted above her head, encouraging Jake to wrap his own around her midriff. He did, stopping carefully below the swell of her breasts. Not that it made any difference to his rapidly stiffening cock. Her body was so tightly encased in the snakeskin dress she couldn't so much as twitch without making him aware of every dip and swell.

"I've always wanted to seduce the pool boy," she continued, oblivious. Or possibly not the least bit oblivious at all. "It's on my list of clichés to live up to. Bad homemade porn with a politician, check. Stint in rehab, check. Twat shots for the cameras, check. All I need to do is bang the pool boy, get caught shoplifting, and, when I'm old enough, become a cougar with killer biceps. I'm halfway there."

"I hate to disappoint you, but my dad doesn't have a pool boy." Jake turned her back around, bringing the ass grinding to a halt. There was only so much of that a man could take in public—and he knew for a fact the bathrooms here weren't ideal for sex. They were so cavernous that even the sound of a condom opening reverberated off the walls with an echo.

"Pool girl?"

"Now you're just being cruel."

She laughed, a soft rush of breath that warmed him from the inside out. "Maybe a little. But it sounds as if your dad intends to keep us for a while—a month, at least. That's a lot of cold fall nights for me to get through alone. And somehow, I don't think Monty would be open to a fling with his little brother's fiancée."

"Don't you fucking dare, Tiger. If you need sex that badly, I'm sure we can figure something out."

She came in for a kiss, twining her arms around his neck and pulling his mouth to hers. Hot and ready, her lips parted to make way for him, and he took full advantage. She made it all too easy—the kissing, the dancing, the near-constant promise of sex. And she did it all with such an honest joie de vivre that he hardly knew how to handle himself. Jake wasn't used to honest *anything*, let alone this blithe approach to affection.

She pulled away, her mouth lifting in a tempting half-smile. "Well, if that's the case, can we start right now?"

Jake could have howled. In frustration. In desire. In rage at finding himself trapped between a rock and a very hard, very unsated place. With all the decency of a man who was fully erect and didn't have any immediate means of alleviating that problem, he gave in and made himself a promise. Until the day their fake engagement ended, all of Becca's needs were his problem.

And his pleasure. They were also his pleasure.

"Right now?" he echoed, his voice low. There was no need to be quiet—the fifty or so half-orgasmic couples on the dance floor provided all the privacy they needed—but his throat was tight, his blood hot. "You may want to be careful what you wish for."

"You. I wish for you."

Consider it done. He slipped a hand between their bodies, not stopping until he reached the hem of her dress. Tight and elastic, the fabric had ridden up as they danced, making it easy to nudge his fingers past fabric to hit the hot, sleek thigh beneath. He enjoyed the silken feel of her skin moving under his fingertips, the way she grew hotter and sleeker with each passing moment.

"Jake." His name came out in a whoosh of air as he nuzzled the back of his fingers against the material of her panties. He felt a surge of laughter rise that tonight, of all nights, she'd actually bothered with undergarments, but as he continued his upward exploration, rubbing the damp, indented fold of her pussy through the fabric, his amusement fled.

So did hers. Her arms wrapped tighter around his neck, making it impossible for anything to wedge its way between them. They were manacled, intertwined, bound so tightly that the movement of his forefinger under the lip of her underwear reverberated in his own cock.

"I should have guessed you'd be a good dancer," she said, gyrating against his hand. "Tall, elegant men always have the best moves. You just have to give a confident twitch, and woman swoon."

"You mean like this?" He gave his finger a *very* confident twitch as she parted her thighs. Her movement was subtle, offering just enough space to let him slide his finger all the way along the unmistakably swollen, slick line of her cunt, but it was enough. He was welcomed in, drawn deeper, and as she grabbed his lower lip in her teeth and tugged her appreciation, he rewarded her with a sharp flick of his nail on her clit.

The noise she emitted was in no way appropriate for

a public venue, but the music and dance floor swallowed them both. There was an anonymity about the raw, almost base way she let him take possession of her body right there. They could be anyone and everyone. They could be no one at all.

"That works," she gasped. "Though you should probably do it again so I can decide for sure."

He laughed against her throat and complied. It would be incredibly easy to spend hours like this—his hand up her skirt, exploring the soft, inviting folds of her body—only seconds and a scream away from making this a front-row spectacle. Something about the idea that they could be caught, that someone paying attention over by the bar might be watching closely and straining as hard as he was for the main event, made Jake's blood boil and his cock pound. A man didn't let as many sex tapes slip through his fingers as he had without a strong river of exhibitionism running through him. And he suspected that Becca, with her own media trail of sexual antics, wasn't immune to the current.

It could always be like this, he realized. Sex on the edge, performances half for the crowds, all for themselves.

Her breath came shorter and faster, her movements almost jerky as he circled her clit over and over again. She tried to keep her mewling to a minimum, but as her chest arched against his and her thighs tensed, he could tell she was close. He waited until the music moved into a heavily thumping refrain before pressing his thumb firmly against her body.

The clenching apex of her orgasm rocked his hand, and he stayed in place for a moment, enjoying her pleasure as it ebbed away against his touch. With a tiny tug to ensure that her underwear slid back into place, he withdrew his hand from between her legs.

"Better?" he asked, his voice low. Heedless of the scent and moisture of her that lingered on his hand, he cupped the back of her neck, his fingers tangled in her hair. Let the world smell her sex. Let them know that this vivid, reckless, damaged young woman was being taken care of for a change.

"Much better." She ran her own hand slowly between them, her fingers walking a trail down to his groin. "The question is, how are you feeling right about now?"

"Not so fast." He pulled away before she got much past his belt. With a shake of his head, he released a soft tsking sound. "I told you—I choose when and where and how."

She stuck her lower lip out in an attractive and patently false moue that had him gripping her neck tighter and pressing her forehead against his. "And no more Monty jokes, okay? If you need something, all you have to do is ask. For the duration of our time together, I'll be the one to take care of you."

"You mean sexually?"

He paused. That was what he meant when he'd spoken the words out loud, but it was impossible to ignore the subtext pulsating between them. He'd spent the majority of adulthood shirking responsibility, doing everything he could to convince people not to rely on him for anything. And he'd been really good at it. His whole life, he'd managed to avoid situations that required staying power. He could walk away, clear of conscience and unattached, from every relationship and every residence he'd ever had.

Until now.

"No, Tiger." He tipped her head up and forced her gaze to meet his. "I mean for everything. You come to me first, understand?"

He thought for a moment that she might get angry at him or taunt him for his overbearing Virgo ways. But all she did was look at him curiously and nod once, accepting his decree with "You're kind of a tyrant when you're engaged, you know that? I pity the woman who does end up marrying you."

She picked up the pace of her dancing and twirled him around, jostling at least half a dozen dancers and causing one man to threaten to punch Jake if they did it again. As the man was a good foot taller and several feet wider than him, it seemed wise to concede him the floor.

"Believe me, Becca," he said, pushing her toward a safer, less-likely-to-murder-him circle of dancers, "the feeling is entirely mutual."

THIRTEEN

"You're looking lovely this morning." Jake nodded as Livvie stepped through Becca's front door, oversized sunglasses covering her eyes and a recognizable slump to her shoulders. It was the slump of defeat, of capitulation, of the impending doom of exercise. "Lulu—you as well. So glad you could make it today."

"Why is he acting like the host of a cocktail party?" Livvie groaned, directing her conversation over his head to where Becca bounced in the background. She'd been up an hour ago, giddy at the prospect of dragging out more unwilling victims on her training session. "And why is he talking so loud?"

"He's gloating." Becca embraced Lulu in a fierce hug, taking a moment to whisper something in the taller woman's ear. He had no idea what she said, but it must have been exactly what Lulu needed, because she lost some of her wide-eyed stare and fell into a smile. "Since you guys agreed to come out with Max and me, he's off the hook for today. From the way he's acting, you'd think I offered him a presidential pardon."

Oh, he wasn't just gloating. He was close to breaking out in song. "Anything you ladies need, you just ask." He took Livvie's jacket and waited patiently while Lulu slipped out of the knee-length wool coat that looked as though it had been recently extracted from her grandmother's trunk. "Coffee, aspirin, Gatorade, a blood transfusion… I'm at your disposal. As long as you re-member never to look him directly in the eyes, you should be fine. And if you need a quick getaway, find a mirror. If you say Mean Max three times, you'll turn him into the Candyman and have a much better chance of getting out alive."

"He's *kidding.* Don't listen to a word he says. Max promised to take it easy on you since it's your first time. He's really quite gentle."

To punctuate her words, Becca reached over and pinched him, a laugh on her lips. Jake felt more excite-ment at seeing that laugh this early in the morning than he ever thought possible. Last night marked the first time she'd slept an entire eight hours without thrashing or waking up halfway through, and it showed. She was radiant. He wasn't sure if was his presence in the bed or the dancing last night or the fingerbang that had done it, but he couldn't remember the last time he'd felt this proud of himself.

I did that. I took some of the shadows out of her eyes.

"Always know your escape route, that's all I'm say-ing." Jake turned to hang the coats in the foyer closet, now neatly arranged and accessible without climbing on top of a pile of boxes first. "And show no fear."

He intended to make himself scarce long before the personal trainer arrived, but Livvie stopped him as he turned to make a discreet exit. The tall model had slipped the sunglasses onto the top of her head to show-case a pair of dark circles around her eyes.

"Did you decide you wanted that coffee after all?" Jake asked politely. By his count, he had about five min-utes of chitchat time or he risked being dragged along.

"This is your fault, you know."

"Probably." He watched out of the corner of his eye as Becca led Lulu to the kitchen, presumably to pump her with fluids and provide a pep talk ahead of time. "But I won't apologize. I've taken my turn twice this week already. I'm not going to be any good to Becca if I can't walk."

"I could have gone the rest of my life, happy and carefree, without ever breaking a sweat."

"It's a good day to set new goals."

"I could have continued turning her down for as long as necessary."

"I doubt that. She's very persuasive."

Livvie glared at him with her dark circles and the wrath of a woman who loved mornings about as much as he did. "But no. You had to ruin it. You had to swoop in here with your chivalry and your tight jogging shirt and your goddamned light shining all over Becca, and now I'll never get my life back. How can I tell her I won't come join her stupid workout when I can see how happy it makes her to have company? I hate you, Jake Montgomery. I hate you so much I'm tempted to tell Becca about that time you hit on me and my sister at the same time."

Jake laughed. "You're part of the village too, huh? I should have known."

Her heavy brows came together in perplexity. "What village? What are you talking about?"

"I'll save you a seat at the next town hall," he promised. He'd always liked Livvie—she was one of those women who took no shit from anyone but still somehow managed to make friends wherever she went—and he liked her even more now. It seemed Becca hadn't been quite as alone as he'd initially feared. "Tell Max I said hello, won't you?"

Without bothering to explain further, he made his escape out the front door. He was sure he could find a coffee shop or a park bench that would provide much more comfort than whatever Max had planned. Besides—he kind of liked the idea of being out this early, of the day stretching ahead of him, holding nothing but promise. He couldn't remember the last time he'd opened his eyes and actually felt excited at the prospect of an open calendar.

"OH, DID JAKE LEAVE?" Becca emerged from the kitchen, glad to see Livvie was still here. She was half afraid her friend would escape the second she turned her back. In the end, she'd only promised to come when Becca said she feared Lulu wouldn't want to be alone with her— and Lulu needed this. She might not know it yet, but she did. "The coward. I never knew men were such wimps until I lived with one for a while."

"Or maybe this particular man feels grueling morning workouts aren't part of what he signed on for," Livvie said archly. "It's a bit above and beyond the call of duty, don't you think?"

"I don't think." Becca held a finger to her lips. "And neither do you. I'd rather Lulu didn't know this is all pretend. For the duration of this morning, we have to act as though Jake is shamefully neglecting his betrothed."

"Oh, really? And why is that?" Her tone was more teasing than inquisitive. "It's the perquisites, isn't it?"

Becca felt herself flushing. It wasn't the perquisites— at least not *just* that. "No. I'm trying to convince her that I'm sane and nice and not at all likely to explode again. I don't think disclosing my fake relationship is going to help any."

"No one is deluded enough to think you're sane, darling."

She didn't have a chance to say more, as they were interrupted by the sound of Max letting himself in the front door. Dressed in what looked like military fatigues this morning, he had an almost reverent look on his face at the idea of not just one, but three women to torture all at once.

She had to laugh at the sight of him, so ebullient as to appear almost kind. It was difficult to tell whether it was she or Max who was more excited at the prospect of expanding their morning routine. It would be amazing to make this a thing, to take women like Lulu and Livvie and herself and provide an outlet, a chance to bond, a way to put all the crap in their lives into perspective.

Men were temporary. Rehab was too invasive. Even revenge only held appeal for so long. Already she was finding it easier to feel more relief than disappointment at not seeking out Dana to force a resolution—especially since that resolution probably didn't exist in the first place. It had been far more therapeutic to go out dancing with Jake, to accept Monty's gesture of hospitality, to be with people she knew cared about her.

Lulu emerged from the kitchen, her hands tucked inside the long sleeves of her shirt, a hesitant smile on her face. "Are we ready to go?" she asked, seeing Max standing there. "I'm excited to see if this magic workout of Becca's is everything she says."

"Oh poor, sweet Lulu." Livvie shook her head and shoved the sunglasses back over her eyes. "You have no idea what you agreed to. The only magic you're going to see today is how quickly the ambulances will come when you black out from overexertion."

"Don't you dare listen to her," Becca said, taking Lulu's arm and looping it through her own. "Ambulances take forever to get anywhere in New York. The magic is in how Max will manage to pull back just when you start to see God."

"Does your dad's chauffeur make it a habit to pick people up in sports cars?" Becca watched as the sky-blue convertible zipped their direction. Defying the laws of physics and all of New York parking, the driver managed to squeeze into a parallel slot the size of a bicycle with no more than a few turns of the wheel.

Although impressed with the maneuver, she cast a doubtful look at the pile of luggage at her side. There was no way all those suitcases were fitting on the back of the car—especially since it looked as if that was where she'd have to sit. Maybe it hadn't been such a good idea to give Liam some much-needed time off after all.

"He does when he's vying for the role of chauffeur of the year," Jake said, sharing none of her qualms. He rushed forward with what had to be the biggest grin she'd ever seen on his face, almost boyish in his excitement.

Huh. Jake, boyish. Over a car, of all conventional things.

"I can't believe you brought Penelope." Jake ran his hand over the hood of the two-seater, his touch equal parts reverence and glee. Becca remembered a similarly erotic movement of that hand against her body and suppressed a twinge of disappointment. He might handle cars and women with the same care, but he had definitely never looked that excited to see her. "What kind of time did you make getting here? Two and a half? Two forty-five?"

"Two fifteen." The driver, a stocky, blond-haired man who looked as though he spent most of his time under cars rather than inside them, tossed Jake his keys. "Though I wouldn't recommend driving her that hard on the way back. I saw a few patrols setting up outside Hartford—I'm not sure you want to risk a ticket."

He noticed Becca standing there and straightened. "This must be your fiancée."

"What?" Jake whirled, as if just remembering he had a fiancée—let alone one standing on the sidewalk behind him. "Oh. Right. Becca."

His breeding finally kicked in, and he made the introductions. "Becca, this is my dad's driver, Ryan Lucas. Ryan, Becca Clare. She's Serena's youngest sister."

Ryan's eyes crinkled warmly at the edges as he strode forward, his hand outstretched. "I think I've seen you around a few times, but we were never formally introduced. I had no idea you and Jake…"

He trailed off when Jake shook his head at him.

"You should tell him the story of how we got together." Becca wound an arm around Jake's waist and looked up at him expectantly, waiting to hear what he came up with. They were going to need to figure out some kind of story. The family driver wasn't going to be the only one wondering at the suddenness of their relationship. "I'm sure he'd love to hear it, Lambkins."

Ryan choked on a laugh, which soon gave way to a cough before turning back into laughter.

"Are you done?" Jake asked when it was clear the chauffeur had no intention of hiding his amusement.

"Based on the amount of coffee my fiancée has consumed this morning, we've got a lengthy drive and several pit stops ahead of us."

"I'm sorry, Jake. I just never saw you as a Lambkins before. I always took you as more of a Schmoopy."

"She's trying out different nicknames, hoping to find one that fits."

"I see."

Jake raised a finger and pointed. "Don't judge me, Car Man. I put up with the moony eyes you threw at my cousin for months, and you don't hear me complaining."

"I won't say another word." Ryan held up his hands and backed away, laughing. "And you owe me one, anyway. One of your dad's town cars is uptown getting re-upholstered, so I juggled things around a little. I'll kill some time in the city and drive it back later this afternoon. I thought you and Penelope might like to spend some quality time together. Ehrm…with your future wife, of course." He swept a mock bow and tugged at an invisible hat on his head as he turned to walk away. "It's lovely to meet you, future wife. I'm sure I'll see more of you back at the Manor."

"Cocky bastard," Jake muttered, but Becca could tell he wasn't the least bit angry. "He isn't even going to help us with these bags. Where is all this supposed to fit?"

"I don't take up much space," Becca promised.

"No, but all your crap does."

"It's not crap. I only packed the essentials."

"Becca, you tried to pack your skis."

She giggled. She'd been using a ski as leverage to shove everything in when Jake walked into the room. He'd taken one look at her suitcases, all of them open and overflowing, and ordered her out of the bedroom. And for the next twenty minutes, he'd forbidden her entry while he painstakingly folded all of her clothes for her—even her bras. She didn't even know you *could* fold bras.

"Well, I wasn't sure how long we were planning on staying away," she said. "And my horoscope today said I need to prepare myself for a major life change. I wanted to be thorough."

"I thought your horoscope told you just a few days ago that you were supposed to hunt down Dana."

She frowned. She'd *thought* that was what it said, but she was beginning to wonder if Dana had been who Madame Pernaud meant. Becca hated the guy, yes. Wanted him to pay for being such a devastating dickhead, of course. But he didn't have the power to hurt her.

Men like Dana made it a lifelong career to prey on the weak, saw a girl like Sara—depressed, struggling, searching for validation in a world prone to judgment—and pounced. In his eyes, Sara had been nothing more than easy sex, an ego-boost, a conquest that was no real conquest at all. And when he got tired of the easy sex a few months later, he left, taking the last of Sara's emotional self-worth with him.

Maybe he hadn't known how much Sara was hurting that night. Maybe he'd thought dumping her in that hotel room was a kindness, ensuring she had bellboys and room service and a concierge desk to turn to for help. But he wasn't the one who got the phone call at three in the morning. The too-late phone call of slurred regrets and a promise to do better next time, as if next time was just a good night's sleep away.

Instead of the usual overwhelming urge to lash out that hit her at the memory, Becca looked at Jake and allowed herself to fall into a smile. Right here, right now, for as far as she could see in the future, there was no way for Dana to hurt her. He'd already taken away one of the best parts of her, and that gave her a kind of freedom and power over him she hadn't recognized before.

"You know what the great thing about life is?" Becca didn't wait for Jake to answer, since he was probably going to say scotch or women who packed everything in one suitcase. "Every day is a clean slate. I slept like a baby last night. Lulu and Livvie are finally speaking to me again after Max tried to kill them. The sun is shining. You have the keys to an adorable itsy-bitsy sports car. I think Sara would want me to enjoy it."

Becca had always hated that expression—it sounded too much like a personal justification for having fun while the tendrils of mourning still clung—but she was beginning to rethink her stance.

When Jake didn't respond right away, she added, "It's what I would have wanted for her if the situation were reversed."

"My car is not itsy-bitsy," Jake said gruffly, but he pulled her against his chest for a quick embrace and an even quicker kiss to the forehead. "And of course that's what she'd want for you. She'd want you to be happy— we all do. Now help me with these bags. At this rate, it's going to take us a week to get there."

He pushed her away, as if the shame of having been caught in the act of such kindness was physically distressing. And in that moment, it was. Becca could only stare, her jaw slack and her heart expanding painfully into her throat, as he eyed the trunk and gauged the amount of space as if it was the only thing that mattered to him.

Oh, shit. Oh, no. Not this.

The pain in her throat only grew worse as she slipped a pair of sunglasses over her eyes, hoping to hide anything and everything they contained. She should have seen this one coming—Madame Pernaud couldn't have spelled it out any clearer if she'd handwritten Becca a letter. Of course the man with the power to hurt her wasn't Dana.

That man was Jake.

FOURTEEN

IT TOOK SOME DOING, but they managed to get all the bags secured—and by *they*, Jake meant himself, lifting and shoving as Becca critiqued his movements from afar.

"I don't think you're doing it right," she said, her head tilted as she watched. "It looks like that top suitcase will fall off if we go over a bump."

"What are you talking about? This is a solid pyramid." He finished lashing the last of the suitcases on the trunk-mounted luggage rack, feeling a trickle of sweat form along the back of his neck. The midmorning sun was doing its best to counteract the brisk fall air, and he'd had to slip out of his jacket and roll up his shirtsleeves. "If it worked for the Egyptians, it should get us out of the city."

"I don't think I've ever seen a man put so much thought into the arrangement of luggage before. Watching you work is fascinating."

"I see you've changed from fun-time fiancée to shrewish wife in a matter of days," he grumbled, though without any real malice. There was something so comfortably normal about preparing for a road trip with Becca, of the traditional roles they seemed to have settled into. The novelty of domesticity would probably wear off soon, but he was enjoying it while it lasted. "At this rate, our eventual breakup won't have to be fabricated."

"About that," she said. "Don't you think we should figure out the details now, while we still have time?"

While we still have time. So ominous, like a death knell sounding.

He covered his sudden sense of unease by holding open the passenger door and helping her slide in to the white leather seat. Penelope was a rebuild project he'd offered Ryan earlier that year, and he didn't regret it for a second. Since Ryan knew so much more about cars than Jake, it had been fun to watch him work. If nothing else, it had passed the time while he was stuck at home, gave him something to do other than standing around feeling ornamental.

"What kind of details do you think we need?" he asked, striving for neutrality. He jumped over the driver's side door without opening it or catching Becca's eye. As it was also necessary to push the seat back from where Ryan's shorter frame had fit, he had a full sixty seconds to force his emotions to return to a more even keel.

"Well, we could probably use an exit strategy. An entrance strategy too. People are going to want to hear everything—your highly romantic proposal, how we got together in the first place. Your family is bound to ask questions as soon as we arrive. Especially since you spent most of the summer with them."

Jake pulled the car out of the parking spot—a considerably slower, more complicated maneuver than the one Ryan had shown off with—before answering. "We've been on again, off again since the wedding. Things got serious when you were released from rehab and I took it upon myself to make sure you were doing okay. I proposed three weeks ago when we took a midnight yacht cruise out on the harbor. And then we forced the crew to swim back to shore so we could make sweet love on the deck under the full moon. You came four times. No— five. It was a big night."

"They'll never believe that."

"Why not? Five orgasms isn't unheard of. I'm quite dexterous."

She giggled. "I meant the rest of it."

"I think it sounds romantic." It made him appear less like a gold digger and more like a caretaker. And the yacht was a nice touch, even if it was in storage right now. He never felt more alive than when he was on the water. If he did ever propose to a woman—an event he'd never imagined before this moment—that was exactly how he'd do it.

"Well, first of all, there wasn't a full moon three weeks ago."

He had to laugh. Of all the holes to poke in his story, that was the one that concerned her the most? "Fine. I proposed under the crescent moon. It was dark. We had a flashlight. I used it to bring on orgasm number three."

"*And* I get seasick."

"Hmm." He frowned. So much for that idea. "Quiet dinner for two?"

"That doesn't sound like you. When have you ever done anything quietly? For that matter, when have I?" She sighed. "Besides, I could never marry a man who would do something so uninspired as dropping a ring in a glass of champagne or having the chef write *will you marry me* in the blancmange. Can you imagine anything so awful?"

"Yes. One of those ballpark proposals."

"I think a sunset walk on the beach would be worse."

"Skywriting."

"A carriage ride through Central Park."

"Wait—isn't that how my dad proposed to Serena?"

Becca released a crack of laughter. "Yes, but she loves that kind of stuff. She's got that whole upright lady, stiff-upper-lip thing going, but she's a total romantic at heart. She's a Taurus. So is your dad, which is why they work so well together."

"I'll have to take your word for it."

Jake had yet to see anything approaching softness or romance from Serena. It wasn't that he disliked his stepmom or anything. As far as placeholder wives went, she seemed to be working out okay. But he didn't really see why his dad had needed to get remarried at all. He already had three grown children—two of whom were more than happy to handle the reins of the family business—and it wasn't as if he needed companionship as he approached retirement. He worked eighteen hour days and rarely emerged from his office for anything but meals.

How was it fair to keep procreating? Lily and Evan, his two-year-old half sister and half brother, were being raised by their nanny, just as he had been. All his dad was doing was creating another generation of children to ignore.

Jake could feel Becca's scrutiny on his profile but didn't turn to acknowledge it, afraid she was going to rise to her sister's defense. But she threw him off-kilter when she asked, "So how did he propose to your mom?"

He tapped the brakes in alarm, his arm automatically shooting over to keep Becca from lurching out of her seat. This, despite the fact that they were going all of fifteen miles an hour through traffic. This, despite the fact that she had her seatbelt on. The forward momentum that propelled her against his forearm was so subtle it barely counted, but he registered the soft, warm press of her body just the same.

"Oh, wow. Is it that bad?"

"No." He managed to get control of the car again, despite the irritated honk of several horns behind him. "I actually don't know how he proposed. I always assumed he wrote up a contract and presented it to her over dinner one night. That sums up what I remember of their relationship pretty well. I can't recall ever seeing them kiss, let alone smile at each other. Sometimes, when I see him with Sere—" He stopped, suddenly aware of who he was talking to.

"Hey." She pressed a hand on his thigh. "It's okay to resent her in front of me. I can't imagine how I'd react if my mom brought home a thirty-four-year-old piece of ass to be my new daddy."

"I can." Jake grimaced. "You'd either fly at his head in a rage or try to seduce him. My money's split between the two."

"Aw, you always say the most flattering things. Did you ever have sex with Serena?"

"What? No. Of course not." Even though she was much closer to his own age than his father's—and even though it wasn't all that far-fetched of an idea for him to make the attempt to seduce his stepmother—the thought had never crossed his mind. From the moment Serena had appeared in his father's life, hanging from his arm at some hotel gala, Jake had felt a wary apprehension where she was concerned. "I'm insulted you'd even ask. I do have some standards."

Becca didn't seem the least bit offended at his mistreatment of her sister's name. "Well, I'm sorry she upset your life so much. And I'm even sorrier you don't know the story of your parents' proposal. I bet it's more romantic than you think." She nodded firmly, as if her misguided beliefs were all that was required to transform supposition into fact. "Every marriage deserves a good proposal story. Even the contractual ones."

Jake slammed on the brakes—this time intentionally, and this time with his arm out and ready to catch her. By this point in their journey, they were midway over the Whitestone Bridge, its suspension lines set against the clear blue sky, making it appear as though they were on the inside of a photograph. At the last minute, he turned the wheel using a move Ryan had taught him, bringing the car to a stop perpendicular to traffic, both lanes blocked. They'd been moving slowly enough that no one rammed into them, but the rancorous honking of several cars squawked up through the air, signaling their discontent.

"Holy Mother. What just happened?" One of Becca's hands clutched the top of the passenger side door; the other held tightly to Jake's arm. "Did the car break down?"

"No."

He rose from his seat and moved around to her side of the car. Since she seemed unable to get out on her own, he reached in and unbuckled her seatbelt, allowing the vinyl to slide smoothly over her lap. Then he promptly lifted her up and sat her on the car's trunk, wedged next to the still-pyramidal heap of their suitcases. She weighed practically nothing, her limbs feather-light as they moved through his. She was flustered but smiling, looking at the growing line of traffic with a laugh on her lips.

"Hey, asshole! What the hell do you think you're doing?" A taxi driver got out of his car and waved a heavy, menacing arm. "This ain't your personal driveway."

"Fuck off," Jake called back. "I'm proposing to my lady. Show some respect."

The cabbie started cursing again, adding to the backdrop of cars whizzing by on the opposite side of the bridge and the painful call of seagulls in the distance. Jake didn't let the cacophony deter him. Hitching his pant leg, he dropped to his knee on the roadway, feeling several small pebbles poking painfully through his slacks. Although he didn't have anything in his hands, he made a pretense of pulling a box out of his pocket and holding it aloft.

"Rebecca Clare," he called, his voice overloud to cover the increasingly loud honking, "you and I have known each other for three and a half years, during which time we've shared a dozen family dinners, nineteen terrible nights of sleep, several relations of a carnal sort, exercise with a man who should be running a large militia, and many conversations I don't care to repeat. I think you might be the least rational woman of my acquaintance. Also, you're terrible at painting and you're a slob. You really need to start hanging up your clothes when you're done with them. Would you do me the very great honor of pretending to be my wife?"

She pulled her sunglasses down from her eyes, allowing him a glimpse of the dancing green irises hiding behind them. Her smile was wide and girlish, and when she jumped down from the car to wrap her arms around his neck, her skirt got caught on the edge, giving the irate cabbie a generous flash of her buttocks.

At least it shut him up.

"Of course I will," she said, her mouth brushing his ear. She wrapped her legs around his waist and pushed him all the way to the ground, landing so that she straddled him, her skirt pushed up to the tops of her thighs. He lay there, prostrate, in the middle of the Whitestone Bridge, pinned beneath a woman he could lift with one flick of his wrist.

She pressed a kiss on his mouth, wet and warm, more playful than serious, though his body didn't bother distinguishing the two.

"You're a snobby control freak with prettier hair than me, and I'm not happy to discover just how tightfisted you can be with the orgasms, but of all my nephews, you're by far my favorite. Nothing on earth would make me happier than to pretend to want to marry you."

He grinned and rolled out from underneath her, being sure to clasp her around one wrist and hoist her up alongside him. With an arm wrapped tightly around her waist, he raised his other fist in the air and shouted, "She said yes!"

A handful of people clapped, a wolf whistle sounded in the distance, and the cabbie offered to drive their car off the side of the bridge in anticipation of the upcoming nuptials. Since he seemed capable—and eager—to make that dream come true, Jake hurried Becca back into the car and pulled into his lane.

"There. We'll have to fudge the dates a little, but how's that for a proposal story?" He ignored the rapid beat of his pulse as he looked sideways at her. It was the adrenaline of stopping traffic on one of New York's most popular bridges, the ebbing danger of a taxi driver eager to make good on his threat to help them swim with the fishes. Nothing more. "Good enough?"

"It was almost perfect."

"What? *Almost?* I thought it was flawless." When she didn't say anything, Jake reached over and gripped the back of her neck, holding tight enough to feel her pulse leap underneath his thumb. "You're tough to please, you know that? I promise to get it right next time."

Fortunately for them both, they hit an open patch of road before he could say more. Jake floored it and forced himself to focus on not getting them killed instead of dwelling on the *next time* he'd propose to anyone.

FIFTEEN

"I THINK THAT MIGHT be the sweetest thing I've ever heard." Serena held her napkin clutched to her chest. "No one has ever stopped traffic for me before."

"And no one is likely to unless you're in need of medical attention," Mr. Montgomery said, though he did it fondly, reaching across the table to pat her hand. The entire family was dining al fresco on the back terrace of the Manor, seated around an enormous farmhouse-style table decorated with the colors and bounty of fall. "As romantic as I'm sure Jake's proposal was, I don't believe in inconveniencing others on a whim."

Although they were dining fairly late, there was enough light provided by the overhead twinkle lights for Becca to make out Jake's jaw firming, his eyes growing cold. It was amazing how walking through the front door of his ancestral home had changed him. Gone was the boyish joy of a too-fast ride in his sports car. Nowhere in sight was the playful, taunting man who'd proposed in the middle of the Whitestone Bridge.

He'd stiffened to lamppost-levels of inflexibility, didn't even blink without first running it through some internal checklist. *This* was the Jake the rest of the world knew, the gorgeous statue of a man who was able to control the beat of his heart and regulate his temperature, the one who didn't let anything touch him.

The one who refused to touch anything in return.

"What I find hard to believe is that he actually got down on one knee in the middle of the road." A wide-smiled, sunny woman who'd been introduced to her as both Jake's cousin and the family nanny winked at Becca from the other side of the table. "All that dirt and motor oil. That's how you *know* it must be true love."

Becca had liked Amy almost instantly. Of all the family, she was the only one who treated Jake with the kind of casual affection Becca herself favored. Amy'd been waiting for them at the door and practically tackled him in the drive. It had been hard to tell if her hug had been driven more by happiness at seeing him or outrage that he got engaged without telling her first.

Becca suspected it was the second one. Mostly because every time she looked up, Amy was watching her as if she was a figment of her imagination, and glancing away for even a second would make Becca disappear back into her subconscious.

"Did you cry?" Amy asked as she speared the asparagus on her plate with a fork. "I did."

"Oh, congratulations!" Becca said. "I didn't know you were engaged too."

She knew Amy was in a serious relationship with Ryan, the chauffeur who'd dropped the car off in New York, but Jake hadn't mentioned another wedding in the family. Maybe they could pretend they wanted to wait for that one first, buy themselves some time to untangle all this.

"Oh, no—not me. I cried when I heard *Jake* was getting married. I was with Evan and Lily at the time. They kept bringing me all their favorite toys to try and cheer me up. The poor things thought I was becoming unhinged."

Serena's eyes opened in alarm, but she didn't say anything—a testament to her sister's good manners. Their mother had sent all four of them to boarding school, but while Serena, Alice and Winnie had enjoyed the experience of equestrian classes and strictly enforced curfews, Becca had been kicked out. Twice.

"I hope they were tears of joy." Jake spoke to Amy, but it was clear he was addressing the whole table. They were all there—his father at the head, looking like Santa Claus in a wrinkled beige suit, Serena her usual svelte self, Monty, Amy, Becca…the only person missing was Jake's younger sister, Jenna, who Becca understood was overseeing a new hotel's construction in Greece. "It *was* happiness that moved you, right?"

He was practically daring someone to contradict him, but no one took up the challenge.

"Of course it was happiness." Amy cast him a curious glance. "Why wouldn't it be?"

"I didn't cry, but I *did* knock him to the ground in my excitement," Becca said, intervening with a laugh. "Which probably wasn't smart, because traffic was still moving in the opposite direction and we almost got run over by a taxi."

"She's exaggerating," Jake said when Serena's hand flew to her mouth. "If the taxi driver was going to maim anyone, it was me."

"Not the safest place for a proposal," Monty said dryly.

"I'm glad everyone has an opinion on the subject, but let me close it by saying I'd never put Becca in any real danger. It's my job to take care of her, and I can promise you all it's a job I take very seriously."

At the head of the table, Mr. Montgomery cleared his throat. At the other end, Amy sniffled.

"Ignore me," she said, waving her fork. "Carry on being adorable. I don't want to get in the way."

Mr. Montgomery spoke up. "Speaking of in the way, Moira should be joining us in a few weeks. She wants to be here to help plan the engagement party."

Oh, dear God. No one had mentioned taking things that far. "Is that absolutely necessary?" Becca asked.

Serena laughed behind her hand, discreet to a fault. "Do you mean the party, or Mom's involvement in it? Neither one is avoidable. She's already started the guest list."

Becca turned to Jake. "I've changed my mind. I'm not marrying you."

He didn't even blink. "Don't be ridiculous. Of course you are."

"Nope. You're hideous and get far too emotional over things. It'll never work out between us."

"It's too late. Weren't you listening? Your mom has already started the guest list. Now be quiet and eat your vegetables."

She grabbed her wineglass and took a deep drink of that instead. "Keep it up, Cuddle Cakes, and I'm going to run away with the pool boy instead."

Monty stopped in the act of bringing his fork to his mouth. "We don't have a pool boy."

Becca made the mistake of meeting Jake's eyes over the top of her glass. His sudden burst of amusement lit him from within, melting away all those layers of ice and stone, leaving nothing but a man so achingly human and approachable it made her want to cry. Cry and hit something and maybe grab her wrist and tap until the urge stopped.

She should never have allowed him to bring her here. The stately house where her sister had found so much happiness might feel like a safe harbor for now, but how would they all feel when she and Jake ended things between them?

"We don't have a pool boy," Jake echoed, a smile lifting his lips and stopping her heart. His voice fell into a low, sexual rumble that she felt clamp in her inner thighs. "I guess you'll have to rely on me instead."

Amy sighed and sniffled again. Since now was hardly the time to tell Jake that it had been a mistake coming here and she wanted to go back to the city, Becca forced herself to pretend that this was exactly how she'd intended things to work out. Her mother would have been proud.

"How are the twins?" she asked her sister, inserting a bright tone as she changed the subject. "I brought presents to give them after dinner. Lily's old enough for play makeup, right?" When she saw Serena's pinched maternal face settling into place, she added, "It's hypoallergenic and washable—made specifically for kids, I swear. I found it at Barneys."

"Oh." She relaxed. "That might be okay. Amy?"

"I'm sure it'll be great," she said diplomatically. They fell into talk of children—not Becca's most well-versed subject, but she knew how important Evan and Lily were to her sister, so she said all the right things and nodded as if she understood the importance of fine motor skills development at thirty months.

"I imagine you and Becca will be wanting privacy as you settle in," Mr. Montgomery said to Jake a few minutes later. He spoke in a conversational tone that made it easy for Becca to overhear. "We'll try not to intrude too much upon your time."

"Monty implied you had a schedule for us."

"*Schedule* is a rather strong word. Think of it more as

a loosely organized lineup of events." He hesitated, as if afraid to push too hard so early in the visit. "I promise to keep your obligations to a minimum. More than anything, we're just happy to have you here."

Becca expected Jake to grow stiff again, but he merely toyed with the stem of his wineglass. "Thanks. I'm happy to be here."

Everyone at the table stopped their conversation at once. It wasn't polite to stare, slack-jawed and incredulous, but that was what they all did anyway. It was difficult to tell which one of them was the most surprised, but if someone forced Becca to pick at gunpoint, she'd say it was Mr. Montgomery.

Jake looked around at each one of them, stopping only when he reached Becca, an amused quirk to his brow. "Was it something I said?"

She released a squeak that was more exasperation than laughter. He was doing it again, playing with checkmates, only moving when he was capable of shaking the whole earth.

Dinner came to an unceremonious end. Although it was meant to be an informal meal, no one got up until Mr. Montgomery stood, pushing back from his chair and dropping a kiss on Serena's forehead. The gesture was sweet and light, causing a strange pang in the region of Becca's heart. It didn't even look as if he was aware of his actions, as though affection for his wife was such an ingrained part of him it required no forethought.

Jake was the next to rise from the table. To his credit, he didn't try to emulate his father's unconscious display of affection. He turned to her instead with a slightly frowning, "You'll be all right?"

"Spending time with my niece and nephew? I think

I can manage. I'm not *great* with kids, but there will be another adult there to protect them."

His frown didn't lift, and she realized with a start that he hadn't been offering support. He was asking for it. This man, who ran marathons in the dark and stopped traffic for fun, was scared to be alone with his family.

On tiptoe, she brushed her mouth against his jawline. To the outside, it looked like a kiss, but she allowed her lips to graze his ear instead. "All you have to do is say the word, and I'll end the engagement so we can escape. I mean it, Jake. Don't feel like you have to suffer through anything for my sake. I'll be okay. I always am."

As he pulled away, his gaze fell on her, soft and warm. His touch was even more so as he tucked her hair behind her ear. "You're not okay, Becca. But you will be."

Was that an…insult? It *felt* like one and it *sounded* like one, but the way Jake straightened his tie and stared at her—as if he might be about to drop an affectionate kiss on her forehead—made her think it might have been the exact opposite.

She opened her mouth to disagree, to tell him that of course she was okay, that no one had mastered the art of survival quite like she had, but he silenced her with a disarming smile. "If you don't mind, I think I'll head up to the nursery with you."

Amy laughed outright. "That's the biggest surprise yet. I never thought I'd see the day you willingly crossed that threshold again."

"If Becca can handle them, so can I," he said primly, and led them all inside.

"IF YOU AREN'T going to have tea with us, you can at least make yourself useful and get some cookies." Becca glanced up from the tiny pink-and-white table set in the middle of the nursery and held up a plastic piece of cake. "These ones are so realistic it's almost cruel."

"Sorry, Becca." Amy looked an apology at her. "I can't send Jake to the kitchen for cookies. Your sister would kill me. Too much refined sugar isn't good for tiny palates."

Becca flipped her pinky up and poured Lily and Evan some more tea, which was really just water in a decorative silver pot. As usual, Jake's half brother and half sister were a mystery to him, and he was grateful Becca seemed to have an idea of how to get along with them. He knew the tiny pair was related to him, and he knew they had brains that functioned on a level equal to that of their peers, but that was all he could say about them with any certainty.

They always seemed happy to see him, though, which was nice. The only other person who managed that kind of regular enthusiasm in his presence was Becca. He should probably take more pains to foster relationships of such unequivocal adoration.

"Serena may be anti-cookie *now*, but you should have seen how much crap she used to sneak me when we were kids."

"Really?" Amy's eyes widened in obvious interest. "Do tell. The only way to get any sugar in this house is to smuggle it in from the outside. I've had serious discussions with Philip's yard crew about growing our own cane."

Becca laughed and sat back in her tiny chair, perilously close to tipping it over. Jake made a motion to rush forward and catch her, but she righted herself at the last minute. He felt more relieved than foolish until Amy saw him and raised a mocking brow. *Damn*. He was likely to hear about that later.

"It was because Serena, Alice and Winnie are all much older than me," Becca confided as if nothing had happened. "By the time I was seven, they were comfortably in their teens and had access to a treasure trove of ill-gotten goods. God, I was so spoiled. They'd give me pretty much anything I wanted. Candy. Nail polish. A sip of champagne when no one was looking. Serena was the worst. She used to keep boxes of Twinkies under her bed."

"I don't believe you," Amy said adamantly. "I think I mentioned Twinkies once in her range of hearing, and she acted like I was talking about flying monkeys."

"You didn't hear this from me, but when she used to get really bad PMS, she'd dip them in mayonnaise." Becca lifted a finger and crossed it over her chest when Amy let out an outraged shout. "On my honor. To this day, I'm pretty sure it was one of the most disgusting things I've ever seen."

"If you give Evan any more of that water, you'll soon get sight of something else disgusting," Amy said. "I don't recommend it."

Jake grimaced as he watched the women interact. He had no idea how his cousin spent eight hours of every day with these children and their bodily functions, but she seemed to like it. He could maybe see the appeal if they were your own, but Amy couldn't even give them sugar if she felt like it. Theirs was a world of restrictions within restrictions—just one of many reasons he found life here so stifling.

Amy clapped her hands, a nanny to the core. "Come on, you two. It's time to get ready for bed."

"Oh, let me do it," Becca said. "You and Jake should take some time to catch up. I can manage pajamas and potty breaks on my own."

"Really? You don't mind?"

"Not at all. I love kids when I only have to see them for an hour and then tuck them in." She leaned down and gave each of the twins' golden-red curls a kiss. "What do you say, Evan and Lily? Can Auntie Becca read your bedtime story tonight?"

The ear-piercing shrieks the pair emitted were all the assent any of them needed. With a cheerful wave and a promise to help the twins with the teeth-brushing portion of events, Becca ushered them out the door and into the hallway, the door clicking firmly shut behind them.

"Oh. My. God." Amy turned on him before he had enough time to do so much as blink. "I love her. I love her so much I want to clone her and keep one version in a closet in case you mess this up."

"Thanks for the vote of confidence." He tilted his head in the direction of the stairwell, hoping to take this conversation somewhere Becca might not overhear. Amy wasn't likely to temper her questions or her volume level for the sake of tact. Her straightforwardness had always been both the best and the worst thing about her. "But one is more than enough."

"One is never enough. I often wish I had two Ryans. One could do helpful things around the apartment, leaving the other free to—"

"Spare me the details Amy, I beg you. It's weird enough being related to you as it is." He waited until her laughter stopped before continuing. "I was sure you'd met Becca before, though."

"Oh, I've seen her once or twice, but I didn't pay attention. That was before I knew you were in lurrrrve."

"How old are you?"

"Lurrrrve. I swear to you, Jake—when we saw the paper announcing your engagement after only a few weeks in the city, I was ninety-nine percent sure you were off somewhere plotting the reporter's demise. I had no idea it might actually be true."

They kept walking, moving through the familiar hallways where he and Monty and Jenna and Amy had been raised by Amy's mom, the family nanny from his youth. When he didn't say anything right away, Amy yanked on his arm, forcing him to stop next to her.

"It *is* true, right? Please tell me it's true."

"Of course it's true. I proposed. She accepted. That's how these things usually work."

"That's not a very romantic way to put it." Amy narrowed her eyes in suspicion. "But I saw you two at dinner. And just now, in the nursery—you were totally going to catch her chair. Not even you can fake that kind of devotion."

"Goddammit. What has Monty been telling you?"

Amy made an exaggerated show of examining the wall behind Jake's head. "Oh, you know Monty. No one listens to him."

"Amy—what did he tell you?"

"He didn't tell *me* anything. But he might have mentioned to your dad that the two of you made a small wager recently."

"He's wrong," Jake said quickly, shutting Amy down before she could say more. "Well, not about the wager, but about the lengths I'm willing to go to win. Whatever he's told you about me and Becca is wrong."

"It *is* awfully sudden…"

"I've known Becca for years. A lot longer than you've known Ryan."

"And there's no denying she has a lot of money, which is something you always seem to find in short supply." Amy bit her lip worriedly. "When Monty told me how much each of the Clare sisters has—"

"Don't you dare." He felt himself bristling. Of all the people he thought he could bristle against, his cousin and one of his closest friends had never figured on the list. Yet here he was, fur flying, teeth bared for attack. "What Becca and I have isn't about money."

"Okay." Amy nodded once. "I believe you."

"I'm fully capable of supporting myself. That bet was made more to annoy Monty than anything else."

"I said I believe you."

"There's no reason why I couldn't march up those stairs to my dad's office right now and get my accounts unfrozen."

"If that's what you want, that's exactly what you should do."

He shook his head and released a begrudging laugh. There were plenty of people on this planet he could intimidate and fool, but this woman he'd grown up with wasn't one of them. Becca and Amy had a lot in common that way.

"That *is* what I'm going to do," he said, "so I'd appreciate it if you didn't spread any more rumors about the bet with Monty. It was a game, nothing more. I mean to do right by Becca, even if that means swallowing my pride and admitting defeat."

Amy let loose a low whistle. "How's that pride taste,

cuz? I imagine that's the first time it's ever crossed your lips."

"Don't you have a boyfriend to go annoy or something?"

"Nope," she said cheerfully. "He had to move all sorts of tasks around to haul your sorry ass out here today, so I've got a good hour to kill before it's time to go home. And I intend to kill it with nosy questions about your lady love."

"Ask away," Jake said, resigned. "But don't be surprised if I refuse to answer."

SIXTEEN

JAKE HAD ALWAYS felt that entering his father's office was akin to being summoned to his death. When he was a kid, he'd done everything he could to render the room powerless. He'd once filled the decanter of brandy on the sideboard with apple juice, emptying the real deal in a potted plant. He'd gone through and reorganized the filing cabinet according to the alphabetical guidelines of Pig Latin. He'd even lost his virginity here, sneaking up with Peyton Packer one weekend while his father was out of town.

In retrospect, that last one had been a mistake. What should have been the ultimate act of defiance had devolved into an awkward, difficult-to-maintain erection as he'd recalled all the times he'd been chastised here, punished here, told he wasn't good enough here.

Although he had yet to resort to sexual antics again, Jake still did his best to transform this pretentious mahogany-paneled room into four innocuous walls. Today was no different. Without waiting for Monty or his dad to invite him in, he strode in and lowered himself carelessly into a chair.

He wouldn't be intimidated. He wouldn't be turned away.

"How nice of you to join us this morning," his dad said without looking up from his desk. Monty lurked over his shoulder, a common enough place to find him during the tediously long work days they both put in. "I thought you'd be out showing Becca the sights today."

"She's with Serena," he said curtly.

"That's nice. Serena hasn't stopped talking about your visit since we first broached the subject. I don't know why I didn't think of it earlier. We should have invited Becca out months ago."

Jake agreed, but not for the reasons his dad thought. He couldn't care less how Serena felt about having company, but it would have been nice for someone to show an interest in Becca's well-being when she first got released from rehab. God knew her own mother hadn't.

"I suppose Monty told you I want the ring," Jake said. He hadn't meant to jump right in, but the alternative was to sit here and dwell on Becca's mistreatment—something that wouldn't end well for any of them.

"He did."

"I hope it won't be a problem."

"Of course not."

Jake was taken aback by this easy acquiescence— so much so that the belligerence slid right out of him.

"I only wish you'd come to me before you proposed. We could have had it cleaned and resized. Becca is considerably smaller than your mother was." His dad made a motion to access the safe behind his desk. Most of the family valuables were kept in a different room—one where the head of security, Alex Morris, could keep a close eye on things. The office safe was reserved for items of a personal nature, the things his dad wanted to oversee himself, since he spent nine-tenths of his life here.

It was strange to think the ring had been here this whole time, close at hand, protected, watched over.

There were so few reminders of his mom in the house anymore.

"Silly me," Jake murmured. "And here I thought I might have to put up a fight to get it."

"Why would you have to do that?"

It was a leading question, a semi-rhetorical one, and one Jake knew it would behoove him not to answer.

He did anyway. "Call me crazy, but I had a suspicion the news of my engagement would be received with something less than enthusiasm."

The air-tight seal of the safe gave a hiss as the door swung open, and his father cast a penetrating stare over his shoulder. Jake hated that stare. It made him feel as if his dad could see right through him. No—*invisible*. It made him feel invisible.

"Of course not. Serena and I couldn't be happier."

Jake wished he was better at reading this man. With most people, he had a fairly good idea what they were thinking, how they planned to act—and if he didn't, he watched and waited until he did. Becca might consider that a personal failing, but it had always served him well in the past. It was better to be certain of your steps than to plunge headfirst into a mess.

"For one, it'll be nice to strengthen our relationship with the Clares further," his dad said, showing his hand and proving Jake's point. That was a tasteful way of saying Becca had a lot of money. Clearly, his father wasn't going to balk at the idea of strengthening his business position by leveraging Becca's name. "For another, I like her. More specifically, I like her for *you*. There. That was brave of me, wasn't it? I hope you aren't going to break off the engagement now to spite me."

Jake gritted his teeth, a surge of anger shaking his

determination to remain aloof. Why did his father insist on twisting everything around? That man's feelings were the last thing he planned to take into account when he broke off the engagement.

If he broke off the engagement.

If.

"And to be honest, I was honored that you'd thought to give her your mother's ring," his father added, his voice softer this time. "I think she would have liked Becca. She's a lovely girl."

"She's a lovely girl, yes, but she's also trouble." Thus far, Monty had been content to take a page from Jake's playbook, standing back and watching the scene unfold, but the reference to their mother proved too much for his restraint. Jake doubted his brother had given the ring a single thought in over a decade, but he couldn't stand the idea that Jake might get something before he had a chance to calculate its worth. "I don't think we can forget some of the more negative attributes her reputation brings to the family."

"That's my fiancée you're talking about," Jake warned. "You might want to watch where you step."

Monty flushed darkly. "It's just so sudden, that's all. If you ask me, you're only trying to win…" As if realizing the severity of the accusation he was about to level, he redirected himself. "I didn't even know you two were seeing each other."

"Oddly enough, I don't find it necessary to email you every time I take a lady out on a date. Is that what you want from me? Details? Pictures? Shame on you. Becca's your aunt. You should show some respect."

"You know what I mean."

"I don't, actually. Why don't you explain it to me?"

It was clear Monty intended to do just that. While their dad rummaged around in his safe—stuffed almost to overflowing—Monty took over the role of disapproving father, looming over Jake and delivering lectures.

"You might think it's funny to skate through life, contributing nothing, but things like our family image affect my day-to-day existence," he said. "Do you have any idea how difficult it is to try and get other businesses to take us seriously when yet another one of your sex tapes is floating around the internet? Not to mention your other exploits. I have to throw money around to get a meeting, and then I get to sit there and pretend that of course I heard about the yacht race and how losing the bet meant you had to dock in Ibiza in the nude in the middle of the day."

"I think you should give me a little credit for that one," Jake protested. "Spain is none too warm in February. You wouldn't believe the wind chill factor."

Predictably, Monty was not amused. At the time, Jake hadn't been either. The damage to the hull that had caused him to lose the race had been what damn near wiped out the last of his bank account. And he wasn't joking about the wind chill. A biting cold like that did things to a man's anatomy he'd rather not announce to the general public.

"The world thinks you're a big joke, Jake. Which, by extension, makes me one."

"No. The world thinks I'm entertaining. They think you're a humorless tightwad. If you have to grease palms to get in on a meeting, it's because they'd rather run naked through Times Square than spend an hour in your company."

He stopped and forced himself to take a deep breath.

This wasn't at all how he intended this meeting to go. According to Becca's misguided sense of logic, he was a man who reacted to situations. He never took any steps on his own, rarely exerted himself to help anyone unless there was something in it for him. He waited for someone else to make the first move and adjusted his strategy accordingly.

Well, his father was moving. He was fishing out an engagement ring for Jake to offer to a woman he actually approved of his son marrying—and he had to know that Jake intended to retaliate in some way. So what was he hoping Jake would do? Go through with the wedding? Fling the ring at his head and run back to New York? Murder his brother in a cold rage and spend the rest of his life in prison?

For the first time in his life, Jake found himself in a situation in which there was no easy solution to the problems unfolding around him. He wanted to do none of those things. And he wanted to do all of them.

"That's actually what I wanted to talk to you about, Monty."

"You want to talk to me about streaking through New York?"

Jake laughed. He wasn't sure if his brother was making a joke or not, but the idea of his straitlaced sibling doing anything exciting in the nude was too good to pass up. "Not quite. I was hoping there might be a way for me to start pulling my own weight around here. I'd like another chance to come work with you."

Monty's incredulity was a red-faced, silent thing that filled Jake with an unaccountable joy. The only thing that could have overturned his brother's rigid sense of the world any more than Jake handing the bet over on a silver platter was if he'd rolled over and shown his belly in a clear move of submission.

"Here it is." Their father turned, holding a flat black box in one hand, ignoring the conversation taking place on the other side of his desk. "I'll have Katie make an appointment with the jeweler, and you can take Becca into the city to get it adjusted."

"That's it?" Monty asked as Jake took the proffered box. His mouth still worked up and down as he processed the scene around him. "You're just handing it over?"

It felt strange, holding something that had once graced his mother's hand. Most of Jake's childhood memories revolved around his nanny—which wasn't the sad, pathetic tale most people thought when they heard he'd been reared primarily by a woman who cashed a paycheck with his father's signature on it. Linda had been treated by his parents as an extension of the Montgomerys, and in many ways, she still was. There had been plenty of physical affection and story times to go around, always a kind face to greet him in the morning.

But his mother held a place in his maternal remembrances, too, however small those memories were. He recalled watching her get dressed for a fundraising event one night—she'd always been more passionate for her charities than for her children—frantic when she couldn't find her ring. It had ended up being inside her vanity drawer, but in the time it took them to find it, he'd been by his mother's side on the floor, crawling as they peeked under beds and inside shoes for the missing piece of jewelry.

It was the first time he could remember recognizing that his mother was a *person*. Not just an aloof adult figure, one half of a parental duo characterized by how little a role they played in his day-to-day life. She'd been real and warm and crying, and for the space of twenty minutes, she'd needed him.

Him. Not Monty. Not Jenna. Not anyone else.

"We'll want to have the insurance policy looked over, of course," his dad said, interrupting his thoughts. "But other than that, I have no objections. Unless you wanted me to keep it for you, Monty? By rights, it should go to you first, but you led me to believe you were giving Jake your blessing."

"Of course he can have it," Monty muttered. "That's not the issue here."

"Don't you want to look at it?" his dad prodded.

Jake shook his head and slipped the box in his coat pocket. He'd wait until there weren't so many eyes on him. His dad had a way of seeing the exact things a man wanted to keep to himself.

"I meant what we were talking about earlier," he said, primarily to distract himself from the heavy weight of the box against his chest, too close to his heart. "About wanting to pull my weight. I've been looking into a few things, and I think I could help with your dismal public relations."

"What's wrong with my public relations?"

"People don't like you. You remind them of their mortality."

"What's that supposed to mean?"

Jake sat still and waited. There was no need to spell it out.

"I'm not that bad," Monty grumbled.

"Well, you're not very good either. Don't misunderstand me—I'm not trying to replace you. I don't want a desk or an executive assistant or even a calendar. And the less I have to see of you, the better. But I'm not the waste of space you've always considered me. It's been recently brought to my attention that the only thing I'm any good at is sitting around and pointing out other people's shortcomings." He smiled, unable to help himself. "I know that might not sound like much, but I think I can help you. I *know* people, Monty. I watch them. I can tell you what they want to hear."

"Oh, please. You don't want to help. You're just scrambling because you're afraid of becoming *that guy*. What's the matter? Is the fact that you're going to have to live off your wife's income for the rest of your life finally sinking in?"

"John, that is quite enough!" Their dad rarely raised his voice, and even more rarely resorted to Monty's given name, a name he shared with his eldest son. His words echoed off the walls, sharp and concise, causing them both to wince. "I want you to apolo—"

"No, Dad," Jake said. "He's right."

Both men swiveled to face him.

"I *am* scrambling, and I *am* afraid of becoming that guy. When I first proposed to Becca, I wasn't thinking of her money. I was only thinking of her. Unfortunately, things have had time to settle since then, and I'm not so sure I like the way they fit."

"I'm sorry, Jake, I didn't—"

Jake held up a hand. "You aren't sorry, and you did. And it's fine. Nothing is going to change the fact that Becca has more money than me, and I'll never be able to apply myself to work the way you do to change that fact. But I can at least do this. I can be more than an accessory to be worn with the right outfit."

"Accessory?" Monty asked, looking a little green around the edges. "Outfit?"

"An inside joke," Jake said. "One I'm not so sure you'd understand even if I did care to explain it."

"Well, I like it." Their dad moved around the desk, his hand outstretched. "You're always saying you don't have time for the more social aspects of running the foundation, Monty. Why not hand them over to Jake? From what I understand, Becca is already a patron of the arts. People will warm to that—to them, as a couple."

"You know about the Artista Theatre?" Jake asked.

"More to the point, *you* know about the Artista Theatre?" his father returned. He didn't wait for a reply. "That settles it. Don't worry about his salary, Monty. I'll make sure it's covered. He's all yours now."

At that decree, Monty gripped the edge of the desk, staring at their father as though he'd just offered to tie the pair of them together and send them over a cliff.

"It's been a good chat, boys, and it's good to see you working together again. I always thought you'd make a great team."

Jake could see Monty struggling to overcome his emotions as their father left them alone in the office. He knew his brother wanted nothing more than to storm out the door behind him, slamming it shut and shaking the whole house in the process. He never would, of course. He was far too proper to do anything that might cause their staff to gossip or anyone to think less of him as a man.

But he wanted to, and that made him just human enough.

"Well, I guess this means you win," Jake said cheerfully. He stood and straightened his cuffs. "I hope you're satisfied. Now I have a real job, just like you wanted. Assistant to the illustrious John Montgomery the Third. I'll make you copies and bring you coffee. Two creams, right? Shall I brew it with love?"

Monty made a snorting sound that was more horse than man. "I don't think this is funny. It's not like you have any usable skills."

"I have usable skills. I use my skills all the time."

"Name five things you're good at."

Jake ticked off his fingers. "Golf. Sex. Skiing. Driving over the speed limit. And I've been told I make a mean martini."

"Fantastic. My dream employee. I'd love to see that résumé get you anywhere in the real world."

"You say that like you've worked your way up from the mailroom floor. Your entire résumé exists because Dad filled the page for you. Face it, Monty—you and I are exactly the same."

"No. *I* never had a choice. You're the one who got to spend the bulk of his life doing nothing but playing games and having fun while I picked up the slack. But it's no matter—everything is forgiven because you suddenly turned a new leaf and brought home wife number one."

Jake wasn't aware how he crossed the room to get up in his brother's face, but he blinked and there he was. Monty's advantage in height and breadth might have made him the more menacing of the two in a boxing ring, but Jake's carefully maintained control had slipped away, leaving him seething, heaving and eager to do something about it.

"Don't you ever say that to me again."

Monty blinked and took a step back, clearly alarmed

at the sudden shift in the air. "But you know it's true. You haven't worked a day in your life."

"Not about the work stuff." Who cared about work? Work had turned his dad into a ghost, Monty into a bore. Work was a means to an end. "You can insult my professional ethics all you want, but if I hear you refer to Becca as *wife number one* again, I won't be held accountable for my actions. You might have a hard time seeing her as anything more than a tabloid sensation, but believe me when I say she's worth a hundred of you. She's my intended wife and a guest in our home, and you'll treat her with respect. Got it?"

"I'm sorry." Monty frowned. "You're right. You're absolutely right. It was uncalled for."

"Good." Jake released a huff and flattened his shirt front. He didn't think he'd ever heard Monty apologize that fast before. Then again, he'd never lost control and threatened bodily harm before. This day was full of revelations. "Now. What can you have me work on? I was kidding about that coffee stuff. Holly would kill me if I started hanging out in the kitchen and messing with her appliances."

Monty's frown only deepened. "I don't know. What *can* you do?"

"Oh, for chrissakes—I can do anything you want. I'm not inept, I'm lazy. There's a big difference. Why don't you give me some people to woo?"

"I guess that might work." He pulled out a day planner from his inside pocket—an actual day planner, with pen and paper and ye olde leather binding—and consulted it. "I'm supposed to be meeting Ben Bridgeport and his son for an eight o'clock tee time on Wednesday. I guess you could be our fourth."

"Bridgeport? Isn't his son Ricky that kid who used to follow us around the grounds when we were young?" Jake snapped. "It is! I remember. We convinced him the gardener's shed was haunted and then dared him to spend an entire night out there. He lasted about twenty minutes, if I recall. We made Amy wear a sheet and clank a bunch of chains on the roof."

Monty chuckled and relaxed into a smile. "Yeah. That's him, though he goes by Richard now."

"Is he still scared of everything that moves? We used to have so much fun messing with him."

"Huh. He *is* pretty risk averse, now that you mention it. I always chalked it up to conservative business morals—the Bridgeports have always been hesitant to diversify—but you're probably right. He's spooked by his own shadow." Monty shook his head, meeting Jake in a rare moment of unanimity. His brother might be a dull lump of a human being, but at least he had a backbone. "I'm surprised you remember."

Jake thought he smelled a compliment in there, unfamiliar but not unpleasant.

"But don't even think about it, Jake."

"You have no idea what I was thinking."

Monty pointed a warning. "Don't wreck this for me. Don't pull some stupid prank at Richard's expense."

"That wasn't my plan."

"Good."

"*Before*," Jake corrected with an easy smile. "That wasn't my plan *before*. But I like your style, Monty. What do you think? I bet we could convince Amy to put on a sheet again. Should we pull out the old haunted fifth hole? Or the ghost of the man struck by lightning when he dared even God to hit a nine iron?"

Jake didn't wait to hear Monty's response as he shoved his hands deep in his pockets and breezed through the door. The tight-lipped frown he received was all he needed to know he'd successfully landed his mark.

That was for insulting Becca.

His hand slipped to his coat pocket, where the weight of the ring box smacked against his chest in time to his footsteps, a reminder that his day's work was far from done. He pulled it out and ran the velvet under his fingertips.

This is for Becca too.

SEVENTEEN

BECCA HELD UP her hand, admiring the way the oversized blue stone caught the light. The Montgomery sapphire was the kind of gem that would demand admiration no matter where it was being showcased. Shamefully big and clear, it could pick up a ray of sunshine in a darkroom, maybe even act as a flashlight in a pinch.

"It's beautiful." She turned and faced the mirror, pretending to go through the motions of everyday life with her new engagement ring intact. There she was, lifting a martini glass to her lips, chatting with friends. Here she stood, casually flipping her hair, looking flirty and fun. Now she was dancing, arms in the air, hands—"Oh, shit."

The ring flew across the room, landing on the swirled carpet near the foot of the bed. Jake bent to retrieve the fallen item, amusement and a grimace rendering him into an uncannily Monty-like vision. "I'm glad to see my family heirloom means so much to you. My great-great grandmother wore that ring."

"Your great-great grandmother must have been a giant. I don't think I could wear that on my thumb."

Jake held the ring between two fingers, transfixed by the shine of it. "Dad figured it would be too big. We'll get it resized."

Becca didn't take the ring when he held it out a second time. It was one thing to see a piece of jewelry like that, to touch it, to indulge in a moment of uncomfortably comfortable what-ifs. It was quite another to accept it—especially since it had the full weight of his family's approval attached to it.

They weren't supposed to approve. She was fully prepared to face her own disappointment when things came to an end. She wasn't so sure she could handle theirs too.

"Why don't you keep it until we visit the jeweler?" she said, hoping her words sounded casual. "There's a good chance I'll lose it between now and then anyway."

"Put it on, Becca."

"It could fall down the toilet."

"I'm not asking."

"I might accidentally feed it to one of the twins."

"While we remain under this roof, you're my fiancée, and you'll wear it. End of story." Jake stalked forward and grabbed her hand, practically shoving the band of platinum around her fourth finger. It was a good thing the ring was so big or the metal would have scraped as it went over her knuckle. "We'll glue it to your goddamned hand if we have to."

"I think that's the sweetest thing a man has ever said to me. Inside that well-dressed exterior lies a true romantic."

He laughed. "Okay—maybe glue is taking things too far." He turned her palm over, fingers lingering on the complex maze of lines she'd always had a hard time reading for herself. "I have an idea. Stay here."

She watched him go, no hurry to his step, into the adjoining room. She'd already spent considerable time snooping in there, so she knew it was a sort of sitting room addition to this, his bedroom. Not that there was very much *him* about either one. She'd hardly been expecting nautical paraphernalia and naked lady posters, but it would have been nice to see some kind of reference to his life growing up inside these walls.

Instead, she was looking at what she suspected was the work of Serena's designer. Like their mother, Serena had a fondness for color coordination. This was clearly the Blue Room. Slate walls, a warmer-hued bedspread with so many pillows they could build a tunnel all the way down the hall to Monty's rooms, even a Picasso she could have sworn—no joke—came from his Blue Period. It was depressing in here. If Becca's apartment was evidence of a last-ditch effort at capturing a virginal innocence she wasn't sure she'd ever possessed, then Jake's rooms were a somber attempt at masculine elegance.

Although maybe she was wrong. Maybe Jake's cold, upright bearing went deeper than she realized. Maybe he was cozy here.

"There." Jake returned holding a length of delicate silver chain. "You can wear it around your neck for now. I know it's not ideal, but it should do the trick."

She stared at the dangling necklace, finding it even more difficult to accept this small gesture than the rock worth tens of thousands of dollars. "Jake, it's not about the fit, and you know it. I can't take the ring. Please don't make me."

He frowned. "You don't like it."

Was he kidding? She loved it. She loved everything about it. It was ostentatious and sparkly and part of a family legacy she felt nothing but admiration for. She loved its history and its elegance. She loved the way Jake's fingers slid over hers as he put it on. She even loved the way he acted like controlling her body's adornment was the same thing as controlling her.

He seriously had no idea. Jake didn't have to *demand* she wear the ring. All he had to do was ask.

"My feelings aren't the point here. It's too much."

"Becca, you have enough money to buy a hundred of these rings. It's not too much. It's barely anything." He offered her a smile—hesitant and slow and all the more powerful because of it. "And you should probably know the ring isn't the only thing I asked my dad for today."

"Oh, God. Please tell me there isn't some family tiara you're going to foist on me. You have to warn me about these things ahead of time."

His smile gained confidence. "There are no tiaras that I know of, and I doubt Monty would let me get my hands on one if there was. But I *am* going to start working with my brother."

The ring slid off her finger in her surprise. Jake was waiting to catch it.

"You? And Monty? Doing what?"

He laughed and slid the chain through the band. "You don't have to be quite so incredulous. So far, all I've signed up for is golf."

"I'm not sure I understand."

"I'm not sure I do either." He held the necklace up in a gesture for her to take it, but her arms were having a difficult time doing what she told them to. "Wear the ring. I already know you hate the idea of being married to me, and nothing about our arrangement is going to change if you accept it. But I need you to stick with me on this for a little bit longer."

"Why?"

"Because." He offered the word as though it was enough, as if nothing at all had changed in the few weeks of their engagement. Probably because for *him*, nothing had. With a sigh, he said, "Because I'm not done yet. Because you're not done yet. And because I think I might actually like the idea of helping Monty out for a change."

She wanted him to say more about why he wasn't done, why she wasn't done, why *they* weren't done, but it seemed safer to latch on to that last one. "You aren't upset at being forced to come here?"

He lifted a finger and grazed her cheek. "No one has ever been able to make me do something against my will, Becca. Not even you."

"You know what I mean."

"Yes. I know what you mean, and that doesn't change anything." He smiled. "It might not be so bad after all, this working-with-the-family-foundation stuff. All those years of sitting around waiting and watching might actually end up being useful. I'm going to become Monty's grease man, using my powers of observation for good."

"Does this mean you're going to start wearing all black and spend three-fourths of your time on the phone like he does?"

"Christ, I hope not." He shook the necklace again, and she had no choice but to lower her head and lift her hair, feeling like Marie Antoinette offering her head to the guillotine. The movement drew him near enough for her to smell the mild tang of his soap, feel the heat rising off his body and encircling hers.

He worked the clasp quickly and neatly, adjusting the billowing white top of her oversized tee as she straightened again. When she caught him staring at her—at where the ring dipped into her shirt, cold against her heart—she shivered. And when he lifted a hand and came close enough to touch it, she almost lost it altogether.

But he pulled back before he went too far. As he always did. As he always *would*.

"Don't get smug, but I think the reason I've always hated working for my family is because I've been *reacting* to the position they chose for me," he said. "Sit behind a desk? Not for me. I never stay in one place for very long. Oversee the international branches? No thanks. I'd rather experience new places nightclub by nightclub. Work in finance? Ha. I don't make money. I spend it."

"So what changed?"

He shrugged the only way Jake knew how, a slight lift of the shoulder and cock of the head, a concise movement you had to be watching for, or you missed it. "They're not telling me what to do. This time, I'm telling them where I think I'll fit." He narrowed his eyes. "Don't say it."

"I wasn't going to."

"Don't even think it."

"I have no idea what you mean. There's nothing in my head but visions of sapphires and vodka tonics."

He growled and took a step forward. "It has nothing to do with me being a Virgo without a Leo cusp. It's because Monty has all the interpersonal skills of a corpse. I can't expect to live off your generosity forever, so I needed a backup plan."

"It sounds like a great backup plan."

"I'm just going to woo a few people, raise a few funds, close a few deals. See if it fits."

"If anyone can woo, it's you."

"If you intend to stand there being obliging, then you also understand why that ring has to stay around your neck. I need some time, Becca, that's all. You have to give me a chance to figure things out before we go our separate ways."

Becca opened her eyes, wide and startled, making Jake feel worse than when he'd forced her into this arrangement in the first place. Though *worse* wasn't the right word for it. He felt bad, yes. Desperate, assuredly. And there was an underlying panic to the entire exchange that left him scrambling for a foothold.

Okay. Maybe *worse* was the right word after all. It was difficult to see how things could get any lower from here, but he didn't know what else to do. Becca wasn't supposed to take one look at the ring and give it *back*.

"Can you do that for me?" he asked, his voice catching. "Can you promise to keep the necklace on until I'm ready?"

She nodded, not losing her startled look in the slightest. "Yes, Jake. I promise."

And that was it. He could get that ring on her finger using force and persuasion, but not of her own volition. He was too much a Virgo, too much a Montgomery, too much a tyrant.

The tyrant in him roared. He'd undertaken the task of making sure she was protected, cared for, able to recover. And he intended to see that task through whether she liked it or not.

"So, how do you want me to proceed?" she asked. "Am I supposed to squeal and jump around and show the ring off every chance I get?"

"I don't know. Is that what you'd do if this were a real engagement?"

She cocked her head, considering. "Probably. I've never been one to hide my light, you know? I think if I were ever going to get married, I'd be dancing on table-tops, flashing the goods every chance I got."

Jake had to smile. That was exactly what she'd been doing the night they'd gotten into this mess. "So do that. We need this to look authentic."

"Okay. Do you want to see my engagement ring?"

"I don't want you to show it to *me*. I've seen it. I just gave it to you."

"I know, but you haven't seen how it looks yet." She pulled the neckline of her shirt out and peered down the front, lips pursed as she examined what lay beneath. She glanced up. "It looks *really* good. I think you'll like it."

He didn't doubt it. Based on the outline of the ring under her thin white shirt, it hit right at that sweet spot, where the twin swells of her breasts came together to create a perfect crevasse. A man could get lost in there.

"That's not what I meant when I said you should show it off."

"You're the one who chained it around my neck." She pulled the shirt out farther, dipping it low enough that he could catch a glimpse of cleavage. "How like a man to tie a lady down and then not stick around to enjoy the show."

"Goddammit, Becca." He allowed himself a brief, sweeping glance down the front of her shirt. And then he allowed himself another one, though it wasn't so brief this time. "Now is not the time to test me."

"Why not? This is the first time I've felt I might have a chance to win."

Not true. She'd won weeks ago.

As her semi-transparent shirt had promised, her breasts were encased in a lacy black bra, which pushed and swelled and made the most out of the natural curvature of her body. The cut was low enough that a hint of nipple arose out of each cup, calling to him. And just above them was the ring. His mark. A promise—however fleeting—that while she was here, she was his.

Aware that he was making a mistake, and all the more determined because of it, he dropped a hand down into her neckline, allowing his knuckle to graze the top of her breast. She arched into it, falling into a purr of softly bound pleasure.

He didn't pull his hand away, opting instead to rub his thumb inside the lip of her bra, moving roughly over her nipple. The body part in question responded almost immediately, puckered and rigid, and Becca's lips parted in a sigh of appreciation. He realized, with a combination of resignation and delight, that she wouldn't stop sighing like that until she got what she wanted.

He had to admire that persistence. Even if it tugged so hard at his cock he wanted to howl.

He rolled her nipple between his forefinger and thumb. "What's your end game here, Tiger?"

"Right now?" She hooked her hands in his belt loops and tugged, forcing him to step closer or risk toppling her to the bed. "I could handle an orgasm. Possibly two."

"And after that?"

"A nap wouldn't go amiss."

He pinched, eliciting a gasp and sending a spike of pleasure through his own body. Spike was an apt description these days. Since stepping up on this strangely noble platform of his, he'd discovered that close proximity to a mewling woman wasn't as easy to cope with as one might hope. All he wanted to do was toss her to the bed and show her how many orgasms she could handle.

But he couldn't. She was in his care. Under his protection. He had never before taken responsibility for another human being, and he wasn't sure he liked it very much at all.

"So like a cat to sleep the day away." He gave up on the nipple, pulling down the top of her shirt to bare her shoulder. He bit. When she let loose a sharp cry, he used her momentary lack of balance to push her to the bed. She fell in a sprawl, legs spread, lips parted—and he was sure she did it on purpose. No one fell like wide-open sex unless she was some kind of evil temptress. "And you know that wasn't what I meant. What do you need, Becca? Other than some time with your sister and a few orgasms?"

She stuck her lower lip out in a pout. "I'd like a lot more than a few."

Jake took a dangerous step forward, looming over her as if he meant to attack. God, she wished he would. For once, it would be nice to force this man to lose a little control, to prod him into a full attack.

But she could hardly say that was what she needed. She didn't *need* anything, though she wanted plenty.

She wanted to avoid rehab, preferably for the rest of her life. She wanted to get away from horrible people like Dana and Trish, who brought up painful reminders of her loss without regard for her feelings. She wanted to spend time with people who actually cared about her.

And if she liked the way Jake's family ring settled on her chest, heavy and comforting, was that really the worst thing in the world? She didn't plan on keeping it. He could have it back the second he asked.

She settled for the answer she knew would get the biggest reaction out of him. "I'm only here because you commanded it." She wriggled her body into a more suggestive pose. "Anything else you care to demand? You *did* promise to sate my every need."

He took a step closer, so near he was one small leap away from covering her with his body. And she wanted him to—all that lean, perfectly contained strength. All those careful Virgo qualities unleashed on top of her.

Her heart leaped as he reached down and unfastened the button of her rocker skinny jeans, his fingers rough as they tugged the fabric over her hips. Finally, he was going to do this properly. She lifted her ass off the bed as he pulled her jeans the rest of the way off, leaving her squirming there with panties so wet the dampness was visible from the outside.

And then he backed away. She was in a shirt and underwear, panting with desire, and the jerk backed away, looking at her as one might an exhibit in a zoo. Well, a sexy zoo. A sexy zoo full of half dressed human captives. That sounded quite nice, actually. Warm heat flooded through her, stopping between her legs and causing her to squirm.

"Do it yourself."

She propped herself up on one elbow. "What did you just say?"

He lifted an arrogant brow, rendering him into a god-like statue of skin and bone. "You want me to make demands? Fine. Slip a finger inside your underwear and touch yourself. I'm tired of doing all the work around here."

Becca felt a slow, satisfied smile creep across her face. The only thing better than having Jake rip an orgasm from her body was to have him watch while she did it herself. She opened her legs wider, allowing him a glimpse at just how wet he'd gotten her with a nipple tweak and the promise of more.

"Don't stall. Touch."

"Yes, sir." She ran her hand over the flat of her stomach, slipping underneath the hem of her underwear, not stopping until she reached her hot, wet center. She tipped her head back and gave herself over to a few long, leisurely draws of her finger along the line of her pussy. "Anything else you'd like to see?"

"Yes. You." As her eyes were closed, she missed seeing him stride forward. But she still felt him draw near, gently lifting the shirt from her body, forcing her hands up as he stripped her.

She tried to adjust her breasts, which he'd made askew in her bra so that one nipple was all the way out, the other sort of half-lumped where it peeked through, but he shook his head. "No. I like it that way." He made a vague twirling gesture near her cunt. "Please. Continue."

She had to laugh at the way he so summarily handled his commands—even more so when he carefully pulled up an armchair, providing himself with a ringside seat. She wouldn't have been surprised to see him extract some popcorn or caviar to munch on during the show.

"You're not even going to return the favor?" She glanced pointedly at his crotch. Although he sat with his usual careful ease, it wasn't difficult to see that he was enjoying this show as much as she was. The firm outline of his cock extended down the right leg of his flat-pressed slacks, showcasing everything from the long, hard length of him to the firmly rounded tip. She wouldn't be averse to watching him stroke a few times. In fact, the idea had her breathing harder.

"Back inside that glorious cunt of yours." Even

though Jake spoke politely, he had to force each word out carefully—otherwise they'd have to be ripped out of him. "You may slip a finger inside if you want, but you have to tell me exactly how it feels."

Becca, bless her, nodded and did as she was told. He couldn't tell if it was a desire to please or to tease him that had her so complacent, but he didn't much care. The sight of her on his bed, disheveled and askew, her expression serene as she slipped her hand back into her underwear and resumed her self-pleasure, was hot enough that he could probably cross his legs and come on the spot. All that was needed to take him from hard to explosive was a half second of friction.

Which was precisely why he didn't move.

"I believe you might be forgetting something," he said, once he was certain of his ability to breathe and talk at the same time.

"Hmm?" Her eyes flew opened, dazed. When she saw his look of warning, she grinned. "Oh, sorry. I got distracted. It feels amazing. I'll take the high road and refrain from words like *saturated*, but I think hot and slippery and tight might fit the bill. Are you sure you don't want in? Mean Max has had me on this Kegel regimen you wouldn't believe. It's like my twat has been replaced by an eighteen-year-old Puritan's. I could crush walnuts in here."

"I'd rather not discuss Mean Max or crushed nuts right now, if you don't mind."

"I'm just saying. It's pretty incredible. I could pompoir you to the next century."

Christ. He could practically feel it—the tightening of her body around him, the rolling sensations as she pulled him up and out of himself using nothing but the muscles of her cunt. "Less talking," he barked. "More touching."

She shrugged and arched farther into her hand, the band of her bra slipping off her shoulder and forcing the jut of her breast to reach up for his touch. He let it jut. He let it ache. But his mouth had grown dry and he slowly licked his lips, imagining what she would taste like right now.

"Slow down there, Tiger," he said, watching as her movements became more intense, her eyes glazed and her breath coming short and fast. If he wasn't careful, she'd make short work of this task—robbing him of the brief moment of pleasure he was allowing himself. A spectator on the sidelines. Forcing himself to sit this one out. "Don't come until I say so."

"Now you're just being mean," she said, but her pace slackened and she released a whimper of protest. "How long are you going to make me suffer?"

"*Are* you suffering?" he asked. He certainly was. The crotch of her underwear was all but transparent by now, and he could catch glimpses of the pink sheen of her bare pussy as she rotated a finger around her clit. The rest of her was also beginning to take on that same rosy hue—sweat and flushed skin, a woman being driven to the edge of madness.

She's not the only one.

"I've felt better," she managed, her breath short.

"I bet you have. I doubt you've ever looked better, though." Since she seemed unable to keep her hands off herself for very long, he decided to increase the element of torture—though he wasn't sure which one of them was the intended victim. "But the real question is, how do you taste?"

Her eyes flared in surprise, her lashes fluttering. As he hoped, surprise gave way to understanding, understanding to capitulation. Without losing eye contact, she withdrew her hand and brought her forefinger to her mouth. Lips puckered, tongue swirled, and she licked a rounded path around the digit. Jake allowed himself one tiny shift in the chair, leaning forward ever-so-slightly, while she slipped her middle finger in.

"Delicious," she cooed, and held her hand toward him, her smile teasing. There was nothing he could do or say or ask for that would discomfit this woman. It was, at once, the most frustrating and the most incredible realization in the world. "Want some?"

He did. He wanted to taste her, devour her, suck on her fingers and her clit until she was no longer able to say her own name, let alone taunt him like that. So of course he just shook his head and sat back. Twirling a finger, he said, "No, but thanks for offering. In exchange for your generosity, I'll allow you to finish."

She didn't wait for any more instructions. Without bothering to pose herself or toy with him or even recognize that he was there, she got to her knees on the bed. He thought for a moment she was going to get up, but she was merely angling her body so she could penetrate her middle finger deeper, riding her own hand to completion. She captured her lower lip in her teeth, and her eyes took on the glazed look of a woman who was about to come and didn't care who was in the room with her.

He knew that without question. Becca wasn't getting herself off because he said so or because she wanted to please him or even because she wanted to toy with him. She was getting herself off because she was hot and horny and those two attributes were the only ones that mattered to her right now.

And he fucking loved it.

She cried out and bucked her body against her hand, her face a gorgeous mask of ecstasy. She lowered herself closer to the bed's horizontal surface, presumably to draw her fingers deeper as her body clenched and unclenched around her. Jake could practically feel it, his own body hot and clenching, his balls tight in ways that were unfamiliar to him.

"That's so much better." Becca fell back to the bed, landing with a soft *whomp*. "Now I feel fantastic." From his vantage point, Jake could see that her panties were still very much askew, the inner lining caught on the fold of her vulva, leaving her exposed and glistening. He got to his feet slowly, enjoying the tight fit of his pants over his engorged cock, reminding him of his desire—and of his ability to place that desire second.

"You did that exceptionally well," he agreed.

With a hand flat on her stomach, he reached closer and slipped his forefinger under the leg line of her panties, drawing his touch along the curve where thigh met pelvis, straightening the fabric. She moaned and shuddered, opening her legs as if to draw him in deeper, but he pulled back and moved on to her bra. With a careful hand, he adjusted each perfect mound of her breasts, returning them to their soft, lacy cups, her nipples so flushed and erect he could have hung clothes on them.

He stopped before fixing the necklace, admiring the view, but that too eventually went in its place. Nestled carefully between her breasts, rising and falling with her slowly normalizing breath, that ring filled him with

a sense of satisfaction not dissimilar to an orgasm of
his own.

"Am I all properly covered now?" She smiled up at
him. Pandered to him, he realized. Mocked him. Then,
lifting the ring he'd so carefully placed, she admired
it for a moment. "I *do* like it. And I promise you don't
have to worry. I'll be careful. It obviously means a lot to
you—and all newspaper articles to the contrary, I don't
always fuck things up."

He smiled, touched by her concern, and ran a finger
along her cheek. "I wouldn't have given it to you unless
I trusted you."

I wouldn't have given it to you unless I cared.

But he didn't say that part out loud.

EIGHTEEN

BECCA WOKE WITH a start, her heart pounding in a slow, rhythmic beat that seemed to be gaining momentum in time to a distant song. Her automatic response to a startled awakening like this was to jolt upright in bed and scream—a fairly common occurrence until a few weeks ago—but the feeling was quashed by the heavy arm wrapped around her waist, the warm press of Jake's body against hers.

"Jake?" She blinked at darkness in the room, rendered all the more shadowy by the lack of daylight streaming in the window. It had to be insanely early, but there was no visible clock for her to check. "Jake—wake up."

"Mumnum," he muttered. His voice was grumpy, but the arm around her waist tightened, pulling her close.

"I mean it. Listen. Is that…is someone playing Eminem at us right now?"

This time, the sound he released was less of a mumble and more of a laugh. "It might be."

Realization crept over her—as did a smile, though it was too dark for him to see it. "Jake Montgomery, is that the sound of Mean Max '8 Mile'ing us out of bed before the crack of dawn?"

"Irritating, isn't it?"

She squealed. "No. It's fantastic. I can't believe you got him to come all this way. I'm almost scared to ask what you had to offer him in exchange. I didn't think Max traveled for *anyone*."

Jake shoved his head under a pillow and held it firm. The music grew louder, moving down the hallway at an alarming rate, and he finally peeked one eye out when it stopped outside the door. Sleep had a way of transforming Jake from the devil to a minor demon, his hair rumpled and his grouchy face on—as if he wanted to stab her with a pitchfork, but only in a good way.

"It's better if you don't know. That way you can claim plausible deniability."

"You're so cute when you're breaking the law for me."

"Oh, I didn't break any laws." Jake rolled out of bed and flipped on the bedroom lights, wincing as the sudden illumination hit his pupils. "But don't be surprised if he's the best man at our wedding. And we might have to fix it so his girlfriend catches your bouquet. Why is it that the biggest, meanest men are always the softest at heart? I do so hate a cliché."

Becca stopped in the act of stretching and stared at Jake. It was impossible to tell if he was joking when he used that tone of voice—the one so dry it crackled in her throat. Of course he hadn't invited Max to the wedding. There was no wedding. There *was* an engagement party—one progressing at an alarmingly rapid rate—but she was trying not to think too much about it.

It was difficult, though. With the weight of the Montgomery sapphire pressed between her breasts all day long, she was having a hard time thinking of anything else. In fact, if Jake's plan had been to get her mind off Sara, he'd done an admirable job. She thought about that ring. She thought about the way Jake watched her get herself off. She thought about how easy it would be to make this her life, this magical country manor where nothing bad was allowed to happen.

She could understand why her sister loved it so much here—why she was happy anchoring herself to her husband and letting him keep her safe. When you had a Montgomery protecting you, not even pain was allowed the get through.

You aren't okay, Becca. But you will be.

That promise scared her—not because Jake couldn't see it through to the end, but because it was beginning to appear as though he *could.* All she had to do was put her happiness in his hands and pray to every deity known to mankind that he wouldn't destroy it.

No biggie.

"Thank you for Max," she said, her heart alternating between light and dark with each beat. "That was really sweet of you."

He just laughed. "Why don't you wait and see if you want to thank me after your workout?"

She wasn't about to let it go so easily. "What'd you really have to do to get him to come?"

"It's not important," Jake said gruffly. "Let's call it an engagement present."

"You're giving me an overly muscled, good-looking man in his prime as a gift?"

"Yes, I am. And I expect him to leave you sweaty and heaving."

She didn't move right away as she struggled to form her next thoughts—thoughts she didn't get a chance to finalize. It turned out there was something to this watching and waiting thing, because Jake sighed and pulled her in for a rough embrace, his body still warm from bed. "You always seem to sleep better on Max days," he said, lips caressing her hairline. Not a kiss, but soothing in ways a real kiss from this man could never be. "That's the only thing I had to tell him to get him to come out for a few weeks. He's on your side, Tiger. We all are."

She nodded into his chest, not trusting herself to speak.

"But you better go out there and tell him to turn his music off, or your sister is going to murder us. We're pretty secluded in this wing, but we're not *that* secluded. That man has no volume controls."

"Does this mean you're not coming with me?"

"I wish. I've got tee time in an hour." He withdrew his embrace, returning to his usual composed self as he stripped off his shirt. God, that man was cruel. He'd button himself up any time they approached the bed, but he had no qualms flashing his perfectly tanned torso everywhere else. "You go exercise your way to serenity. I'm going to golf my way into Monty's good graces."

"That's not fair. Yours is easier."

His eyes flashed with humor as he turned to the closet. "You've obviously never golfed with my brother before."

"I CAN'T BELIEVE you hit a birdie on that last hole."

Jake stood with Richard Bridgeport in the golf course parking lot, his hand out to accept the tee that had remained carefully tucked behind Ricky's ear for the entire back nine. His lucky tee, he called it, unearthed from the seventeenth hole at St. Andrews, a treasure he'd sworn had allowed him to go over a hundred games without losing.

He gestured at the tiny white splintered piece of wood as he handed it over. "And take good care of that. I hope you know I wouldn't have wagered it with any other man."

"You've always been a superstitious bastard," Jake said, but he slipped the tee carefully in his pocket all the same. He had a feeling Becca believed in things like lucky tees—throwing it away probably equaled twenty years of bad luck or something. "Wasn't it you who didn't change your gym socks for an entire year when the rugby team had that championship run? By the end of the season, I'm pretty sure we could smell them all the way in the chemistry lab."

Ricky laughed and nodded. Jake could tell he wanted to clap a hearty hand on his back in the manner of Good Old Boys Clubs everywhere, so he stepped carefully away. Yes, they'd bonded over Monty spending ten minutes teeing up every shot and generally sucking all the fun out of life. And yes, he'd done an admirable job of playing into every one of Ricky's weaknesses—jokes in bad taste, embellished stories of the halcyon days of boyhood—but back-slapping was taking things too far.

"Yeah, well. It worked, didn't it? I still have the trophy at home. The wife likes to take it out and polish it every now and then."

"I'll bet she does." Jake winked.

Over the top of Ricky's head, he caught Monty's eye and allowed a look of satisfaction to cross his face. It had taken him all of five minutes to move from Richard to Ricky, fifteen minutes to get him laughing over the memories of once having scared him into a state of incontinence, twenty to extract an invitation to visit the Bridgeports in France during the frigid Connecticut winter. This wooing stuff was easy.

"So you'll come to Nice, right?" Ricky asked as

their caddies loaded up the cars. "In January? We have a week-long house party every year, but nothing we say will tear your brother from his work long enough to stop by. We'd love to see a representative from the Montgomery Foundation there this year."

A week in the Mediterranean? Yeah. He could manage that.

"I'm sure I can figure something out," Jake promised.

"And of course you'll bring your fiancée. A couple of high-profile guests like you two is always good for our image, if you don't mind my saying. And I believe Tilda went to school with a sister of hers and Serena's. I can never remember her name—she's the one who works over in Seattle now."

"Alice," Jake supplied. He'd only met her once, but she seemed nice enough, if indistinguishable from the rest. After a while, all the Clare women started to blur together.

Well, all of them but Becca. Becca was the bright spot in the family, the highlight of his day. Her small, unimpressive form had made its mark on his life in a way he wasn't sure he could ever undo.

"That's her." Ricky nodded. "Tilda is always talking about how much trouble they used to get into together—but I probably don't need to tell *you* about that."

Jake felt his pulse pick up to dangerous levels, but he forced himself to turn to Ricky with a semblance of calm. Forget his promise to help Monty smooth things over. Let this man say one word against Becca, and he'd set all of Nice on fire. "Oh?" he said tightly. "And why's that?"

Ricky laughed, ignorant of the fury that was about to be unleashed upon his head. "No one got into more trouble than you, Jake. The stories you could tell will keep us entertained for months."

MONTY DROVE LIKE he golfed—which was to say they wound their way through the countryside at a painfully slow pace. At this rate, they'd get home from the course sometime late tomorrow night.

"You wouldn't have *really* done anything to jeopardize our relationship with the Bridgeports." Monty glanced at Jake out of the corner of his eye—a brief look, of course, since his eyes had to remain sealed on the road, his hands in place at their customary position on the wheel. "No matter what he said against Rebecca."

"Don't be too sure about that. I was this close to shoving his lucky tee up his ass." Jake sighed. "I can see why you have a hard time playing nice with him. That was the most tedious game of golf I've ever played. He tried calling me Old Sport."

Monty chuckled. "I think you might be my hero now. I've been hearing about that tee for five years' worth of golf games. He's lucky *I* didn't shove it up his ass."

The thought of Monty doing anything so untoward put a smile on Jake's face, and he felt himself relaxing against the passenger seat. This being-helpful thing wasn't so hard, now that he was reconciled to it. And he liked golfing. He liked Nice. He even liked feeling as if he'd accomplished something today.

"I appreciate your help," Monty said, breaking into his thoughts. "I know being an ordinary, agreeable human being isn't easy for you, but you did a lot of good today. I think Ben is finally ready to move forward with the foundation merger. They're even going to let our side manage the assets."

"Stop right there." Jake held up a hand. "Monty, I'll golf with any man, woman or child you send my way. I'll drink cocktails and travel to Nice and chat with dried-up foundation heads like yourself until I collapse from exhaustion. I'll even go to brunches and lunches and tea if I have to. But I refuse—absolutely refuse—to talk about assets and mergers with you."

Monty chuckled again—which made two such out-bursts so far, some kind of record for them both. "Fair enough."

Jake glanced at him out of the corner of his eye, un-sure how far he could push things on this, their first day as allies. He'd sneaked a peek at his horoscope over his morning coffee, and Becca's guru mentioned something about leveraging relationships. What the hell, right?

"I do find myself curious about how you pick orga-nizations to give money to, though," he said, as casu-ally as if they were discussing the weather. "The vetting process, if you will. From what I gather, we focus mostly on education."

"Choosing grantees is rather involved," Monty said warily. "There's a whole team in charge of it. Protocols and paperwork—stuff you wouldn't be interested in."

"You're trying to tell me you have no say in the mat-ter? You never get to make a suggestion?"

"Well, of course I have a say. But it's not like I sit on a throne making decrees."

"Okay." Jake nodded, satisfied with that answer for now. He was only feeling his brother out anyway. He wasn't even sure what he was asking *for*, except to better understand this world he'd shunned for so long. From what he gathered, all Monty did was spend fam-ily money—and if the articles he read had anything to say about it, at a much faster rate than Jake did. He just had a different shopping list.

His quiet acceptance must have found favor with his brother, because Monty offered a genuine-sounding, "I guess Dad wasn't so far off after all. There's something to be said for the two of us doing this together."

"Really?"

"Really." He grimaced. "I hate this side of stuff. No matter how hard I try, I can't get past the hypocrisy of it all. We sit there and drink our hundred-year-old wine and visit our vacation homes in France, and then we impose ridiculous financial restrictions on our grant-making efforts. I know that's how it works—believe me, I *know*—but I'm not good at pretending I don't see it. And unfortunately, people like the Bridgeports can tell."

"That's supposed to put me in my place, I imagine."

"No." Monty's foot touched the brakes in surprise. "That's not what I meant at all. That's how the game is played, and *someone* has to represent that side of us. I only wish I'd thought to ask you years ago."

"It's better that you didn't. I wouldn't have accepted."

Monty paused. "But you will now?"

"I will now."

He paused even longer the second time. "Because of her?"

Jake didn't grace the question with a response. Even if he *was* in the habit of opening his heart and pouring its steaming, fecund contents all over his brother, there was no easy way to answer that question.

There was no easy answer to anything right now, so he focused instead on the familiar sights of fall settling on the Connecticut countryside. Once upon a time, he'd loved it out here, would spend hours doing normal boy-hood things like climbing trees and murdering insects with a magnifying glass. A quarry over one hillside had been a particular favorite once he'd reached the age where common sense took a backseat to his burgeoning sense of adventure.

It was difficult, now, to remember when it was he'd lost his love for this place. He'd long since replaced climbing trees with clubbing, hiking the quarry with skiing in Switzerland.

"Stop the car, Monty."

"What?" Monty slowed but didn't stop. "Look, I'm sorry about mentioning your fiancée, okay? I didn't mean it as an insult."

"Stop the car, Monty."

They rolled to a halt on the gravel side of the road. "I wasn't demeaning her or your relationship, I swear. I can see now—"

Jake made a shushing noise and peered out the window. What had seemed at first glance to be a sight of mild interest was now one that required his full focus. "Up there, at the top of the hill—do you see anything?"

"Yes, now that you mention it. It looks like some-one is yelling at a tree. Actually—" Monty shot Jake a nervous glance, "—it looks like *Rebecca* is yelling at a tree."

Jake sighed and unfolded himself from his seat. "That's what I was afraid of."

"Am I allowed to ask?"

"Unless I'm mistaken, she's got a man treed up there." And here he thought the cats were the ones who ended up in the branches. "Just cross your fingers it's not Mean Max. I don't relish the thought of getting him down."

"Do I WANT to know why there's a strange man in this tree, or should I just go get a ladder?"

Becca wasn't surprised to hear Jake's low, cool voice at her ear. He had an uncanny way of showing up exactly when he was needed, a savior in form-fitting pants. She barely blinked when he took a spot next to her, glancing up at where Greg clung to a branch, a camera swinging from his neck.

"No. No ladders." Greg shook his head, and then thought better of it as the movement caused him to swing precariously to the right. "Don't let her anywhere near me. She's gone crazy."

"I'm not crazy." In fact, she was being more than reasonable. She'd tapped four times on each wrist before she made any threats. If you asked her, things were going quite well. "All he has to do is hand over that camera and we can all go on our merry way. It's his own fault he's stuck up there."

"That seems a reasonable trade." Jake held out a hand. "You heard the lady. She'd like your camera."

"Well, she can't have it! And if I could reach my phone without falling to my death, I'd call the police. You can't corner a man and make threats. This is America."

Becca had to laugh. Greg was acting as though she'd waved a gun in his face and forced him to scale walls. He'd already been in the tree when she walked past, enjoying a moment of quiet before she headed back into the house. She wasn't sure which of them had been more surprised, but she suspected it was Greg.

"You're absolutely right. What was I thinking?" Jake gestured to Monty, who lurked a few steps behind, looking as confused as she was sure Jake felt. It was difficult not to compare the two men—and even more difficult not to realize how far superior Jake was to his elder brother. He might not have any idea what was going on, but no one watching the scene from afar would feel that Jake was in anything but complete control of himself.

"This man is in America," he said calmly. "Of course he wants to be paid for his camera. Bubbly Face, how much would you like to pay him for it? Monty rarely carries more than a few hundred at a time, so we may need to offer him a trade."

"I don't want to pay him anything, Boo Bear." She crossed her arms. "Don't you recognize who that is?"

"Should I?" Jake turned his attention back to the man, a look of concentration moving over his features as he tried to place him. "Hmm. He does look familiar."

"Pay very close attention to the scar on the forehead and that lovely scowl of his. He always wears it when he's on the job."

She knew the exact moment Jake figured it out. It wasn't so much a flash of recognition as an inferno of rage that swirled in his eyes. But as he always did, he kept his emotions in check, tightly reined, likely to cause him a heart attack well before he reached the age of fifty.

"Hello, Greg," he said, the ice in his voice giving lie to his fury. "I didn't recognize you upside down. It was nice of you to come all this way to see us, but I think it might behoove you to do as my fiancée asks. If you think *she's* crazy, I'm afraid you're in for a big surprise when you discover what I'm about to do."

"You can't have my camera!"

"So you keep saying. But I think perhaps you're underestimating how persuasive I can be when I'm feeling…shall we say annoyed?"

"Do you want me to get Alex?" Monty seemed more concerned for his brother's well-being than Greg's. "Maybe we should let security handle this."

Jake didn't look over, though Becca noted the firm set of his jaw. "Yes. That would be wise. Why don't you take Becca and head back to the house. I'm not so sure I want witnesses for this next part."

"Oh, I'm not missing this," Becca said. Not for the world. She might not mind Greg when she was at home or on vacation, where it was practically expected of him to pounce out of the bushes to catch her making a fool of herself, but out here at Montgomery Manor was a different story. Jake's family was here. Serena's *children* were here. "Just remember to be careful of his asthma."

"I'll bear it in mind." He began to slowly unclasp the watch from his wrist. "It's always nice to know a man's weaknesses before I head in."

Jake felt a strange sense of calm washing over him as he handed his watch to Becca for safekeeping. Nothing would make him happier right now than to forcibly remove this man's camera through whatever means were necessary—the more gruesome, the better.

This was his family estate. Private land. The one place where Becca should get a break from the constant vigilance of the media. *Christ*. They weren't happy sitting back and waiting for her to snap. They were practically causing her to in the first place.

"He has a backup SD card in his hip pouch," Becca said as Jake circled the base of the oak tree, looking for a foothold. He didn't recall ever climbing this particular variety before—he'd always been more of an orchard dweller, making off with fruit in exchange for his labors—but he was always willing to try new things. "I saw him slip it in there when he thought I wasn't looking."

"It will be my honor to retrieve that as well."

Jake only got as far as the lowest branch, which he used as a sort of leverage bar to get his momentum going, when he felt himself lifted from below. He glanced down, startled, to find Monty giving him a boost.

"I'd appreciate it if you didn't kill him," Monty said wryly. "If we hide any more bodies in the quarry, people are going to start asking questions."

A startled noise escaped Greg's throat.

"I'll do my best," Jake promised. "But we could always use the old mill pond if things get out of hand."

Climbing a tree was a lot like riding a bicycle, as it turned out. Jake wasn't sure he'd touched those particular muscles anytime in the past two decades, but with Monty's help, he managed to get his body up over the bottom fork of the tree with relative ease. From there, he was able to pull himself up the three branches required to reach where Greg was perched on high.

Below him, Becca broke out in enthusiastic applause. Monty, to his credit, nudged her away from the tree and positioned himself in front of her. Jake wasn't going to say he *liked* his brother yet, but he was feeling closer than he had in a long time.

Family comes first. It was an adage none of them seemed able to escape.

"You must be one hell of a dedicated photojournalist," he said as he inched his way to where Greg clung. The branch creaked with his added weight, and he paused as several of the yellowing leaves flitted to the ground. "How long have you been hiding up here?"

"I wasn't hiding." Greg's voice turned high and nasal, signaling his fear. "If you want to know the truth, she chased me up here."

He moved closer. "You fled for your life as a hundred-pound woman in high-heeled boots chased you up a twenty-foot tree? Are you absolutely sure that's the story you want to stick to?"

"Well, I wasn't on this branch. I was down on that one." He pointed at a thicker branch a few feet below, and Jake noticed his hand shook before he quickly returned his grip. "She was clearly the aggressor—and so are you. You can't attack me like this. I'm unarmed."

Right. Because the only tools a man could wield against a woman like Becca were ones forged of steel. "I'm not attacking you. I'm robbing you. If you're going to file a police report, at least do it correctly."

"He's also trespassing," Monty called up. He unclipped his cellphone from his belt and waved it. "That might have some bearing on this situation. I'd be happy to put a call in and find out. I haven't talked to Sheriff Nolte since the retirement party for his lieutenant last month. I'm sure he could sort this out in a matter of minutes."

Jake didn't bother to hide his smile. He'd forgotten how handy Monty could be in a fight. He played fair—he never played anything but fair—but he knew how to use his strengths in a way that felt anything but. As a kid, his strengths were usually his ability to tattle or to make the person caught in the act feel like shit. *Jake, if you sneak out and get caught, Linda will probably get blamed for it. Jake, if you have to pick on someone, pick on me. I can take it.* Hell, those were his strengths as an adult too.

"I want the camera and the SD card and anything else you may have snuck into that bag." Jake held out his hand, being careful not to actually touch Greg and give him any cause for complaint. There was no law against sharing a tree with a man. At least not that he knew of. "Now."

"It's not like I got anything incriminating."

"That doesn't make it okay." Jake peered over the side of the branch in an exaggerated gesture. "I can see pretty nicely down my fiancée's shirt from here. How do I know you're not snapping boob pictures to go home and upload to porn sites?"

"I'm not that kind of journalist."

"Oh, I'm sorry. I didn't mean to insult your professional integrity. My mistake."

Greg flushed. "I just wanted some family shots—you know, all of you together, a big happy celebration."

"We hire a public relations specialist for that." Jake stuck out his hand to ask for the camera one more time. As much fun as he was having getting splinters in his ass, the role of knight errant was getting tiresome. "Don't make me ask again."

Greg finally realized the precariousness of his situation, and with a cautious maneuver, he managed to get the camera unhooked from around his neck and extended toward Jake. Unfortunately, his movements were too nervous, too jerky, and the branch decided it could no longer bear their combined weight.

To the symphony of an ominous splinter and Becca's cry, Jake felt the rough pull of bark under his legs.

And then he was falling.

NINETEEN

"THIS REALLY ISN'T NECESSARY." Jake lay on the ground, his head resting firmly in Becca's lap while she picked out leaves and other debris from his hair. Despite Jake being injured, a heavy branch at their feet and Greg moaning nearby, his locks managed to capture that perfect combination of charm and windswept ease. "I can sit up."

"Yes, but your brother is afraid you might punch Greg in the face. I've been told to keep you in place, and keep you in place I will." She moved from his hair to his neck, running her fingers in a soft pattern along the tendons, lingering at his chiseled jawline. Opportunities to simply sit and enjoy this man's body were rare, and she intended to get the most out of it. His bulk was heavy but not unpleasant on her legs, and her lower half reacted to the reassuring weight of him with a familiar, pooling warmth.

She liked the sensation of a man on top of her. She especially liked the sensation of *this* man on top of her. Too bad it took a tumble from a tree to get him there. She had a feeling that life with Jake would always be like this. She'd be the one crawling on him, asking for his touch, begging for more. He'd only return the favor when he slipped and fell—something he spent every minute of every day striving to avoid.

A loud groan rose up behind her, and Jake lifted his

head enough to look at Greg sitting a few feet away, slumped against the tree trunk. Greg had softened the fall for Jake—probably the only generous act the man had performed in his entire lifetime—which meant he'd taken the brunt of the impact. She was no medical expert, but his arm was bent at an awkward angle that indicated there were some not-so-comfortable bones in there right now.

An ambulance was already on its way, and Monty had walked down to the road to greet them, leaving the three of them alone. Becca, as the only one with full mobility, had lost no time swiping the camera away and holding it safely in her lap next to Jake's head.

"I told you there weren't any bad pictures on there." Greg scowled as she scrolled through the photos, deleting with reckless abandon.

"What about this one?" She held up the screen for Greg to see. Although distance prevented him from making out the exact details, it wasn't hard to discern her shape in Jake's super-comfortable silk robe as she'd stepped out on the terrace that morning.

"I took that with a telescopic lens. I was outside the gate—fully within my legal rights."

"Uh-oh. My finger slipped. It's deleted."

Jake laughed softly and then winced. He'd stubbornly refused to let her look under his shirt, but the way he was favoring his left side indicated something had been smashed or bruised under there.

"Ew. Is this selfie porn?" She held the camera out again, this time for Jake's edification. Greg was a fairly attractive man, clearly working hard chasing down celebrities, but if that wasn't a sock shoved down the front of his briefs, she'd, well, eat that sock. "Dear God. Who were you planning on sending that to?"

Jake shielded his eyes. "Take it away, Becca. I can't defend myself here. Delete them all. Or better yet, just smash the damn thing and spare us the commentary."

"Oh, but I'm leaving the selfie. *Only* the selfie. Greg can take it to his boss with my compliments. You're still working for that Janine woman, right? I bet she'd like this one."

Greg let out a howl of protest that set her laughing, but she noticed Jake didn't share her amusement. He grew still and silent—and not, she was sure, the result of his injury. "You know the name of his boss? Just how long has this guy been chasing you?"

Becca released a chuff. "Are you kidding? Greg and I go way back." She tilted her head and examined the man. Despite the fact that his face was drawn tight against the pain and she had his livelihood in her hands—literally—she had a hard time mustering up sympathy at the sight of him. For the longest time, she'd tried to humanize her captors, a sort of Stockholm Syndrome coping mechanism. She'd brought the paparazzi camped out in front of her apartment fast food, offered them lattes, asked about families, kids, wives.

It had never worked. She knew Greg didn't like onions on his cheeseburgers. He preferred cappuccinos with extra foam and two sugars. He had no wife or kids, but he took good care of an elderly mother he feared was showing the early signs of dementia.

She knew all that, and he *still* sold a picture of her sunbathing topless on her apartment roof to the highest bidder.

"When was our first meeting, Big G?" She pretended

to think about it. "I was, what, fourteen? Fifteen? You remember—I was being harassed by that group of college guys outside the zoo."

The flash of recognition that crossed Greg's face filled her with an odd sense of buoyancy. Of course he remembered. That had been the start of a long, fruitful career for the both of them. He couldn't have been more than twenty himself at the time.

"I don't recall the specifics."

"Sure you do. You snagged a picture when the one with the backward baseball cap grabbed me and pushed me against a rock. That was some headline, wasn't it? *Clare Heiress Welcomes an Opportunity to Molest the Animals.* Tabloids used to be a lot more clever back then. I miss that."

"Hey—it looked like you were enjoying it. How was I supposed to know they weren't your friends?"

"That part where I looked you straight in the eye and called out for you to help me...that wasn't a clue?"

"They were only messing around. You were never in any real danger."

She decided to delete the selfie after all, extending the camera his direction and giving it a waggle so he knew he could have it back. Which was why it was so bizarre that it went flying out of her hand and smashed against the trunk of the tree, narrowly missing Greg's head. He flinched and ducked, but there was no amount of movement—short of flapping his broken arm and flying away—that would have saved him from the sudden figure of Jake looming over him.

She didn't know a man could move that fast after he'd fallen from a tree. She didn't know Jake could move that fast, period.

"What are you doing? Your brother said you need to stay resting until you can get checked out."

"Is it true?" Jake ignored her, holding himself stiff. His nose was inches away from Greg's, and she could tell, from the fear twisted on the other man's face, that Jake had surpassed anger and gone somewhere she wasn't sure mortals could follow. "You stood there and watched while a teenage girl—a kid—begged you to save her? You let those bastards *touch her* and lived to tell the tale?"

"It was a long time ago." Greg cast a wide-eyed, frantic look her way. She scrambled to her feet, unsure what was expected. Was she supposed to save him from Jake? *Yeah, right.* She couldn't even save herself. "I was just starting out. She was dressed in this short skirt and—"

Jake punched him. The sound was a dull thud, a slight crackle, the meeting of bones and skin. And it wasn't nearly as loud as the howl of protest Greg let out in response. His good hand flew to his nose, which bled freely as Jake pulled back his fist to do it again.

Holy shit. Jake was going to do it again.

"Slow down there, Tiger." She sprang to his side and laid a hand on his forearm. His muscles strained under her fingertips, taut and wiry and strong enough to set her pulse leaping. She couldn't tell if her reaction was adrenaline or fear or the exhilarating realization that every ounce of that strength was being used in her defense. "Take a deep breath. Tap your wrist. Look at me."

He only complied with the last one. His brilliantly blue eyes turned her way and held firm. Like fire and ice in that brief space of time where they were allowed to coexist, he burned across the spectrum, taking her with him.

"I don't think you want to hit him again," she said quietly.

His gaze only intensified. "But I do. I really, really do. What he did—"

"Sorry, Tiger, but you're about a decade too late. The damage has already been done."

"It's. Not. Too. Fucking. Late." Jake inhaled slowly, his mouth open to say more. But he settled for another vehement *fuck* before shaking himself off. "He's lucky I didn't brain him with that camera."

As if realizing how close he'd been to stepping over the edge, Jake straightened his stance and his shirt, working his fist, his movements slow as the adrenaline of the moment ebbed away to leave only pain. "Okay. Tell me. What else can be laid at his door? I want specifics."

Becca bit her lip and thought about it. Greg wasn't her only camera shadow, though he was by far her most diligent one. "I want to say he was crotch shot number one. He was definitely the graduation party in Belize that got out of control, and the rooftop tan was his most famous one to date. He was also that time I tripped on the sidewalk and broke my ankle…oh! And the hotel room with the senator's son had his signature all over it, though he chose to remain anonymous for that one. From what I understand, there were political implications."

Jake had managed to reach a dangerous level of calm. "Are there more?"

"Maybe a few," Becca lied, thinking of the number of times she'd appeared in print. "But none worth mentioning. Besides—it looks like our cavalry has arrived."

Jake followed the line of Becca's finger, where a figure dressed all in black approached. It took him two seconds to recognize Alex, his father's head of security, stalking across the grass as if approaching the front lines.

Dammit. He should have gone ahead and punched Greg a few more times while he'd had the chance. From the way Alex's face was set in a firm scowl, it was obvious all the punching would now take place in an official capacity.

"What's going on here?" Tall, muscled as hell and visibly angry, Alex made an excellent bodyguard. Even Jake admitted to a slight quiver of fear at the sight of him. "How long has this guy been hanging around the house, and why haven't I been informed of it until now?"

"From the pictures Becca deleted, it looks like he arrived a few days after we did," Jake returned as calmly as he could. "And I'm sure we would have been happy to apprise you of the fact if we'd known. He's been peeking in windows."

"*My* windows? He dared to peek in *my* windows?" Alex pushed Jake out of the way, reminding him he had some very sore ribs that required tending. As a child, falling out of trees meant a scrape and a tumble. His adult body had much less agility in the reflex department, and he'd fallen like ten sacks of potatoes lumped together. "I sure hope it was worth it, little man. I take it as a personal insult when anyone puts the Montgomery family in danger."

"No—wait." Greg shot a scared, bloody look Jake's way. With a broken arm and what looked like a similarly situated nose, there was little he could do short of rolling down the hill in hopes of escape. "It wasn't like that. I only wanted to get pictures of the happy couple. Good press. Positive coverage."

"When have you ever bothered with positive coverage?" Becca scoffed. She slid behind Jake and placed a gentle hand on his shoulder. He was still buzzing from the adrenaline, his knuckles throbbing in time to the pounding of his heartbeat, but at her slight touch, he felt his fight draining away. "Sit down already. You look like you're about to pass out."

"I'm the one who broke news of your engagement," Greg said. "That picture of you two kissing in the park. Janine loved it. They're already saying it's the story of the year."

"So you thought you could come out here and see what you could dig up on our relationship?" Jake asked angrily. Becca was tugging on his arm, causing his side to flare up in a searing pain, and also reminding him that he'd flown off the handle once already. Once was going to hurt tomorrow. Twice would probably keep him confined to bed.

"No—not at all. I want the good stuff. Kisses. Romantic walks. Okay, if I caught the pair of you in an interesting position, I might have used it. But tactfully. *Tactfully*, I swear."

An ambulance siren sounded in the distance, and Jake realized with a frown that they were going to have to bring a stretcher out to haul Greg away. It would take them at least five minutes to make it up the hill with all that equipment, and he wasn't sure he could stand here listening to this man's half-assed justifications for that long.

Chasing a grown woman through the park was bad. Taking naked pictures of one was worse. But actually standing by and watching a child—watching *Becca*—get sexually assaulted and then selling the photos for profit was up there in the ranks of fucking evil.

"I suppose I can trust you to stand guard until they get here?" Jake asked. Needlessly, as Alex had crossed his arms and was looming over Greg in a way that would make CIA torturers tremble. "I'd like to go out and meet the medics. I don't know how much more of his bullshit I can take."

"Oh, I've got this." Alex threw a wink over his shoulder. "And the fewer witnesses, the better."

"Thanks." Jake took a tentative step forward and found that although all of his limbs worked just fine, putting weight on his left half was proving to be a bit much. Without having to say a word, Becca ducked under his arm and arrayed herself at his side.

"Okay, Tiger," she teased. "Since you suck so bad at sitting still and following orders, we can go."

"I got your camera, didn't I?" he growled, but he was grateful to have her there to support him. "And what happened to Love Muffin? I like that one better."

She giggled and started leading him toward the direction of the flashing red lights, their movements slow. "You hated Love Muffin."

"I changed my mind. It's Love Muffin or nothing."

"Sure thing, Tiger."

TWENTY

"He punched the guy in the face? Just like that—and after falling out of a tree and breaking his rib?" Amy shook her head. "It's fabulous. It's so fabulous it hurts."

Becca smiled and relaxed against the leather ottoman currently providing her backrest. Curled up on the floor next to a roaring fire, hot tea in hand, chatting with one of the only people in the world who seemed to care about Jake as an actual human being—she couldn't remember the last time she'd felt so good.

Yes, I can. The day in the Artista Theatre. With Jake. The day she'd painted her living room wall. With Jake. Coffee with Jake. Dinner with Jake. Waking up with Jake.

There seemed to be a disastrous pattern emerging here.

"I don't know that *fabulous* is how he's feeling right now." Becca took a long sip of her drink to distract herself, and it worked. She didn't know what kind of magician they had working in the kitchens here, but this wasn't just tea. It was some kind of herbal manna. "I can't imagine falling out of a tree is very pleasant."

"It's not." Amy laughed. "We used to climb out there a lot as kids. Don't tell your sister, but I'm dreaming of the day I get to teach the twins how to find the best footholds."

"What was he like, growing up?" Becca shifted so

that she faced the other woman more squarely. It was
past Amy's work hours, but in light of the recent security breach, Ryan had been recruited to help examine
the rest of the grounds, so she'd decided to stick around.
"Jake is one of those men who acts like he emerged from
the womb fully dressed. It's hard for me to picture him
running around and getting messy like normal boys."

A wistful smile moved across Amy's face. "Well,
I'm four years younger than him and I wasn't as much a
part of the family as I am now, so my perception is also
pretty skewed. But he was untouchable, even back then."

"Untouchable?"

"Yeah—you know. Aloof and distant. Always in
charge." She nodded as if those adjectives were sewn
into his skin. Becca had a hard time contradicting her,
even though there was an emotional depth to Jake few
people understood. There was no question the aloof stuff
was a part of him—placed there by the universe itself—
but that wasn't what had transformed him into the man
few people dared get near. Oh, no. That was neglect,
plain and simple. If you asked her, no one had ever cared
enough to *make* him participate in his own life.

"I think I need examples," Becca said.

"Oh, I have examples," Amy replied. "He learned
early on that he could use his natural authority to get
whatever he wanted out of the downstairs staff. If being
charming didn't work, he'd do this thing where he sat
absolutely still for as long as it took for things to go his
way. Like, we all wanted this plate of Christmas tarts
one year, but they were supposed to be for some big
party of his parents'. No amount of tears would work—
and believe me, we tried. So Jake went down to the
kitchen and parked himself. He didn't say a word, didn't

make a single request, just sat there at the big table and watched Patrick—he was our cook—as he went about his work. After about forty-five minutes, Patrick caved. He was *certain* Jake was doing something sneaky when he wasn't paying attention."

"And was he?" Becca asked. That sounded exactly like something a young Jake would do.

"Nope. He didn't lift so much as a finger the entire time. Patrick gave us the entire plate of tarts and made a new batch for the party. God, that was a fun day." She laughed. "Probably detrimental in the long run, though. I think it marked the first time Jake realized he could get the most out of people by doing nothing at all."

Becca didn't have a chance to respond before Amy reached over and squeezed her hand. "Which is why it's all the more surprising that he went to such lengths to avenge you against your cameraman. I never thought I'd see the day he'd resort to physical violence over a woman."

"It's not *that* strange. You know how overprotective he gets."

"But I don't." Amy leaned over the ottoman, her eyes wide. "Tell me. Tell me all about how he gets."

Becca coughed uncomfortably and studied the milky swirls in her cup. She wished there was more to the way he treated her than overprotective urges—God, how she wished there was more—but there was no denying the realities of their situation. Their very fake, very messy situation.

"He likes how out-of-control my life is, how different it is from his own." It was the ultimate cycle of act-react-act-react. As long as Becca kept struggling, kept hurting, kept falling, Jake had a reason to hold her at night.

He could step up to play the rescuer when the situation called for it, send for Max to help her sleep, command orgasms when she got out of her mind with desire.

But that didn't mean his feelings for her were real. It didn't mean this ring around her neck was hers to keep.

She clamped her hands more firmly around her cup in an effort to keep herself from pulling the necklace out and staring at it in the firelight. "He's the kind of man who has to be needed—*really* needed—before he's moved to protect. But when he does…it's big. And it's good. And it's hard to remember how I ever survived without him."

Amy laughed. "Are you sure we're talking about the same Jake—*my* Jake, the Jake who never thinks of anyone else if he can possibly help it?"

Becca didn't feel like turning this into a joking matter. There was too much emotion moving down her throat, transforming the tea into broken glass. "You are aware you're speaking to the woman who loves him?"

"Of course he's different with you," Amy rushed, not missing Becca's tone. It was a desperate tone, a truthful tone. *The woman who loves him.* "But you have to admit—he's not exactly next in line for the Nobel Peace Prize."

"It's probably better if we change the subject now," she said tightly. She didn't feel an urge to attack Amy, which was good, but she wasn't sure if that was due more to Jake's influence or the fact that she'd just admitted to being in love with her fiancé. The fiancé who didn't love her back. The fiancé who couldn't even bring himself to have sex with her. "I don't think Jake would be very pleased if I insulted you to your face."

Amy fell into a peal of laughter and, without warning, pulled her into a hug. "You're so perfect for him I have a hard time believing you're real," she said, her words fierce, her arms even more so. "I always knew that a wife was what he needed to pull him together, but I had a hard time seeing how that could happen, given his lifestyle."

"You mean the lifestyle of going to parties and making highly public, highly regrettable mistakes?"

Amy had the decency to blush. "Well, that just goes to show. I always assumed he'd need a tough-as-nails businesswoman who could whip him into shape. Possibly with chains. Maybe with actual whips. I've never been so happy to be wrong. He worships the ground you walk on."

Becca felt herself growing flustered—not from anger this time, but from embarrassment. "*Worship* might be pushing things."

"It's not." She shook her head firmly. "And you can insult me to my face all you want for that one. I've known Jake my whole life, and I have never—*never*—seen him look at anyone the way he looks at you."

Becca knew she shouldn't ask. It would be better to leave things right there, unsaid and unfinished, safely kept behind the lines. Jake was only on loan to her. His calm presence. His ability to soothe her. The way he took over her life. The way she let him, as if her whole happiness depended on it.

She asked anyway. "How does he look at me?"

"Like he'd break through the gates of hell in order to make you happy," Amy said. "Like he'd tackle the devil himself if he dared to hurt you."

She tucked a strand of Becca's hair behind her ear and

buried her under a smile so warm, so honest, she felt she might suffocate under the affection of it.

"But what if he's the devil?" The question slipped through Becca's defenses before she could stop it. There was no way to take it back, so she let it sit there between them, wobbling like gelatin. "What if *he's* the one person in this world who can hurt me most?"

"Oh, honey." Amy sat back with a sigh. "He's always been the devil. It's why no other woman would do."

TWENTY-ONE

BEING TRAPPED IN bed with a bodily injury was the worst thing that had ever happened to him.

"What do you think you're doing?" Jake tried to scoot up against the headboard and out of Becca's reach, but there was only so far a man could go when his ribcage looked like a patchwork quilt done up in purple. "And what are you wearing?"

She looked down at herself with a start. "They're my pajamas. You told me I was not to cross this threshold without them."

"Those are very clearly *not* pajamas." Miniscule tap shorts and a billowing silk tank top weren't the sort of thing sensible women wore to bed. Not if they expected to get any actual sleeping done. "I meant flannel. Layers of it. And why are you carrying a tea tray? I have a broken rib, not the flu."

She set the tea tray—an antique set he was pretty sure no one in the family had ever used before—on the side table and sat on the edge of the bed, her form making almost no indentation on the mattress. "Poor baby. Being forced to acknowledge your own human weakness makes you cranky. How are you feeling?"

"I'm feeling like I don't trust your smile. What are you up to?"

It was bad enough being forced to stay immobile for the next twenty-four hours, ineffective and restrained.

Having a scantily clad Becca nurse him was just plain cruel. Especially since she laid a hand on his thigh, the pressure of her fingertips strong where she gripped, intent on squeezing the life out of him. *No.* She was squeezing the restraint out of him. It was like bedding down with a hungry, man-sized snake.

"You have a few choices here, my friend. I know how much you like to be in control of things, so I thought giving you options would be kinder than waltzing in here with an ambush."

Too late. He was already ambushed. He was so ambushed he could taste it.

Her hand slipped higher, moving along the muscle of his inner thigh, running perilously close to his groin. He could have stopped her with one grip of the wrist—he was injured but not *incapacitated*—but he relaxed his head against the headboard and let her have her way.

He didn't know what else to do. What had once been nobility was quickly becoming farce. The sexual push-and-pull with Becca had made sense before. He wanted but didn't take, put her well-being before his own and found satisfaction enough in leaving it there. But somewhere in the past few weeks, *her* well-being and *his* well-being had become intertwined.

He knew it. He felt it. It was branded on his soul.

"Is one of my options sexual assault?" he asked, looking carefully at her hand. A few more inches to the left, and he wasn't sure either of them would leave this room alive.

She laughed, unaware, as she always was, how fine a line she walked with him. "Yep. The idea of you being unable to fight back has had me worked up all day. What would you say to a nice, warm sponge bath for two?"

He shouldn't answer her. He shouldn't even acknowledge that she'd spoken. "I'd say you're heartless."

"Maybe." She averted her gaze and shrugged, causing the thin pink strap of her tank to slip down her arm. He indulged in one finger traveling the slope of her shoulder, under silk and over it, to put her back to rights. "But I'd be good at it. I can be thorough when it comes to the sensitive bits, and I'm not afraid to get wet."

She was goading him now. He cleared his throat, forcing his tongue to uncleave from the roof of his mouth. "So far, I count sexual assault, a sponge bath and what looks like a tea party among my options. Am I missing any?"

"No, that about covers it." She lifted her hand from his leg, allowing blood and oxygen to begin flowing again. "Although it's not a tea party I have in mind. I want to read your leaves."

"Nope. Nuh-uh. Not going to happen." Jake gauged the distance from the bed to the door, his entire side throbbing at the idea of making the attempt. He might be willing to lie here and accept her sexual overtures, but there was no way he was letting her near his future. He wasn't so sure he wanted to know what it contained. "Take your heathen beverage and go spin fortunes for Serena or Amy. They probably love that stuff."

"Suit yourself." Without waiting for him to respond, Becca got to her feet and carefully moved the strap back down her shoulder. All his hard work, all his self-control—she was swiping it away with one flick of her wrist. Her movements were designed to taunt, and as the silken material slumped to one side, he could make out the hint of her breast preparing to emerge. "I like this option better anyway."

"I haven't picked yet," he protested, his voice rough. "Maybe I was going to go with the bath option."

She reached to the other strap and ran her thumb slowly under the band. "I have to be naked for either one. These pajamas are silk. I'm not ruining them with all those bubbles. I intend to work up a *very* substantial lather."

Jake drew in a shuddering breath and closed his eyes, as if taking her out of his line of sight would make this easier. If anything, the loss of one sense only heightened the rest. He could hear the soft exhalation of her breathing, smell the herbal tea that wafted up from the bedside. And he could taste her. He could taste the salty-sweet essence of her skin, feel the way her entire body loosened under his lips and tongue.

His cock shifted, making up his mind for him.

He sat up with the full intention of making good on his baser urges. He wasn't feeling pity or protective or as if he might regret his actions later. The only thing he wanted was for Becca to know that the choice was her. For sponge bath or tea leaves, New York or Connecticut, richer or poorer—it was always her.

But his body screamed a warning. A broken rib was one of those things that always sounded minor, a useless body part that could be easily dispensed with, but the truth was the exact opposite. He couldn't even breathe without feeling the limitations of his body. Sex with Becca would bring more pain than pleasure—and he was pretty sure she'd known that well before she'd slipped in here with a silver tray containing his fate.

"Fine. You win. Read the tea leaves." When she didn't respond right away, he focused on her expression, which looked more starkly desolate than any other he'd seen on her yet. He blinked and it was gone, so quickly he wasn't sure it had been there are at all.

"Why aren't you gloating?" he asked, concerned. "It seems like you should be gloating."

"You were supposed to pick the sponge bath."

Ah. Sexual frustration. That would account for it. He knew the feeling. "If it helps, it was a pretty close run."

"But never close enough." She pulled her strap back up. Not much more of her was covered up, and despite his soreness, he felt the keen spike of desire move through him again. This was the different kind, though—the kind that sprang from her most natural actions and movements, the kind she seemed totally unaware of.

It was the much more dangerous kind.

"One of these days, I'm going to catch you by surprise and you won't be able to help yourself."

He couldn't help but smile at her casual confidence. "Big words from a small person. Want to put a wager on it?"

"Nope. If you ever give in, I'll have already won." She didn't elaborate. With a none-too-gentle push on the leg, she forced him to scoot over so she could sit. "Now—I'm using green tea, because it has some good anti-inflammatory side effects, which I figured might help with the pain."

"You're reading medicinal tea? Doesn't that mess up the results?"

"It's not a magic trick, Jake. There aren't rules."

"Fine. Pour. But you should probably know that I hate green tea. It tastes like fungus."

Becca rolled her eyes as she got their things ready, grateful for the distraction of the ritual. She'd come in here without much of a purpose, but at the sight of him leaning against the headboard, his bare torso wrapped in a white band, looking exhausted and in pain, she felt an ache in her heart that clarified things. She wanted him to choose sex with her because he couldn't go another day without it. She wanted him to choose a sponge bath because he trusted her enough to take care of him as well as he'd been taking care of her.

But all he'd done was reluctantly accept his fate. That was all she was to him.

She stifled her sigh and put a pinch of tea at the bottom of each teacup before pouring a generous amount of hot water over the top. Jake eyed the proffered cup doubtfully but accepted and took a deep drink.

"Slow down." She checked his hand. "Give it a few minutes to steep. The leaves need time to unfurl."

He didn't appear convinced. "Why is this so important to you anyway? You've been trying to get your hands on my fortunes since that first morning."

"I've been trying to get my hands lots of places," she corrected him, looking pointedly at his groin in its encased cotton pajamas. "Maybe I'm greedy."

He adjusted his position on the bed, moving his bandaged upper half with more care than usual. She hadn't seen underneath the wrap yet, but if his stiffness was any indication, he was in quite a bit of pain.

"What are you hoping you'll find? Evidence of my gilded soul? Evidence of the exact opposite?"

"It doesn't matter what information I find. It matters what you do with it." She gestured for him to go ahead and finish his tea. It was still hot, and she sipped hers carefully, watching Jake over the top of her cup. He grimaced as the last of it went down.

"There. Now what?"

"Now is when I ask if there's any specific information you seek."

His brow came up.

"About your love life, about your family, about your job. The usual stuff."

"Do I have to?" he asked with a sigh. She let the question answer itself. "Right. Sorry. Let's see…you're my love life right now, so you know how well that's going. My dad has yet to say a word to me about physically assaulting a man on our property, so the family side of things is grim. And I imagine the job situation is directly related to the family stuff. That about covers it. Life holds no mystery for me anymore. I'm done."

"Jake—humor me. Please." She tried to keep the stricken note out of her voice, but it didn't work. And she didn't dare look up for the full minute that passed, aware that he was watching her closely.

"Okay. I want to hear about the love life one."

Her eyes flew to his, startled.

"What?" he grumbled. "You said I had to pick one."

She nodded and focused her attention back on the cups. It wouldn't do to read too much into this situation. With Jake, what she saw was what she got. "Go ahead and tip it upside down on this cloth, but do it gently. You don't want to jostle the leaves too much."

"God forbid."

She set her own cup aside, determined to take a look at it later, when Jake wasn't around to witness the results. She expected to see quite a bit of heartache inside her fortune. That was what happened when you fell in love with a man who didn't love you back. Your heart ached.

"Okay," she said as soon as the tea had enough time

to drain and the leaves to settle. She flipped his cup. "Now we look."

She felt his breath still as she made her initial perusal, an action that was pretty typical as far as her readings went. For some reason, everyone seemed to expect neon lights and firm answers. When it was clear she meant to study the cup for a minute, he resumed a more normal pattern of breathing. "You see this snake right here? And don't you dare say it looks like a tea leaf. I know it does. Pretend you're a kid again, making animal shapes out of clouds."

"Sure. If we're playing the cloud game, I can see how that might be a snake."

"Okay. Well, a snake signals danger of some kind."

"My love life is in *danger?* Is it too late to change my question?"

"Yes." She tilted the cup and frowned. "A snake can also be an enemy, but that's not always the case. And this particular snake breaks up that long line of tea leaves around the rim, see? It's breaking up a journey of some kind. So your path to love is threatened by danger or an enemy."

"Well, I *did* drive all the way here from Manhattan. And that cabbie *did* almost try to run us off the road. It was touch-and-go there for a while."

She stifled her laughter, unwilling to let him derail her. "That's a pretty literal interpretation. Think along more metaphoric lines." She moved closer, feeling the warmth of his body at her side. She was unwilling to let that derail her either. "Okay, now here—those dots scattered at the handle? Those signal wealth, which makes sense, given your family circumstances."

"I suppose that's a comfort."

"But this—this is where you need to worry." She pointed at a cluster near the center. "It's shackles."

"Shackles? No way. That's a kangaroo."

"It's not a kangaroo. There's nothing remotely marsupial about it. They're definitely shackles. Chains." Her heart sank. Chains in a love life prediction would be a man like Jake's worst nightmare. "These bind you to your fate irrevocably."

"You just yelled at me for being too literal. I don't think that's a very creative reading of shackles." Jake took the cup from her hand and shook it. A few of the smaller clumps of tea moved around, but the major points stayed intact. "And I still say it's a kangaroo. What does a kangaroo mean?"

She bit her lip, thinking. "It could be one of several things. Preparing to jump an obstacle is a popular one, but some people think it signals contentment at home."

"Yep." He handed her the cup. "It's definitely a kangaroo."

She turned it clockwise. Was that a kangaroo? No. It was definitely handcuffs.

"So this is how you make life decisions?" he asked—not unkindly, but with a quiet air of contemplation. "Riches are guaranteed, but a dangerous enemy impedes my path to love. If I want to overcome the obstacle, I have to make like a kangaroo and bounce my way over it. That's it?"

"It wasn't a kangaroo."

"It *was*, and I fail to see how your way of making life decisions is better than mine."

"I didn't say it was better. I said it wasn't worse."

He narrowed his eyes and studied her. It was the kind of gaze that made it difficult to breathe, skimming over

her outside parts and zeroing in where she didn't want
him to see. "So you want me to use this as a basis for deciding what I should do next? To complete my journey?"

"I wanted you to opt for the sponge bath."

He paused, a lock of hair falling as his brow wrinkled
with concentration. She leaned close and ran her fingers
over his forehead, lingering on the worry lines, smooth-
ing them with her touch. His skin felt overheated and
alive, and she wanted to keep her movements going so
much it was a physical ache.

He held still long enough for her to complete her min-
istration. "I'm *trying* here, Becca. I know it's not easy
for you to look at me and see anything but the cruel,
overbearing son of a bitch I've always been, but I'm
trying to see things from your point of view. You have
to believe that."

She reached for the necklace. "Does that mean we
can be done pretending now?"

His jaw settled firmly, the chiseled line of his mouth
so tight it could crack. He placed a hand on hers, almost over her heart. "No. Leave it on. You promised
you would."

"You're only making it worse," she said, despairing.
"Every day that goes by, every family member we win
over, every man you chase out of a tree for me, the harder
it will be to bring this to an end."

"I'm not worried about that part." He held her hand
firm. "I can handle the family fallout. You have my word
on that. Whatever happens, this is on me, and I'll make
sure everyone knows it."

"That's not—"

"Stop arguing."

"I get a say in this. It's my life too."

"I know it is." He spoke so quietly she wasn't sure he knew it at all. "But if I were to ask you to sleep in the guest room down the hall tonight because of my injury, what would you do? How would you sleep?"

Not nearly as well—and he knew it. But that wasn't fair. He shouldn't get to hold her hostage because she'd come to see him as a glorified teddy bear. That was her fault, and she was sorry she'd let herself use Jake's attention as an alternative to working through things on her own, but the reality was clear.

Jake wasn't going to be around forever. He was being incredibly patient and kind with her, but that was only because he hadn't fixed her yet. Jake was a man who arranged his suits neatly in his closet according to cut and color. He ate his food in a clockwise rotation, starting at the top of the plate and working his way around. He loved to gamble—not because he needed the money, but because he liked to sit down and learn each person's tell, to best them in a game against themselves.

He was neat and he was careful and he didn't like it when the things in his life were disorganized. And she was disorganized. She was a hot freaking mess.

"I'm not ready to let you go yet, Becca. How about we leave it at that?" His hand lay flat against her sternum, stilling the motions of her heart slamming painfully into her chest wall.

She took a page from Jake's playbook and held herself firm, watching and waiting to see what came next. Let her be more than a project to push to perfection. Let him offer to help her because it was what he wanted, not because he thought it was what she needed. Let him promise to heal her by spending every night in her bed for the rest of her life.

Nothing came. He outwaited her.

"People are going to start being hurt by this, Jake."
People that included her. People that were *especially* her.

"Give me two weeks. Let's see this engagement party
happen, and then we'll call it off."

"Why? What's going to happen at the engagement
party? What's going to change between now and then?"

He smiled. "Apparently, I've got to find a way to demolish the snake in my path."

Oh, hell. What had she done?

"And I will demolish it, even if I have to be a kangaroo to do it."

"Will you stop with the stupid kangaroo? It was a
lump. Make-believe."

He made a soft tsking sound. "How dare you—reading tea leaves isn't a joke. Someone wise once told me
that it's all about taking reality and turning it into something more."

She took it back. She took it all back. She wasn't prepared for this reality any longer.

"Besides—I kind of like this new proactive Jake. You
wanted me to stop sitting around and waiting for other
people to do things. Well, you got your wish. I'm taking
care of this, Becca. I'm taking care of you."

Her throat hurt with a thousand unspoken words, but
she nodded and let him leave things there. It was just
a ring. And just an engagement party. And just a few
weeks. She'd withstood greater, recovered from worse,
got back up and danced in the face of so much more.

Jake wouldn't break her.

But damn, he was certainly giving it his all.

TWENTY-TWO

"EVERYBODY HOLD THAT POSE. And one, two, three."

The flash of a camera going off a few feet away set an autonomic response flowing through Becca's veins—one that warned her to run, panic, act out in ways that would give them something to talk about for months. It was a grab bag of reactions, all of them familiar in their own way.

Too bad none of them fit the scenario. As Greg repeated the command several times, holding his camera as best he could with one arm, Becca had to remind herself to smile and relax.

Right. Relax. While she was posed with the rest of the Montgomery family under a massive oak tree, all of them strategically arranged around bales of hay and dressed in the coordinated colors of fall. She had on a red sweater and jeans, and there were cowboy boots on her feet. She'd never worn cowboy boots anywhere but city streets and costume parties. The crunchy grass felt odd underfoot.

Jake had been wrangled into a sweater in a shade of deep, rustic orange, but he'd drawn the line there. "We're not the twins you're dressing up for some mommy-and-me time, Serena," he'd said. "Touch my footwear and you'll discover how difficult I can be."

"Okay. Just a few more of the happy couple, and we

should be all set. Do you think I can get you two on the horse?"

"No."

Becca smothered a laugh. Jake had been against the horse right from the start.

"How about next to it? Becca can have one foot in the stirrup while you look up at her from the ground."

"No."

"In the pasture? As backdrop?"

Jake tugged at the sleeves of his sweater, which he'd insisted were too short, and sighed. "Why do I feel as though you're purposefully antagonizing me now?"

"I'm not," Greg rushed. "Of course I'm not. Absolutely no horse shots. Got it. Let me set a few things up and we can call it a day."

Poor Greg. Becca almost felt sorry for him, jumping whenever Jake spoke, his eyes never quite still, as if he expected brimstone to start raining from the sky at any moment.

"That man isn't a very good photographer." Her mother planted herself at Becca's side as the men moved a few bales of hay around. She'd also managed to skip the cowboy boots, but she looked quaintly rustic in a close-fitting velvety brown dress, purchased specifically for today's theatrics. "I sent Serena the contact information for the woman who did the Halstead engagement photos. What was wrong with her?"

"Jake wanted Greg."

"But that's absurd. He's a nobody. What's he done?"

Becca stifled a laugh. If her mom had any idea how many Clare photographs could already be attributed to that man's name, she'd storm back up to the house and refuse to leave her room for days. She'd arrived yesterday and had already threatened to stay in her room four times. No one took her seriously. It was common knowledge her mom would gladly pack up all her life belongings and take up residence in the mother-in-law suite the second anyone asked. She loved this place even more than Serena and Becca did. These sixty acres were the Clare family weakness.

"He doesn't even have full use of his arm. Does his injury have anything to do with Jake's?"

"There might be a minor correlation," Becca lied. "There was a mishap on the grounds a few days ago. A tree branch proved unstable."

"Well, I'm just glad you two decided to do this thing up properly." Her mom turned to her and nodded once. It was a good nod, the kind that signaled approval, and Becca was moved to wrap her arms around her mother's waist and squeeze. Maybe it was all the down-home sentimentality wafting about, but she was glad to have her mom around right now. She wasn't a bad woman when all was said and done—she just had no idea what to do with a daughter like her. The rest of her brood had turned out amazingly well. "I'll admit I was a bit shocked at first, but I've always liked Jake. He's a nice boy, and he'll take good care of you."

"I love how everyone seems to think that's enough," Becca said, mostly to herself.

"What's that, sweetie?"

She sighed. "I was just wondering when taking care of me became the collective family goal. Wrap me up, hold me tight, pose me and ask me to smile."

"But Becca—don't you *want* to marry Jake?"

"Of course I do," she said quickly. Too quickly, desperate with the truth. "I share your reservations about

Greg, that's all. I wish we could have had some other photographer."

But Jake had insisted, and no amount of attempted arguments on her part would sway him. Greg, apparently, was a snake. An enemy snake. A tea snake. And since Jake was a big proponent of the keep-your-friends-close-and-your-enemies-closer school of thought, he'd decided the only way to prevent the man from hurting Becca in the future was to offer him the opportunity of a lifetime. Exclusive coverage of the Montgomery-Clare nuptials…and an ironclad contract that he'd never again so much as *look* at Becca without permission.

Greg's turncoat situation wouldn't make her nearly so annoyed if she'd thought it was a bad idea. But it wasn't. It was genius. With a single easy tug, Jake had managed to remove one of the biggest thorns in her side. She should have felt relieved and grateful and happy.

She *was* relieved and grateful and happy. But she was also devastated. This new proactive Jake had wasted no time in tackling his promise to make her okay. He was wiping out her obstacles and clearing her path. He was handing her a better life on a silver platter.

All so he could walk away, guilt-free.

From where he stood chatting with his brother, Jake paused long enough to seek her out, falling into a smile as soon as their eyes met. It was just a tiny lift of the lips, but one that lifted her heart a thousand times higher before dropping it again. Her heart didn't fare any better when Mr. Montgomery came up to shake her hand, informing her mother that Lily and Evan had requested their grandmother's help in leaping into a pile a leaves.

For all her faults as a parent, her mom made an excellent grandma. She'd deny those two kids absolutely nothing. With a fond pat on Becca's cheek, she left her standing alone with her brother-in-law/pretend future-father-in-law/one of the most powerful men on the East Coast. Oh, Lord. She defied anyone to find a situation more fucked up than hers.

She turned to face the head of the family, a man who looked no more powerful than a used-car salesman, his face lined and warm, his body a testament to countless hours behind a desk. "Well, my dear—I think we've pulled this off quite credibly." He gestured at his family with all the satisfaction of a man who knows he's worked hard and done well. "This should be a good story to sate the masses. If there's one thing they love more than scandal, it's a royal wedding."

"I hardly think Jake and I qualify as royalty."

"No? Then let's call it the next best thing. Nobility." He nodded, finalizing his argument in that one gesture. It was so much like Jake—despotism at its most refined—that Becca had to smile. They might not share the same physique, but the two men were incredibly alike. "And it's likely to stay that way now that you've granted this Greg fellow exclusive rights to the story. Exclusivity has a way of piquing interest like nothing else I've encountered in business. It was a great idea."

"Oh, it wasn't *my* idea. I'd have been happy never to see Greg again. This was all Jake."

"Really? How extraordinary. Every day with you under my roof is turning out to be a revelation." He nodded at where Greg, Monty and Jake were setting up. "It appears they'll be busy for a few minutes. Walk with me a ways? Between Jake and Serena making demands on your time, you and I haven't had a chance to talk yet."

She smiled nervously. It wasn't fair to blame Jake and

Serena for that—much of her scarcity was due to her careful avoidance of the head of household. She liked Mr. Montgomery, she really did, but he was too much like Jake. A watcher and a waiter. A man who saw almost everything.

"I'm sorry," she said as they moved along a narrow footpath leading back up to the house. "It's been kind of a busy few weeks."

"And likely to get busier. Your mother and sister don't take this wedding-planning stuff lightly, let me tell you. I think I sampled forty different kinds of cake before they finally picked one—and that was only because I threatened to go into a diabetic coma if they kept it up much longer."

"Oh, I don't know that we want to rush the wedding." It was bad enough now that they had Greg involved and formal pictures with the whole family. The second deposits started being made, she had a hard time seeing her way out of this. "We're not in a hurry."

"Of course you're not," he said cheerfully. "This one is purely selfish on my part. I'd like to see the two of you settled down sooner rather than later. You're good for him."

"You mean he's good for me."

There was that look. The watching look. The waiting look. "That too. You've both reached a kind of equilibrium as of late, wouldn't you say?"

Equilibrium was one word for it. Dependency was another. Desperation also fit.

He patted her hand gently, taking note of the ring, which she'd taken off the necklace for the photos. She had to hold it in place by clasping her thumb in her palm, but it worked well enough for the day.

"It suits you," he said, touching it lightly around the edges. "A nice, solid stone."

She glanced down at her finger, at the showy sapphire nestled among the more valuable diamonds, unsure what to say. She felt awful having it on her finger, filling Mr. Montgomery with so much hope, knowing it wasn't hers to keep.

"It *is* lovely," she eventually said.

"I saw the gem on its own once." He tucked her hand back in his arm. "I had them reinforce the setting before I married Nancy, and they asked if I wanted to hold the sapphire while they had it out. I'm glad I did. I was struck at how fragile it looked without all those diamonds protecting it."

"It's probably not the same without the fancy setting."

"No, not the same," he agreed. "But the jeweler laughed when I told him how breakable it looked. He said the only way it would shatter was if I took a hammer directly to it—and even then, it wasn't a sure thing. The diamonds only give it an illusion of strength. They set it off and, in my opinion, make it better, but they don't change the integrity of the stone. Nothing can do that."

She continued crunching her cowboy boots along the path, *really* unsure what to say this time.

"I think they're ready for you now." He pointed her back in the direction of the photo shoot. "I believe Jake is planning on taking you into New York soon to get the ring resized. I'd like for you to know you have my blessing to get it reset while you're there. No—don't argue. Just because the ring was given to you in one form doesn't mean it has to stay that way. It's yours as much as it is ours."

"I don't—"

He didn't let her interrupt, Montgomery to the core. "Keep the diamonds if you want. Wear it as a solid gem. Find a new, different look that works for you. No matter what you choose, it won't change your standing with me, you understand? You're part of the family now."

Becca was left gawping for something to say as Jake strode toward them, the extra-stiff movements of his upper half the only indication that his bones were still knitting back to health inside him.

She knew how he felt. He could try to hide the pain behind a charming smile and a careful walk, but it was there all the same. The best they could do was grin and bear it.

"Are you ready?" he asked, his crooked smile catching on her heart. "We're almost done now."

She swallowed and nodded. That was exactly what she was afraid of.

JAKE SAT IN his father's office, leaning back in the expensively leather-bound chair bearing the worn impression of an indefatigable work ethic.

It was a little beneath him to sit on the authoritarian side of the desk, but he needed all the extra confidence he could get for the interview to come. There was nothing his dad could say or do to ruin his life—he knew now that only one person had the power to do that—but he'd never before tried to talk to his dad about something this personal.

"I'll need you to help draft up the assessment, Katie," his dad's quietly firm voice said on the opposite side of the door. His personal assistant, a meek woman who would have been better off as a librarian somewhere, pushed open the door as the familiarly rotund figure of his father bustled through. "Ah, never mind. It appears I have a visitor. See that no calls come through, if you please."

Jake made a motion to rise from the chair, but his dad held up a hand. "Oh, no—stay put. You're supposed to be taking it easy. Between you, your photographer friend and about half of the downstairs staff who got talked into working out with Becca's personal trainer this morning, I feel as if we're running an infirmary."

Jake chuckled and relaxed into the chair. It *was* comfortable—his side felt much better here than it did lying on his back. "I should have warned them not to take Max up on his offer. I'm surprised there's anyone still standing to run this place."

"It'll take much more than a man named Mean Max to bring my enterprise to a halt." His dad spoke with his usual calm confidence and settled himself in the chair opposite the desk. He looked just as at home on that side, settling his hands over his stomach and blinking at Jake expectantly.

Jake's automatic response was to clamp his lips shut and outstare his dad. Outstare, outlast, outsilence. Win.

He decided to laugh instead. Becca was right. It was an annoying trait to wait and watch, refusing to make the first move. How many times had he stood in front of his dad, squirming and uncomfortable, thinking that exact thing? *If only he'd say something. If only he'd give me some indication how he's feeling.*

"I wanted to talk to you about Mom's ring," he said, refusing to play that game any longer. He'd never be *great* at opening his mouth and pouring out his feelings, but this seemed as good a place as any to start.

One of his dad's bushy eyebrows rose. "Is something

wrong with it? Did Becca say something about the setting?"

"Not exactly." Jake studied his fingernails before realizing that that, too, was an affectation of his father's. A stalling tactic, a way to make the other person uncomfortable. He forced himself to meet his eyes across the desk instead. "I wanted to know how you proposed."

"To your mother?"

Jake nodded, not trusting himself to speak. It was ridiculous to get sentimental over this. He hadn't shed a tear or spared a thought for his mom in years, was long past the age where he felt her loss as anything more than a dull ache of what might have been. And he'd certainly never cared about his parents' romance before. Like most couples in their socioeconomic circle, the reality of their relationship was much less important than the image of it—and he'd never been allowed to believe they were anything but content with one another.

"Becca seems to think it's odd that I don't know how you asked her to marry you," he said by way of explanation. It was only a small portion of his motivation, but it was the easiest to explain. "She thinks everyone deserves a good proposal story."

His dad laughed softly and settled more comfortably in his chair. "A good proposal story along the lines of stopping traffic on a bridge in the middle of the day?"

"Or something else," Jake said quickly. He was uncomfortable dwelling too long on what had—or rather, what hadn't—happened on the Whitestone Bridge. He'd meant every word he said that day. She was messy and irrational and there was no way to accept her without accepting that her life would never be normal.

But that wasn't what he needed her to know. That

wasn't why he had to get the next proposal perfect. He would get it right because it was what she deserved. He would get it right because it was what *they* deserved.

All his other decisions as of late had been easy. He'd sat down with Greg and offered him a way to start repairing some of the damages he'd wrought in Becca's life—an offer the man wisely accepted when Jake made it clear what the alternative would be. He'd also sat down with Monty and asked to learn more about the grant-making process—more specifically, how he could help select the organizations the Montgomery Foundation served. A lifetime of watching and waiting had rendered him good for almost nothing in this world, but if Becca had taught him only one thing, it was that passing judgments on other people's hard work was something he *could* do.

So there. He'd dazzle the world with checkmates that mattered for a change.

This last decision, the most important of all, had been easy to make but not so easy to put into execution. Never before had an outcome loomed so heavily. Losing this— losing Becca—wouldn't be like losing a yacht or a bet or his dignity. It would be the end of him.

"I know so little about your lives before you got married," he said, forcing himself to keep his tone level. "Growing up, you were always both so busy with your work—you never really talked about anything personal. I think I knew more about the staffs' lives than yours."

His dad lost some of his casual ease, and Jake could tell he was about to close himself off, his defensive hackles on alert. He knew, because that was what he'd do in the exact same situation.

"I'm not complaining. I'm just curious." He paused.

"If I'm asking Becca to wear that ring for the rest of her life, I think it's only natural to want to know its history."

His dad jerked out of his seat and grabbed the brandy on the sideboard, pouring himself a liberal two fingers. Since it was rare for his dad to drink before five o'clock—and even rarer for him to drink under any but the most comfortable social or business circumstances, Jake felt a jolt of alarm. "Is it *bad?*"

He didn't get an immediate answer, which meant *bad* barely even began to cover it. Great. He'd given Becca a cursed ring and forced her to keep it on at all times. No wonder things were so unsettled between them, why he felt as if one wrong step would have her closing the door in his face without a chance to outline all his reasons why they should make their engagement real.

"We were lucky in those days that the media wasn't as involved in our lives," his dad said, doing little to ease Jake's mind. "I honestly don't know how your mother and I would have fared if we had to deal with the same issues you and Becca have ahead of you."

"Somehow, I have a hard time imagining cameramen chasing Mom around in hopes of a strong wind."

His dad took a long, bobbing drink. This VSOP wasn't the cheap stuff, so the fact that he was swilling it like ale was pretty telling. "Don't be so sure. Oh, I know she'd settled down by the time you kids were old enough to remember her, but there were a few years there…" He paused, smiling tightly, before changing the subject. "Do you know why I froze your accounts?"

Jake frowned at the sudden shift. He hadn't come here to talk finances. He wanted to talk love. "Because I've made no positive contributions to society and you were tired of footing the bill for it?" he asked, hoping bluntness would help them move on more quickly. "I'm not stupid, Dad. I know what you think of me."

"No. You don't know what I think."

"I have a few ideas."

"You *don't*." He set his glass down with a start. "I'm not blaming you, Jake. It's my fault. I know that. I wasn't there for you kids when you were young, and I've made few efforts to change things since then. But you have to understand—most of your childhood years were spent building the company up, and it was always so hard to pull myself away from work. By the time your mother passed away and I realized how far away from me you all were, it was too late. The damage was done, and most of it to you. Monty and Jenna were always able to demand at least some of my time—Monty because he put in long work hours beside me before he began talking; Jenna because she doesn't let anyone stop her from doing or having what she wants—but you. *You*."

The profligate sheep swathed in black. The monkey in the middle.

"You were so much like me it was painful to watch. It still is sometimes."

Jake paused, waiting for the punch line, but there wasn't one. This was the joke that never ended.

His dad's shoulders sagged, as if suddenly tired of holding the world in place. "The day I proposed to your mother was the worst day of my life."

Jake shot to his feet. "What?"

He had the audacity to chuckle. "Sit back down. You're going to make your rib worse. I don't mean it was literally the worst day of my life. But at the time, I thought it was."

Jake sat. There was no way he could walk out after a confession like that.

His dad looked at him carefully. "It's not something many people know, but there was a baby before Monty. A baby we never got a chance to meet, and one neither of us particularly wanted in the first place."

"You mean—"

"Yes. That's exactly what I mean. It wasn't so easy to get away with that sort of thing back then. We were young and reckless and thought nothing could touch us—and for a long time, nothing did. But it all came to a crashing halt with this baby, this supposed miracle of life. It was either get married or face your Grandfather Hawthorne's wrath. I proposed to your mother out in the formal garden where no one would hear her scream. She cried for three hours."

Jake thought of his maternal grandparent, long since gone but a man he remembered as so stern no one knew for sure if he had lips under his mustache, and held back a shudder. That was not the sort of man whose daughter you knocked up and walked away from. That was the sort of man whose daughter you took advantage of and then burdened with a ring she didn't want. A marriage she didn't want. A life she didn't want.

Christ. It was more than a cursed ring. They were a cursed family.

"So you never even loved her?" Jake asked, his voice a scooped-out hollow. "She never loved you?"

"Not at first, no. And don't look so stricken. We went on to have an eighteen-year marriage and three perfectly healthy children. I like to think we worked a few things out."

"I don't understand. What does this have to do with my financial status?"

His dad ran his finger around the edge of his glass. "More than you think. Before I got married, I was a lot like you. Oh, I was never as good-looking as you are, and I certainly never reached your level of—ah, notoriety, shall we call it? But I had my fair share of escapades. I even took to sailing for a while. There's something about the wide expanse of the ocean that frees a man, isn't there?"

Jake only nodded, worried lest his father veer too far off point. Or ask to go with him next time he took his yacht out. It was a small yacht. There was one stateroom. And getting Becca her sea legs would take every ounce of concentration he had.

"What I'm trying to say is that it took the responsibility of a wife and impending fatherhood to finally settle me down. I was considerably younger than you are now, but it was the kick I needed to put my life in order. Since I wasn't aware of your, ah, long-standing relationship with Becca, it seemed to me that marriage was out of the question for you. And I could hardly force you to care about a business you've always disliked. So I did the only thing I could think of to thrust you into the same kind of responsibility."

"You took away my independence."

"Hardly. I never had any doubt you'd do anything but land on your feet. I just took away the cushion at the end of your fall."

Jake let his father's meaning settle, hoping that in doing so, he'd see a clearer way to the finish line. But as everything came into focus, he found himself more confused than before. Was his father encouraging him to marry Becca—forcing her into it if he had to—because a marriage of convenience had worked for him? Or was he telling Jake to let her go?

"Do you regret it?" he asked suddenly. "Marrying Mom?"

"No," he said after a thoughtful pause. Jake appreciated that he didn't lie or rush to reassure him. "We were content together, and I could never regret having you and Monty and Jenna. But I think I could have been happier. I think *we* could have been happier. When I found myself faced with a pregnant wife and then a not-pregnant wife and then an emotionally devastated wife, I threw myself into work. All this—these four walls, the long hours away, the business trips that never seemed to end—was my way of coping with a woman I didn't really understand. A not very great way of coping, as it turned out."

"I had no idea."

"Of course you didn't. That's the way I wanted it, so that's the way it was." *Ah.* There was the father he recognized. Jake felt much more comfortable with the megalomaniac than the man. "But that's also why I'm so glad you have Becca. Not because I think you need a wife, necessarily, but because I can tell you won't be repeating my mistakes."

Jake felt himself stiffen. "I'm not so sure about that."

"But I *am* sure," the megalomaniac said. "For one, I don't see you becoming a workaholic anytime in the near future."

Jake choked on a startled laugh. "I'm glad to find your expectations remain realistic."

"I'm not displeased with the way things have turned out. Do your part to help Monty, carve yourself a niche, and keep up the high profile, and I'll be more than happy with your contribution. Did you know our shares have gone up fifty points since you and Becca got engaged? They're predicting twice that once the wedding actually goes through. Don't you dare mention this to Monty, but having an infamous scoundrel like you for a son has done more for the hotels than anything he'll ever accomplish. We paid for the new Paris facility with the affair you had with that shoe designer in Milan."

Jake veered toward outrage—he'd gotten hell from Monty for the bad publicity on that one—but it hardly seemed worth the effort now. "You mean my primary function in this family is to create scandals?"

"You don't have to sound so offended. It's not as if you aren't any good at it."

"Thank you?"

"And of course I suspected you were just toying with your brother when I heard of your engagement, but after seeing you and Becca together, I know you're making the right choice. Asking that woman to marry you was the smartest thing you've ever done." His dad flashed a rare grin and picked up his glass of brandy again, holding it up in a toast. "Or it will be, once you gather up the nerve to actually do it."

Jake was too exhausted to show his surprise. "Isn't there anything that goes on in this family you don't already know about?"

"Of course not." He preened, a peacock showing his feathers. "Just make sure you don't screw it up, will you? I'm not sure I care to live under the same roof as Serena and Moira with a canceled wedding hanging over our heads."

TWENTY-THREE

"I PROMISE TO make it quick and painless. You'll barely know I'm in there."

Becca laughed as she got out of the sports car, helped along by Jake's waiting hand. He was opening doors for her now—this was how far into farce they'd gone. The man could barely walk, shouldn't have been driving, refused to take any painkillers that might put him at a slight disadvantage, but he still made her sit in the passenger seat while he pulled open her door and went through all the steps of a regular courtship.

"I bet you say that to all the girls."

"Only the ones who are skittish."

She planted her feet on the sidewalk. "I'm not skittish. I'm annoyed. I told you from the start how much I dislike this idea." They stood between Jake's highly illegal parking spot and a blithely understated storefront. The jeweler they were visiting was housed in a nondescript brick building in an out-of-the-way location, one of those companies that had been in place since the nineteenth century and had no intention of changing to suit the modern era. Of course the Montgomerys wouldn't do things the normal way with Cartier or Asprey, the whole flash and bang.

Somehow, this age-old family establishment made things even worse. She had almost talked herself up to striding through the doors of Tiffany's and listening to a carefully blasé sales clerk talk about platinum settings and diamond quality. But this? A sweet old man with an eyepiece, a close-walled room where every Montgomery bride-to-be for the past century had sat and made plans for the future?

Nope. She wasn't doing it.

"What time do they close?" she asked, taking a large step back.

"They don't."

"I'm serious, Jake." She grabbed his wrist and glanced at his watch. "It's ten o'clock now. If they close at six, that'll give me eight hours to enjoy what remains of my conscience before I destroy your family legacy. Would you mind? Just a normal day in the city? No weddings, no families, no anything?"

He held perfectly still as he looked down at her. "They don't close at six."

"Okay, five then. Or seven. Whatever. Please?"

"Piers will stay open as late as I ask him to, even if it's the middle of the night." He twitched his fingers, as if he wanted to make a move toward her. But as always, he held firm. "How many hours do you need to be okay with this?"

A hundred. A thousand. Not even one. "What time would he close if you were a normal human being who didn't get to command the world at your leisure?"

His lips relaxed in a smile. "I believe his sign says eight."

Ten hours. That was even better. A lot could happen in ten hours. She might even be able to persuade the most stubborn man on the face of the planet that vandalizing his family heirloom wasn't in her life plan. "Okay. What if I promise, absolutely pinky swear, that we'll come back and take care of the ring at eight? Can we forget our deal exists until then?"

He wanted to argue with her, she could tell. He always got this combined look of exasperation and amusement, as if he wanted to put his imperious foot down but knew, deep inside, that he'd have a lot more fun if he didn't.

"I guess it doesn't matter if we drop the ring off now or in a few hours." He looked a warning at her. "As long as it gets done."

"When I make a promise, I keep it." Which was part of this whole problem. She'd promised to wear his stupid ring. She'd promised to let him dissolve this on his own terms. *This is the last time I make a deal with the devil.*

"Shall we shake on it?" He turned his wrist and slipped his hand in hers. Firm and cool, he waited for her to make the first upward motion. And then he didn't let go. He held her hand in a gesture that was more authoritarian than romantic, but which made her pulse leap all the same. "The day is yours to command. Where do you want to go?"

She made the sound of a buzzer. "Wrong question. I never thought I'd say this, but I'm exhausted with everything being about me. If you do one more unselfish thing to try and make my life better, I'm going to kick you in the ribs."

Jake released a startled laugh, wincing as it shook his side. He'd done a fairly good job so far of stifling laughter and rage and all other emotions in the name of pain management, but Becca had a way of catching him off guard. "I don't think anyone has ever accused me of being not selfish enough before. I thought you hated my perfectionist Virgo tyranny?"

"I *do*." Becca's fingers slipped casually through his,

forcing their hands into a more natural embrace. He stared down at where their palms touched, curious at how comfortable it felt. He wasn't sure he'd ever stood on the sidewalk and held hands with a woman before. "And despite my better judgment, I'm holding out for the day you realize that asking me what I want is more effective than telling me. But today we're doing what *you* want."

"That's easy." He tugged her in the direction of the jeweler's bright red door. "I want to go in there and fit your ring."

"Anything but that. Did you miss the whole first part of our conversation?"

If he weren't still injured, he'd be sorely tempted to lift her over his shoulder and haul her into the jeweler's despite her protests. Okay, so it wasn't the most romantic of gestures—some might even call it barbaric—but he didn't think he'd be able to relax until he knew Piers was in there working his magic. He could be romantic afterward. He could be selfish or unselfish or whatever Becca wanted.

If only she'd fucking *relent*. They might joke about his tyrannical qualities until the sun came down, but the truth was that she commanded his every movement, his every thought, his every desire. There wasn't a thing in this world he wouldn't do for her. This was no engagement of convenience. This was no relationship built on obligation. He wanted Becca so much he couldn't think of a single thing he wouldn't do to have her.

"Where should we go first?" she asked, smiling up at him. She'd dressed for a day on her feet, comfortable in leggings and flat boots that slouched around her ankles. Her hair was knotted casually over one shoulder, her smile lighting her eyes from within. It was difficult to remember how he'd ever thought this woman was just another pretty face in the crowd.

Rebecca Clare wasn't *just* anything. Those laughing eyes could as easily fill with pain as joy. Those sweet features hid a core of steel no amount of his might could bend. The trusting way her body molded to his at night made him feel alive and strong and so unworthy of her it was absurd.

"Pretend you can travel back in time to a few months ago," she said when he didn't respond. "You just got to New York. Your pockets are full of money. Your favorite sports car is parked at an awkward angle and is ready for you to take it anywhere. Your sole task is to enjoy yourself. What does a day in the life of Jake Montgomery look like?"

He considered her question carefully. Too carefully and too long, the moment stretching well past thoughtfulness into shame.

"Uh-oh. Is it one of those things you don't want a clingy, prone-to-seasickness fiancée to do with you? Does it involve bevvies of supermodels and international travel and yachts? Maybe I can take some Dramamine or make myself scarce."

"No." He frowned, his brow feeling heavy. "No, that's not it at all."

"Do you want to get a manicure and shop for shoes? Is it worse? A pedicure and underwear?" When he still didn't respond, she tightened her hold on his hand. "Hey—why so serious? This is supposed to be fun."

"Empty."

"What?"

"Empty," he repeated firmly. "That's what a day in my life looked like a few months ago. If we turned back the hands of time and filled my pockets with money, I can tell you exactly what I'd do. I'd go nowhere important, see no one who mattered, do nothing that made an impact on anyone else's life."

"That's not true. You impact lots of people's lives. You're always out doing something."

"Oh, I might play a round of golf if someone needs a fourth to make up their numbers. Go out to a club if someone wants to get noticed and invites me along. Stop by one of my dad's hotels to run up a bill and make sure he knows I still exist."

That wasn't a life. That was a sad and lonely man passing the time until he died.

He didn't glance down at Becca, even though he could feel her gaze searing into his profile. He didn't want her pity. He didn't want her to smile and tell him it was okay. A man who'd wasted as much of his life as he had didn't deserve pity. And it wasn't okay.

That kind of life wasn't okay with him at all.

"Time travel in the other direction then." Her words were calm, containing nothing but warmth. "Let's fast forward a few months. You still have pockets full of money. You still have your tiny, overcompensating car—which, by the way, is about to get a ticket—and a full day in New York. For the first time in weeks, you're blissfully free of wedding plans and family obligations and Monty making you be nice to the people he sucks at pretending to like. What do you do?"

His first instinct was to go over there and talk his way out of a parking ticket, but he found he didn't care to divert his attention right now. He liked the picture Becca was painting too much. The painting was crowded—none of that watery Monet stuff—bursting instead with the vibrant red of her apartment wall. His family. His job. His fiancée dragging him away for a much-needed break.

His life could be full. If he let it. If she let him.

"I think I'd go see a show," he said.

"I like the sound of that. What show are we going to see?"

"I don't know. What is the Artista Theatre playing today?"

Her laughter filled the air, causing the scowling cop to look up from the task of writing what was probably going to amount to a several-hundred-dollar fine. "You're cheating. You only want to go to the Artista because you think it's what I want to do."

"Wrong," he said. He left the cop and the car, taking Becca by the arm instead as they moved away from the jeweler and in the direction of East Harlem. "I want to go there because I have fond memories of getting drunk below the stage with an infuriatingly careless woman who has a sentimental attachment to it. And because the acting is exceptional."

"Okay, we can go to the Artista," she said, her pace matching his. "But you better start thinking about what you want to do afterward, because we're doing something *you* actually want. Something I've never done before."

"Well, that'll be easy. I'll just think of all the activities a sane, sedate woman might do on a trip to the city. I doubt you've ever gone anywhere near those."

"THIS IS MY APARTMENT." Becca stood in her living room, twirling slowly as if expecting surprises to pop out of every corner. "I hate to break it to you, but I've already done pretty much everything a woman can physically do in here."

"Oh, really?" Jake couldn't keep a note of interest from out of his voice. Two hours of sitting next to her in a dark theater, watching what had to be the worst modern-day retelling of *Don Quixote* ever made, and his *interest* was very much at the forefront of his mind. His interest wanted to kiss her until words stopped making sense. His interest wanted to ask her for another strip-tease in front of the red wall. His interest wanted to rip her leggings off with his teeth.

He settled instead for a casually inflected, "Define what you mean by *everything*, if you please. In detail. With hand gestures."

"I mean there's no position ignored, no lingerie untorn, no hole unplundered."

He almost choked on his surprise. He'd been spending so much time trying *not* to think about sex with Becca that he'd forgotten how wonderfully depraved this woman could be.

"Do you still want hand gestures?" she asked sweetly.

"No, thank you. I changed my mind."

"I thought you might." She paused, frowning. "Seriously though—are we stopping here to pick something up? Because I know your idea of a good time isn't sitting at home watching television."

"I have it on good authority that there is *one* thing you've never done in here before. Something messy. Something fulfilling. Something delicious." He took a predatory step forward, and she licked her lips in response. Dipping his head to the side of her neck, he lowered his voice to a whisper. "You've never cooked dinner in your kitchen."

She squealed in outrage as he pulled away—and not a moment too soon. A few more seconds in that intoxicating space below her ear, and food would be the last thing going in either of their mouths. "You bastard. It'll never work. I don't have any food in there."

"Good thing I texted Liam and had him pick up a few supplies for us while we were at the Artista."

"You did? Really?" She caught herself in the middle of an excited clap and sobered. "Nice try, but this can't be your big plan. Cooking for me can't be the last thing you do before we head back to the jewelry store."

"Why not?" He unbuttoned the cuff of his shirt sleeve and began rolling the fabric up. "We have to eat. You said it had to be something you've never done before. And I can't think of anything I'd rather do than spend time with you."

"Jake." Her voice was strangled.

"Becca." His, on the contrary, had never been more calm. "You told me to fast-forward sixty days into the future and create my perfect day. Well, here I am. A few months older, a few months wiser and ready to tackle a shrimp scampi."

"But you said we only had to do this a little bit longer. You said you'd have everything settled by then."

"I did, and I will."

"So you and I..."

"Are going to cook dinner," he said firmly. He knew that wasn't the question Becca was asking, but he also knew that the wild-eyed look in her eyes was composed of equal parts desperation and fear. It was her trapped-animal look, the look that made him want to tuck her away in a cave where he could stand guard and protect her from the world.

There was no doubt in his mind—if he told her right now he had no intention of dissolving their relationship either in a week or in a decade, there was a very real possibility he'd be returning to Montgomery Manor alone. She wasn't ready yet. She needed more time to get used to the idea. And he'd promised her that day on the bridge that the next time he proposed, he'd get it right.

He would. He'd get it right. He'd get it so right there'd be no way for her to say no.

"I suppose I *am* hungry."

"That's a good girl." He wouldn't acknowledge how relieved her words made him feel, as if the tight band around his heart was loosened enough to let him live for one more day. "I should probably add the caveat that this is the one and only dish I know how to make. I don't want you to get your hopes up, thinking you're engaged to some kind of kitchen mastermind."

"And here I was planning on chaining you to the stove for the rest of your life." Becca followed Jake into the kitchen, admiring the easy way he finished rolling up his sleeves and rummaged around in the paper bags that Liam had dropped off earlier. One look at him, and you'd think he'd been living in her apartment forever, cooking dinner and making her feel like the only woman in the world. "Shrimp scampi seems awfully complicated if you're only going to learn how to cook one dish. Why not cereal? Or toast?"

"This is my seduction meal. No woman is impressed with toast."

"I'd be impressed with toast," she said.

Who was she kidding? She'd be impressed if he pulled out a slice of bread and started tearing off pieces to throw at her. Everything about this day was perfect—

the wind-whipped drive in, the amazing afternoon at the theater, the domineering way he took up the reins of domesticity. With Jake, even dinner was a carefully contrived experiment in control. He decided what they would eat and where they would eat and even how the meal would make its way onto her plate.

She hated that about him. She also loved that about him, and she desperately wished she knew which sentiment was stronger. Right now, love was winning. Love had pulled miles ahead and showed no signs of flagging.

He pulled out an enormous block of butter and handed it to her. "Yes, but I think we've already determined your standards are notoriously low."

"That's where you're wrong. My standards are incredibly high." Becca tossed the butter to the side. For most of her life, she'd been good at listening when the universe spoke. She read the stars and adjusted her actions accordingly. She never defied predictions or tamped down that niggling feeling in her gut when she felt something was wrong. But ever since the day Jake Montgomery sauntered into her life, she'd done nothing but ignore the signs.

Madame Pernaud had warned her against digging in too deep with a relationship, but she'd grabbed a shovel and dug anyway. Madame Pernaud told her to confront Jake weeks ago, but that breathless proposal on the bridge had knocked the reason right out of her.

She was about to do it again. Despite the rapid-fire beat of her pulse, which screamed at her to run away as fast and as far as her feet could take her, she was about to let this man cook her dinner in her own home, to give in to feelings that scared the absolute shit out of her. She was about to give in *so freaking hard.*

And she couldn't even find it in her to care.

"What are you doing, Becca? Stay where you are."

"I can't be seduced with a fancy meal, but I might fall prey to a tall, tyrannical scrap of a man. The taller and more tyrannical, the better."

He stepped back, wielding a package of linguine at her like a lance. "But I haven't started cooking yet."

"I don't want your stupid food, Jake. I want you."

"But this wasn't part of my plan—"

"Drop the pasta." She trapped him against the counter, pinning him with her proximity. No part of her body touched his, but she was close enough to feel the power rising off his perfectly rigid form. "You can cook me dinner later. You can cook me eight dinners later, and even stand over my chair watching to make sure I eat every bite. I'll probably need the protein."

The package fell to the ground, shards of dried pasta scattering from the point of impact. "Becca, I can't—"

"Yes, well *I* can." She brought her hands up to his chest, settling them firmly over his heartbeat. It was regular and strong, though pounding hard enough to set her fingers tingling. "And if you're having problems on your side of things, I think that might be something we need to have looked at."

"You know that's not the case," he growled, still not moving.

"Do I? I haven't seen any evidence so far."

"I know what you're doing," he said. "I know you're trying to get me to react."

She didn't care if he knew it. She didn't care if the whole world knew it.

Apparently, neither did he. His heart gave one giant leap under her fingertips before she felt the back of her neck being pulled roughly forward, forced to meet his lips in a searing kiss.

It was the kiss she'd been waiting for. It wasn't a teasing, playful promise of things to come. It wasn't the rough, angry tangle of tongues a man driven to the limit might be expected to offer. It wasn't even one of Jake's carefully controlled kisses, intensifying along a perfect incline to maximize her pleasure.

It was honest and real and hot in ways she never knew existed. He fought at first—against himself and against her—but when he opened his mouth to let her in, he let *all* of her in. His grip on her neck grew stronger, crushing her to him. She tried to be careful of his side, but his hold on her was too powerful and she inadvertently slammed the sorest part of him.

He groaned into her mouth as the kiss fell sharply away.

"I'm sorry," she said with a wince, seeing the pain he struggled to hide on his face. "I was trying to be careful."

"I wasn't." His lips lifted in a smile. "Which is why maybe you should let me cook instead."

"No." She took him by the hand and tugged. "This is maybe why you should let me take care of you for a change."

He didn't want to move at first, but when she pulled hard enough to cause another flash of pain to cross his face, he complied. She moved insistently toward the direction of her bedroom, which was clean for probably the first time in years, since she'd been living elsewhere for the past few weeks.

He stopped in the doorway, propping his arm on the frame to keep her from budging him another inch.

"Tempting though the offer is, I'd rather wait until we can do this properly."

"I know. That's why we're doing it now." She didn't look over her shoulder as she pulled back the comforter. Crisp sheets awaited a man to muss them up. "Take off your clothes and get your beaten-up ass on the bed."

"That's the least sexy command I've ever received," he said, eyebrows lifted. "You could at least take off your shirt first."

"I swear to God, if you don't let me do this my way, I'm not coming back to the Manor with you."

It didn't seem possible, but his brows came up even higher at that. "Are you giving me a sex ultimatum?"

"I'm giving you a regular ultimatum. I get it, Jake, I really do. You like to be in charge. You want to throw me to the bed and rock me seventeen different ways. You want to make me dinner and lock me in an ivory tower and slay my dragons." She smiled sadly. "I'm not against the idea of an ivory tower, mind you, but I need to know that you can let me down sometimes. I need to know you're physically and emotionally capable of allowing me to have my turn."

They stared at each other for a full minute, neither one of them blinking or backing down. She would have liked to think that she was matching him alpha for alpha, stubbornness for stubbornness, but the truth was that she felt trapped in his gaze, pinned in place by the natural authority he would never be able to shed.

And that was okay. She could accept that Jake would never be able to fully let go, that the stars overseeing his birth decreed his path to be one of eternal struggle for supremacy. But she needed to know that he could set it aside when she asked. She needed to know that even though it pained him, he could allow her to have her way when it mattered.

It mattered right now. If she was going to take a risk on him—if she was going to throw all of her better judgment and life experiences out the window and trust him with her heart, even if it was only for a few days—he needed to get on that bed and prove he was capable of trusting her to lead the way.

He blew out a long breath, and his shoulders came down a fraction of an inch. Not much, but enough to signal she was making headway. "This isn't about sex, is it?" he asked.

"Not even remotely."

He nodded once and pushed off from the doorframe, preparing to divest himself of his slacks as he did. His movements were efficient as he undid the button at his hips and tugged on the zipper. One wouldn't think, to note the casual way in which he pulled the material down, that he was the least bit interested in relations of a carnal sort. But as he stepped out of the pants and began carefully working the buttons of his shirt, it was clear to Becca there was a stiffness to his movements that had nothing to do with his injury, a hitch in his breath that made her heart skip several beats.

She stepped forward to help him out of his undershirt. She let her fingers skim the warm expanse of his stomach, flat from midnight marathons and tanned from a summer of indolence. Those qualities mattered much less to her than the way his skin rippled under her touch, his body unable to suppress the longing he felt—if not for her, then for what they were about to do.

"If I hurt you, you have to say so." She lifted the shirt over his head, pausing as she took in the line of deep purple ringed in the yellow of a fading bruise. Moving slowly enough that he couldn't mistake her intention, she leaned in and kissed along the edge, her lips gentle where they landed.

"Do I need a safe word?" he asked, amusement alongside desire in his voice.

"No. A simple *ouch* will suffice." She stepped back and admired the man standing in front of her. He was naked save for his form-fitting boxer briefs, which slung low on his hips and molded to his lean, muscular build. There wasn't an inch of fat on him that didn't belong, his muscles unfolded along every limb so that he was a marvel of well-maintained architecture, an Eiffel Tower of human form.

And to make matters even more unfair, the bruise only added to his appeal, a slash of color and imperfection on an otherwise flawless body. She tilted her head, considering him. "Do you know, I've never seen you naked before? I've seen all the parts, but not at the same time."

"If those are the qualifications for nudity, then I haven't technically seen you naked either." His glance told her he wouldn't mind rectifying that situation.

"Oh, you will. But you have to get on the bed first. And finish stripping."

"Your wish is my command." He whisked off his briefs and moved toward the bed before she could do much more than gape at him. Semi-erect, his interest stirred but not overtaking him, Jake's cock was some kind of miracle. So too was the fact that there wasn't an ounce of modesty in him as he settled himself on the mattress and crossed his legs at the ankle.

"Will it hurt you to put your hands behind your head and hold them there?" she asked.

Jake considered Becca's question carefully. "Do you mean will it cause me physical pain, or will I pout and throw a fit?"

She laughed and licked her lips as she approached the bed. "The first one. You can pout all you want, but it won't change my mind."

No—he could see that. There was a determination to her words and actions that had every single one of his nerve endings on alert. Danger, wariness, pleasure— they were all there, spiking his blood and stirring his interest.

"I can handle it," he said, and lifted his arms to prove that he could do as she asked.

His side protested only slightly as he linked his fingers behind his head and rested against the headboard. Stretched but not beyond endurance, the pain was an almost welcome sensation. At least it gave him something other than the pounding, demanding coil of need that was making itself known between his legs.

"Good." She smiled—that catlike smile, the one he knew belonged to neither tiger nor kitten, but to her and her alone. "Keep them there. No matter what I do, you aren't to move them. Understand?"

He narrowed his eyes. That was asking quite a lot. He wasn't a man who played well on the sidelines. Especially not when all he wanted to do was cover her body with his and find a thousand ways to pleasure her. "You aren't going to go to the kitchen and try to cook without me, are you?"

"No, Jake." She slipped off her boots. "I'm not leaving this room until we're both satisfied."

There was nothing for him to do but watch as she stripped off the rest of her clothes. In true Becca fashion, she didn't bother making it a show. This was a serviceable removal of her clothes, an action to reduce the number of barriers between them and nothing more.

He could have watched her for hours, not touching, not thinking, just admiring this woman he intended to keep forever. But when she was down to nothing but a pair of floral-sprigged panties and a bra, she made a move for the necklace that hung around her neck.

He sat up. "What are you—"

"Hands behind your head." She spoke with a severity he'd never heard from her before. A rising panic filled his throat as he realized she meant to take it off and tuck it in the drawer beside her bed. He knew this moment was important, that what she was asking of him was more than a physical release, but he couldn't help but feel tricked. What if this was nothing more than an elaborate ploy to avoid getting the ring resized? What if she meant to take it off and never put it back on, using sex as a pretext?

And what if he'd fallen for it?

"This wasn't part of the deal," he said desperately. "I like the way it looks on you."

"Good thing this isn't about you. It's about me. It's about *us*."

She slammed the drawer shut, her movements jerky as she climbed onto the bed and on top of him. He would have been lying if he said the sight of her, angry as she straddled his legs, didn't fire his blood. That was the tiger he'd fallen in love with. That was the tiger he never wanted to lose.

"If I want to take off that ring, I'm going to take off

that ring. And you can glare all you want, but it's not going to change the fact that *I* decide when I want to wear it."

"Yes, ma'am," he said quickly.

She flicked the clasp of her bra open and shrugged out of it, unleashing the full power of her sex-starved nipples, pulled tight against the waiting air. "And if I want to touch your cock, I'm going to touch your cock without waiting for you to demand it."

"Oh, fuck."

There was no mercy in her grasp as she pulled the most sensitive part of his body like it was a stick shift. Long neglected and desperate for her touch, his erection felt as if it might burst under her cruelty.

She leaned forward, her mouth hovering over his own. "And if I want to kiss you, that's exactly what I'm going to do. I like the way you kiss, but I like the way *I* kiss too."

He allowed his lips to fall open as she teased herself forward, her hands not stopping their relentless up and down movement on his cock, her nipples just brushing his chest, sending jolts of awareness through him.

Her lips touched his briefly before pulling away again, teasing and taunting. If she was trying to prove that she was the one who could command the pace of their lovemaking, she'd more than succeeded—and for naught. He could have told her weeks ago that the sight of her smile alone was enough to have him falling to the ground in thanks.

He wasn't in any physical pain as she lifted herself up on her knees and reached back into the drawer, this time to extricate a packet of condoms. But he felt the strain of keeping his hands behind his head in ways that were foreign to him. It would have been easier if she'd restrained him, if she'd pulled out a playful set of handcuffs or used a pair of silk stockings to secure each hand. At least then there'd be a physical force holding him in place. His passive acceptance would be less of a choice and more of a game.

As it was, he had to bite on the tip of his tongue to stop himself from running his hands all over Becca's body. He wanted to take her breasts in hand, feel her nipples harden under his thumbs, rock her hips over his until their bodies fit perfectly together.

"Hard, isn't it?" she said, laughing. She tore the condom package open using her teeth as leverage, that gleam of pearly white so ruthless as to elicit a groan from him. "I'm surprised you've made it this far, to be honest."

"I'm stronger than I look."

She stopped her movements, hands suspended in midair, condom dangling to one side. "So am I, Jake. That's the one thing you've never been able to understand."

Before he could ask what she meant by that, she brought the condom to his tip. Without gentling her actions in the slightest, she rolled the latex over the length of his cock, rough and squeezing, a low hum escaping her throat as she worked.

"Christ, Becca." He rolled his head back, fingers tugging at his hair to redirect some of the sensation from his groin. "You mean to do this thing properly, don't you?"

"You have no idea." With another flash of her teeth, she lifted her body, neatly pushing her panties aside to reveal the soft pink flesh of her cunt. It looked warm and gleaming and exactly where he wanted to be right now. "Because when I want to fuck you…"

"Yeah, yeah—I get it. When you want to fuck me,

that's exactly what you're going to do." He spoke with gritted teeth. "Believe me. I get the point. You win."

"You don't get the point at all. I'm not trying to *beat* you at anything. I'm trying to make you realize that any power you have over me, you have because I give it to you. I don't submit meekly to your protection because I don't know any better. I do it because I trust you."

He didn't move as she brought her body down to his. Agonizingly slow and somehow so fast his head whirled, her slick pussy grabbed the tip of his cock and teased it with its beckoning heat.

Her hands braced each of his thighs as she looked down at him. "I do it, Jake, because I—" Her words were lost in a gasp as she brought herself the rest of the way down. The sudden change from yearning to possession rocked through him in so powerful a jolt he didn't have the time or brainpower to wonder at the rest of her statement.

"Oh, sweet fuck," she cried, biting her lip. "It's been too long since I've done this."

All of his promises to keep his hands behind his head fled at the pain in her voice, and he brought his touch to the taper of her waist, prepared to lift her off. "Are you hurt? Can I help?"

"Just—" She released a shaky laugh. "Just give me a second."

Since she wasn't demanding he put his hands back yet, he brought one to her face and cupped her gently, loving the way the sweet curve of her cheek fit so naturally in his embrace. He could have stayed that way for as long as she needed, but she got a seductive glint in her eye and let her mouth fall open enough to pull his thumb in. Hot and wet, her mouth wrapped around the digit the same way her body wrapped around his cock, and she started moving against him in a way that left no room for anything else.

There was only the two of them, reduced to nothing more than this moment. He forgot all about pain and promises, lost instead in the overwhelming feeling of rightness that being with Becca caused. This was no hard and fast fuck to pass the time and make a statement. This wasn't about pleasing himself or even about pleasing her. Sex with Becca was so much a part of his soul that he cried out in ecstasy long before his body reached its climax. And when he was finally unable to take another second of her softly mewling cries, her body's undulations, the flare of her hips over and over again as she brought herself onto him, he realized he'd done the unthinkable and come before her.

Never, in all his years of meaningless sex and meaningful sex and everything in between, had he left his partner anything but sated. Furious with himself and overwhelmed with the sudden urge to prove he could do this as many times as Becca needed to finish, he almost didn't notice that Becca smiled and said, "Finally," before she brought herself down onto his semi-erect cock one more time and fell into a cry of pleasure.

He felt every cresting wave of her orgasm, acutely aware of where their bodies fit together. The pleasure that rocked through her felt better than his own had been—something he hadn't thought possible.

He hadn't thought a lot of things possible, including the fact that she'd waited for him. She'd planned on fucking him until he had no choice but to lose himself inside her, and then—and only then—did she plan on letting herself go.

Because she was the one in charge. Because he would be given the opportunity to protect her only when she allowed it.

He almost laughed at how foolish he'd been all this time. How had he ever thought this woman was the one who needed him? Nothing he did or said or planned would change her. Nothing he demanded would make a difference in her life. She was the snake in his path, a pair of shackles he had to willingly slip on his wrists. If he wanted her, he had to *earn* her.

"How's the rib holding up?" she asked, rolling carefully off him and settling her naked body lengthwise against his. She took a moment to take her panties off, allowing him the full nudity he'd been denied until this moment.

"It hurts."

She frowned into the muscles of his shoulder, where she'd buried her head. "Too hurt to make me dinner?"

He turned carefully over and held her body to his. After dropping a kiss on her forehead, and her nose, and her cheeks, and spending a good five minutes on her mouth, he decided it was a good time to recover some of his lost ground.

With any luck, he'd be spending the rest of his life trying to keep up with this woman.

"Oh, I'll make you dinner," he promised. "But not until you put that goddamned ring back around your neck. And we're still stopping at Piers's to get it resized on the way back to the Manor."

She looked up at him, a playful smile on her lips. "Yes, master. But you have to promise me something in return."

"Anything."

"You have to stop blindsiding me with chivalry. No more surprises. I appreciate you bringing Max out to the Manor, and I think the deal you struck with Greg was brilliant, but enough is enough. I know it goes against every Virgo fiber that thrums in your body, but you have to let me have a say in my own life."

She was right, of course. The Rebecca Clare he'd come to know made mistakes, lots of them, but she willingly paid full price afterward. Her life was a constant balance of staying true to herself while facing the collective judgment of the media, her family, her friends, the world. She faced each night with a quiver of fear and got up every morning with a smile on her face.

She was twenty-four freaking years old, and somehow the wisest and most innocent person he'd ever met.

"I reserve the right to one more surprise," he said, his throat tight. Her eyes flashed a warning, but he refused to give this last one up. It was too important. They'd come too far and been through too much. "The engagement party. I just need until then."

"I don't think—"

"It'll be the last one, I promise." And he pulled her close before either of them made the mistake of saying more.

She'd given him power over her. She'd given him her trust. She'd given him her body.

The only thing he had to give her in return was his name. He desperately hoped it would be enough.

BECCA ENDED UP asking that the ring's setting remain intact. Piers, every bit the wizened old man she'd hoped he would be, applauded her decision, saying that nothing became a sapphire so well as a bed of precious stones that, though flashy and secure, would never rival it for beauty.

She made the mistake of glancing at Jake when Piers said that, and the affectionate way he smiled snagged her heart and tore her open. It would have been a great opportunity for him to drop to one knee and propose for real this time, to promise that she could keep the ring forever, that the diamonds would always be there to protect.

But he didn't.

And even though she knew it was silly, she didn't breathe the entire way over the Whitestone Bridge. Although they wouldn't get the ring back for a few days, she desperately hoped he'd pull another jerky stop in the middle, lifting her to the trunk of the car and declaring that his desire to take care of her went further, extended deeper, meant more.

But he didn't.

"I had fun today," she said as the car's wheels left the bridge and returned to solid ground. "Too much fun. It's going to be hard to get back to life as usual at the Manor. Pictures with Greg, an engagement party with all our friends in attendance…"

He didn't take the bait. "It's only for another week, and then I think we can make our discreet exit." He slipped his arm over the seat and rubbed the back of her neck, weakening her knees and her resolve. "Think you can make it that long, Love Muffin?"

If you promise to never stop touching me like that? She could make it forever.

TWENTY-FOUR

THE ENTIRE WEEK before the engagement party found Montgomery Manor full of guests, brimming with excitement and luggage and so much free-flowing alcohol Becca had to wonder if there was a distillery somewhere on the grounds.

The high level of activity was exactly what she needed. While she was busy entertaining guests and helping friends find their way through the massive house, it was easy to pretend that everything was as it should be. She was floating on a sea of love and champagne, buoyed by the secret smiles Jake threw her way when she caught his eye across a crowded room. The only thing missing was a declaration of love and a ring.

Mere details, really.

And if she found herself sometimes wondering *why* they didn't speak again about what happened in New York, she wasn't selfish enough to bring it up. There weren't very many things she'd been able to give Jake thus far in their relationship. Temporary lodging, a fledgling love for the theater, a cracked rib. Allowing him the playing field—a chance to do things on his own, tightly wound Virgo terms—seemed the least she could do.

She just wished she knew exactly what his tightly wound Virgo terms were.

Fortunately, she didn't have much longer to wait. The

day of the engagement party had dawned clear and bright, and even her horoscope prophesized a good turnout.

> *Aries (March 21-April 19): Today is one of those rare days in which your hard work becomes evident in a big way. Surround yourself with family and friends to make the most of it. Remember that alcohol has calories too.*

Madame Pernaud never told her to just sit back and enjoy herself. It almost felt like an omen.

She blew out a long breath and examined the contents of the closet in Jake's bedroom, where her clothes took up exactly half the space. For the first time in days, she was entirely alone, left to her own devices as she got ready for the evening. Her dress code requirements included nothing more than to look put together and happy, with an added bonus of hopefully driving her mother crazy.

But it was so *quiet* in here. So empty. It was the first time in days she hadn't been surrounded by other people, and she wasn't so sure she cared for it. Her doubts had taken on a sonorous clang at the base of her skull, another one of those sneaky headaches she rarely saw coming.

"There you are, you little bitch. I've been looking everywhere for you."

The door to the bedroom flew open. Becca glanced up, only momentarily startled. She'd know that voice anywhere.

"Livvie!" She tossed aside the dress she'd been considering and rushed to hug her friend. Her timing couldn't have been better. "I didn't know you were coming. We didn't get an RSVP."

"Are you kidding?" she exclaimed, smiling widely. "I wouldn't miss your engagement party for all the money in the world. I even got up at seven this morning to fly out here. That's how dedicated I am."

Becca took a step back and glanced over her friend, taking in the short silver dress, smudged eyes and still-gloriously-waterfall-like hair. "Liar. You haven't gone to bed yet."

She laughed. "Not true. I napped on the plane."

They fell into companionable chatter as Becca returned her attention to the closet. It was a familiar feeling, getting dressed and hearing about Livvie's latest photo shoot, a pair of women unconcerned with anything but enjoying one another's company. The entire thing would have been perfectly normal if not for the sly looks and lengthy pauses Livvie tossed in every few minutes, as if waiting for Becca to fold.

"So," she finally said, once Becca had narrowed down her choices, her discarded dresses not quite tossed on the floor but piled semi-neatly on the bed. "You're going to make me ask, aren't you?"

"I don't know what you're talking about," Becca lied.

"Good try, darling. This is either the most realistic fake engagement I've ever seen in my life, or you've been playing a deeper game than you let on. The papers have had nothing but nauseatingly sweet photos of you and Jake for weeks."

"You're the one who told me to ride the positive publicity wave."

"Oh, no, you don't. You're not pinning this on me. I meant for you to go to a few parties and get free shit.

I didn't tell you to go hang out with your families and wear matching sweaters on a hayride." She took a dress from out of Becca's hand. "And don't wear this shade of pink. It washes you out."

"I know, but it's the twenty-third. I received some advice that pink was my color for tonight, and I don't dare contradict it." She tugged the dress back and held it to her chest. If a girl couldn't be superstitious on the day of her engagement party, when could she? She'd defied Madame Pernaud far too many times over the past few weeks. It seemed dangerous to push things any further.

She stepped out of her yoga pants and slipped the fabric over her head. The dress was demurely cut across the top and flared in the skirt, fifties-style, though the cutaways on either side of her waist saved it from being too sedate. A Montgomery party this might be, but her name was still on the invitation.

She only got as far as putting her arms through the sleeves before she lost it. "Oh, Livvie. What if I'm wrong about everything?"

Livvie rose and came to her aid, tugging on the zipper and securing the fabric snugly into place. "It *is* still a fake engagement, then?"

"Yes. No. I don't know." This was supposed to be the happiest day of her life—or one of two—and she'd never felt so close to bursting into tears. She had no ring, no fiancé, no idea what to expect out of the evening except for some kind of surprise and everyone she'd ever known in attendance. She was pretty sure at least half of them had come to see what kind of a spectacle she'd make of herself, how far she'd fall now that she'd risen so high.

Not that she blamed them. She was rather curious on that subject herself.

"Oh, darling. Surely it's not that confusing. Either he loves you or he doesn't."

"It's not that easy, unfortunately. You have to understand how the Montgomery mind works. The people in this family don't do things in half measures. There are times when I'm absolutely certain Jake means to propose tonight, and there are times when I get the feeling I'm just a project he's putting the final touches on."

"A project? Jake?"

"He thinks I'm his responsibility. He has from the start."

"Then that's your answer right there. Jake Montgomery has never been responsible for anything since the day he was born."

Becca smiled and nodded, but she knew no amount of explaining would bring Livvie around to her point of view. Because the reality was that Jake was one of the most responsible people she'd ever met, second only to his father.

It was why he'd spent so much of his life avoiding any and all claims of adulthood. His subconscious mind knew, even if he didn't, that when he took on a task—whether it was getting dressed in the morning or winning a bet or pretending to fall in love—he would see it through to completion. He couldn't leave a loose thread any more than he could stop breathing, and rather than become like the man who'd sired him, a man who picked up every responsibility that came his way, he'd picked up none.

Until she came along.

"Well, I still say that's not the right shade of pink for you, but you look delicious." Livvie straightened the dress with a grin. "If he hasn't popped the question yet, it's only because he hasn't caught a glimpse of the killer side boob you've got going on over there."

Becca groaned. "No man is moved to commit to a life of monogamy because of side boob."

"And it's a good thing too," Livvie said. "If every man who's seen my tits felt the urge to propose marriage, I'd be in real trouble."

"You look amazing." Jake had to stop himself from grabbing the ring out of his pocket and falling to his knees right there at the base of the stairs. Becca made an entrance worthy of a woman used to the limelight, her steps smooth and confident, her dress a playful mixture of propriety and in-your-face scandal. She was every inch herself.

She was gorgeous.

"Why, thank you. You're not so bad yourself."

He'd taken considerable pains to get dressed for the engagement party, aware that he and Becca would be on the receiving end of a hundred dull, well-meaning compliments—as well as the flash of Greg's camera, omnipresent and eager to catch them at either their best or their worst. And that was fine. Jake had taken his father's words in the office the other day to heart. If he needed to make a highly public impression on the world in exchange for the right to direct his life the way he saw fit, then he'd pour himself into a tuxedo and do just that.

He only hoped Becca would consent to do it with him.

Alex and Ryan had been recruited to stand guard outside either door to the foyer where Becca was making her grand entrance, affording him a necessary few minutes of privacy to get this right. He couldn't count the number of times his family and well-meaning guests had asked why Becca wasn't wearing her engagement ring, but no amount of prodding on their part would get him to hurry. There would be no party unless she said yes, which meant getting her to say yes was going to happen if he had to take four days to get it right. The rest of them could drink champagne and wait.

He took her hand and helped her down the last step, refusing to give up his hold on that delicate assemblage of bones and muscle and skin. Her hand was small in his, but strong—something he'd failed to recognize when he first offered to take care of her. She was stronger than him in every possible way. It had been ridiculous to think she could ever need him the way he needed her.

"What's wrong?" she asked, when he took a moment to gain his bearings. His pulse leaped in ways that were entirely new to him, agonizing and exciting and scared all at once. *This is what it feels like to put your life in someone else's hands*, he realized. *This is what it means to truly let go.*

"Nothing is wrong, Becca. Not anymore. Not after tonight." He smiled as her eyes flew open, her mouth falling in surprise. She knew what was coming—how could she not know?—but he appreciated that she could still be as flustered by this as he was. This was new territory for them both. "That day in New York, the day we had the ring resized, I promised you there'd only be one more surprise, one more unfinished matter to take care of."

Her breath caught, and he pulled her to him in a warm embrace. "I'm a control freak and I'm arrogant and I wait until other people make mistakes before I swoop in and show them up. I'll never be good at punching a time clock or putting others first. In fact, the only thing

I've been able to do with any success is take care of you. Which is why—"

He was interrupted when the door guarded by Ryan swung open to reveal a squat, powerful-looking man striding toward them with his hand thrust in his pocket. It took a second to recognize the figure as Dana Carstairs.

"I tried to stop him, but…" Ryan, also dressed for the evening's events in a tux, wasn't too far behind. "He insisted he had to talk to you. He said you'd want to see him."

"There you are," Dana said, not slowing down. "Why's it so fucking hard to find you in your own house?"

Jake had no immediate reply. He'd been too focused on his proposal and the woman in his arms, and he was having a hard time switching his emotions over. *He*, the man who was never at a loss for words. *He*, the man who never let anything or anyone catch him off guard.

Becca was much quicker to pick up on the change in the room. Her face drained of all color as Dana approached, and she pulled away from him with a sharp cry. "Jake? What is this?"

"It's…" The words died away. He had no idea what this was.

"Okay. I'm here." Dana planted his feet in front of them, arms crossed over his chest. Like everyone else in attendance, he was dressed up for the night in a well-cut suit and red power tie, but no amount of polish would make him look like anything more than a thug.

Seeing him standing there, glaring mulishly, it was difficult for Jake to remember just what it was about this man that had once attracted him. Dana was amusing and wealthy—two qualities he used to think mattered—but a lifetime of self-indulgent dissipation had also rendered him cruel.

Jake wasn't sure he cared to consider how far along that same path he must have been not to recognize it before.

"What now?" Dana barked. "Do you want me to apologize? Beg for forgiveness?"

Jake's attention came back with a snap. The first thing he needed to do was get this man out of here. He didn't care for the way his heartbeat was picking up in the other man's presence, like iron fillings reacting to a magnet—and he *really* didn't care for the way Becca had turned an unnaturally pale shade of white, setting off the color of her dress in stark contrast.

"I believe both of those things are in order, but not to me," he said coolly, and gestured for Ryan to step closer. He knew the chauffeur's stocky strength would come in handy someday. "I'm not the one you hurt."

"Well, how was I supposed to know?" Dana cast a look of loathing at Becca. "I didn't get a detailed itinerary along with my invitation."

"Itinerary? Invitation?" Becca wasn't getting any of her color back, and she stepped away from Jake by a distance of several feet. It might as well have been miles. "You invited him to our engagement party? *This* is your surprise? The final hurrah?"

"Of course not. This isn't the final anything." It was the start. It was the beginning of their lives together.

"Look—I'm sorry, all right? Will that make you feel better? Will that get you off my back?" Dana's voice rose to a dangerous level, and Jake could see that a few people were streaming in through the open doors to locate the source of the yelling. It was almost fitting, having an audience gathering for this. The people would always love a good Rebecca Clare scandal.

Jake shook his head in warning, but Dana either missed or chose not to see the dangerous gleam in his eyes.

"It's not like I even did anything illegal. I was the last to see Sara that night, I admit, but I didn't put the pills in her mouth. I didn't hold the bottle to her lips. I'm sorry she took things hard, but you can't hold me accountable for her actions. She was already messed up by the time I got my hands on her."

It was the worst possible excuse Dana could have offered—tantamount to standing idly by and snapping photos while a teenager was harassed in the park—and Jake reacted the same way as he had that day with Greg. It wasn't all right to ignore someone else's suffering because it was convenient. It wasn't all right to hurt the woman he loved.

With a firm step forward, he prepared to lay Dana flat and have Ryan drag him out by his heels, if that was what it would take to get him out of their lives for good. He'd get a restraining order. He'd hire someone to find Dana's darkest secrets—have him locked away for tax evasion if he had to.

"Don't you dare," Becca said. He assumed she was talking to Dana, but when he looked over at her, her full anger was turned his way. He recoiled at the power of it—at the *pain* of it. The only other time he'd seen her like that was when she'd attacked first Dana and then Trish. This was the pain of when she'd been pushed to the brink. This was the pain he'd promised himself he'd spend the rest of his life trying to save her from.

And it was directed at *him*.

"I can't believe this is what you thought I wanted. Revenge. Closure. An eye for an eye." The pain turned to tears, and he found himself drowning in them, choking as he struggled for air. Why was it so difficult for him to find the words? He was good at words, at saying what people wanted to hear.

"Becca—" he pleaded.

But she shook her head, her expression brittle. "You have no idea, do you, Jake? I'm not some doll with a broken arm for you to tape back on or a closet you need to rearrange. I'm a *person*." She lowered her voice so that only the two of them could hear. "I'm the person who trusted you. I'm the person who loved you."

Jake didn't know what to do. He was being pulled too many directions at once. He wanted to haul Dana out by the seat of his pants. Clear the room, telling everyone to get their kicks at someone else's expense for a change. Take Becca into his arms and tell her how wholly and completely she was loved back.

Fuck this. Action, not reaction. He was going to do all three.

"All right, everyone. Show's over." He made eye contact with Alex and Ryan, and they took his hint almost immediately. They transformed into a pair of tuxedoed bouncers and began corralling the guests back into the ballroom. "Except you, Dana. You stay put."

The man halted in the middle of beating a hasty retreat, unable to back down from the command in Jake's voice. "You'll stay here until we have a chance to chat," he said. "Don't you dare try to leave these grounds, or I'll use the full capacity of my family's resources to hunt you down. Nowhere is far enough for you, got it?"

Dana scowled but nodded, and Jake felt a sense of

triumph fill his chest. He was beginning to see why his dad liked playing the hard-assed businessman so much. With two down and just one to go, he spun, prepared to pull Becca into his arms and whisk her out of here while she was still on two feet. If he wasn't careful, she'd probably beat him to it and tear Dana down before he got a chance.

But as he spun again, his gaze skimming wildly over the glittering dresses departing through the open doors, he realized Becca was gone.

No. His heart stopped as he caught sight of her heading up the stairs. *Not gone yet.* Relief washed over him as he darted up after her. It was a moment almost worthy of thanks to deities of the northbound kind.

Becca knew the exact moment Jake flew up the stairs to follow her, his tread light and his tension high. It was about one minute too late, sixty seconds *after* he started cleaning up her messes again.

Given the way he was reacting, barking orders like a general, it was obvious he wanted her to stand there and wait while he adjusted the environment to his exact specifications. It was textbook Jake. Clear the room of onlookers and scandal. Force Dana to stay in place until he could wrest an apology from his lips. Try to cure Becca of her sorrow, just like everyone else, because the damaged girl inside would never be good enough.

He grabbed her roughly by the arm and twisted, forcing her to turn back and face him. "Becca—wait. I'm sorry it had to happen like this. This isn't at all how tonight was supposed to go."

"No? Imagine that." She gave a bitter laugh. Poor baby. He'd probably been hoping to produce Dana all by himself, like pulling a rabbit out of his hat.

"No." He frowned at her. "Of course it's not. I understand that you're upset with me, but you can't just walk away like this. Hit me if you want to. Fly into a rage. Attack. Do *something*."

"Would that make you feel better?" She'd never felt less like attacking anyone in her life—at least not anyone but herself. God, she was so *stupid*. Building this night up as something more. Pinning all her girlish dreams on a man like Jake. "Should I pull a Rebecca Clare for the cameras? Should I throw a tantrum in front of everyone and kick Dana in the balls? Would that work?"

The color drained from his face. "You know that's not what I mean."

"I'm not so sure I do. From where I stand, that seems to be all you've ever wanted from me. As long as I'm fucking things up and overreacting, you're perfectly happy. I think you could be happy forever that way— me breaking things, you fixing them." She tried to tug her arm back but he held it firm. "It bothers you that I might not actually need you anymore, doesn't it? That I might be okay without you?"

Except she wasn't. She wasn't okay at all. But he wouldn't release her arm, and she didn't know how else to get away.

"I'm sorry to disappoint you after all your careful planning, but I don't hate Dana. I don't feel anything as far as he's concerned. I'm not sure when it happened, but somewhere between Max and Madame Pernaud and yes, even you, I figured out there were much better ways for me to expend my energies."

"Good for you."

"Don't you dare patronize me." She wouldn't be talked down to. Not now. Not when everything else was falling apart. "Maybe this whole night is my fault for getting my hopes up, for not listening when all the signs warned me away from you, but I'm not going to act out just so you can feel like you have a purpose."

His hand finally fell, though she felt the ghost of his fingers gripping her skin. "You aren't even going to give me a chance to explain?"

"Explain what? I understand what you were trying to do, Jake—and a few weeks ago, I probably would have thanked you for it. You were holding up your end of the bargain, making sure I got the closure I needed."

You were taking care of me. It was the only thing he'd ever offered, and she'd been a fool to see it as something more. A sad, pitiful fool. The type of girl she'd promised herself—promised the memory of Sara—she'd never be.

"I practically begged you to take me to see Dana back in New York, so it makes sense you'd finish things off this way. It's brilliant, actually. Just like the Greg solution."

"And that's it?" he asked, looking at her with a queer frown. "That's all I get? Your gratitude?"

"What else do you *want?*" she cried, her voice tinged with desperation.

"I want you, Becca. You're all I've ever wanted." His frown didn't lift. "But if this is the kind of man you think I am, then I understand why you might not want me back."

She searched in vain for something to say, for some insight into the wild, almost frantic look in his eyes, but nothing came. All she could do as he turned and walked out of the room was watch him go, her breath suspended and her head pounding. She could have screamed or flown down the stairs after him, but what was the point?

Because you can only muffle the sound of a heart breaking for so long before it breaks everything else, a niggling voice said.

She did her best to ignore it. Her damnable intuition might be right on that score, but it didn't take into account the fact that she was already broken to begin with. Rebecca Clare had learned a long time ago how to walk on unsteady legs. They would carry her anywhere she needed to go.

TWENTY-FIVE

BECCA QUICKLY REALIZED there was nowhere in this house full of hundreds of people she could go to be alone. Guests spilled out from the ballroom, taking up residence in hallways and drawing rooms. The staff area was a hub of activity tonight. And Jake's room was of course out of the question.

The only place she might have been assured of some peace and quiet was the nursery, but Serena had a night nurse who seemed pretty vigilant in her care of the youngest Montgomerys.

She slid through a hallway on the first floor, bypassing the ballroom in hopes of a closet somewhere she could hide, but most of the doors were locked tight. How ironic that this giant manor, this fortress where she'd felt so protected a few days ago, had now become a house of mirrors.

The overwhelming urge Becca felt to seek comfort in Jake's arms was another piece of irony she could do without. She wanted one of those briefly gruff hugs he sucked at. She wanted him to adjust the skewed skirt of her dress and send her back into the party. She wanted to grasp at the feeling of rightness that came simply from knowing he was near.

And that was why you didn't put your heart in a man's keeping, why you held fast to your promise not to grow attached. *He* was the one who'd hurt her, yet she'd fall into his arms if he walked around that corner right now.

He didn't walk around that corner. But someone else did.

"It's you." Dana noticed her the same time she noticed him, though his surprise was much more palpable than hers. Backing away, his hands up, he said, "Don't attack me. I was on my way out."

"You're still here."

"Only because Jake told me to stay. He was very persuasive."

Of course he was. Fixing Becca had been his duty. You didn't get between a Montgomery and duty.

"I think it's probably okay for you to go now," Becca crossed her arms and leaned on the wall to show him she meant no harm. "You've served your purpose. No one here will miss you."

Dana paused, looking warily at the open hallway. He reminded her of a dog trying to sneak past a particularly nasty housecat. "It wasn't my fault. I didn't know what she was going to do."

The familiar snag of loss moved through Becca. Unlike the first time she'd confronted Dana, the sensation didn't catch on her insides. It moved through and lodged in her heart—a place she knew it would always be. No amount of vengeance against this man would change that, and she wasn't sure she *would* get rid of that ache even if she could. It was part of her now, a reminder of Sara and how far she'd come in her grief.

"It wasn't her fault either."

"And it's not like my life is a cakewalk now. You know how many women want to date the guy whose last girlfriend killed herself?"

She pushed herself off the wall, almost laughing when he visibly recoiled. Whatever else Jake had done here tonight, he'd certainly put the fear of the devil in this man. "I think it was better when you didn't talk. Come on, I'll walk you out. Let's get your coat."

Dana backed away even farther, her overture of a truce proving too much for his tiny, shriveled heart to contemplate. "What are you going to do to it?"

"Douse it in gasoline and then force you into it before I light a match. You can be the after-dinner fireworks show." She rolled her eyes and walked away, sure he'd follow. Getting help in escaping this place wasn't an offer you turned down. She was still looking for her own exit.

Since she had an actual destination this time, it didn't take long to lead Dana to the first-floor study, where a good-looking young man—perfect for a pool boy—had set up a coat check.

"Please get this man his coat. He won't be returning." There were hundreds of jackets and wraps for the boy to push through, so she and Dana had a few minutes to themselves. Although she willed herself to keep her mouth shut, to not prod at subjects best left unaired, she couldn't help herself. "What did Jake say to get you to come out here, anyway? I'd have thought this was the last place you'd willingly show your face."

"He didn't say anything. I got an invitation in the mail a few weeks ago." He paused long enough to take his coat and slip the boy a bill. "I was sure he did it just to scare me—to show he had the upper hand. I figured I'd call him on it."

Another snag made its way into her insides, but this time, it stopped in her gut. "What are you talking about?"

"That's a little marriage advice from me to you. Always call Jake Montgomery on a bluff. Nine times out of ten, the bastard's got nothing in his hand, but few people are brave enough to throw their chips in to find out."

"You got an invitation? That's it?" Becca tactfully ignored the *bastard* reference. Her mind was much more taken up with the first part of Dana's disclosure. From the day the words "engagement" and "party" had first been uttered, her mother had guarded the task of sending out the invitations as if she was the head of security at Fort Knox. Becca hadn't even been allowed to look at the prototype until they were already sent out. "Was it postmarked in New York?"

"I don't know. Yes? What difference does it make?"

It made a difference. It made all the difference in the world. "So you never talked to Jake about coming? Never heard from him since that first day?"

"No, I haven't," he said with a look of loathing. "And believe me, I'd like to keep things that way. I might be the asshole who dumped a girl the night she committed suicide, but this whole family is fucking crazy."

Those were all the parting words she got from him. Without waiting for the fucking crazy to make itself known again, he pulled his keys from out of his pocket and fled.

"Are you okay?" the coat check boy asked. She hadn't realized until he spoke that she'd been standing there, unmoving, for several minutes. "Should I get someone?"

"No." Becca's voice sounded miles away to her own ears. "No, I'm fine."

"Maybe you should sit down," he suggested. "You look pale. I have like twenty furs back here if you're cold."

She almost laughed at the absurdity of it, of someone telling her she was pale and weak, that her passivity was a cause for concern. So much of her life had been spent flying out in passion—anger and excitement, pain and euphoria—that the idea of her falling into a decline now, of all times, was preposterous.

What am I doing, just standing here? Rebecca Clare was not a woman to sit idly by while life happened to her. She wasn't a woman to let the pain of loss define her. And most of all, she wasn't a woman to run away and curl up with her pride when she realized she'd wronged the man she loved.

She had to find Jake. She had to find Jake and call him on the bluff of walking away.

"I SHOULD HAVE let you explain." Becca found him on the roof. It had taken over an hour of frantic searching before Ryan pointed her in the direction of the widow's walk at the very top of the house. "You didn't invite Dana here tonight, did you?"

He didn't turn to acknowledge her. Silhouetted against the night sky, his dark figure could have been that of any man from any era, a Montgomery from over a hundred years ago. But she knew the long, lean lines of his bearing as though they were written in her hand. That was why she'd never been able to make much sense of her own palm readings before. It was *him*.

Cold but unwilling to let that slow her down, she wrapped her arms around her and moved forward. "Jake, I'm sorry. Would you believe me if I said I overreacted?"

"Everyone is still here," he said, ignoring her apology and gesturing at the lights below. Laughter rose up through the still night sky, the glittering gowns and clinking of glasses signaling how well the party was going. "You didn't send them home."

"I wasn't aware I was supposed to," she said. "Is it time? Did you want me to have my big diva moment and end things?"

He finally turned, such a stark expression on his face she immediately ran forward to wrap her arms around his waist. He didn't stop her, but he didn't return the embrace either.

"I'm sorry," she said again, this time into his lapel. "I talked to Dana before he left. I know it was just a misunderstanding. My mom probably sent the invitation, thinking he was a friend of yours."

Jake gently pushed her away. With a sigh, he shrugged himself out of his jacket and dropped it over her shoulders. "It's too cold out here for you to stand around in that dress."

"Still taking care of me?" she asked, her voice wobbly. The jacket smelled so much like him, sandalwood and rose, its warmth moving straight from his body into her own.

"Becca—" His voice broke off, and he gripped the railing of the walk. "Do you have any idea how you made me feel down there? This is our engagement party. Our big night."

"I'm aware of that. But I saw Dana and panicked. How many times can I tell you how sorry I am?"

"None. A hundred. It doesn't matter." He shook his head. "I know I'm not the most emotionally expressive man, but I thought you knew me better than that. I thought you, of all people, believed in me enough to know I'd never do something to hurt you."

"I *do* believe in you."

"No. You don't." His lips firmed into a line. "You thought I'd bring your worst enemy—a man both of us abhor—to confront you without even warning you first. You thought I'd subject you to that kind of pain and humiliation on what was supposed to be *our* night together."

What could she say? She *had* thought he'd done that. She was half afraid he might do it again someday.

He wasn't done. "That day at your apartment, the day we made love, you told me you trusted me. You told me that any power I have over you is there because you allow it."

She nodded, remembering.

"But you lied," he said starkly. "You don't trust me. You don't trust me at all."

"Of course I do, Jake. All I've ever done is trust you. From the day I let you take me home from the club, I've put myself in your hands."

"No. You haven't. Not completely. You've allowed me to join you on your workouts and sleep in your bed at night and bring you home to my family, but there's a part of you that's been held back this entire time. There's a part of you I can't get near."

And then he did it again. He watched. He waited. He pulled out the full Virgo and set it in the dead space between them.

"What are you afraid of?" he asked after what felt like an eternity. A long, cold eternity—one not even the devil could warm up. "What is it that you think I'm going to do to you?"

She felt tears welling up in her eyes. Not because he spoke harshly or because he was wrong, but because he was kind and he was right. And he deserved better.

"For as long as I can remember, I've defined myself by my ability to take the blows life deals me." She spoke slowly, carefully, aware she'd only have one chance to say this. "The media, my family, Sara—all of it. I don't necessarily make the right choices, but I always own my mistakes."

"I know. I love that about you."

Oh, God. He couldn't say things like that or she'd never finish. "But I'm not unbreakable, Jake. I have limits." She'd been so good at pretending she could survive anything that she'd forgotten she had vulnerabilities too. And those vulnerabilities were a big part of her. The *biggest* part of her. "No matter how much I might want to be with you, you'll always be a Virgo. No—don't get mad. I don't mean it in a negative sense. I just mean that you'll always want to have everything perfectly lined up. You'll always try to have everything your way."

"I can do better. I can let some things go."

"But can I?" She wasn't so sure. "I think I'll always see myself as a burden you picked up along the way. A wrinkled shirt. A disorganized closet."

"Becca…"

She drew in a shuddering breath. She still had more to say. "And maybe I could handle that. Maybe that would be enough. But I'm not so sure I can just tie my happiness to yours and let it go. I can't become the kind of woman who would rather take her own life than face a day without you."

Jake understood in a flash of his brilliantly blue eyes. He pulled Becca close, crushing her, crushing both their outfits, crushing her heart. "You won't. Of course you won't. I won't let you."

"What if it's not up to you?" she asked, her voice muffled by the press of his chest and her mounting tears. "As much as it will pain you to hear it, you don't control the universe. What if you're not there when it happens?"

"I won't let it happen because I'm never going to leave you. And because you're a survivor." He pulled back and lifted her chin, the move that was so condescending and delicious and totally *him*. "I know I'm overbearing and overprotective. I know that marrying into my family is like becoming part of a cult. But the good news is that they like you a hell of a lot more than they like me. You're not Sara, Becca. You're not alone. You're strong. You're beautiful. And you're *fantastic*."

She choked on a watery sob and examined his shirt-front, stained from her makeup and disheveled from her touch. She pointed at it with a frown. "You're a mess. You always will be if you keep me around, you know. There will always be scandals and public breakdowns and cameras there to catch them. There will always be wrinkles. You hate wrinkles."

"Yes, but I love *you* more," he said. "I might not have always been open to the idea of such a disordered existence, but I can't imagine anything else now. You may not be aware of it, but when you put your life and your struggles in my keeping, I received an unexpected, heavy, glorious *gift*. I know you've been through a lot this year. I know you may never get over what happened to Sara, and that you'll have just as many bad nights as good. And I know that all of this—the joy and the despair, the process of rebuilding your life—will take place in the spotlight. All I'm asking for is a chance to share the spotlight with you."

A sob filled her throat. He did love her. He did mean to see this through. He was asking her to *give* him the power to hurt her, and she couldn't think of anything else in the universe she'd rather do.

"Trust me with your happiness, Becca. Please. Let me be there to catch you when you fall. And be there to catch me when I do."

The sob escaped, and she didn't wait for him to lift his arms this time. She fell into him, colliding with the warmth of his chest, wrapping her arms tightly around his waist, determined never to let go. "I'm sorry for not believing in you. I'm sorry for not believing in myself. After everything I built up inside my head about tonight, I saw Dana and thought—"

"Yes?"

"I thought it was the end. I thought you were trying to figure out a way to fix me so you could move on. I thought all my fears were coming true."

"Goddammit. Don't you know by now? I don't want to move on from you. I want to spend the rest of my life with you." Without waiting for her reply, he reached in his pocket and extracted the ring. Even under the half-moon sky, it was sparkling, radiant, protected by the diamonds she couldn't ask Piers to remove. "Won't you please marry me?"

His proposal—long awaited, so anticipated—was terse almost to the point of nonexistence, not even remotely as romantic as traffic stopped on a bridge.

It was perfect.

"Yes!" she screamed out and grabbed him, more forcefully than she intended. He winced and backed away, his ribs not quite up to their full capabilities yet. "I'm sorry. I'll be gentler next time."

"It's okay," he said, looking at her with so much warmth she thought she might go up in flames right there. "You can't hurt me. In fact, you're welcome to try as often as you like."

"But I don't want to hurt you. I want to take care of you. I want to support you in the manner to which you are accustomed and bind your wounds and read your tea leaves and help you calm down when you're about to attack harmless cameramen in trees. You're my tiger, Tiger."

He gave an exaggerated sigh. "Is that really the one we're sticking with?"

"Yep."

"You know that tigers bite, right?" He wrapped an arm around her waist, his hand slipping under the jacket and into the cutaway panel on the side.

"Go right ahead."

His hand skimmed over her stomach, his fingers moving over the taut lines of her belly and heading inexorably southward. "And they growl."

"I'm looking forward to it."

"No, Becca." He brought his lips to hers in a warm kiss, promising a lifetime of such embraces. "*I'm* looking forward to it—and to spending the rest of our lives getting into messes together."

EPILOGUE

"I SWEAR TO GOD, if you bring that shrimp scampi anywhere near me right now, I'm jumping overboard."

"You have to eat, Becca. I promised Max I'd get three square meals in you every day. Even though he's busy getting your stupid Better than Therapy Boot Camp up and running, I don't care to cross him right now. That man needs to get back together with his girlfriend. Soon."

She glared at him from where she lay curled on the deck, the spray of the ocean on her face doing little to ease the overwhelming nausea she'd known would hit her. She hadn't been kidding about being prone to seasickness. Even looking at pictures of boats made her dizzy. "I told you this was a bad idea. There's no way I'm making it to Nice. Drop me off somewhere on the Amalfi Coast. I'll swim the rest of the way."

Jake laughed, and she was pretty sure she'd never heard a more cruel sound. This wasn't funny. She was dying.

"I'm not abandoning my wife in Italy because she can't find her sea legs."

He set down the plate of food he'd been bringing her—downwind, thank God—and settled on the boards next to her. *Sara's Voyage*, as the yacht had been re-christened before they'd set sail, was a gorgeous expanse of hardwood and complicated rigging. She hated it almost as much as she loved it.

It was kind of like being married to Jake Montgomery, now that she thought about it.

"Here." He lifted her head and settled it in his lap, his pants wrinkled and his shirt askew. He was wrinkled all the time now. That part she didn't hate so much. "I brought you something."

"Is it a helicopter come to whisk me out of my misery?"

"No." There was that chuckle again. "But I was reading up, and it sounds like some of your silly wrist acupressure points are used to control motion sickness."

She sat up a little, feeling a smile touch her lips. "You mean you've been reading up on alternative health methods? Have you discovered my trove of Traditional Chinese Medicine textbooks?"

"Maybe. Don't gloat." He pulled out a pair of wristbands that looked like cheap plastic watches. She watched, amused, as he lifted her hands and secured each one in place, lingering over her left hand, where her ring was now a permanent fixture. He dropped a kiss to each palm. "There. Give it half an hour. If they don't work, we can head back to Naples and get you your helicopter."

"Oh, that's so sweet. If I had a dollar for every time a man offered to get me a helicopter…"

She wasn't sure if the nausea was abating yet, but Jake began running his hands through her hair, bringing her another kind of comfort. A familiar kind of comfort—the kind of comfort entire lives could be built on.

"I hope it won't be too boring for you, staying with the Bridgeports," he said, working his magic while the wristbands worked theirs. "We don't have to do this, you know. I can call Monty and tell him to fuck off. It'd be my pleasure, actually."

"It's okay. I like it."

"That's probably because you haven't met Ricky and his wife yet."

"No, stupid—I like this. You and me, sharing our lives. Me adding some excitement to your boring house parties. You forcing the Montgomery Foundation to invest in struggling theaters in the city. We're like a power couple now."

"To be fair, I get half my pleasure in doing it to thwart Monty. He hates the arts. He and your mom's financial advisor have that in common." His hands moved down her hairline to her neck, slipping surreptitiously down the collar of her striped boat-necked tee. She might not feel like a sailor, but she certainly looked like one. "Feeling better yet?"

"A little." She sat up, looking over the rigging and beams and all sorts of things she didn't understand but was rapidly coming to appreciate as all that stood between her and sudden death. "But shouldn't you be hoisting the mainsail or something?"

"Nah. This old girl practically sails herself." He smiled, slow and tiger-like, a grin he reserved for her and her alone. "Besides—there's supposed to be a crescent moon tonight."

"A crescent moon?"

"Oh, yes. We may even have to get out the flashlight."

* * * * *

Want more Montgomery Manor? Keep reading for a sneak peek from BECAUSE I CAN, the next book in the series from author Tamara Morgan.

"WHO, MONTY? HE'S A solid ten, no questions asked."

Monty skidded to a halt as he prepared to round the corner. It wasn't a customary habit of his to lurk along the hallways where the Montgomery Manor staff was hard at work, but he'd been feeling a desperate need for caffeine today. He'd also been feeling a desperate need to unchain himself from his desk for a few minutes, so heading down to the basement-level kitchen to refill his cup had seemed as good an excuse as any.

The eavesdropping was an unexpected perk.

"A ten? Are you sure we're talking about the same man? Monotonous Montgomery? Drudgery John?"

"Absolutely. I'd let him bend me over a table or two."

"You're crazy. Jake is the more attractive brother by far."

"Yeah, but you also admitted you like men with those curly mustaches. I think your taste is flawed."

Even though Monty knew it behooved him to clear his throat or stomp his feet or otherwise put an end to the conversation currently underway behind the swinging metal doors, he leaned forward, straining to place the voices. If he wasn't mistaken, the woman with a flair for the hirsute was Holly, the family cook. He had yet to determine who it was that considered him a ten.

And he *really* wanted to know. As his all-too-familiar nicknames indicated, women weren't in the habit of looking at him and visualizing a sex object. He was too old, too boring and much too tightly wound for that—a vintage toy soldier with moving parts. And not the *good* moving parts either.

"Jake has that whole naughty-playboy thing going for him," Holly said. "Or he used to, before he got married."

"I know, but Monty is bigger. I like a man with some meat on him."

"That's because you're only sexually attracted to guys who can beat you at arm wrestling, which is like twelve people overall."

A robust laugh escaped the kitchen as the pieces fell into place. That sound could only belong to Georgia Lennox—and so could the conversation, now that he thought about it. The owner and operator of the Handywoman Express had never struck him as the type of woman to speak in maidenly euphemisms, and, truth be told, she probably *was* able to beat most men at arm wrestling.

His dad had been utilizing Georgia's services for almost two decades, even though she couldn't be more than thirty years old. He remembered her as a gangly, toothy kid a few years younger than himself, riding over on her bike with a tool belt strapped across her chest like a bandolier, asking if there was anything she could do around the place to pick up some extra cash. Despite her tender years, she'd gratefully accepted his dad's request to build a bridge to continue the footpath that stopped at the West Creek.

And it was a good bridge too—solid oak, a few feet across, still standing to this day. It probably intended to keep standing forever, out of fear she might come at it with a hammer if it didn't.

Georgia was scary. In fact, he wasn't at all convinced he *could* win against her in an arm-wrestling match. Or that bending her over a table would result in anything but immeasurable bodily harm.

"I don't think a few muscles is too much to ask for in a man," Georgia said, her voice still overloud in its low, deep-throated tone. "It's impossible to look at someone naked and feel all hot and bothered if he has spindly arms. The T-Rex look isn't attractive on anyone."

"Fine. You can give him his ten. I wish you both very happy."

"Oh, no. He's a solid ten in the looks department, but you have to knock off at least half his points for personality. As soon as I was done, ah, admiring his arms, we'd have to exchange a few words."

Monty almost dropped his coffee cup. This was the price of hulking in doorways, listening in where he wasn't wanted, but all the same he couldn't prevent the sense of indignation that rose to the surface. He wasn't that bad. Certainly not a *five*.

"Ha! You're right. He'd probably stare at you for ten minutes before finally offering a few tips for improved performance next time." Holly lowered her voice in what he assumed was an emulation of his own. "Less tongue, I think, could enhance the experience for both of us."

"Is there a reason you kept your eyes open the whole time? I found it quite unnerving."

"How would you rate it when I flipped you over and came in from behind? Three stars? Four? Would you consider it a *bold* move on my part?"

Bursts of feminine laughter had him sneaking slowly away from the door, fearful lest his footsteps sound in the tiled hallway. He only got about five feet when his back hit something soft and warm, and he spun to find himself face-to-face with Amy—yet another staff member, this one the nanny to his three-year-old half brother and half sister. At least he didn't have to fear any sexual judgment from the tall, sunny blonde. Cousinship rendered her safe and neutral territory.

"Oh, hey, Monty." She lifted her empty coffee cup in a show of solidarity. "Mondays, am I right?"

He blinked. "Are you right about what?"

"The daily grind? The need for liquid sustenance? No?" She examined him with pursed lips. "How about this one? I heard they're making this new caffeinated soap so you can skip the coffee and wash the energy boost right into your skin."

It took him a moment to register that she was making small talk, offering those bland bits of conversation that normal people—people who weren't nicknamed Drudgery John—needed to make it through the day. He studied his cup, where a residual pool of ice-cold coffee sloshed, and decided he could go without a refill. Too much caffeine always made him feel jittery and out of control of himself anyway.

It would be a *bold* move on his part to have another one when it wasn't even eight o'clock yet.

"I doubt skin absorbs chemical compounds the same way your digestive system does," he said when it became clear some sort of response was required.

Amy, a woman he knew to be blithely unconcerned for the social comforts and discomforts of others, somehow interpreted this to mean he wanted more coffee. She grabbed the handle of his cup and brushed past him. "Come on. We'll go sweet-talk Holly into giving up some of her wakey-wakey juice."

Monty did a quick mental calculation and decided it would be less disastrous to follow Amy into the cavernous, glistening metal hull that was the kitchen. At least this way, the other two women would assume he'd come down with his cousin and allow him to save face. There was no reason anyone had to know he'd been shamelessly eavesdropping.

A ten, dropped to a five for my terrible personality.

He had no idea how to handle that kind of insult, but his earlier sense of indignation wasn't abating any now that it had time to settle in. He was a man who paid his taxes on time. He didn't use foul language in the presence of children. He didn't even miss appointments unless there was an emergency, since he hated throwing other people's schedules off.

Apparently, none of that mattered as much as the ability to parry with words. A man could be a charming serial killer and be more likable than Monty. That was where he ranked on the social hierarchy. Right below people who stored dismembered limbs in their freezers.

Amy made enough noise as she walked into the kitchen that the conversation came to a halt long before they became visible. From the scene that unfolded before them, it was clear the two women in the kitchen had been enjoying a comfortable chat. Holly always looked as if she belonged in a five-star restaurant—she was the consummate chef from the tips of her plastic clogs to the top of her dark brown hair, pulled back into its customary braid—but for the moment, she was lounging against the counter sipping her own cup of coffee. And Georgia defied explanation most days, so she could have been hanging from the ceiling by a pair of Spider-Man web-slingers, and it wouldn't have taken him more than a second to adjust. The fact that she was kneeling on top of the stove with her head inside the vent hood, the clank of metal on metal signifying some kind of work taking place, wouldn't stop her from venturing opinions on the state of his manhood.

He'd almost never seen Georgia in a state of inaction, since she was always in the middle of some kind of project around the house. He'd also never seen her in anything but the navy blue coveralls and heavy work boots that comprised her self-imposed uniform. A red bandanna knotted above one knee added a touch of adornment, but he knew from experience it would be the only decoration she'd bother with.

"Hey, Holly. Hey, Georgia. I need some coffee, stat." Amy strode forward and shook the two empty cups until Holly took them. "So does Monty. He was skulking in the hallway right outside the door. I think he was afraid to face you on his own."

Holly turned an alarmed look his way, but it was the echoing laugh of Georgia in the stove hood that arrested him.

"Skulking?" She poked her head out. As he expected, she wore no trace of makeup or jewelry, her tangled brown curtain of hair pulled back in its invariable ponytail. *All* of her was invariable. Although she'd grown out of the gangly, toothy stage from her youth, she hadn't moved an unrecognizable distance from it. Her lips were still thin, her features still prominent, and her complexion bore a windswept ruggedness that would have better served a sea captain or lumberjack.

She wasn't beautiful. She wasn't even pretty. But as the hammer in her back pocket attested, she was more than capable of making do without.

She grinned, bringing life to her features and making Monty long for the kitchen tiles to devour him whole. "Then it's good we weren't talking about anything inappropriate. I can't imagine how uncomfortable that would make things."

Any chance Monty might have had of playing cool disappeared. One would think that thirty-five years of life on this planet would give a man a certain amount of panache in awkward situations, but one would be wrong. Like a prisoner trapped in solitary confinement, Monty found that the more time he spent on his own, the less panache he was capable of. The less *everything* he was capable of. Even the Count of Monte Cristo eventually discovered a kindred spirit on the other side of the stone wall to save him from the monotony of his own company.

Monty's stone walls kept going forever.

"I wasn't skulking." He couldn't think of anything that might serve as a reasonable excuse, so he left it there.

Holly handed his coffee cup back to him, offering it handle-side-out to prevent their fingers from touching. "You didn't have to come all this way for a refill," she said uneasily. "I could have sent someone up."

"You forget that Monty and I are slaves to our duty," Amy said. "If we didn't break away every now and then, we'd become nothing more than drones of productivity."

Then, as if realizing a drone of productivity was basically all Monty was, she also fell into an uncomfortable silence.

That was his cue to leave. He might not always land on the right thing to say, but he did know how to make a timely exit. In fact, one of the best moves he'd made recently as the head of the Montgomery Foundation was handing over the social obligations to his brother Jake. The division of labor worked so well that Monty had been able to sever most of his ties to the real world and hide away in the Manor with only his spreadsheets for company. He'd never been more popular now that no one had to actually interact with him. He even got fan mail sometimes.

"Thank you for the coffee." He raised his cup in a gesture of appreciation. "I'll let you three get back to work."

It should have been an easy escape, an only mildly distressing break to his routine, but in this, as in all things, he missed his mark. His comment sounded less like a polite parting and more like a boss jumping on his employees' backs for standing around talking when they should have been working.

Technically, they weren't even *his* employees. He didn't own this house, and they weren't hired to cater to his whims. He lived here and he labored here, but he drew a paycheck with the Montgomery name on it just like everyone else. At least the three other women had the option of leaving to go work somewhere else if they wanted. The thing about having your name on the wrought-iron gate leading in was that it worked an awful lot like a cattle brand. He'd always bear the marks.

"You're right," Holly said with a tight smile. "I've got lots of deep cleaning I could be getting done this morning."

"And if I don't go relieve the night nurse of her duties in the next five minutes, she might refuse to come in early the next time I beg," Amy said.

Only Georgia didn't seem to be in a hurry to jump when he barked, but that was probably because she hadn't stopped working the entire time he'd been present. She leaped from the stove and brushed her hands on the seat of her coveralls.

"I'll walk you out, shall I?" she said cheerfully. "I'm about to head to the garden shed to clean the gutters. The glamorous life of a handywoman never ends."

He couldn't think of a polite way to demur, so he waited while she gathered up her toolbox and provided some parting advice to Holly about changing the filters before accompanying her out the doors.

"I'm glad to catch you this morning," Georgia said, as though there was nothing odd about the two of them chatting as they moved through the maze of hallways. Just two people, one of whom apparently harbored table-rocking sexual fantasies about the other, their footsteps so long they were practically running. What could be weird about that? "I wanted to ask you again whether you'd be willing to help out with Homeward Bound."

"Homeward Bound?"

"Yeah." When he didn't say anything right away, she supplied more information. "The charity that builds houses for families in need? The one I've been volunteering for since I was eighteen? I got put in charge of the local chapter last year when I finally got my contractor's license."

The name and premise were well-known enough to strike a chord, but that was where the familiarity ended. Thousands of grant applications crossed Monty's desk every week, and it was impossible to keep track of all the organizations that needed funding and were turned down. Once upon a time, he'd tried to keep a more accurate personal count, but he'd learned that if he wanted to preserve his sanity, it was better to focus on the people he *could* help, rather than the ones he couldn't.

"What is it you want?" he asked warily.

Her face fell, cheeks heavy with the weight of her disappointment. "Oh. You don't remember our conversation?"

"No, I..." *Shoot.* There was no way to pretend he had any idea what she was talking about. It seemed that unless this woman was rating his sexual prowess, he didn't pay attention to what she had to say. How charming of him. "I'm so sorry. It's not ringing a bell."

"Never mind. I figured getting you to participate would be a long shot anyway." She waved him off with an attempt at a smile. "Forget I said anything. It's not a problem."

But it *was* a problem, and he felt that fact more keenly than he might have a few hours ago. Not only was it remiss of him to forget about Georgia's charity work in the first place—his dad would never overlook that sort of detail about anyone on his staff—but he was in the bizarre position of wanting to impress her. This woman, a woman he rarely saw and barely knew, thought his personality sucked.

Well, it *did* suck, but he didn't care for people to actually know that. Or discuss it amongst themselves in the family kitchens.

"Have you applied to the Montgomery Foundation through the traditional channels?" he asked. "It's not exactly sanctioned, but I'm sure we could expedite the proposal given your years of service to the family."

He passed a hand over his eyes, barely stifling a groan at the familiar drone of his voice. He was doing it again, speaking as if he'd swallowed a business report and was doomed to a lifetime of churning it out piece by piece. "If it's something you'd like, that is," he added lamely.

"Oh, no. We're a local chapter of a state organization, so the money's already taken care of." She spoke loudly—more so than usual, obviously hiding her disappointment. "It's not a big deal. I always seem to be running short on able-bodied young men to do the heavy lifting, and you look like you know your way around the free weights. I thought you might be able to lend some muscle, that's all."

"You want me to help you build houses?" An oddly sweeping pleasure took over. Not only did Georgia think he was a ten in the looks department, but she also considered him a bastion of strength. His spine straightened, naturally puffing his chest out a few extra inches.

She promptly deflated it. "I've already hit up everyone else around here. Ryan and Alex stop by occasionally, but they're busy most weekends."

"I see," he said dryly. "How gratifying."

"I *did* ask you a few months ago," she pointed out.

Again, he found himself at a loss. Chances were she was telling the truth, and her request, like so many others, had become part of the monument of missed opportunities that loomed over his day-to-day life. If only happiness could be measured in parties unattended, people unentertained, friendships untenanted. He'd be euphoric.

"I can understand why you might have blocked it out," she said. "It's a lot of hard work, and I think we've acquired a total of eighty-seven stitches all told."

"How…tempting?"

"Well, since all the work we do is unpaid, we try to have a good time while we're out there. Stitches are the price we pay, but it's fun."

Fun?

He must have done a poor job of hiding his disbelief, because she continued with that same deep-velvet laugh from before. "But it's also a big commitment, and I know how busy you are. Some other time, maybe."

They reached a breakaway point in the hall, two paths laid out so clearly they might as well have been memorialized in verse. Monty would head upstairs to once again pick up the reins of industry while Georgia journeyed outside, where birds chirped and the sun shone and manual labor was considered a source of entertainment rather than a means to an end.

Unaware of how deeply he felt the differences between them, Georgia stuck her hand out and held it inches from his own. Her palm bore every appearance of being strong and callused, an extension of a woman who could only be described with the exact same terms. "I wish there was something I could do," he said, and since there didn't seem any way around it, he slipped his palm into hers. Predictably, her skin was rough and coarse, but it was also hotter than expected, as if proximity to her hammer gave her excess energy, rendering her a Thor in blue coveralls. "Unfortunately, my schedule doesn't leave me much room for extracurriculars."

"I won't mention it again." She didn't let go of his hand right away, and he had to wonder at what possessed her to keep it going so long.

He found out a few seconds later.

"We were just blowing off steam in there, by the way. I don't know how much you overheard—that ventilation hood magnifies sound like whoa, damn—but we didn't mean anything by it."

"I don't know what you're talking about," he said, snatching his hand back.

"You didn't pick up on any of our conversation? Maybe a little something about numbers?"

"I was only a few steps ahead of Amy the whole time."

"Okay." She nodded, but the smirk lifting her lips marred what would have been an otherwise perfect get-away moment. "Then it's probably safe for me to tell you I changed my mind. Plus one for being such a good sport about it."

Despite his determination not to admit he'd overheard anything untoward, he smiled. "Only one?"

"For now." She winked. Like old men who smelled of licorice and sea captains everywhere, she was oddly able to pull it off. "Maybe you could swing by some time and earn a few more. We could admire your arms together."

Admire my arms? He blinked. Surely she wasn't suggesting what he thought she was suggesting. Despite her earlier revelations, there was nothing about this woman that belonged in the sexual portion of his thoughts. She worked for his father. She carried a hammer in her back pocket. And the most attractive thing about her was the fact that he didn't find her the least bit attractive.

So why was he suddenly picturing her naked?

She waved and headed for the outer door, her not-naked form moving with a confident swagger, rendering him a fool. "See you around, Monty. Those gutters aren't going to clean themselves." She paused and winked again. "Bow-chicka-bow-wow."

ALL OF GEORGIA'S BEST Monty fantasies involved an apocryphal rescue of some sort.

Even though this part of Connecticut was protected from every natural disaster known to mankind—barring the occasional winter snowstorm—her imagination seethed with volcano eruptions, tornadoes and devastating floods that should have made her ashamed of herself. But she wasn't. She wasn't ashamed at all. She gleefully killed off everyone within a hundred-mile radius so that in the midst of the rubble and devastation, only two souls remained.

Her favorite scenario was an earthquake that trapped Monty inside his office, where he always had some sort of body part pinned and unable to get free. Through diligence and the use of her trusty hammer, Georgia broke through the giant pile of boards and rocks only to suffer an aftershock that buried them together.

She always got them out, of course, but only after they'd given up hope and decided to make the most of their last twenty minutes on earth. With sex. Lots of sex. Sex that was desperate and seedy and could only be the action of two people for all intents and purposes alone in the world.

Inside her head, Monty was exceptionally skilled at that kind of desperate, seedy sex.

Inside her head, so was she.

Georgia continued her assault on the minor ecosystem that had developed inside the garden shed gutter, lying prone on the roof as she basked in the double glow of the morning sun and her imagination. There weren't many situations in which the unattractive, unkempt handywoman in coveralls was able to land the six-foot-two gorgeous mountain of a millionaire, and that she was required to concoct elaborate doomsday scenarios to make it happen would come as no surprise to anyone. In a doomsday scenario, it didn't matter whether your underwear came in the form of tiny scraps of lace from

Victoria's Secret or enormous cotton briefs from the bargain bin at the grocery store.

In fact, giant bargain bin underwear was probably preferred. If it came down to it, they could turn the briefs into a slingshot and use them for hunting.

"And this is why we don't proposition the man of the Manor, Georgia," she muttered. "Because we probably *could* kill grouse with our panties, should the situation call for it."

To convince herself that she wasn't hurt by the day's interaction—that rejection from a man like Monty wasn't only likely, but carved in stone—she shoved her gloved hand deep in the gutter, scooping out slimy bits of decaying leaves and what looked like a slug colony. She heaved the handful into the plastic bucket propped next to her and scooped again, finding the repetitive motions soothing.

Although most people wrinkled their noses and looked down at her when she mentioned what she did for a living, she'd always found that manual labor had a way of bringing clarity, of stripping everything else away so she could just breathe. She'd tried to get the same kind of focus through yoga once, but it had been impossible to concentrate when her ass was in the air and the spandex pants she'd bought for the occasion were riding.

Some women might be skilled at daintily extracting fabric from between their butt cheeks, but Georgia Lennox wasn't one of them. Which was fine. Whatever. She'd had her Girl Card taken away from her much too long ago to regret its loss.

Well, she didn't regret it *much*. There were times— times that coincided with a chance encounter with the

well-groomed, well-packed millionaire she'd somewhat unwisely chosen as her ideal physical specimen
of man—when she wished she were better at being a
woman.

As if to prove how far from femininity a human being
could reside, a sleek black sports car pulled up the cob-
bled drive, coming to a stop a few feet below Georgia and her bucket o' muck. The woman who emerged
from the driver's side door was *exactly* who belonged
on the arm of a man like Monty. Even from a good ten
feet above, Georgia could see the sleek lines of a pair of
legs straight out of a forties film. Everything about her
was Hollywood-glamour perfect. Bouncy hair, perfectly
painted lips, the way you could tell she had a throaty
laugh and drank alcoholic beverages inexplicably made
with vegetables.

And Georgia couldn't even find it in her to hate the
woman, because when her perilously high heel lodged
between two of the cobblestones, the woman let out a
"for motherfucking Pete's sake" like a real champ. She
swore even louder when she lifted her foot only to keep
the shoe and leave the heel behind.

Since this was as close to a rescue scenario as Georgia was going to get anytime soon, she set her bucket
aside and rose to her feet. Skipping the hassle of climbing down the ladder set against the back side of the shed,
she gripped the edge of the roof and swung herself down.

"Jesus H. Christ!" the woman screamed as Georgia
fell in a neat crouch a few feet from where she stood.
"Where did you come from?"

She pointed straight up. "I was doing maintenance."

"In the sky?"

"Close. The roof." She laughed. "Sorry to scare you like that. I should have called down first. I'm Georgia."

She could feel the weight of the other woman's scrutiny as she cast her initial judgments. It was a weight—a burden—Georgia knew well, and she didn't take it amiss when the woman didn't appear to be impressed with the outcome. It was cool. Few people were.

Still, as she stuck her hand out, waiting for the other woman to shake, she couldn't help but note the differences between them. The woman's hand was nicely formed, the sort of limb that could be described with phrases like *soft* and *silky*. Nothing about Georgia was silky. She spent so much time out of doors she was practically sheathed in leather.

But the woman took her hand anyway. "Ashleigh. Are you some sort of staff member? Perhaps you can help me. I seem to have broken my shoe on the walkway."

Georgia reached down and plucked the rogue heel from between the flagstones. "Not a problem. I don't suppose you have any superglue on you? Or chewing gum?" At Ashleigh's blank stare, Georgia sighed. "I'm not surprised. No one does anymore. I blame four out of five dentists."

She didn't wait for Ashleigh to muster up a polite response—it was one of Georgia's many curses to be unable to interact with the rich in any way that approached sanity—before she dipped into the tool belt strapped around her waist. Although her oversized white truck had a more comprehensive array of tools and fasteners, there was a double-sided nail in a side pouch that would do the trick. With a few efficient movements, she managed to wedge the nail into the heel portion.

From there, she only had to flip the shoe over and jam the broken part in.

See? Easy-peasy. She didn't even need to pull her hammer out.

"Voilà." She gave the heel a wiggle before handing it over. "It's not perfect, but it'll hold."

Ashleigh looked at the shoe and back at Georgia, her brows pulled together in obvious concern for her footwear. "Oh. Um. Thank you?"

"You're welcome. It shouldn't stab through to your foot, but if it does, you may want to hunt down some of that chewing gum after all. You can use it to pad your heel."

Ashleigh gave a reluctant laugh, and Georgia couldn't help but feel smug at the sound of it. She'd totally called it—that was the very definition of throaty.

"Do you *really* work here?" she asked.

"As in, am I a vetted professional, or am I the cheerful homeless lady who wanders the grounds? Strange though it may seem, it's the first one."

"I didn't mean—"

"And I'm sorry if I scared you before," Georgia added, interrupting Ashleigh before she bothered with a halfhearted attempt at backtracking. There was no need. Of all the insults Georgia had withstood in her lifetime, being looked upon as a cheerful homeless lady was quite nice. Because of her work with Homeward Bound, she'd known quite a few such women and counted them among her personal heroes. "I saw your heel break off and figured I could help. Can I point you where you need to go?"

"Oh, not me. I know my way." Ashleigh turned her leg and slipped the heel back on, a smile curving her lips as she tested it with her weight. "Hey—that's not bad. I can't even tell it was broken. What did you say your name was again? I'll be sure and tell Monty about your assistance. Maybe he can work you in a raise."

Georgia felt a whoosh of air leave her lungs before she immediately sucked it all back in where it belonged. She was *not* wasting perfectly good oxygen on this situation. Of course this woman was here to see Monty—Georgia had surmised as much the second she'd seen those legs emerge from the car. And of course she looked at Georgia as the help.

Georgia might technically own her own company, but she *was* the help. The slightly eccentric, ungainly help. The slightly eccentric, ungainly help who harbored an unhealthy crush on the drop-dead-gorgeous scion of the household.

The chasm between the two of them couldn't have been wider if it was the Grand Canyon.

Still… "My name is Holly," she lied. "Holly Santos. I work in the kitchen."

"Are you sure that's what you said before?"

Georgia didn't lose her wide and slightly crazed smile. "Absolutely."

Though she couldn't quite say why, she didn't want Monty to know she'd served his girlfriend in a menial capacity. It was one thing to look at him and feel her own lack of worth, but it was another to have that belief reflected back at her. She was always on the lookout for ways to feel *more* equal to him, not less—it was why she kind of liked that he was such a clod in the conversation department. It leveled the playing field. The Bore and the Beast had a much better chance of success than that other silly story.

Ashleigh thanked her again for the shoe repair and turned to go into the house, and even Georgia had to admire the way she walked, a film vixen right down to the sway of her hips.

She tried to give a little sway herself, but there was gutter goo under her boot and she almost lost her footing. With a sigh, she hopped up the ladder and made her way back to the garden shed roof instead.

At least she had a pretty good view of the grounds from here. She might never own a place like Montgomery Manor, with its sixty sprawling acres and enough room to stretch her legs, but she did get to visit whenever she felt like it.

It was a lot like having your Girl Card revoked but retaining the body parts, now that she thought about it. She might not get to be an active member of the club, but at least she got to stop by from time to time.

Some days, that was even enough.

Don't miss BECAUSE I CAN by Tamara Morgan,
Available now wherever Carina Press ebooks are sold.
www.CarinaPress.com

ABOUT THE AUTHOR

TAMARA MORGAN IS A contemporary romance author of humorous, heartfelt stories with flawed heroes and heroines designed to get your hackles up and make your heart melt. Her long-lived affinity for romance novels survived a BA degree in English literature, after which time she discovered it was much more fun to create stories than analyze the life out of them.

Whether building Victorian dollhouses, consuming mass quantities of coffee and wine, or crying over cheesy 1950s musicals, Tamara commits to her flaws like every good heroine should. She lives in the Inland Northwest with her husband, daughter and variety of household pets, and only occasionally complains about the weather.

REQUEST YOUR FREE BOOKS!

2 FREE NOVELS
FROM THE ROMANCE COLLECTION
PLUS 2 FREE GIFTS!

YES! Please send me 2 FREE novels from the Romance Collection and my 2 FREE gifts (gifts are worth about $10). After receiving them, if I don't wish to receive any more books, I can return the shipping statement marked "cancel." If I don't cancel, I will receive 4 brand-new novels every month and be billed just $6.49 per book in the U.S. or $6.99 per book in Canada. That's a savings of at least 19% off the cover price. It's quite a bargain! Shipping and handling is just 50¢ per book in the U.S. and 75¢ per book in Canada.* I understand that accepting the 2 free books and gifts places me under no obligation to buy anything. I can always return a shipment and cancel at any time. Even if I never buy another book, the two free books and gifts are mine to keep forever.

194/394 MDN GH4D

Name _____ (PLEASE PRINT) _____

Address _____ Apt. # _____

City _____ State/Prov. _____ Zip/Postal Code _____

Signature (if under 18, a parent or guardian must sign)

Mail to the **Reader Service:**
IN U.S.A.: P.O. Box 1867, Buffalo, NY 14240-1867
IN CANADA: P.O. Box 609, Fort Erie, Ontario L2A 5X3

Want to try two free books from another line?
Call 1-800-873-8635 or visit www.ReaderService.com.

* Terms and prices subject to change without notice. Prices do not include applicable taxes. Sales tax applicable in N.Y. Canadian residents will be charged applicable taxes. Offer not valid in Quebec. This offer is limited to one order per household. Not valid for current subscribers to the Romance Collection or the Romance/Suspense Collection. All orders subject to credit approval. Credit or debit balances in a customer's account(s) may be offset by any other outstanding balance owed by or to the customer. Please allow 4 to 6 weeks for delivery. Offer available while quantities last.

Your Privacy—The Reader Service is committed to protecting your privacy. Our Privacy Policy is available online at www.ReaderService.com or upon request from the Reader Service.

We make a portion of our mailing list available to reputable third parties that offer products we believe may interest you. If you prefer that we not exchange your name with third parties, or if you wish to clarify or modify your communication preferences, please visit us at www.ReaderService.com/consumerchoice or write to us at Reader Service Preference Service, P.O. Box 9062, Buffalo, NY 14240-9062. Include your complete name and address.

ROM15

REQUEST YOUR FREE BOOKS!
2 FREE NOVELS PLUS 2 FREE GIFTS!

HARLEQUIN®

American Romance®

LOVE, HOME & HAPPINESS

YES! Please send me 2 FREE Harlequin® American Romance® novels and my 2 FREE gifts (gifts are worth about $10). After receiving them, if I don't wish to receive any more books, I can return the shipping statement marked "cancel." If I don't cancel, I will receive 4 brand-new novels every month and be billed just $4.74 per book in the U.S. or $5.49 per book in Canada. That's a savings of at least 12% off the cover price! It's quite a bargain! Shipping and handling is just 50¢ per book in the U.S. and 75¢ per book in Canada.* I understand that accepting the 2 free books and gifts places me under no obligation to buy anything. I can always return a shipment and cancel at any time. Even if I never buy another book, the two free books and gifts are mine to keep forever.

154/354 HDN GHZZ

Name	(PLEASE PRINT)	
Address		Apt. #
City	State/Prov.	Zip/Postal Code

Signature (if under 18, a parent or guardian must sign)

Mail to the **Reader Service:**
IN U.S.A.: P.O. Box 1867, Buffalo, NY 14240-1867
IN CANADA: P.O. Box 609, Fort Erie, Ontario L2A 5X3

Want to try two free books from another line?
Call 1-800-873-8635 or visit www.ReaderService.com.

* Terms and prices subject to change without notice. Prices do not include applicable taxes. Sales tax applicable in N.Y. Canadian residents will be charged applicable taxes. Offer not valid in Quebec. This offer is limited to one order per household. Not valid for current subscribers to Harlequin American Romance books. All orders subject to credit approval. Credit or debit balances in a customer's account(s) may be offset by any other outstanding balance owed by or to the customer. Please allow 4 to 6 weeks for delivery. Offer available while quantities last.

Your Privacy—The Reader Service is committed to protecting your privacy. Our Privacy Policy is available online at www.ReaderService.com or upon request from the Reader Service.

We make a portion of our mailing list available to reputable third parties that offer products we believe may interest you. If you prefer that we not exchange your name with third parties, or if you wish to clarify or modify your communication preferences, please visit us at www.ReaderService.com/consumerschoice or write to us at Reader Service Preference Service, P.O. Box 9062, Buffalo, NY 14240-9062. Include your complete name and address.

HARI5

REQUEST YOUR FREE BOOKS!
2 FREE NOVELS PLUS 2 FREE GIFTS!

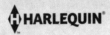

ROMANTIC suspense

Sparked by danger, fueled by passion

REQUEST YOUR FREE BOOKS!

2 FREE INSPIRATIONAL NOVELS
PLUS 2
FREE
MYSTERY GIFTS

WESTERN WP PROMISES

YES! Please send me **The Western Promises Collection** in Larger Print. This collection begins with 3 FREE books and 2 FREE gifts (gifts valued at approx. $14.00 retail) in the first shipment, along with the other first 4 books from the collection! If I do not cancel, I will receive 8 monthly shipments until I have the entire 51-book Western Promises collection. I will receive 2 or 3 FREE books in each shipment and I will pay just $4.99 US/ $5.89 CDN for each of the other four books in each shipment, plus $2.99 for shipping and handling per shipment. *If I decide to keep the entire collection, I'll have paid for only 32 books, because 19 books are FREE! I understand that accepting the 3 free books and gifts places me under no obligation to buy anything. I can always return a shipment and cancel at any time. My free books and gifts are mine to keep no matter what I decide.

272 HCN 3070 472 HCN 3070

Name _____ (PLEASE PRINT) _____

Address _____ Apt. # _____

City _____ State/Prov. _____ Zip/Postal Code _____

Signature (if under 18, a parent or guardian must sign)

Mail to the **Reader Service:**
IN U.S.A.: P.O. Box 1867, Buffalo, NY 14240-1867
IN CANADA: P.O. Box 609, Fort Erie, Ontario L2A 5X3

WPBPA16R